DOUBLE IDENTITY

DOUBLE IDENTITY

❀

A Texan in Hitler's Reich

A Novel

Robert Spoede

iUniverse, Inc.
New York Lincoln Shanghai

Double Identity
A Texan in Hitler's Reich

iUniverse books may be ordered through booksellers or by contacting:

iUniverse
2021 Pine Lake Road, Suite 100
Lincoln, NE 68512
www.iuniverse.com
1-800-Authors (1-800-288-4677)

ISBN-13: 978-0-595-36926-3 (pbk)
ISBN-13: 978-0-595-81337-7 (ebk)
ISBN-10: 0-595-36926-X (pbk)
ISBN-10: 0-595-81337-2 (ebk)

Printed in the United States of America

Contents

❖

Glossary

❀

Ach	Oh
Arzt	Physician, doctor
Auf Wiedersehen	Goodbye [Until we see one another again]
Aus	Out
Bestimmt	Of course/For sure
Bitte	Please
Bürgermeister	Mayor
Danke	Thanks
Das ist gute	That is good
Ein moment	One moment/a moment
Ersatz	Substitute
Frau	Mrs.
Führer	Leader
Gute	Good
Guten Abend	Good evening
Guten Morgen	Good morning
Guten Tag	Good day
Guten Nacht	Good night

Gymnasium	Secondary school
Hauptmann	Captain
Hausfrau	House wife
Herr	Mister
Ja	Yes
Kristallnacht	Crystal night/night of broken glass
Mein	Mine
Nazi	Short for National Socialist
Nein	No
Raus!	Get out of here!, get way from here!
Rucksack	Back pack
Schweinhund	Pig dog [literally]
Schloss	Castle
Sehr	Very
Schutzstaffeln [SS]	*Nazi* Security Agency (began as body guard for Hitler)
Sicherheitdienst [SD]	*Nazi* secret police [to include informers]
Sturmhauptführer	Captain in the *SS*
Sturmmann	Lance corporal in the *SS*
Verstehen Sie?	Do you understand?
Vielen Dank	Many thanks
Von	of (or "from")
Was ist?	What is that (this)?
Wehrmacht	German army as opposed to *SS*
Wie gehts	How is it going?
Wie geht es Ihnen	How is it going with you?
Wie gibt?	What's up?
Wunderbar!	Wonderful!

Note: German society tended to appreciate titles—the wife of a professor holding a doctorate might well be called Mrs. Professor Doctor Jones [Frau Professor Doktor Jones.]

CHAPTER 1

❀

April–May 1942
The Hospital

If only his eyes could see! Everything was a white blur! All Carl sensed was white. Even his perception of the whirling white fog kept drifting in and out. He heard a comforting woman's voice call to him as through the white Texas summer clouds he had flown through in his training, "Friedrich! Friedrich! You must wake, Friedrich!" His heart longed to cry out but his lips could only whisper, "Mama! Mama!" Everything was a struggle. He felt as though there was great pressure upon him. Why was everything white? Where was he? Sounds of voices faded in and out. His mother's mother had called him Friedrich because that had been her father's name. Was she here? Where was here? Where was he? Searing pain wracked his entire body. As he tried to answer the calling voice only guttural moaning whispers, almost whimpers, came forth. Hours passed. Then he remembered some of the nightmarish events that brought him here. A flak blast had destroyed the Wellington and caused the certain death of his newfound friends, Captain Geoff Townshend and other crewmates of the Royal Air Force. Now he was in a hospital where the people spoke German.

He had lived! His parachute had delivered him safely to German ground. He forced his mind to recapture reality. He now knew that he had evaded capture in the countryside. As his mind began to clear so did his remembrance of his entry into the city. He was a fugitive in the enemy's country. The voices beside him continued to speak German but who were they? Then consciousness graciously slipped away as the pain deadener took its effect.

Carl would never have a clear memory of anything other than an infernal wave of flames coming to flood over him. He remembered nothing of the shouts of "Save him! Save him! Save the hero!" He would never recall the doctor who, seeing his foot under the burning beam, had severed muscle, tendon, and bone to remove him. His mind would forever obliterate the wild ride to the hospital, a tourniquet squelching the flow of blood from his severed leg.

For more than a week, Carl existed in a world of fuzzy whiteness deadened by the pain that alternated with morphine. He was aware of German voices as he drifted in and out of conscious thought. There was warmth and there was pain. His right leg hurt. His face seemed aflame but the greatest torturing throb came from his left side. Each time he moved, it seemed an invisible knife peeled away flesh and skin.

He was unaware of the days that passed before he became minimally alert to his surroundings. The first words he heard, and he did not think that the speakers were aware of his understanding were, "It was a reasonably good reconstruction of the face and there is no infection in the burns on his side or on his hands. But it's too bad about the leg."

A woman's voice made contact with him. The first words to which he responded were, "Are you awake, Captain?"

Captain? No, he was a first lieutenant. However, he had better play along.

"Yes," he finally responded to the voice emanating from a body bending over him. Then, with difficulty, "Where am I?" Because he had been addressed in German, he responded in the same language.

"Why, in the city hospital. Do you need anything? Are you thirsty or would you like a little broth?" The fuzzy face both responded and questioned.

Then once again he slipped from consciousness.

When again at least partially aware of his surroundings, he concealed his wakefulness in order to determine his status. Had the *Nazis* penetrated his false identity? Was he a prisoner? Would they cure him to shoot him? Had he unconsciously betrayed himself? However, she had said the "city hospital" and not a military hospital. He determined to listen and learn although he would have to make his needs known. Therefore, he would rest quietly, keep his mouth shut, and seek to discover as much as possible about his situation.

He heard the voice of a woman, sounding far away, "He is doing well. Much better than could be expected with the trauma he has been through."

Then a man's voice, equally distant, replied, "*Das ist gute.* That is very good. Keep me informed immediately of any change. Berlin wants a report two or three times a day."

One day passed into another, with his faculties becoming sharper daily. He felt the tight bandages that bound his face and body and became more and more aware of conversations not only in the room but also in the hallway outside his door. He mentally composed and directed upward sentence prayers of thanks for both his survival and for his knowledge of German. He became aware that he was not the only patient in the room. As his eyes traced the walls and took in all the room, he saw that there were three more beds, all occupied. He struggled to keep every sense alert.

As he lay placid and resigned he overheard, not in a cloud of semi-consciousness, but clearly and lucidly, "How is *Sturmhauptführer* Schleiter, *Frau* Oberholzel?"

A female voice answered "As well as one would expect, doctor. He rests quietly and does not speak a word. I don't think he has become conscious."

"That is very understandable with the blow to the voice box. It might well pain him to speak. That is another memory that he will know all his life. If he were a tenor he would now be forevermore a bass."

Then again the nurse's voice, "Such a brave young man and such a shame that he had to lose his foot."

A deep cold cut into the marrow of the being of the young Texan. Two thoughts penetrated his mind as he remembered that he had taken on the identity of a Captain Schleiter. They must be talking of him. But the other communication, "…he had to lose his foot!!" How could that be? He could move his left foot and see the bed cover move. Pain filled his right foot. It had to be there for it hurt and throbbed with a burning intensity. Never had he experienced any thing to compare with his present suffering. How could his leg hurt so much if it were not there?

"Keep me informed as to when we can have visitors. There are many waiting to see him," intoned the male, surely a doctor's voice.

Carl's curiosity would have divulged the rapidity and strength of his recovery had his actions been observed by any of the hospital staff. Anxious to be sure that his foot was gone, he waited until his roommates were asleep or facing away from him and the nurse was out of the room and then began to lift the blanket covering his legs with his hands covered with mitten-like bandages. His fears were realized when he beheld his leg swathed in bandages that ended halfway between where his knee was and where his ankle should have been. He fell back onto his pillow with a loud moan, a moan loud enough to bring attention from a nurse in the hall.

"What's going on?" she queried. "Coming out of it, are we? Well, maybe we can finally get some food through that mask of yours and onto your ribs!" Turning on her heels, she left the room. She soon returned with another woman who carried a vessel and a straw much like the ones in drug stores at home. While the second woman held the container the nurse carefully inserted the glass tube through the facial bandages and between his lips and commanded, "Now suck it in!" Suck he did and the feel of the warm broth stimulated hunger even more. The second woman then remarked, "He is a hungry one, no?"

The days passed with all the discomforts, awkwardness, and embarrassments of hospital life. Increasingly with the passage of days, the young American gave thanks once more for the German spoken in his family's home and refined into excellence by *Tante* Anna.

In about ten days the doctor named Aschenfelter who had been seeing him routinely came once more, but this time accompanied by two others in the gowns of physicians. Aschenfelter, ignoring Carl, explained to the others, "Here is our hero. He has made a remarkable recovery considering the nature of his injuries. Remarkable recuperative powers. We have sealed off his leg and the wound is nice and clean, there should be no trouble there. There appears to have been no damage to his ribs or back and no internal trauma to the organs. He took a strong blow to his throat and voice box that has limited his speech. He will, I am afraid, always speak in a different tone although there is no reason to believe that his ability to talk will in any way be limited. His voice will simply always sound differently than it did before the injury. You see we still have his whole head wrapped and protected. His features have been severely damaged. That's why I asked for you to come to see what you can do, doctor."

The younger of the two accompanying Aschenfelter, but still approaching middle age, responded, "Well, we will just have to take a look. We all know who our captain is so we will give him the best care we can."

"Yes," replied the first, and finally, "*Sturmhauptführer* Schleiter, this is Doctor Bacher, the *Reich's* leading reparative surgeon. He wants to look at your face."

Without waiting for permission the process of removing the gauze from Carl's face began. Slowly the physician unrolled the wrappings as two nurses watched. As long as cloth left cloth there was no pain but slowly the pain increased. When the removal reached the bottom layer and laid bare his wounds, the pain became intense. Carl gripped the bed iron with all his strength and grit his teeth until his jaws hurt in order to avoid screaming his anguish. All of this was done with the sounds of "Ah, so" and long "hummms." Carl watched through slitted eyes as the doctors and the nurses gathered ever closer to observe. Finally, the process seemed over, although much of the fiery pain remained, as the doctors stood back and considered, chins encased in sterile fingers.

Aschenfelter observed, "You see there were major contusions to the face, the nose is destroyed and broken many times over, and the lacerations to his face are deep and severe. Without your skills, Dr. Bacher, he will be a monster to behold. You see that we have assisted his breathing with a nasal ventilator."

As Doctor Bacher's hand stroked his chin, saying nothing, Carl noticed that the two other medical men emulated the cosmetic surgeon in putting their hands to their chins to communicate their deep consideration. He thought of the statue of "The Thinker." Finally, Bacher turned to the other two and asked, "Do you have any idea of his facial construction before these injuries? I would like to have a plan to see what I should attempt to make him look like, although he will never be as handsome as he was. But I would like to, as builders say, have a blueprint for what I should do."

"We have his identity card with his photo attached. He truly was an ideal German lad for whom *Reichsführer* Himmler has great concern. Could you work from his identification picture? We have it here in his records." Pulling the identification card from a folder, he handed it to Bacher.

Bacher looked at the two others as though they were blithering idiots. "Why do you think I have been sent here? Do you not think that I know that! We all know that *Reichsführer* Himmler himself is interested in this officer. The *Wehrmacht* medical services ordered me to get here as soon as I could."

Then, carefully examining the photo on the card, he continued, "Yes, this will do, although I wish it were larger and the lighting was better. However, it will have to do. We will make what we can with it."

Continuing to study the face on the identification card, he commanded, "Get him ready for my procedure as soon as possible! When will his condition enable him to stand up to it? I do not mean when it is convenient to you! When will he be strong enough? I must return to my work on the front in the east."

"Considering that he has lost his foot and part of his leg and much blood, he has come back extremely well," parried the familiar Dr. Aschenfelter, "I think we can do the job two days from now."

"Good!" commanded Bacher, "Have him in surgery at 8:00 hours sharp on Thursday. Maybe I can get a train to return to my work with the soldiers at the front that evening."

"We have all heard of the great work you are doing with frostbite injuries to the faces of our men. We hear that they have lost ears and noses from that hellish cold on the front," interjected the third doctor who had remained silent until this time.

Herr Arzt Bacher softened a little as he made a request, "Dr. Hildendorf, you are the head of this hospital, I ask you to treat those who come to you from the front as the heroes they are. The war against the Bolshevik barbarians is nothing like the war was in the west where we fought against honorable and civilized men and not such cold and mud and ice and snow and wind and rain and sleet. However, enough! Please help our men as much as you can."

Carl had two nights rest before being wheeled into a surgical room. No one bothered to ask if he desired the surgery. He knew that he had no control over his own destiny, but with confidence, he interceded for help from above even as the nurses wheeled him into the operating room. In preparation for the ether mask, the medical staff once more removed the two day old bandages. When the attendants had finished removing the gauze, Bacher noticed that the patient closed his eyes and moved his lips in apparent prayer.

"Aha, a praying *SS* man! Now, we know that pigs can have wings!" he casually commented to himself without further thought.

The nurse pressed the ether mask over Carl's face and ordered him to breathe deeply.

When Carl fully regained his senses his face both burned and ached even more than it ever had. He sensed that bandages covered all of his facial features. As awareness returned he discovered that he was in a room, a rather large room. There were no other beds in the chamber. Moving his head as little as possible, he rolled his eyes to take inventory of his surroundings. His most important discovery was that a bulky female attendant, possibly a nurse, sat in the chair with a full view of him. Even in his condition he thought, "Even German nurses sleep on the job." He observed her closed eyes and her head resting on the wall behind her chair exposing her more than ample neck.

"Well," he thought, "I might as well get some service if I am being watched. I hope that nothing gave me away while I was unconscious. Any effort to get to Switzerland or Holland will have to be postponed; there is no way I can move about now. I must keep up the pretense." With those thoughts in his mind, he uttered a low moan, watching the woman to see her reaction. Her nap had not been deep and she started and rose from her seat.

"Yes, yes, good captain. Are you awake?" she asked.

Through the bandages he managed to mumble "*Ja*"

She responded, "*Ein moment*," stepped quickly from the room and returned with Dr. Aschenfelter.

After examining Carl's face the doctor coughed, carefully covering his mouth, and expressed to no one in particular an opinion for which no one had asked. "Yes, very good, all seems very good. Of course, the bandages must stay on much longer. All seems to be doing well. Yes, we have done well."

For a little over a week Carl was left to himself except for the ministrations of the hospital personnel and feeding, first through that straw. Thick soup came first, when much to his joy, the doctor ordered the nurses to loosen the bandages sufficiently for him to take food orally. Within days he progressed to solid food. The care also included a change of the bandages every other day and the scrupulously cautious removal of his light blonde whiskers. A nurse did this time-consuming semi-shaving with scissors. The shaving occurred often enough to keep the stubble from entering his surgery wounds but not every time they changed his bandages. He felt his strength growing every day. The pain of the facial reconstruction abated as his stamina increased. He attempted to push from his mind the loss of his lower leg as he exercised his arms and shoulders against the iron bed frame.

The patient now began to recollect how he, an American airman, came to be in a hospital of the enemy. He remembered his assignment as an intelligence liaison with the Royal Air Force because of his total fluency in the language of the foe, the flight over the land of his forebears, the destruction of the British aircraft and the death of his new English comrades on the Wellington, the parachute drop onto enemy soil. He recalled his relief at not being captured immediately and evading the enemy in the countryside as he attempted to do his duty and work his escape across the land to the Netherlands. Finally, he had entered the city to find a way across a wide and swift flowing river only to find the English air force again striking the city....

A building abandoned by workers during the raid appeared sturdy. If his eyes could have seen through walls, they would have seen that this was a plant for making gunpowder for the weapons of the *Third Reich*. Nevertheless, based on his judgment and need for concealment he hastened through the door and into the building. As he trod down the well lit hallway a figure appeared from a doorway and drew a wicked-looking pistol from its holster demanding, "Halt! Who are you?"

Dumbly, he could only make the silly response of "*Freund.*" as he remembered the "Who goes there, friend or foe?" line from his reading of adventure tales.

The figure that faced him in the uniform of what Carl took to be a German officer wore a black uniform with a black "Sam Brown" belt and an ornamental dagger. Black boots encased his feet and calves, extending almost to his knees. "Almost like senior boots, but probably not as good as Mr. Holick's at A&M," came the involuntary and inane thought to Carl's mind. His confronter's high peaked cap curved above Carl's height two or three inches; his face showed a slight bristle of blond whiskers.

His blue eyes glistened with the high excitement of the capture. Exclaiming, "You *schweinhund* of an English aviator, I'm going to put a finish to you!" as he raised the hand weapon to line up directly with Carl's face..

The officer seemed bent on summary execution right there in the building and Carl never knew why he did not carry out his decision immediately. Suddenly the aim of the pistol lowered to his mid-section; Carl clearly understood the instructions of "*Aus*! Put your hands over your head and go back outside! I'll shoot you there!"

While Carl questioned whether he could move his head sideways quicker than a finger could pull a trigger, he knew that his body could not evade a bullet. So he turned, conscious of the gun two or three paces behind him, and went back the way that he had entered. Once outside the German commanded, "Up against the wall!" waving the gun to indicate what Carl was to do. The commands were given in German and Carl never was to know if his captor would have ever questioned to himself why his captive obeyed the orders quickly. As he faced the young officer, who could not have been much older than himself, Carl noted that now the enemy, realizing what he was about to do, began to tremble slightly.

As if to justify his own violation of the law of war, the pistol wielder now began to recite loudly the crimes of Carl. "You are guilty of bombing the cities of the Fatherland and killing and wounding people of the Aryan race. I find you guilty of obstructing the future of evolutionary progress! I, as an officer in the State Security Force, condemn you to summary execution! You can not understand this but you need to say your prayers to any God you have!"

Carl had no time for prayer. Suddenly, as one more English bomb fell on German soil, a tremendous blast at the open end of the alley way sent debris flying. Carl sensed but never saw an object hurtling through the early dawn air. The German's head twisted grotesquely to one side at an impossible angle and a large object dropped to the ground even before the dead body of his intended executioner fell.

The flying block of wood propelled by the blast had snapped the German's neck and death had been instantaneous. The cap lay a few feet away and the dead body reposed in peaceful order. The deathblow caused no blood to flow. No moisture had appeared that could have resulted from death-loosened muscles. Carl's first instinct, to run, quickly deferred to second thoughts. The uniform provided a great disguise. The air assault continued and no witnesses observed the incident.

He picked up the pistol and put it in the holster on the enemy's belt. Putting the SS cap on his own head, he then hooked his hands under the shoulders of the limp and still warm body and pulled it back into the building.

Feverishly he stripped the body down to the skin, removing all, even a watch. The tattoo under the left armpit of the dead man indicated his blood type, and being the most common of all types, matched that of Carl. He then removed all of his own clothes, including his underwear, and replaced them with the German's clothing. Everything was exchanged; watch, undergarments, socks for stockings. With amazed satisfaction and assurance, he noted how similar he and the German were in height, weight, and coloring. The uniform fit as though it had been tailored for him. As he placed his flight uniform on the body, he puzzled over what to do with his "dog tags," the two metal pieces of identification that provided his name, serial number, and blood type. If captured in the German uniform without the tags he risked execution as a spy. But then, he had almost been shot when wearing the combat uniform so what was there to lose? He slid his dog tags into the pocket of the German uniform he had donned.

He quickly took time to examine the contents of the pockets of the uniform. He learned from the identification card in the dead man's wallet that he had borne the rank and name of Captain Friedrich Schleiter. He had worn the uniform of the *Schutzstaffeln* or SS. The captain had been born a year and eleven months before Carl. Military orders and leave papers as well as quite a large amount of money also appeared. He realized that these were important items of which to be aware. The orders accounted for the *Nazi's* presence in the city. He was to inspect both the military troops in the city and "to arrange for the relocation of Jews, gypsies, and other undesirable elements of the population of the city to the eastern territories." The orders clearly stated that the captain, regardless of his relatively minor rank, acted as the personal representative of *Reichführer-Schutzstafelln* Heinrich Himmler. Further searching of the pockets of the military blouse revealed a numbered key with the identification registration form of the *Grand Hotel*.

After Carl pulled the body, now dressed in his flight suit, into the slight shadow at a corner of the hall, he boldly exited the building and walked with what he imagined a German officer's walk would be. Outside he discovered that his friends in the English air force had continued their strike on the city but with even more force and determination. Bombs had continued to fall. Buildings had exploded although many of the bombs had fallen on streets.

He continued to negotiate through the streets and had gone about two blocks when an explosion like none he had ever heard or would hear again in his lifetime, occurred behind him as a bomb fell through the roof into the basement of the powder plant. Reinforced by the explosives stored in the building, the bomb left only a crater where the building and the body had been.

The young American continued to hurry down the street as he thought, "It is probably wise to get away from this spot as quick as I can. There may be someone who could recognize Captain Schleiter of the *SS*. The further away I am, the safer I am from recognition."

...His reverie of remembrance was cut short as hospital attendants began to swarm over the room, cleaning all the windows, scrubbing the floor, and changing the bed; sheets, blankets and all. Carl wondered, "What is going on? Everything is normally very clean but they are really doing it up fine. Something must be happening. Could it be a Red Cross representative? No, I am sure that they still think I am Captain Schleiter."

His curiosity was satisfied when, later that day, his nurse excitedly informed him, "You are going to have a visitor today. A high ranking visitor accompanied by a whole delegation of important people. We must make sure that you look your best with clean clothing." All was made ready for the appearance of his mysterious but important visitors. At the appointed hour he heard the rhythmic steps of clicking heels echoing from the hall and through the door into his room. First came in a man introduced as the head of the district; and then followed names too rapidly to be grasped. Their positions included the district party leader, the mayor of the city, the chief of internal security for the city and other functionaries whose position he could not identify. They all crowded into the room.

After the necessary right arm salutes to the health of the *Führer,* the district leader began an address, which stated in part that Captain Schleiter had shown remarkable bravery in saving the lives of three children at the definite risk of his own. He had amply demonstrated the standards expected of the officers of the *SS* and all German forces to the highest degree. The *Führer* has desired that Captain Schleiter receive the Iron Cross, Second Class. The award was not only for his rescue of the children but also for his administration of the relocation of undesirable populations to the eastern territories. At this time an officer stepped forward and laid a medal with a red neck band about three-quarters of an inch wide upon Carl's chest as he lay in bed. Again there were the *"Heil Hitler"* salutes by all in the room save Carl who could be excused because of his wounds.

It was then that a woman rushed forward to hug him tightly around the neck, causing more pain as her shoulders encountered his face bandages. As she stepped back he recognized her as the mother of the three boys in the burning building. Then another man edged forward and diffidently stated, "You are a very brave man, Captain Schleiter. Your conduct made us ashamed of ourselves for doing so little." It was then that recognition of the fireman who organized the blanket holders flashed into Carl's memory.

The mother then stated to the fireman, "You too were brave because you made the men rescue the captain when his leg was pinned by the burning beam. It took a doctor to free you, captain, because he had to remove your foot caught under that beam."

Then several bottles of wine, along with five colorful bunches of flowers, were produced along with tall thin glasses and toasts were offered to the brave captain, to the *Führer,* to the Third Reich, and to victory. Carl observed wryly to himself, "It seems everybody is enjoying my injuries and hospital stay except me." With a few more *"Heil Hitler"* salutes the party then left, their heels hammering the hall floor in unison.

"Me, an old farm boy from Texas, now a *Nazi* hero!" Carl reflected. "If I get out of this mess I will have something to tell when I get home. It won't make my family any more proud of me than they were. Have they heard? Is Mama crying for me? I wish I could let them know that I am alive. I wonder what is next. I'm going to have a hard time hitting the road on one leg and I don't want to go to the Russian front as a one-legged *Nazi* officer. My future's really out of my hands without some outside intervention. As Papa said many times it is possible to sure get in the pickle barrel."

In the quiet of the hospital room he returned to his recollection of the past....

After assuming the guise of the *Nazi* officer, he reached the point where the street merged into another. He discovered that the bombs had ceased exploding but that fires were consuming several buildings. Vehicles, equipment and both men and women hurried to the fire sites. The German population's desire for order had kept the turmoil to a minimum. Carl noted the citizenry leaving basements and other shelters from the air raid. If he had rendered a damage report of the war making capability of the industry of the city he would have had to report it minimal. The exception was the tremendous explosion that had occurred in the building where death had come so close. Women, clad in robes and other nightwear, escorted similarly dressed children back into the buildings. It seemed that things quickly settled back into a semblance of normality.

The large metal hotel key that he felt in his pocket kept reminding him that he was exhausted and hungry. Venturing boldly in his new disguise, he asked a passing woman for the directions to the hotel. She informed him, "It is by the rail station just outside the walls of the old city. Just follow around the wall and you will see it on your left in about one kilometer."

He easily followed the directions. He crossed two streets and soon saw the walls curving in a great arc. Following them he soon saw his objective. Having the key and the room number in his possession there was no need to stop at the hotel reception desk. He turned into the doorway, and hiding his face by slowly removing the headgear and lowering it gradually to his side attempted to pass without notice. The old clerk on duty nevertheless called out a loud greeting (it paid to be in favor with the National Socialist elite), "*Guten Morgen, Herr Sturmhauptfüher. Wie gehts?*"

Carl fixed his attention on the iron grill surrounding the elevator shaft and pushed the button to bring the conveyance to his level, all the time acting like the grill was the most fascinating piece of art ever seen in the western world. The elevator came and he ordered it up to the fourth floor where he disembarked, and moving cautiously in his nervousness, eventually found a door with a number corresponding to his key. The key worked. Opening the door he discovered a room with rich brocade drapes reinforced with lace-like netting. The carpet appeared thick and luxurious; the bed spread wide, and to one who had lacked sufficient sleep for days, inviting. He restrained the impulse to throw himself on the bed and surrendered to sleep as he continued his examination of the room.

Within a minute the phone in the room rang. Startled, he examined his options. There was danger both ways. If he answered, he might be revealed through his lack of real knowledge about the dead man's mission. If he failed to answer there might be an investigation because the hotel personnel knew that he had come into the room. Even though they thought he was the German captain, if he failed to answer some one could well come to check. Deciding that to answer was the lesser risk, he lifted the instrument and greeted, "*Guten Morgen.*"

"*Guten Morgen, Herr Sturmhauptführer,*" responded a voice. "This is Heinz at the desk. I thought that you might want another woman this afternoon or tonight."

Shocked at the brazen approach Carl restrained his indignation with a fervent, "No!" Then he thought quickly and decided it might be wise not to act outraged. The key word that he had heard was "another." So Schleiter had indulged his hormones at least once before. He amended his earlier denial with, "No, not today. I have been awake all night and need to get a very good rest. But thank you for considering my desires."

"Think nothing of it, good captain. All of our people appreciate the strain of your duties in behalf of the *Führer* and thus in behalf of the people. Again, good morning and have a good rest."

Thinking quickly, Carl asked, "Is there food available at this hour?"

"For sure," came the response. "Our dining is the best in the city. It is always open for one of the *Führer's* close staff. Just let me know when you want to dine and what you would like."

"Thank you very much," acknowledged Carl, "would it be possible to send some eggs, ham, and bread up soon?"

"*Bestimmt, Mein Herr*! Although it may be three quarters of an hour because the stoves have not yet been heated."

"That is good because I would like to wash first," the American temporized.

There was a toilet room with a vast tub, deep and long. Throwing caution aside, he turned the handles and filled the tub with water as warm as he could stand it. Stripping off the German uniform, he lowered himself into the water and felt strangely at ease in his false role as an *SS* officer. The muscles in his body relaxed and he had to fight the torpor of sleep that assailed his wakefulness. To fight the onslaught he soaped and sponged himself off briskly and rose from the tub feeling too much at peace for his own ease of mind as he remembered, "eternal vigilance is the price of liberty." Toweling off and then wrapping the towel around his mid-section he found the shaving equipment of the dead captain, brushed up a rich lather and spread it over his face.

When the razor had scraped off the stubble, he felt clean and refreshed. He then re-entered the bedroom and searched the drawers and the closet. The captain had been traveling light with only one other pair of trousers, one other shirt, and two sets of under linen and stockings. Carl put on the trousers, the shirt, and a set of fresh underwear. As he dressed, he saw what appeared to be a brief case in the corner of the room.

Hardly had this been accomplished when he heard a soft rap at the door, which he had not locked with the key upon entering the room. Carl hurried to the bathroom, closed the door to leave it only about four inches open and exclaimed in a strong voice, "Come in." He heard the door open and then a voice said, "*Heil* Hitler. It is your food, *Mein Herr*. Should I put it on the table?"

The impostor, beginning to try to act as he thought Schleiter would, exclaimed, "*Bestimmt*! Do you think I want it on the bed! I will settle the bill at the desk."

A response came, "Thank you very much, sir. May you have a good appetite. *Heil* Hitler!" Then he heard the sound of the door to the hall closing. He reminded himself again that he was in another place where greetings were different. "Must remember to 'Heil' rather than 'Howdy' or even 'Good Morning.' I must be careful. I must observe and do as the Germans do. I probably should be more German, no, more *Nazi*, than others. I should talk only when necessary."

The breakfast items were on the table when he once more left the bath chamber. Famished, he wolfed down the breakfast offerings before him and then fell on the bed. Exhausted, hunger satisfied, clean all over, he departed into a deep, and hazardous, sleep. His subconscious must have been more alert than his conscious for he only slept eight hours when his eyes opened. He leaped from bed, startled and disoriented. He staggered as he rose from the bed, rubbed consciousness into his eyes, and generally reoriented himself and his situation even as he turned the light switch. Here he was, in the middle of the enemy's land, well fed, now well rested, and soon to be dressed again in the uniform of one of the enemy elite. In the security of the room he re-examined the papers found in the uniform as well as those in the brief case. He particularly studied the orders. They stated that he was to go to four cities, of which this was the last, and initiate the "enforced relocation of Jews, gypsies, and other undesirable persons to the occupied land in the newly acquired eastern territories." He was unsure of what that meant exactly but it did not sound good.

He searched the case for papers and letters and found that its bottom was composed of several layers of loosely glued leather. Being able to separate the top layer from the next, he slid his identification tags that identified him as an American and the *New Testament* he had carried since leaving college between the layers, and pressed the layers firmly together. He thought that if he was captured carrying the case at least he would possess identity as an Allied soldier.

Now after days of evading and escaping the enemy out in the open countryside he began to feel penned in and endangered in this room from which there was little avenue of flight. Again dressing in the complete uniform of the *SS* captain he left the room and walked the steps to the ground floor. He took the steps because he wanted to stretch his legs and there was less likelihood of getting into close proximity of someone who knew Captain Schleiter well. Entering the lobby he turned away from the reception counter and the clerk there and toward a hall that, according to a sign, led to the hotel's dining room. Before arriving at the restaurant he spotted an exit out to the street and left the hotel. Outside he found that it was growing dark and again noted the number of men in the gray uniforms of the *Wehrmacht*, some moving in groups in unison, some singly, and some in groups but not in unison. For the first time, now rested and alert, he noticed that "*Heil* Hitler" was used as a greeting and a farewell many times, but not always.

Sauntering casually down the street, responding to the salutes and "*Heil* Hitler's" of passing military he was careful to salute if not saluted first. Sometimes arms rose from the side almost concurrently. After several blocks a restaurant caught his attention, and hunger having revived, he entered. He was surprised at the great deference shown to him as one who appeared to be in authority. A middle-aged man, either the host or the headwaiter, greeted him and instantly seated him at a table that seemed a privileged place. His escort informed him, "We are honored to have one so young but such a great servant of our *Führer* dine with us. If there is anything, absolutely anything you desire, please, please ask! But may I recommend the pork, potatoes with parsley, and cabbage, with one of our golden tarts to finish?"

The *ersatz SS* answered, "That will be fine. But I wonder if you have some good coffee." Then truthfully, he added, "I have not had any really good coffee for some time."

"Bestimmt, Mein Herr, Bestimmt! We will have a special pot prepared just for you. Thank you ever so much for your dedicated service to the Fatherland."

From that point, until he paid his bill Carl wondered if the appreciation would be reflected with a free meal but no reward there. An above middle age waiter, who, like the headwaiter, was apparently too old for military service, provided his service. The meal went down to his stomach well and satisfied his hunger even more. While he was eating, the room filled with men in uniforms mostly of gray and blue colors. He was glad when he noted that no one entering wore the black uniform of the SS. A band took its place on the stage and began playing both old romantic German folk songs that he had heard from childhood and new ones unfamiliar to him. One was a particularly haunting melody that came after members of the audience called out for *"Lili Marlene."* Several couples took to the floor wrapped in the strong embraces of wartime romance. Then an officer in a blue uniform called for more patriotic songs. Those were accompanied by loud singing from the customers. Carl caught furtive glances directed at him as he ate but no one, he was thankful, approached him.

Finished with his dinner Carl first checked the watch on his wrist and observed that it was eight o'clock in the evening. After settling his bill through his waiter, he went to the street and began walking toward the rail station to check on the possibility of catching a train to the vicinity of Holland. Walking slowly and casually he was startled to see a group of military stopping and looking at what seemed to be the identity cards of pedestrians on the street. They were moving very slowly in his direction and while he thought that he probably could get through this check, it was better to avoid it if he could.

At that moment, he was standing in front of a movie theater looking at the posters of the current attractions and it seemed normal to go in. The movie featured an actress name Zarah Leander, a name that stuck in his memory for two reasons. First was the odd spelling of a name he thought must be akin to "Sarah." The second was that a Texas hamlet near Austin bore the same name as the actress' family name. In fact, there had been a cadet named Lahrer a year ahead of him from Leander.

A feature self-identified as "news" was on as he entered, and it showed the *Luftwaffe* destroying British and Russian planes by the tens. The newsreel, as these movie features had been called in America, showed the bullets of German fighters ripping and tearing at the fuselages and wings of the planes of their enemies. It showed night scenes of anti-aircraft guns firing at targets illuminated in the sky by searchlights. There was even one of a British bomber, whether it was a Wellington or not could not be determined because of the dark of the night, flaming downward through the teepee-like poles of lights seeking their way to the sky. "This," declared the narration, "shows the futility of the efforts to the British and certainly they should see that their continued struggle against the people's *Reich* is in vain and they must make peace. They will see that their real enemy is Bolsheviks on the eastern front."

The main feature exalted a young woman, portrayed by the blonde actress, speaking German with a slight but pleasing accent and prolific in bearing children of the pure Aryan race for the glory of the Fatherland. Her greatest delight, after the hope of bearing children for the *Führer*, seemed to be planting and harvesting crops to feed the German people. The actress played a role that showed her, the epitome of a Nordic bloodline, as a stalwart in the war against the Bolsheviks, portrayed as seeking the destruction of German culture, and Jews, who sought to mongrelize the German genetic heritage.

Well into the film, he remembered that he was seeking a way out of Germany. Upon leaving the theater, he recalled that his leave orders gave him permission to go to a town in an area called Württemberg. He did not have the slightest idea where that province, if that was the right word, was. He surmised that it might be possible to discover its location at the rail station.

At the station, he went to a ticket window and asked, "What is the best routing to Littach by Donaueschingen in Württemberg?" Carl did not understand that this address indicated that Littach was a town near the larger town of Donaueschingen.

The agent, checking his tables, informed him that, "You must go to Frankfurt-on-Main, change trains for Stuttgart, change again to the Donaueschingen connection and then change once more to go to Littach.

He parried, "Here are my leave orders and this is my destination," showing with his fingertip the address on the papers.

The location seemed to send the agent into a rhapsody of contemplation, "Oh, what a beautiful area for a hero of the Reich to rest in. You may see the mountains from there and will be so close to the Bodensee! What a joy! So far from England and the bombs! So close to Swiss chocolates! I thank God in heaven that a worthy young man like you will have such a nice rest from your sacrificial service!"

Switzerland! Not Holland but even safer! It was a neutral country although surrounded by German and Italian territory. At least his parents could get the news that he was alive and well.

"Please give me tickets to that destination. And, please, when does the train leave? *Ach*, and what track will it be on?"

"The next departure is in two hours and seventeen minutes on track 4. As you know, we try to run the trains at night to keep the *schweinhund* English bombers from interfering." It took a moment for the seller of train tickets to step back and pull several pieces of cardboard off a dispenser, stamp them and prepare to return to the window. While the ticket seller had his back turned, another man in a more impressive uniform approached the ticket seller and whispered in his ear. Tremors ran down the back of Carl as he thought that his deception had been discovered.

When his tickets arrived at the window the ticket agent pled, "Oh, sir, please forgive me! I did not know-ah-I did not understand that you, that you were so intimate—so close an aide to *Reichsführer* Himmler and the *Führer* himself! *Heil* Hitler"

"*Heil* Hitler," the Texan responded, unsure as to how to act in the face of the statement but decided on, "Yes, Herr *Reichsführer* Himmler has been considerate of me and I consider myself fortunate." Much relieved and breath escaping from his chest, he paid, received his tickets, and turned back to find a seat.

He had hardly gone fifteen steps when the second man called and asked for a moment of his time, "Sir, *Heil* Hitler, I am the station master. We would be pleased if you would allow us to show you the hospitality of our station. If you would follow me I will take you to the lounge for significant persons."

After rendering the omnipresent "*Heil* Hitler" and a short pause, Carl observed the diffidence of the stationmaster and willingly followed him to the lounge. There the seats were chairs, soft, padded chairs rather than the hard benches where he had been preparing to sit.

"Would you like a little *schnapps* or beer, or maybe a cup of coffee or tea?" was proffered.

"No," he replied, "I will just sit and look at some work I need to do but many thanks." Your kindness will always be remembered, *Heil* Hitler," he flattered the station host.

Bowing obsequiously and once more hailing the leader of the German government the stationmaster excused himself to return to his duties.

The stationmaster had not been gone five minutes when the sound of sirens broke through the din of the station. "Another raid!" cried voices outside the lounge. "Don't the Englishers have anything else to do? This is the third raid in ten days," declared another. "Where are the damn shelters? We had better get out of here!"

Carl agreed that it would be good to get away from the rail station for he remembered from his briefings that the rail yard was a primary target of the bombers. It would be strange indeed, if bombs did not fall on or near the station. It was near the railroad yard where several lines joined. So he moved quickly with the others and away from the station. They led him to a basement that was strongly built and reinforced with additional supports of its ceiling. A half-hour after entering this shelter came the sound of anti-aircraft guns firing at the air-raiders. The sound of much stronger explosions came nearer as bombs began to explode. The explosions of bombs bursting outside their shelter, together with its walls, prevented any noise of the British planes overhead. As they huddled together in shared anxiety and fear, it seemed that they grew closer together. When one explosive dropped so near that the building above them shuddered and dirt and dust fell upon them, a little girl, curled beside a woman who must have been her mother, turned for security and solace to the arms of Carl, the man in the uniform of her nation. Carl noticed that the adult woman clutched an infant to her breast, softly rocking back and forth on the bench and singing to the baby. The child in his arms received little attention from the woman and so she turned to Carl. Her body, sobbing and shaking, moved closer and closer into his embrace. Like an echo ringing down the halls of his subconscious he sang the comforting songs and made the comforting sounds that his mother had crooned to him.

As the sounds of the war outside slowly diminished, the wails of the terror inside did also. The mother turned fully to confront Carl and said to the man in the SS uniform, "Sir, please accept my deepest thanks. My husband is serving at the eastern front and we have not heard from him since December. Thank you for caring for my little Monica."

"*Bitte*," he responded, "She also was a comfort to me. I think that in times like these we must all be comfort one to another. May we meet again under happier circumstances. I hope that you will soon hear that your man is well and happy and that Monica can be in his arms and not in a stranger's."

To himself Carl thought, "I wonder if this means that I have consorted with the enemy and given aid and comfort to them like the Articles of War say? If the Germans catch me I will be shot at dawn and if I violated my oath my own people may shoot me." He knew that the last was only a humorous thought to relieve the tension of his flight and plight.

Soon all the occupants of the shelter were out into the night air…air filled with the smell of cordite, smoke, the wailing of sirens, and the shouts and screams of people. The size and the tempo of the air raids had begun their ever-increasing upward curve. Looking back to see about returning to the train station in order to catch his train, there was no order there. He discovered that the escape from the station had been wise. The ruined building now burned with intense heat. In the yard, steam engines, passengers cars, and freight cars lay strewn around as the playthings of a great giant's child. Escape from the city by way of the rail line was not to be accomplished this night. Carl thought, "Boy, the RAF did a real job tonight! They hit the target right on the head. It will take two weeks or a month to get this mess back in working order. Is there another way I can get from here down to near Switzerland?" Carl needed time for thought but the environment was not conducive to planning with the noise and pandemonium all about him. He thought to himself probably the best place to do this was back in the hotel room.

Less than half a block on the retrace of his route a whole company of men, firemen, police, soldiers, and civilians, battled a blaze that burned fiercely in the lower stories of what appeared to be an apartment house of four floors. Men attempted to control the fires with jets of pressurized water spewing from hoses. Two men on the sidewalk were unable to control the power of the water-pressured nozzle. Without thinking, but only seeing that there was a job to be done, he let his hands join the hands of the men to control and direct the stream of water into an upstairs window. One of the men shouted above the din, "*Vielen Dank, Hauptmann*" and then lapsed into silence as conditions allowed no time for appreciation. In the process of handling the powerful stream, his uniform became soaked through to his skin.

Now, above the general noise, Carl heard the screams of both those in the burning building and others on the street. One woman, collapsed to her knees on the street, cried in supplication, "My children, my children, Oh, God, please save my darlings. Please! Please! Please! Will not someone help me?"

Carl heard a fireman ask, "Where are your children?"

She looked at him in consternation, "Why, in my apartment in that building, you idiot!" Carl had time to shake his head at the way people acted in emergencies and their failure to communicate clearly in disaster.

The fireman tried again, "On what floor are they? How many are there?"

She cried out an answer, "On the fourth floor. There are three, Wilhelm, Erich, and little Hansel," reinforced by the shout of people pointing upward to the top of the building where the three could be seen screaming in fear just above the tall flames licking up the side of the building.

Murmurs around Carl piteously consigned the three tots to what appeared to be a sure fate. Impulse and some strange drive took over in Carl as he saw these younger versions of himself in peril. Seeing a stairway not yet consumed by flames, although the inferno ranged dangerously close to the steps, he instinctively broke from the crowd and raced into the building. Holding his dripping uniform sleeve over the lower half of his face he bolted through the open door of the building to the shouts of crowd, "No! No! You can do nothing! Stop! Stop him someone!" No one reached out to restrain him and before he could think, he was halfway up the first flight of stairs leading to the second level.

As he, in a blind and unthinking action, raced up to the second level, and then the third, and finally the fourth, he felt the heat searing toward him. Tongues of fire leapt like those of hell and reached out to embrace him with the hug of hate. Even in his closed-minded fixation on his self-assumed task, he was aware of the tentacles of fire and their accompaniment of crackling small and larger explosions. As he rose higher in the building, the smoke grew thicker and more suffocating. The only advantage that Carl had over the claims of the fire and its smoke partner was the moisture of the uniform and particularly the sleeve, which he held as tightly as possible over his mouth and nose. Even here the heat was so strong that his clothing seemed to dry instantly.

When he reached the fourth floor he raced the few steps to a door that he thought must lead to the apartment of the children. Leveraging the heated door handle, he thrust the door open and beheld his objects. Panic-stricken and crying out their fear the three moved away from him as he approached. He surprised himself by addressing them calmly, "Come children, your mother sent me for you. She wants you to come with me." The two smallest, although still weeping, seemed slightly quieted with the mention of their mother and came to him. Still the largest shied away as Carl thought of the tales he had heard of horses preferring the remembered security of a blazing stable to the unknown of the outside. Firmly, he told the largest, "I am going to carry these two out. You follow me! Do you understand?" A mute stare and movement even further away from his would-be rescuer greeted his directions.

Carl considered his options. The situation of all four grew steadily worse as the fire found fuel. Thinking, "I must save at least these two!" the would-be savior grabbed the two youngest and moved to the stairs. As he descended, the licks of flame were even closer now than at his ascent. The sounds of wooden beams splitting were louder and the heat more intense. Still the stairs held as he came to the third level, then the second level, and finally he broke out into the smoke filled air around the building. His emergence was greeted with great cheers from all the crowd but one.

Grasping the two from his arms the mother cried in anguish, "Where is Wilhelm? Why did you not bring my Wilhelm out?" And then with a cry that Carl thought came close to that of a banshee she screamed, "You must go back for Wilhelm! Save Wilhelm!"

Asking the hose handlers to soak him once more Carl broke for the entrance. As he raced to the second level, it was obvious even in his driven state that the supports of the stairs at this level were weakening by the instant. Nevertheless he was able to negotiate his way to the top floor and once more to the apartment where he had last seen little Wilhelm. Even during this time a humorous thought raced through is mind, "Why couldn't little Wilhelm have been a good Kraut and just follow orders?" There was no more time for idle thoughts and he entered and found his target cowering in a corner. Striding quickly to the terrified child, he picked him up, uttering comforting words as he did so.

Now the boy clung desperately to Carl's neck and even seemed to want to wrap his legs around his protector. Wrapping both arms around the child Carl once more made his way to the stairs. Even in the few elapsed minutes, the fire had increased in strength and destructiveness. The flames rose through the openings in the stairwell as though it was a chimney suited for its own purpose. By the time the two, rescuer and rescued, reached the last flight of stairs any option of using it to carry the boy down was obviously vain. Carl did see an open window at that level and moved to it.

Carl shouted, "Get below me and catch the boy! Hurry! Hurry!" The crowd saw and heard his commands but, intimidated by the fire and the danger of collapsing walls, only a few moved at first. Again Carl repeated his commands, "I tell you to get to the window and catch this child! Right now! Move!"

Now a dozen men, mostly older men beyond the age for military service and cautious in maturity, edged closer to the building. The authority in Carl's voice demanded obedience. One, a fireman emboldened by Carl's urgent commands, organized them by snatching up a blanket on the ground and stretching it out to form a rescue net held open by the hands of a dozen or so. The fireman, warning all that they must grip the blanket firmly before the child landed on it, then turned his face upward and communicated, "We are ready, Captain. Do you have more orders for us?"

"Just make sure the young lad is safe. I am going to have to throw him away from the building."

Upon hearing these words from him little Wilhelm clung even tighter to the rescuer he had so recently shunned. The boy's embrace made it impossible to gain separation between the two until Carl with force removed the little arms entwined tightly around his neck, saying, "Wilhelm, you must jump to those men! There is your mama over there. Do you see her?"

Wilhelm nodded, "Yes," tears rolling down his face, and released the grip of his legs about Carl's middle.

Carl turned him so that he faced to the street and ordered, "Close you eyes. Get stiff. You are going for a ride."

The boy complied with the order. Carl put his right hand under the crotch of the child, brought him to shoulder level and launched him out of the building to the waiting blanket below. Finally thinking of his own predicament, Carl only caught a glimpse of the child in the blanket held firmly in the arms of the men.

He had only time to turn to seek the best avenue of escape. As Carl rushed to the stairway and attempted to leap over the gulf of flames, he sensed more than saw a great wall of fire flying toward him. Then all consciousness was gone....

He wakened from the trance-like nightmare he had endured. His alertness, heightened by the realization of his continuing peril, sharpened. He abandoned the still so vivid past and focused on his present situation.

The doctor inspected his leg that day and concluded that it would take another ten days before the patient could stand safely. Addressing the injured youth with a broad and beaming smile, he exclaimed, "But there is great news for you. Your wife has been ordered and granted permission to travel here to the city to visit you and arrangements have been made for her stay in a room here in the hospital. Of course she cannot stay in this room for we do not want any, uh, ah, excitement to irritate your wounds. I am sure you understand all my meaning. You know the difficulties and the restrictions by the authorities on travel in these times but you have influence in high places and the wheels were greased. She is expected, let us see, today is Thursday, and then there is Friday, and Saturday, ah, yes, she will arrive Sunday. That is just three days. Just think that in three days you will see your woman, Captain Schleiter."

It was good that the bandages still completely covered his face for Carl felt the blood rush into the pit of his body. A wife! Someone who knew his now dead captor intimately. Someone who probably knew every bump, every facet of her husband's body. Small differences, such as the shape of a fingernail, not only could but also probably would reveal him as the impostor he was. He was helpless and could only wait for the revelation of his double identity. He searched for hope. The bandages still on his hand and his fingers took care of the fingernail matter. Conversation was the real danger: talk of friends and acquaintances; intimate moments shared; places they had visited together; yes, these were the danger points. He vowed to say as little as possible.

CHAPTER 2

✿

May 1942
The Wife

The Countess Marlene simply had endured as she traveled, forehead against window, eyes moist with unshed tears, as forests, hills, and communities rolled by the window of the train. The order, not requests, not permission, had been mandatory and arbitrary. She would go to be with her husband and to be prepared to escort him to Littach. As she thought of Friedrich her mind forced her to remember the night they were wed. It had been by any measurement, a brutal night, not to be gauged by the brutal lechery but by her husband's obvious desire to humiliate her. Almost uncontrollably, he had ranted about her noble birth, indeed, all nobility, especially her father. She had always desired bride hood, womanhood, motherhood. Her bridal night shattered the adolescent dreams with purgatorial assaults on her emotions, mind, and body.

Was God exacting justice from on high on Friedrich Schleiter for that night? Was it for the detestation that consumed him for all who were not like him. She had known him for years as a man filled with a consuming hatred for Jews, gypsies, and Godly believers. She believed that all humans were depraved and some, from a human viewpoint, more so than others, but she had never in her innocence suspected that anyone could have sunk to the depths she had seen in this *Nazi* officer.

She acknowledged to herself that wrongful acts brought their own consequences. She had married Friedrich Schlieter for what she felt were good reasons but without a consecrated love. Would providence permit a desecration of her body because of misjudgment? All the teaching her father had given her told her that God wanted to fill her life with joy. She felt violated and not joyous. What had happened to God's promises? Why had God permitted evil to triumph among her beloved German people? God had promised that the gates of hell could not stand against the gospel of Christ but it appeared that the demons of Satan sallied forth from those gates to destroy those who believed.

Now she was to face him once more. He had the power of the government on his side, and humanly speaking, she was powerless. Even as she uttered silent petitions questions continued. Was this injury punishment on him? Was she now to endure sharing her body with a sadistic, disfigured, and horrifying ogre? He was powerful and had connections to those with far more power than he possessed.

In desperation, she turned to One who knew and prayed. For some reason the story of Esther flooded into her mind with the words, "for such a time as this." She had done what she thought had to be done. The gravest consequences afflicted her and she was willing to bear them for the life of her father.

A different fear and trepidation gripped Carl Solms the days he waited in his hospital room for the arrival of his "wife." What would the Germans do when the woman exposed him? They would certainly want to know who he truly was. Would they try him and execute him as a spy? Would they even give him a trial? Would they summarily execute him as a spy? Would they accuse him of the murder of this fellow Schleiter and execute him? His best hope was to spend the rest of the war in a camp as a wounded, one-legged prisoner. He could do nothing but wait and so resolved to keep his silence as much as possible in his "wife's" presence. He did not even know her given name. Was there a way he could discover it before her arrival? It would be good to say something like, "Oh, my darling Lisa, you don't know the joy it gives me to see you." Surely something more than, "*Wie geht es Ihnen?*" must be said by husbands who have been separated from their wives for an extended time.

On the other hand, did German culture differ? His parents and grandparents were not demonstrative. Possibly it was part of Teutonic culture. Certainly the young patient had no knowledge or experience in these marital situations. At least he should know her name. For the first time he consciously empathized with the creatures snared by his traps in the river bottom back in Texas. They too had no way of escape and only waited for the executioner's blow. He possessed one advantage over the little victims of his traps. His hunters did not know yet that they should search for him, that he was a quarry. His little prey had been physically caught and their identity known but his true identity was not established yet.

Now, recognizing the danger of extra talk, he determined to engage the hospital staff in as much conversation as possible. He forced himself to speak despite the pain that the movement of his jaws and lips caused and his difficulty in forming words. This must be done. When an attendant entered the room once more Carl rasped, "I believe it would be good to exercise my throat by speaking. Could you find time from your busy duties to talk with me?"

"Ah, yes," responded the nurse, just a little flattered that her diligence had been noted, "I have some time now. Does it not pain you to talk? What would you like to talk about?"

"Well," came back the invalid, "What is the news of the war?"

"You probably know more than me but the radio says that we will capture the great cities of Russia very soon. Our boys are driving triumphantly on Leningrad, Moscow and the mountains of the Caucasus. Mr. Goebbels has reported that the Russian government has fled Moscow and that peace will soon follow the capture of that capital. It is reported that General Rommel and his *Afrika Korps* will soon take Cairo and drive on to Mesopotamia. Yes, all is good."

"And what of the British? Do they still bomb?"

"That is for sure," retorted the woman, "but not on our city since the raid in which you were injured. They seem to have moved on to other places. My cousin, who lives in Bremen, said they got it good and many homes were destroyed. I do not understand the English; do they not know their real enemies are the Bolshevik Russians? The English are really Aryan, you know. Many of us and many of them are of Saxon blood, you understand. Why do they not stand with their blood kin? We all know that the *Führer* will lead us to victory. He is our greatest genius since Frederick and we know what that great king did."

"Well," thought Carl, "she does want to talk."

His next line of dialogue proposed a game, "Do you know my wife's given name? No, then let us see if you can guess. If you do, you may take a vase and bouquet of these flowers home with you."

"How should I know your wife's name?" was her come back, "Do you think I'm a gypsy that I should have special vision?"

"I thought you might fool me and have seen the records." he suggested as a hint, "But if you can't guess I get to keep those lovely, bright flowers."

"Well, keep your crazy blossoms. I haven't time to play guessing games," was the impatient retort.

"Well," thought the one-footed patient, "Nothing ventured, nothing gained. That was a failure."

He was mistaken. The next time the nurse appeared she beamed and acted as though she was the mistress of all knowledge. "For sure you are the wise one. You wanted me to know how well married you are! Indeed, a countess twice over yet!"

Playing along, Carl stated, assuming that what she said was true, after all, the captain did have connections, "Sure, she is a countess but you can't guess her name. That was the deal."

"I most certainly can. You married the Countess Marlene von Krönitz and Ritterbach, daughter of Count Erich Albert von Krönitz and the Countess Theresa von Ritterbach. Her father once had large land holdings until the *New Order* came to Germany. When her mother died, she should have inherited more great holdings in Württemberg by the Black Forest. She is known as Marli to those who are close to her."

"You didn't guess," complained Carl in mock petulance, "You must have read my records in the hospital office or something. But I'll keep my word and you can have your pick of the flowers." The most beautiful arrangement of flowers presented to him disappeared from the deep sill of the casement window in his room that day.

So his supposed wife was of noble birth and named "Marlene" but was "Marli" with her friends. Should he first greet her as Marlene? Germans, he knew from personal experience with his parents and grandparents can be formal. His *Omas* still referred to their husbands as "Mister" even after more than four decades of marriage. In moments of emotion or intimacy, Schleiter may have whispered, "Marli." He decided just to greet her with what seemed natural.

The conversations with the staff members continued and he learned that the shelves of stores were becoming more barren each week; the losses of the Royal Air Force on their bombing raids were immense; German submarines were successful in sinking almost every Allied ship in the Atlantic. Wearied by his queries and acknowledging his special standing, the staff offered to bring a radio to his room so that he could hear of the great victories of the Germans and their Allies. The Japanese were expected to occupy the Hawaiian Islands within months to compliment their conquests of the Philippines, Malaya, the East Indies, and the islands of the Pacific. "Will I, and can I, maintain this deception for the remainder of my life in the event that we lose the war?" Carl questioned himself.

He continued to do every exercise that he could think of in his bed to maintain the strength of his muscles, pulling and pushing the iron bed until his muscles ached. He also lifted his legs up against the bed covers as far as he could and maintained them there as long as he could to strengthen his stomach muscles. The exercise had given him a strong appetite and the food was pleasing and would, as his father's mother had often said, "stick to his ribs."

He knew that two critical moments lay in the near future. The first would be the confrontation with the countess/wife. She might well sense and expose his masquerade. The other decisive moment would be when the doctor removed the bandages and his facial features were exposed. He did not fear the second occurrence as much as the first for his overall coloring matched that of the dead German. Same color hair, eyes, height, and weight. Sure, his voice tones were different but the blow to the voice box could excuse that. He hoped, however, that every time he looked in the mirror to shave that he would not frighten himself with hideousness.

He was curious as to his supposed wife. Was she a plump *hausfrau* like so many he had seen? Was she a horse-faced aristocrat? He applied this mental picture of female faces at the top of a pear shaped figure with too broad hips and a flat chest to the aristocrats of all nations. Was she a *Nazi* zealot? Probably, because it seemed that her husband certainly was close to the top circles of the *Nazi* Party. Was she sharp, alert to details and contradictions? Was he a father? Were there children to be accounted for? He hoped not, for he was sure to have slips in recognition and many other things. There was nothing he could do but wait and see how long it took him to be exposed as the impersonator he had been forced to become.

In the wait until Sunday, he continued his talks with any of the medical staff who would listen and talk. He asked if any had been to the town specified in his leave orders. None had been but they told him of the charms of the Black Forest in that part of Germany and the glistening beauty of the *Bodensee*. It took him some time to realize that to the Germans what he had learned as Lake Constance was the *Bodensee*. His knowledge of geography had never revealed that name to him. As to the land of Count Krönitz in the state of Hanover, all the hospital staff knew was that it had included a lot of land before Hitler. He had learned that the family Krönitz rightfully claimed distant relationship to the royal family of England. So now he knew that his supposed wife was related, although distantly, to the king of England. This sure did not paint a pretty picture but one of a cold and snobby better-than-thou woman. Served the good *SS* Captain Schleiter right; they deserved each other, a cold aristocrat and a vicious *Gestapo* officer.

No daughter of a Protestant protester, a dissenter of the policies of the National Socialist regime, could have expected the privileged treatment that the Countess Marlene Schleiter received upon her Sunday arrival at the rail station in the city. An *SS* lieutenant, a driver and a large car waited to take her to the hospital. The officer, whose name she never bothered to remember, was unctuous in his attention to the degree that she longed to be free of his toadying presence. As they drove, she saw for the first time the damage inflicted on this and other cities of the Reich. Somehow, the sight assured her of the reality and justice of her God.

At the door of the hospital the fawnery continued as several people awaited her arrival. After all, her husband, although low in rank, certainly had the ear of the *Reichsführer-SS* and possibly the *Führer* himself. In the old days she would have been a rich woman of consequence and famed nobility.

In keeping with the training in graciousness from childhood she responded to the flattery with smiles and kind words reinforced by a touch of her hand on an arm of one of the male escorts. She felt no apprehension of or resentment toward these medical people who did their job. She turned a *faux pas* of an accompanying nurse into humor shared by the party as she set the pace with purposeful stride under the direction of the staff.

As the room of Friedrich Schleiter grew closer some of the escort faded away to their own responsibilities having satisfied their desire to bask in the acquaintance of the young noblewoman.

If only they knew of her real opinion of their hero of the *Reich*!

On Sunday morning the nurses were officious in their care of Carl. They removed the blood-tinged bandages on his face, even more carefully removed facial hair, his body thoroughly bathed, his hair combed and plastered down, and a generous application of scented, stinging *Kolnischer Wasser* was applied before they replaced the bandages. In short, they made him ready for the visit of his wife. His pulse did beat with a strong thump in his chest but not for anticipation of seeing a loved one or the physical drive of the appearance of a mate. His chest beat heavy with the strain of the test he feared he would have to undergo and the care he would need in every word that he spoke to this woman who should know him so well.

On that Sunday morning Marlene Schleiter, *Countess von Krönitz*, *Countess of Ritterbach*, and legal wife of *SS* Captain Friedrich Schleiter, marched purposefully along the hall of the city hospital. Her heels clicked in rhythmic and steady beat upon the anesthetically clean floor. She paid little heed to the physician who had greeted her as she stepped from her transportation.

"Welcome to our hospital, Baroness Schleiter. Your husband is recuperating wonderfully, I am sure you will be happy to hear." Seeking her favor, he informed the lady, distinguished by birth and by her husband's service to the *Reich*, the details of her husband's care: the name of the doctors to include the skilled repairer of facial damage, the special diet that had been prepared, and even her husband's room number.

Now, eyes ahead, shoulders back, her dress swaying in rhythm with her stride, she marched toward the designated room without waiting for the medic who scurried along beside her. "What pain she must be in! What love she must have for this man! She is truly Spartan! What a tragedy that she must now face this lover who may be like the creation of Doctor Frankenstein! I will not tell her anything as to what to expect. She will soon discover it herself when the bandages are removed. I will not know and will be innocent."

As they neared the room nurses and another doctor joined the party as it grew from two to three then to five. The countess, although she continued in a fixed and determined way, graciously returned the greetings extended to her but with little warmth. Recalling the immediate reason she was in this place at this time those about her excused any appearance of hauteur.

"The decision was made for me. Had I a choice I might not have come, but the authorities ordered me to attend my husband. I question myself as to what I would have done if those two had not come to my home. It was not that I feared an air attack on the train; but to me, there was no need to come. Oh, well, I am here and will soon see him, damaged as he is."...

The mayor of the town of her residence as well as the county leader of the National Socialist Democratic Party, known to the world as the *Nazi* Party, represented the "authorities". The two identified themselves through the speaker at the gate and requested admission. She opened the gate electronically and watched as they approached her door.

She acknowledged them with "*Guten Morgen, Bürgermeister* Schlenkmann and *Kreisleiter* Greider. What brings you this way?"

She refused to say that it was a pleasure to see the mayor whose broad face and body and wide but tight-lipped smile was in keeping with his character. She recognized the second man as the ambitious-beyond-his-ability official of the *Nazi* Party, dressed in his brown greatcoat and uniform, black boots, and small pistol as his honor weapon. While restraining a smile of welcome for the two, she continued with caution, "Please come in from the rain and I will have *Frau* Weber prepare some tea. I trust your wives are well."

After the ubiquitous "*Heil Hitler!*" the two men glanced at one another before Greider answered, "Baroness Schleiter, you are very gracious and we thank you for the invitation," thinking to himself that the woman should be sitting when she heard the news. Not that he felt warm toward this woman but he should keep up appearances of caring until it was no longer useful. As the two stepped into the residence the Party leader observed with covetous eyes the nobility of both the furnishings and classical elegant walls and ceiling arising through centuries of aristocratic good taste.

She contemplated, "Why are these men here? Has something happened to Papa? Has he been taken into custody? Is he sick? Is he injured? Or are they going to require something of me?"

"May I ask again the reason for your welcome visit to my home? It is not often that we have visitors from the town," as she reached for the handle of a teapot that an older woman had placed before them.

Greider, the senior party leader of the area, thought that he had the responsibility of presenting the news of the woman's husband.

"Baroness, we bring disturbing news of your husband. He has been seriously injured but is alive and receiving the best of medical care. The first reports stated that his injuries came from heroically rescuing children from a burning building following an air attack upon the city. His duties called him to the city where he was serving the *Führer* and the *Reich* faithfully. We have been informed that he suffered serious burns and other injuries, but none are life threatening. There is also some question about other injuries. We make this visit at the expressed direction of *Reichsführer* Himmler who we all know thinks highly of your man. *Reichsführer* Himmler has directed that we pass on any additional news to you as quickly as possible."

"Do you desire sugar, Burgomaster Schlenkmann? Milk?" the hostess asked with equanimity. "And you, *Kreisleiter* Greider? Sugar? Milk?"

She continued in the same cultured and reserved voice, "Do you have means to communicate my appreciation to the *Reichsführer* for his concern for the wife of one of his men? If so, please do so. I do thank you for your trouble in coming to my home in this weather to inform me. You will keep me informed of any change in Friedrich's condition? Please take a piece of the little cake. It is very good. *Frau* Weber is a wonderful cook. It does appear that we are going to have a late summer, does it not?"

"We will, of course, keep you informed. The main office of the *Schutz-staffeln* instructed us to direct you to be prepared to go to the hospital. There you will visit your husband and escort him to this residence when the doctors say he can be moved. We regret that we cannot authorize your journey now. The exigencies of war and the condition of Captain Schleiter rule against it at this time. You are right, Baroness, this cake is delicious but we must be going. We regret that we have had to deliver such troubling news but it could have been worse for your husband yet lives. Please excuse us. We will show ourselves out."

Seizing the opportunity to use this excuse to escape the company of the men a bit sooner, she only nodded as she cast her eyes toward the floor in order that her relief remained hidden from the mayor and the *Nazi* leader. As soon as she heard the front door close behind the men, she lifted her gaze and moved briskly into the kitchen.

After more than two weeks' wait, *Kreisleiter* Greider informed her by telephone that the order for her trip had arrived. He added that his sedan would be at the residence to take her to the train station the next mid-morning. Having readied her appearance early the next morning, the double countess went quickly to the vehicle even before it came to a complete halt on the gravel.

The Party official then presented her with tickets and travel papers. These not only permitted her to travel, but also gave her no choice, by order of *Reichsführer-Schutzstaffeln* Heinrich Himmler. Some authority provided a detailed train schedule with all the necessary tickets needed to transfer between trains. *Kreisleiter* Greider informed her that a representative of the *SS* would meet her at the station in the city. The hospital director would provide her with a private room in the hospital.

Her mind said, "The old aristocracy may be condemned but there is now a *Nazi* privileged class. It is strange that I should get its benefits."...

It was half past eleven when one of the nurses came laughing into Carl's room and ostentatiously began fussing with the remaining flowers. First they moved them this way and then back again that way. He could see her sending glances at him all the time. "This is going to be worse than I expected. Everyone will watch me and this woman's reaction like hawks. If there is one inconsistency, I'm cooked!"

Finally, he heard voices and steps in the hall, although this time the steps were not in cadence and someone's heels did click sharply on the floor. Listening he tried to catch a female voice but only heard male voices. Even from his position, he realized that they were seeking to impress the countess with the care her husband had received as well as the honor they had been granted. Finally, Carl observed Dr. Hildendorf standing outside the door, which had been propped open, and wave to communicate to someone to enter before him. In stepped the someone.

She came dressed in a gray loose dress best called colorless under an equally drab black full coat. As she quickly removed a black hat of the style of the 1930's he saw that she had tied her hair in a tight bun. Her face contained little color and seemed pallid, entirely devoid of rouge or lipstick. Carl thought "Very severe. Harsh and hard but not really the face of a horse!" Her entire ensemble as a middle-aged *hausfrau* belied the fact that she appeared to be much younger. Although bulky and drab in dress, her age might be from twenty to thirty-five but because her husband was essentially Carl's age, he assumed that she was at the lower end of that range. She walked into the room and greeted, "Hello, Friedrich. I am glad you survived and I am genuinely sorry for the injuries you have suffered."

"We do have one cold fish here," Carl mentally noted to himself. "What did she mean by 'genuinely'? I probably should maintain that mood."

"And how are you, Marlene? How was your journey?"

"Very good, Friedrich," she answered with just a trace of surprise in her voice at his gentle inquiry. Appearing to become uncertain and aware of the onlookers she decided she would be expected to show a little emotion even before the onlookers. She leaned over the bed and gave a peck of a kiss on his hair above the bandages.

"A mummy!" flashed through the mind of the young wife. "He looks like the pictures of a mummy that are in my books. But he asked about my journey! That is a first!" In spite of her deep revulsion toward him, some force within her forced a feeling of compassion toward her tormentor. He had been an active and viral youth, loving physical games. But, she continued in her thoughts, he always played to win at any cost, both viciously and cowardly, and though he had the ability to win seemed to take pleasure in cheating.

"*Danke*, Dr. Hildendorf. You have been very helpful. Will you please leave us for a half-hour so we can be alone?"

"*Bestimmt*, Countess, and if there is anything you want just pull the cord there and the hospital will be at your service. Is there not something we can get for you, a cup of tea or coffee, a nice little glass of good Moselle wine, or a bite to eat?"

"Not at the moment but perhaps a little later. I want to be alone with Captain Schleiter now. I will call with the cord if we desire anything. Thank you." The last was far more a dismissal than a phrase of appreciation. The hospital director so understood it and quickly shushed the rest of the group from the room.

As soon as the doctor and his staff cleared the room, the woman turned to the bed occupant, surveyed him slowly, and finally said, "So you were a hero and saved three children? What happened? Did you go out of your head?"

Carl thought, "She cares about her Friedrich and cannot stand the idea of her love taking such risks." Aloud he tried to be indefinite, "I don't know. It just happened." He did not think it wise to go into a long explanation of how some irresistible instinct assumed control. His response caused her to shake her head as though in wonder.

Marlene *von* Krönitz Schleiter then opened her purse, a sensible and spacious bag, and drew forth a bundle of envelopes bound with twine. Carefully and calmly, she untied the string to free the envelopes and offered them to Carl. Reaching out to take them he asked, "Have you read them?"

Her reply was taut, "Of course not! Some are official."

"I can not see well with these bandages and all. Will you open them and read them to me, please?"

"If attitudes were weather there would be ice in this room," thought Carl. "She sure isn't demonstrative."

He had asked her to open the letters and read them to him because he had discovered that the bandages made it difficult to get a clear view of reading material.

She had turned and was approaching a chair when his request came to her. As she spun around her face communicated total shock and surprise. "Just when did it become correct for me to read your correspondence?" She demanded, and continued, "Almost all of these envelopes show that they are official party matters. I do not believe you want me to know their content and I certainly do not want to share in them. Read them yourself when you can!"

"Oops. That was a mistake! Gotta be more careful. She is and her husband was German. He was definitely the boss and did not let her do anything. But, boy, she can be a Tartar. Something doesn't figure. She keeps her place as wife with the letters and then kind of tells him off!" he told himself. He then put the correspondence on the bed as though reading it was too exhausting and difficult, and turned on his side away from her.

At this movement she announced, "I am tired after traveling all day. I will go to my room and rest. I will send the nurse in. You may want something." With this pronunciation, she disappeared through the door.

After she left he considered, "She didn't even tell me that I looked like a mummy or a zombie! Doesn't she want to have a sense of humor?"

When the nurse entered, he, for the first time, asked for a sleeping draught and a glass of water. These were provided and the chemicals did their duty and he soon slept soundly.

In her room, Marlene threw herself on the bed, shuddering with grief, longing for the comforting arms of her father. No longer could she restrain the sobs that wracked her body as the memories of her relationship with Friedrich Schleiter tortured her mind. Resolving, she regained control and mouthed a petition heavenward. "Why? Why? Why do I have to bear this burden?"

She had struggled to obey God and to protect her beloved father but…now? Married to a disfigured sadist! "Why? Why?" God had let her union be worse than anything she could have ever imagined. "Why?"

What kind of wife should she be? Coerced into a secular marriage filled with detestation and void of affection, what would God want of her? She had been taught that the wife was to be submissive to her husband. But this man? His conduct had been that of a depraved beast before and his appearance might well portray the inner man that she knew. Her mind searched for purpose but could discover none.

She decided that her only course was to trust and take the next step and be prepared to take another.

That evening Carl asked the nurse to help him open the mail and hold it at his eye level so he could read it. Unless it was in code, it was entirely insignificant and pertained to *Nazi* Party matters. It also included hopes that his leave time with his new bride would bring him great joy.

"New bride!" Now that was news indeed. Relief flooded because the marriage relationship had not been long and there should be gaps in familiarity. Almost certainly, he did not have to ask about children! There was mention of the great work he had done in the movement of people to the east. What was that about? He should know so he must guard his tongue. Tiring he asked the nurse to read and she, obviously impressed, informed him from a letter that the *Führer* himself had commented on the zeal and effectiveness of the young Captain Friedrich Schleiter

In the morning soon after his meal, the woman Marlene appeared once more. This time there was no kiss but only the minimum "*Guten Morgen.*"

Seeing the letters she had brought lying scattered about the bed and floor where they had fallen from the bed during the night, she muttered, "What have the nurses been doing?" She then proceeded to pick them up and lay them on the bedside stand. She did not utter another word.

"Well," he reflected, "if she wants to be silent that suits my needs perfectly. I can't give myself away with anything I say if I don't say anything."

Silent moments passed while the seated Marlene read. Nurses entered and left two times, casting curious glances at the young couple. He had time to examine her closely as she looked down at what she read. There was no blemish to her features other than, as he had noted before, they appeared hard and cold. The padded shoulders combined with the utter shapelessness of her dress caused him to think, "She must be one of those women called 'stout.'" Her hair, pulled into a tight bun, removed any softness from the flesh of her face. Had Carl used one word to describe her physical appearance he would have answered, "Strong." She seemed to want to hide the identity of the book she read and Carl was satisfied to let her have her privacy.

Occasionally she looked up to let her gaze fix on him as though he was a strange and puzzling creature. When she did, he could see that her eyes were Aryan blue. Finally, the supposed wife said, "I noticed a little chapel in the hospital. This is Sunday. I will go there for a while to pray." With this remark she peremptorily rose and left.

Concerned and a little frustrated at his helplessness, Carl determined to violate the orders and test his balance and strength by standing by his bed. Rotating his hips around he swung his legs over the side of the bed and watched to see if there was any rupture of the sutures where his right leg ended. Waiting for about two minutes, he observed that all seemed well. Now he ventured a little further and, grasping the highest point of the bed, stood erect on his leg. The act of standing and the descent of blood from his head caused a slight dizziness for a moment and then again all seemed well. Hopping on his foot along the wall, he approached a chair by the window that looked out from his room. He lowered himself gently into the chair. There was some discomfort where his leg had been severed but it was well worth it to be able to see outside.

He noted that the grounds of the hospital were rather extensive and well groomed. To see the sun and the interplay of the sunshine and the shade gave him exquisite pleasure in some most satisfying way. The beauty of the rays filtering through the budding limbs of the trees promised that after the darkest period there were promises of light and life. Possibly his mood shift came from a change from the antiseptic bareness of the four walls of the room. It may well have been the reassurance that the world continued despite the delinquencies of mankind. Lost in his meditation, he was unaware of steps in the hall until the sharp words came, "What are you doing? Were you not told of the danger of bleeding! Captain, we are responsible for your care so please be careful. But let's take a look at your wound while you are up." Turning his head, he observed an ashen-faced Dr. Hildendorf and the buxom nurse.

The doctor bent and looked at the bandaging at the end of his leg muttering "hmmm" and "yes" and other sounds impossible to understand. Finally, he said, "Amazing, very amazing. Your leg has scabbed over wonderfully. You did nothing to cause bleeding but we must be careful. I will order crutches for you to see if the sutures continue to hold and excessive bleeding does not occur. There will be some moisture for weeks but we don't want the arteries to rupture when you are away from the hospital."

Moving to another seat, Hildendorf began to write on a small pad for a minute or two and then looked up.

"Now, let me look at your face and see how it is doing." As he began removing the bandages they stuck to the incisions. Carl caught himself drawing his breath and trying to make comic sounds when the pain became strongest. The doctor, when finished, sympathetically said, "You stand pain well. The removal had to hurt but all is well." An examination of the surgery also pleased Hildendorf because there was no bleeding and all the incisions had closed nicely. "*Sehr Gute*! Very good!" he pronounced. "Soon we will be able to release you from our hospital. Now let's get you back to your bed."

Carl had not settled in bed long when the countess returned. The doctor described to her Carl's venture to the window and how nicely his wounds were healing. She received this news with calm and made no response. Dr. Hildendorf told Carl to be careful as he left the room.

Silence returned with the doctor's departure. Eventually, Carl, being thirsty, asked for a glass of water. He listened as his supposed wife's steps echoed down the hall and heard her greet the nurses. There followed laughing and talking from the nurse's station. Listening carefully, he could hear them congratulating her on her husband's quick recovery. Her responses were open and gay. She asked of them, their families, and of their work in the hospital. When she returned to the room with the glass, she was once again the reticent sphinx and remained so for the remainder of the afternoon. As darkness approached, she said she must leave and bid him good night.

Carl puzzled over what her emotions would have been had she known that her husband was not merely injured but was dead. He had a suspicion that she would have demonstrated little more grief than she had shown to date. When she had gone, Carl asked for and received a mirror. The reflection he saw bore little resemblance to the young Texan who had landed in Germany from a burning aircraft. His nose had been reshaped and bright red wounds extended over large areas of his face. His nurse told him, "When the wounds heal the scars of the surgery will fade a good bit. You truly will be like an aristocrat who is honored with many university saber scars." With that, he surmised, he must be satisfied. Then, remembering, he asked for the identification card. Comparing his new face with that on the card, he decided that he looked more like Friedrich Schleiter than Carl Solms and that might be good.

In the morning, with the countess present, Dr. Hildendorf entered with the buxom nurse carrying a set of crutches. "Please get out of bed, Captain, to see if you can use these," requested the medic. Taking them, Carl slid his legs from the bed and stood with the wooden aides under his armpits. With the assistance of the two supports, he negotiated his way around the room and into the hallway. His first thought of joy: "No more bedpans!" He wondered what this strange woman who was supposed to be his wife was thinking. She had no trouble talking to the doctor and the other hospital personnel but with him she kept her silence.

After a quick but thorough examination of the wounds on both his face and amputated leg, Hildendorf said, "I am glad that you are mobile because we must now release you from the hospital. Berlin has told us that we must receive fifty per cent of our capacity from the armed forces. With the civilian casualties from the bombings, we will be over-taxed to meet our responsibilities. So tomorrow you will be dismissed. Your wife will take you to your home in the south. We will give some antiseptics for your wounds and trust your wife to care for you. We will also give you any additional travel documents you might need and papers for an extended recuperation leave issued by Berlin." Turning to the nurse who was present, he ordered the prescribed medicines to be delivered to Captain Schleiter the next morning.

On Monday morning, hospital attendants brought in the briefcase and suitcase that the *SS* captain had left in the hotel before the fire. It contained the freshly cleaned and pressed uniform with which Carl had disguised himself at the death of the German officer. It also included bathroom items such as shaving gear, a comb, and after-shave lotion. All had been neatly folded and packed, possibly by the hotel staff. Because bandages encased his hands and much of his body, Carl required the assistance of hospital personnel to get dressed in the clean uniform. His right trouser leg was neatly folded and pinned over the stump-ending limb. The boot from his missing leg was also presented to him and later, in a private moment he was relieved to find that his identification tags and the slim New Testament were still secure.

Now his alleged wife arrived and the couple was escorted to a waiting ambulance. With several "*Heil* Hitler" and "*Sieg Heils*", the driver helped Carl into the back of the ambulance with his purported wife following him inside. He settled on a heavy cloth bench stretched on one side of the vehicle while the woman sat opposite him. He noticed that she had not changed her clothes although as he brushed against her dress it felt smooth and fine and was not the rough material that he had first assumed. He thought, "That feels like a rich girl's dress."

Her manner remained as aloof as ever although she showed compassion in aiding him on entering the transportation. With his head near the driver's compartment and with no windows on the side of the vehicle there was no opportunity to observe their progress. The woman maintained her silence for reasons of her own and he was more than satisfied not to risk exposure through idle conversation. Total, and to him, frosty silence reigned in the back of the ambulance.

One thing he did want to know, however, was their destination so asked. "Where are you taking me?" She replied cryptically, "*Schloss Altburg.*" He certainly could not ask the location of the castle for she obviously expected him to know. He just responded "Oh." and thought, "So the countess lives in a castle and wears a non-descript and shapeless dress made of finely woven wool. Well, that's probably the way of the continental higher classes: plain, snooty, and rich."

After several brief halts the ambulance came to a final stop and Carl heard the driver's door open. Then the rear doors opened and the driver said, "We are at the station. Will you help me, *Frau* Captain, in getting your husband out?" Carl found it strange that she was referred to by her husband's rank although he realized that the driver probably had not been informed that she was a countess. In any event, she readily agreed and the strength in her grasp surprised Carl and pained him through the sterile wrappings. As she took one of his arms and the driver the other he was soon aided and lifted through the rear door. She continued to hold him as the driver retrieved the crutches.

The driver then questioned, "Will you need my assistance in getting into the station, *Frau* Schleiter?"

She replied, "No, all is fine and I can manage him by myself."

Carl and the countess maneuvered their way onto the curb and the driver after expressing his appreciation with "*vielen Dank*," and an "*auf Wiedersehen*" took his place at the wheel of the ambulance and pulled away.

Marlene asked, "Do you need my help?" When he too said that he could make it without aid, she picked up the very light clothing bags and pointed the way they were to go.

Now Carl observed how the air raids had damaged the station. It had taken several hits. The workers had made good progress on large holes in the roof. Beyond the station, other laborers were putting their efforts into repairing the damage to the rails that led into and out of the station. Carl thought it amazing how much repair had been done following the raids.

The countess told him, "We will find a place for you to sit with your leg elevated so the blood will not press on the wound. The doctors said that we must see to it that the veins and arteries are not opened." When she had him settled, she informed him "I will go get the tickets while you sit here. Remember to keep your leg on the bench." With that, she disappeared behind him. Alone and almost unable to move on his own, he felt forlorn as he had not before.

"What a strange turn," he considered, "a short while ago I was in England with two legs and known to all in my true identity as Lieutenant Solms. Now I am a one legged captain of the *SS* sitting in a rail station in Germany waiting. I have a supposed wife who is a countess but who will hardly speak to me although she is taking time to care for me." He heard again the plaintive wail of the trains entering and rolling through the station and on to their destinations. In spite of the bombing, the people seemed to be going about their affairs calmly. Both soldiers of the *Wehrmacht* in their gray uniforms and the blue clad members of the *Luftwaffe* strolled about eyeing the damage done by the Royal Air Force. Adolescents in leather shorts proudly wore the crooked cross of the *swastika* on their arms. He surmised that they were members of the much-publicized Hitler Youth. The women looked as drab and colorless as the Countess Marlene did.

While waiting, a uniformed ticket agent who he finally recognized as the one who had provided the ticket before the fire, approached and exclaimed, "Things are really different, now, are they not, good Captain. When you were here a few weeks ago, my rail station was whole as you were. Those dog-mothered English have hurt my station and you. When I read of your bravery in the *Zeitung* I remembered you and thought even then that you had the real bearing of a hero. You did not just strut around but were kind and considerate to all you met. Did you hear of the stationmaster? Well, he did not make it. He refused to leave his post in his station and his office took a direct hit. He died instantly. Oh, I see your lady returning. It was good to see you again and to know that you at least survived."

When Marlene arrived she reported, "We can board the train in half an hour but we must eat first because we have not eaten this morning." She continued, "I have obtained some bread, sausage and wine." Although he had never been a wine drinker he thought it best that he wash the solids down with several sips thinking that maybe he "should take a little wine for his stomach's sake."

The food tasted so good and he was so appreciative that he automatically blurted out, in German, "*Danke*, Marlene." She turned her head at the words of appreciation and shot a quizzical look at him. "Have I goofed?" but everything quickly returned to what had been. Then it was time to board the train.

She carried the clothing containers belonging to both of them again and guided him to the track of their train. As he moved with the crowd toward the train, he could hear low voices commenting "hero," "Russian veteran," and "poor brave young man." Marlene's jaws clenched tight as she heard these comments. Uniformed men carefully checked most of the passenger's authority to travel and identity cards at the entrance to the train. Carl would never know whether he resembled Friedrich Schleiter enough to have passed through the checkpoints in his uninjured state. His facial bandages combined with his lost leg washed away any inclination for the examiners to doubt but they examined the woman's papers closely. Assisted by the men and his alleged wife at the steps to the train he entered the rail car. Once more, the woman led the way to an unoccupied compartment

Once she settled on the bench seat across from him, she ordered, "Raise your amputated leg up onto the seat to guard against bleeding." As she said this there seemed to be a twitch in his heart at the sad, somber look on her face when she turned from him to fix her gaze purposefully out the window. There was a slight lurch and jolt as the car started in motion. Soon the station had disappeared and rail yards were about all that was visible for several minutes. Then the buildings of the city came by the windows of the rail car. The houses and buildings of the city quit flitting by eventually and the morning light revealed open country. It became clear to Carl that their train was an express of some kind as they passed though station after station without stopping.

Marlene ignored both the passing scenes of well-kept fields and many villages to concentrate on a book she had drawn from her ever-present handbag. Curiosity as to what could be of such interest to her nagged at him until he discovered that she was studying some theological work. She seemed careful that no other person could see what she read.

In about a half-hour they entered a city designated as Frankfurt by signs in the station and the train stopped for passengers to leave and arrive. When they continued at a high rate of speed for an hour and a half, Carl noticed that they crossed a four lane divided highway on which could be seen significant military and civilian truck traffic. Marlene commented, seemingly without thinking, "The *autobahn.*" As the hours passed they stopped in one more city and then another. At last they rolled into a station clearly labeled Stuttgart. Carl had enjoyed the beauty his eyes beheld through the window, the neatly cultivated small fields, the many tiny villages, and the open and well-groomed woods that he had observed on foot. He considered this land as well kept as any city park he had ever encountered.

A careful observer would have noted that the woman turned no pages as her mind drifted to the person of the semi-prone figure across from her. Their communication had been scant but there was something emanating from him that perplexed her. Before his injury, he had never expressed appreciation, especially to anyone lower on the social scale, now he did! He even seemed somewhat considerate of her although he remained typically aloof.

Changing the focus of her gaze, she considered the lovely landscape, green and growing greener with each passing spring day, that rolled by. The hills, soft and promising, seemed to have a maternal love for the villages nestled in their curves. People, strong and industrious, some men, many women, made their way from the hamlets to the fields. Fragments of thought kept invading her mind. Good people. Individually good people. Industrious people. Beautiful land. Productive land. Now?

A beautiful land she loved penetrated by horror. Diabolical hatred and viciousness had overtaken the people, once good, whom she loved. Why? How? The only answers she could draw forth were that the root of bitterness had penetrated deep into the heart of her people and had triumphed and produced hatred. Sincere love and forgiveness had become the signs of weakness to her people and not the strength that, in truth, had to underlie them. Only the strong can truly forgive. The infinitely strong had forgiven infinitely. The strong can love with a sacrificial love while the weak love for their own being.

These somewhat chaotic thoughts brought reassurance. She had sacrificed for love of her father. All his life he had loved her and cared for her. He had loved her before she knew the meaning of love. His love had given her the strength to present herself, her body, in a sacrificial way to serve him. Suddenly her heart filled with joy, a joy that washed away the bitterness and anger toward the man sharing the compartment with her. She lifted hr face upward for only a second to give thanks for her rescue from dark thoughts. Now her heart, while not thoroughly happy, was joyous in service.

In the Stuttgart station, she told Carl they had to make a change of trains and so they should dismount. He followed her slowly and haltingly with the crutches. Carrying all their belongings, she gave him little assistance but the conductor rushed to help him so that he left the car without incident. Marlene informed her injured companion that she would check on connections after she had him settled on a bench with enough room for his leg to stretch out.

His feelings told him that those who passed looked at him with a mixture of emotion. The glances that were cast his way expressed silent attitudes of respect, "Thank you for serving the Fatherland and *Führer* so ably and bravely." At the same time, the prolonged looks also expressed either pity or sympathy. In about fifteen minutes, he saw the woman in the ample gray dress working her way through the people toward him.

She reported, "We board the train in an hour and twenty minutes." She then asked, "Do you want to go with me for lunch or would you prefer for me to bring you something?"

His answer was instantaneous although he was puzzled as to why he was so quick to answer, "I want to go." He then added as a reason, "The exercise will strengthen me," to disguise the growing pleasure he had in her presence.

As they made their way to the restaurant the people parted, as did the Red Sea for Moses, when they noticed his approach. He thought to himself, "I do even better than Moses because I don't even have to hit them with my rod or my crutch," and then laughed aloud. The woman looked at him with a hint of bewilderment but said nothing. Although the room seemed full, the head-waiter insured room for the injured *SS* captain and his woman became available.

The master waiter, napkin over his forearm, escorted them to a table where Carl made a futile attempt to help seat the woman. She was much too quick and independent of mind to wait for him. In fact, he doubted her awareness of his intent to do as he had been taught. It was probably a sign of his recuperative powers that his appetite was sharp and the plate of noodles topped with bits of meat and gravy, with cabbage, quickly disappeared. He desperately longed for an American style soft drink but he recognized that was impossible. The menu offering apple juice, he satisfied himself with that. The meal passed in silence and an avoidance of eye contact. As they finished eating, Marlene informed him they could now board the train.

Again, they found a compartment with sufficient room for them. A young member of the army and a girl, whose head rested on the soldier's shoulder, occupied the compartment when they entered. Marlene seated herself beside them and indicated to Carl the empty cushioned bench opposite was for him and his leg. A moment of self-pity afflicted her as she considered that the soldier's girl had been free to make her choice. Then she remembered her prior thoughts and girded herself once more. As the train moved out of the Stuttgart rail yards the young soldier remarked that he was glad that they had left the area where the British bombers struck. Neither Carl, apprehensive in fear of error, nor Marlene, lost in her own thoughts, responded to the overture. The stars outside shone brightly as the train entered the Donaueschingen station.

His companion informed him that once again they would change trains.

She emphasized that she did not want to reach their final rail destination in the middle of the night, which they would have been sure to do if they departed Donaueschingen on the next train, scheduled to leave just before midnight. She, knowledgeable of the city, led the way to a hotel near the station where they found that there was only one room available, which, after considering the situation, she accepted.

Carl, troubled by the demand he was inflicting on the woman, felt helpless. There was nothing more normal than husband and wife sleeping in the same room, indeed in the same bed. A boy carried their light luggage to an elevator that took them to the third floor hallway. There they followed the lad to their assigned bedchamber.

Marlene's fists clenched in tenseness as she faced the ordeal of sharing a bed with her brutish *Nazi* husband. Despite her resolution to be strong, she dreaded the corruption of her body more than the physical and emotional pain he might inflict as on the first two nights following the marriage. She entered the room with chest constricted to the point of pain. In order to gain perspective, she immediately headed for the bath where she remembered a prayer in a garden. There One better than she had committed Himself.

When she re-entered the bed chamber she was first surprised and then alarmed that the man was in the bed. Was it impatience to have her or, hopefully, was he too exhausted and wounded? Both in order to buy time and because it was her custom, she sat before the mirror and brushed her hair that, loosened, cascaded down the back of her gown.

When the lady Marlene first went to the bath off the hall, Carl dressed in the nightclothes provided by the hospital as quickly as possible. She was gone for a considerable time during which he both tried to sleep and then pretended to be asleep as the door opened for her return. He did not observe as she removed her dress and donned a gown for the night. When the light stayed on, however, he looked to see what she was doing and saw that she had taken her hair down from the bun and was brushing it.

He was shocked to see that she was not heavy when the extremely loose dress was removed but that she was beautifully formed. Her lustrous brown hair that flowed down her back to her clearly discernable waistline fascinated him. When she turned in the light, the complexion that had seemed so pallid and frozen had taken on life from the fierce rubbing of the washcloth. He was amazed at her change from a dowdy woman to a beautiful young girl. He had truthfully pled tiredness as they had entered but when the bed depressed as she entered it he felt a hunger in his loins. He turned his back to her, determined to attempt to sleep, praying that he had the strength to resist the sin that his body craved. He drifted into a deep sleep after lying still for an hour. Tired and weak after the trauma of the last days even the racing of his blood could only keep him awake for that period.

When the sun's rays shone upon their heads through the window whose curtains Marlene had parted during the night, they both awakened. Their bodies had slid together during the night with their backs touching. The woman, with the beams striking directly into her face, was the first to awake. She seemed to be out of bed as quickly as her eyes opened. She, without conscious thought, gave thanks for the deliverance of the night.

Carl turned and saw that she was preparing to dress. He felt obligated to keep his back to her for both his and her modesty although he longed to watch. When dressed she again journeyed to the bath and returned with the same pink and healthy color in her face that he had first noticed the previous evening.

While she was in the bathroom, he clothed himself, although he had to hop to some of his clothing. The trouser leg of his missing foot remained securely clipped. Upon her return to the room, she examined the appearance of the wound and made minor adjustments to his uniform by straightening his tie and fiddling with the leather strap over his right shoulder. He pondered this strange female who obviously desired to conceal her beauty.

"What is this woman about? Why did she almost totally refrain from addressing me in conversation but was so friendly and open with all others?"

he mentally questioned. He remembered that her coolness toward him protected his secret but he did desire to exchange thoughts with her. Her marriage to the *SS* captain was troubling. It probably indicated she had a strong sympathy for Adolf Hitler and the *Nazi* party. Then again, she read religious books. How could she seem to have two such different personalities? On one hand she showed kindness to him because of his injuries and favored strangers with what seemed inherent charm, but in their relationship she was arrogantly cold. He remembered with delicious pleasure the times that there had been touch between them. It may have been only a slight brush of their hands or her holding his arm in assistance. Above all, her unmasked beauty of the previous night sent a surge of energy through his body.

Seemingly totally unaware of his thoughts, she led the way from the room down to the dining area of the hostelry where they were able to obtain a breakfast of bread, meat, preserved fruit, and cheese, with coffee. The food satisfied so much that he began to fear complacency. All was so easy that he found it difficult to remember that if his identity were penetrated his death might well follow. He reminded himself, "I must control my feeling of being alone and, most importantly, my tongue. If I say something to ease loneliness, it may compromise my identity. For now the past is washed away. I must let this girl lead me. It is strange that I no longer think of her as 'just a woman' but as a 'girl.'"

Men in the uniforms of Germany; army, air force, labor service, and security police, occupied the dining room. Feeling safe because of the "altered" appearance of Friedrich Schlieter, he nevertheless feared that someone would recognize Marlene. Again, a "comrade" might come to talk of things with which an *SS* officer would be familiar. The couple, silent with each other as well as with those about them, to his relief, was left in their quiet contemplation. "What is she thinking?" was the question that both fascinated and irritated Carl.

After breakfast and settling the cost of their meal and the room, the two returned to the station to wait the time to board. The hour hand of the station clock almost made a full circuit before they boarded a local train that stopped at the stations in small towns and even villages. During this time, his companion stated that she must get a message to *Kreisleiter* Ernst Greider. The identity of and what connection his companion had to this person puzzled Carl. He relaxed as she explained, "Greider became the Local Group Leader when your friend Gert Malstein gained promotion to District Leader of the Party." She added, "When the order arrived for me to come to you, he delivered it and said that when we returned he would be honored to greet you at the station." Carl understood that he must learn quickly of this party rank and hierarchy to maintain his masquerade.

The rail route led first by high hills and then across rolling topography marked by, what seemed to him, high hills and deep valleys. This scenery ended soon after leaving a small city when the route followed the path of a stream. To the west of the tracks were high conical hills that faded further west as they continued to travel south along the serpentine stream. Copses of evergreens lay scattered like shadows over the rolling hills. The small patches of tilled ground continued to fascinate Carl because of their great difference from the fields to which he was accustomed. "Must take a great deal of labor just to sow and harvest those patches much less keep them as neat and clean as they are."

The dead *Nazi's* watch showed that it was just before two in the afternoon as the rail car slowed once more upon entering a rail station. Keyed up and alert, Carl noted the sign that designated the station for "Littach". He watched his female escort gather their belongings in preparation for dismounting. Balancing himself on his crutches, he struggled to give the woman Marlene assistance but a worker on the train rushed to assist, saying, "*Heil* Hitler. *Kreisleiter* Greider told me to assist you, Baroness. The whole town knows that your husband is a hero of the *Reich*."

"A baroness! I wonder what the difference is between a baroness and a countess."

She interrupted his thought line, "I know that *Kreisleiter* Greider will insure a warm welcome for one who is not only a child-saving hero but also a member of the *Schutzstaffeln* and an aide to the *Reichsführer-SS* Himmler."

"Was there a note of bitterness in that statement?" he asked himself.

Marlene approached a rather small, mustached individual in a brown uniform standing on the station platform. After speaking to him for a brief moment, she led him back to Carl. His arrival before Carl was accompanied by a strong, "*Heil* Hitler" united with a raised right arm in the prevailing honor to Germany's *Führer*. Carl responded with as much verve as he could muster and hoped that his physical state would cover for his hesitation to join in the salutation. The man had the same small mustache as his *Führer* although, in Carl's mind, he seemed a bit better fed. He was four to six inches shorter than Carl. Without giving Marlene an opportunity to make the introduction, he identified himself with evident pride as *Kreisleiter* Ernst Greider. Marlene turned her back on both of them and stepped a few paces away.

This squat, broad-headed local *Nazi* leader, with short arms gesticulating and heavy legs moving in what could have been dance steps, was effusive in his address to Carl, "We of Littach are deeply honored to have you with us for your recuperation. We are proud that one of our noble ladies has taken you for her husband. Many in the town will want to see the medal that we understand the *Führer* himself authorized for you. We have heard that you earned it more in your performance of duty than by the simple saving of those children."

Unable to restrain his enthusiasm for this contact with one who saw the *Führer* often, he moved closer and inquired, "Has the *Führer* ever spoken only to you? Have you ever spoken directly and personally to the *Führer*?"

Would it be better to say "Yes" or to deny that access with a "No?" He responded, "Yes, but understand that I only spoke when I submitted reports. He only spoke to me when he wanted more information relating to the reports. I never remember speaking to him on a social basis."

CHAPTER 3

❀

May–June 1942
The Castle

Greider reported that his car was waiting to take the captain and the countess to the castle. Carl struggled to maintain a straight face when Greider used the word "castle." When the countess had told him that they were going to Altburg, he had assumed it was a village near Littach. Where was this castle? Whose castle was it? It probably belonged to the countess. It did not seem to be a place of incarceration by the way he was being treated. She was a countess so she could well own a castle. The order Greider gave to the driver to go to "*Schloss Altburg*" satisfied him as to the name of the castle. The *ersatz* captain and his innocently false wife carefully arranged themselves in the back of the black sedan. The woman he increasingly thought of as Marlene inquired of someone named the "Webers" and if they knew of her return with Captain Schleiter. Greider answered affirmatively that all should be in readiness for her return. *Herr* Weber had assured him that all would be prepared for the arrival of the countess. Increasingly Carl's suspicion that the castle must be the home of the countess became confirmed.

Seated beside the countess Carl once more touched the material of her dress, which felt like the soft skin of a woman. With the driver and another soldier in the front seat and with the countess flanked by Greider and Carl in the back, the car proceeded through the small city of Littach and entered the countryside. En route Greider inquired, "Just how serious are your injuries other than the loss of your foot? Do you think it will be long before you return to your duties? Every Party member knows of your fervent performance of your duties of relocation. We are sure that you will be anxious to return to the work of your heart and will be joyous when you can. Your injuries will prevent you from frontline action in the east to your great disappointment. That is where the promotions are, fighting the Bolsheviks, although you have done well for yourself being a captain in your mid-twenties. I am sure there are many staff positions you can handle and free some whole man for combat duty."

Carl replied, "My injuries are quite severe, the doctors say. They instructed that I was to take an extensive time for recuperation. I can hardly handle my crutches and I have difficulty getting about. As you can see, I took quite a blow to my face. The doctor's have done a great job in repairing the damage but there remains a great deal of healing needed. I also suffered burns, particularly on my left side up to my armpit. No, it looks like it will be months at least before I can get back to my duties. Even now I am exhausted from our travel. Possibly we can discuss it some other time. Thank you for your interest."

Greider seized the opportunity by declaring, "My wife, *Frau Kreisleiter* Greider, would be honored if you would receive us, Countess. Can you give me a day when we may come and pay our respects, no?"

The baroness paused briefly and then replied, "I would be delighted to receive you a week from this Friday."

Greider was tenacious, "There are some other ladies, and in fact their husbands, who also would be pleased if they might call on you and your hero husband."

The countess' graciousness rose to this challenge, "Certainly our friends from town may call. I only ask that you supply the names of those who will attend."

They drove down a narrow, escalating road curving between heavily wooded hills for a third of an hour before coming to an iron gate. There waiting beside the gate was a man who Carl guessed was in his middle fifties. When the car stopped Marlene hastened out and ran to the broad built man as she exclaimed, "Hans, it is so good to see you and to be home." With that, she threw her arms about him and gave him a kiss on the cheek.

He returned the affectionate display but with diffidence and responded, "It is good for us to have you at home once more, Countess Marli. I will see to your luggage at the residence."

The older man's greeting of the men in the car was more reserved to the point of coolness as he addressed them formally by their offices and names. Carl began to think that he himself must be the odd man out as far as his supposed wife's affections were concerned. She had certainly displayed more affection for this man than she had for the one who was supposed to be her husband.

"If she knows I am not her husband why does she not expose me?"

The countess returned to the car; the gate opened, and after the vehicle passed, closed. Hans stood on the running board as the vehicle continued up a driveway even narrower than the roads. The ascent of the vehicle continued as the lane twisted up a sharp hill. After a final hairpin turn, a hybrid building loomed before them. The light of the afternoon sun revealed the trace of an ancient and immense castle. It took only a moment to know that the outer walls, now virtually destroyed by time and men, at one time in the past encompassed more than five acres of the hilltop. As they prepared to enter one of the wings of the structure, Carl saw the ruins of another wing across the courtyard. It was obvious to the American that the past proprietors had restored one wing and a good amount of the center section.

Entering the restored wing before them, the skill of the restoring craftsmen and the quality of the material used proclaimed themselves. The restored wing of the structure appeared quite old by American standards but not nearly as old as the castle ruins. Much of the stonework of the other wing and its turrets was missing. A heavily graveled courtyard of more than thirty by fifty yards lying in front of the center section and between the wings provided a stopping place for the car.

Immediately the door of the house opened and an older woman hurried out to the car arriving just as the baroness exited the vehicle. She and the woman embraced warmly as the woman exulted, "Come in, my lady, come in. All is ready. Thank God that you traveled safely! We prayed and lit candles for you that no bombs would fall on you. He answered!"

"Oh, little mother, you are so good. Yes, I am glad we had a safe trip. There is bomb damage in the cities in the north it is true. Train travel is particularly dangerous. It seems that the rail yards and moving trains are attractive targets for the English. Captain Schleiter is fortunate to have survived the bombing in the city and I hope that he knows it and gives thanks."

In spite of all her display of affection for the countess, Carl received only a nod from the woman. Carl guessed that this couple must be the Webers and could not but observe that their greeting for him was cold to the point of offense. At least the older couple saw fit to acknowledge his presence with a nod while the local Group Leader of the Party failed to receive even a glance. When the man, who did indeed turn out to be Weber, took the suitcases, he motioned Carl into the house. His injuries and crutches prevented Carl from moving quickly and he noticed that Greider failed to receive an invitation to enter.

The *Nazi* official, nevertheless, followed them into a foyer with walls of plaster and a high vaulted ceiling and from there into a spacious room with similar walls and ceiling where small cakes with pastry plates, saucers, and cups stood waiting. Weber placed the bags near a door exiting the room while Marlene, who seemed perfectly at ease, seated herself. The *Nazi* Greider moved quickly to take a seat beside her on the sofa while Carl had to crutch to a seat across the room. He watched the interplay between the local official and Marlene with interest, wanting to determine, as they said back home, "the lay of the land." Was she a committed *Nazi*? Was she supportive of the programs and policies of Hitler?

The official enthused, "Your residence is very lovely, Countess, very impressive. I understand that the first castle was built in the eleventh century. That is true, no? Was it not once the seat of your ancestor, the margrave, during the Peasants' Rebellion in the sixteenth century? Even then, the Bolsheviks were raising their heads. Now radicals threaten us again. Have you heard of the heroic efforts of our men in throwing back the Russian offensive in the east? Soon we will once more be on the offensive and we will occupy Moscow and own the oil of the Caucasus. The Russkies cannot last long now. We are capturing all their industrial towns and they will be reduced to axes and pitchforks for weapons. How blessed we of the German nation are to have such a glorious leader as our *Führer*, do you not think so?"

The noble woman looked at the man with eyes that appeared as serene as the ocean on the calmest of days. Carl thought, "Her eyes look like deep blue mirrors. They deflect all inquiry but at the same time are sympathetic and kind." Now it seemed as though he saw the dark but open blue that normally shone from her eyes suddenly alter. Her eyes that had seemed as refreshing as small blue mountain pools turned quickly into the hardness of cold blue marble.

"I think that girl could be tough and strong and not brook any nonsense," Carl reflected to himself.

Her response was cryptic, "I trust that God's purposes shall surely triumph and that His justice will rule."

"Yes," returned Greider, "I have heard that you speak of God often but do you really believe we need that crutch now?" At the word crutch he looked at Carl and changed his subject, "I am sure that you do not depend on otherworldly sources but know that the genius of our *Führer* will lead us to total triumph. *Heil* Hitler!" it seemed that the thought of Germany's master delivered him into a state of ecstasy that could only be satisfied with the hailing of that human.

Carl, hesitantly replied, "That is a strong thought, Greider." He chose to treat the party official with familiarity because he had increasingly realized that Schleiter had been in a powerful position. His position seemed far superior to that of a local leader at the edge of the Reich.

Greider demonstrated his recognition of the connections that Schleiter had in high places, "My car is available to you for a tour of my area if you will just let me know in advance when you would like to go out and see how we do things here. For sure we never had many Jewish swine about but we will soon round up those who are in our small towns. It will be good to see them relocated and out of our sight, the filthy pigs."

The countess broke in, "Your offer to my husband is kind but we have a car, although it is quite old. It will, however, suffice. Of course, if Captain Schleiter desires or needs to do much traveling may we call on you for fuel?"

Greider thanked her and said that the captain would have all the fuel needed in his duties.

Carl thought that a significant glance passed between Marlene and the woman called *Frau* Weber as the latter set down a teapot swathed in a gloriously colorful tea cozy. Marlene then poured the tea, asking, "What will you have, Friedrich? *Kreisleiter* Greider, will you take sugar? Milk?" When Carl, not understanding perfectly, volunteered that he wanted both she questioned, "When did you begin adulterating tea, Friedrich? You never did before."

"A mistake! I made a mistake then." he gasped silently but quickly covered, "Oh, from work. I often felt I needed more energy to get the job done over the long hours."

No one followed up on the question of tea, sugar, and milk as *Frau* Weber brought him a pastry plate with two cakelets and a cup of tea with milk and sugar. The conversation then turned to the expected agricultural production from the land surrounding the castle. Greider wanted to insure that his area made a large shipment to the government. *Herr* Weber, who had disappeared with their bags after a whispered conversation with Marlene, returned, interjecting, "Oh, my, the winter has not been good and it has been difficult to prepare and plant the fields. I do not know what we would have done without the French help these last months. They are fairly good workers. Of course, we could do more if the government had not taken the majority of the estate.

There is little German labor available because of all the men in Russia and Africa. The French help keep the house and grounds decent but the little land left barely provides for needs of the estate."

From this byplay, Carl surmised that the government requisitioned all farm produce for use as it saw fit and guessed that Weber did not totally approve of the taking of the fruit of the land. It also appeared that the government had taken much of the land itself. This thought led him to wondering about the relationship of Marlene to the Webers. In many ways, they had the demeanor of servants but if so, they were privileged servants with a close relationship to the lady.

"I hope my wife will be able and welcome to call and pay her respects to you, baroness. It would be a great honor to her and she would love to see the noble furnishings of the castle. This fortress and your family have been so important to this region of the Reich," Greider importuned.

"Oh, you do remember that I asked her to visit a week from this Friday. Please have her call at any time. We are busy about the land, so please have her telephone before she comes so that we insure that we will be at home. Is it settled? Can you accept for her, that we can expect her on the second Friday from today?"

"Oh, pardon my forgetfulness. It is a burden to lead the party in this district. Berlin counts on us doing our job of rooting out hoarders, profiteers, Bolsheviks, Jews and other traitors at the local level. There is so much on my mind that it escaped me that I had asked and you had graciously agreed."

From the failure to set a specific hour for the engagement Carl assumed that Europeans, at least Germans, had a set time to have "tea."

The county leader accepted with alacrity, "For sure, I know that she is free on Fridays."

When tea drinking ceased, Greider took his leave and left. The countess went to the door with him and wished him a good trip. Upon return, Marlene said that *Frau* Weber had informed her that dinner waited if they would enter the dining room. Carl thoroughly enjoyed the ample provisions and, pleading fatigue, asked to be excused for the night. Marlene falteringly said, "I asked that your things be put in the Bach room. I thought that you might rest better there than in my room. You know, I, uh, I don't want to injure your. . your wound while sleeping."

"That's good," Carl sincerely replied for he did want to avoid the temptation of her body next to his in bed. "I also could well disturb your rest with my tossing and turning." He worried as to how he was to identify the Bach room.

"How did it get to be called that? Is she saying "Bach" or "back"? Well, she wasn't speaking English so it must be "Bach" but I'll begin in the back of the house—I guess upstairs."

"Forgive me! I really didn't mean to be thoughtless of you." she apologized with grace. "You will need help in negotiating the stairs and with the lights. Let me summon Hans to help you and I will go ahead and turn on the lights so that you don't fall."

She then called out in a strong but gentle voice for the man and he entered from the kitchen almost immediately. He followed her instructions with no expression on his face. The widow of Friedrich Schleiter led Carl, helped by her servant, to a large and well-appointed room on the second floor. A bed stood high off the floor to invite a wounded and tired young man into the realm of dreams. She pointed out a pitcher and a basin for any personal washing. She added that *Frau* Weber would fill the pitcher with warm water from the kitchen soon. Almost before she completed the promise, a slight rap at the door presaged the arrival of the hot, not warm, water in another container. The countess praised, "How alert of you, *kleine mutti*, to know that he would need to wash."

Carl quickly recognized a chamber pot in the room because they were familiar vessels to a Texas farm boy of the 1920's and 1930's. Making short use of this vessel, and tenderly washing his face, Carl hastened into the covers and to sleep.

The young lady of the old castle felt relief flood over her as soon as the door to the room assigned to Carl closed behind her. More than relief surged through her. Why did he not require her to sleep in the same room? Were his injuries continuing to affect him so that he really wanted and needed the rest? If this were so, how long did she have before he would demand his marital rights? Was the center of his manhood impacted by his injuries?

Again, she could only wait for future developments and continue to seek the strength that would carry her through.

It was so good to be in this building and to have the assurance of the presence of the Webers. They were strong and dependable. They loved her with an accepting love. She shared almost all with the older woman and felt free to weep in her presence. Marlene von Krönitz and Ritterbach had always depended on the advice and counsel of Annaliese Weber and she intended to continue to do so.

Leaving the room, she walked the halls, first on the floor she was on and then moved to the floor above and finally to the ground floor. As she walked, she examined closely the portraits of her forebears on the walls. What crises had they experienced? She knew of some of those recorded in history books but she also knew that her ancestors suffered through personally agonizing moments beyond her comprehension and that history had not stopped with them for they and the family survived. As she had grown older, these halls and likenesses had become increasingly hallowed to her, and now in her distress, even more so.

Then her mind turned once more to the man in the bed in the Bach chamber. He did not seem the man she had known and despised since childhood although the efficient records of the German state proclaimed his identity. A degree of courtesy had replaced arrogance and pride. There had been instances of humility where none had been known before. The answer must lie in the horrific injuries that he had suffered. Then again, was it believable that Friedrich Schleiter would risk his life to save a child or children, whether they were dear to him or not? She could not explain to herself the actions of the *Nazi* captain in rushing into the fiery holocaust. She could not understand an action so totally lacking in self-interest.

Because he went to sleep well before the others, Carl was the first to rise in the morning. The view from the windows with their deep sills revealed rain falling from a sky as gray as the uniforms of the *Wehrmacht*. Carl had to note the difference between these windows and those in America. These had handles and opened ever so slightly at the top, being hinged at the bottom and seemed to give better protection from the weather. When he checked the water in the pitcher he found it cold. An inspection of the wardrobe in the room revealed additional uniforms and some non-military men's clothing. He saw that there were an extra pair of boots and two pairs of shoes. All of this apparel was the same size. After donning the non-military dress, Carl decided he would explore as much as he could. The long hall connected to the stair had more than half a dozen doors opening off it, apparently to more sleeping rooms. He wondered what door Marlene was behind but had no thought of trying to discover it. Stairs leading upward to a third floor promised more rooms. When it came to the stairs going down to ground level, he stopped to consider the best way of dealing with them with his crutches. Wanting to be sure that he did not fall he decided the best thing he could do was to slide down them on his rump, lowering himself with his arms one riser at a time and moving the crutches along. After two or three minutes, he was at the bottom, and using the post of the stair rail, rose.

He then moved as quietly as possible from the room where tea had been served to a dining room and then on into the kitchen. The ceilings of the rooms were much higher than he had ever seen at home or even in England. The kitchen had several appendices that included a pantry and a room for the storage of meat. Hanging on the wall of a small room adjacent to the kitchen he discovered a shadow box. In the dark wood frame were three Maltese cross medals with explanatory script. These citations indicated that one Heinrich Stephan Weber had distinguished himself in the face of the enemy at the great battle of Tannenberg in Prussia in August, 1914, in the battle of the Somme in July, 1916, and on the Marne in September, 1918. Now he knew that the older man was a brave man and a national hero with a great commitment to his nation. He had also been a fellow soldier with his cousin *Tante* Anna's husband in the Great War. Weber had risen to the rank of what Carl took to be a senior sergeant of some kind.

Retracing his steps he found a huge room lined with book-filled shelves. "Got to be the library," he was sure. Another large room contained a piano, and standing in the corner a harp. Continuing his exploration, he discovered another room even larger than the library with a hard wooden floor and furnished with armchairs with high backs and several small tables. Two great rugs that would have been called Persian back in Texas covered less than half the floor space. The molding of the room, like that of the "tea" room seemed authentically aristocratic to his uneducated conception. Yes, he could imagine the highest of society inhabiting these rooms, walking about and talking to one another.

In addition to the large rooms, there were several small rooms, one with a desk and office appointments and another prepared for sewing and needlework. Retracing his way to the library, he began to examine the works there. The vaulted ceiling of this book room he estimated to have a height of about twenty feet. The plasterers had worked the plaster of the walls of all the rooms other than the great huge hall wondrously smooth. The huge room with its great fireplace was finished with what seemed to him as fine wood to a height of about ten feet and then plaster above. Heavy drapes set off all the windows of the lower level of the residence. The shelves of the library rose to a height beyond his reach. A rolling ladder sitting in the corner made the works out of reach available. Unable to inspect the volumes stored high up he did begin to examine the titles at eye level. There he found a wide variety of works. He was familiar with some, generally aware of others, and many were completely unfamiliar. When he came to the collected works of several American authors, his interest became more intense. Among these were Mark Twain, James Fenimore Cooper, Edgar Allen Poe, and a complete collection of the American transcendentalists his college English professor had loved.

Proceeding further along the stacks he found a section apparently devoted to theology. This was an area of literature of which he had scant knowledge. His reading since becoming a believer was mostly of scripture and devotionals. He recognized a few of the names: Martin Luther, Philip Melancthon, Ulrich Zwingli, and Desiderius Erasmus. As he moved, supported by the crutches, down the line of books he came upon many by English, Scottish. French, and Russian, in addition to the expected German writers. He moved back and explored the volumes in the English language. From these he selected one of the works of Dickens, *Great Expectations*. Looking around the room, he saw a comfortable seat located at a table but facing away from the entrance to the chamber.

He had read a short distance into the work when the countess' voice coming from the door behind him startled him.

"Hello! Have you become a reader? Did you find something of Hitler, or Dr. Goebbels, or is it Nietzsche's writing that appeals to you? You will not find *Mein Kampf* here!"

He closed the book as quickly as he could and slid it to his lap to conceal it. "Friedrich Schleiter probably did not read English," he considered and then responded aloud, "I was very bored and had nothing to do, so I was examining these books. They appear to be expensive. Are they worth anything?"

Having turned, he was able to view the blood rise on her face as she exploded, "Only if you can read and have taste but they would not have value for the ignorant!"

Holding the book casually and looking at it as though it was an oddity, he limped on one crutch back to the shelves in the wrong place as though he really did not know the English language or topic. He then turned and bid an expressionless "Good morning." She then turned on her heel and strode from the room, "Food will soon be ready."

As she stepped from the room the strange conduct of the man who was her husband perplexed and confused her once more. The man she had known, at least casually, since childhood had never shown interest in books. Now he investigated the library before the liquor cabinet. He brandished a book before grabbing a goblet! Where there had never been shame, he had shown shame for being caught with a book and attempted to hide it from her. Had her prayers been answered? Had his injuries changed him to the point that she should tolerate living with him? "I will ask Liese!"

As she entered the kitchen, safe from being overheard, she asked her substitute mother, "Can a leopard change his spots or, rather, can a jackal change to a retriever?" She then quickly described the riddle of the behavior of the man called Friedrich Schleiter. She discovered that her account of Friedrich Schleiter's demeanor only puzzled the older woman as well.

Carl once more counseled himself that he must be vigilant if his impostor role was not to be revealed. He considered how he could find out more about Friedrich Schleiter. The marriage of Marlene and Schleiter bewildered him. There certainly did not seem to be either familiarity or affection between the two. In the false role he was playing, his sympathies were with the woman. "Probably because he was such a scum of the *SS* and she seems like she might be a real fine girl."

He was surprised that the older couple joined them for the first meal of the day in the small dining area adjacent to the kitchen. Alert to everything about him, he noted that his seat was at the end of a small rectangular table with his purported wife at the other end. *Frau* Weber's seat gave her ready access to the kitchen. There was little conversation at the table, as it seemed that the countess had been brought up to date the previous night about the occurrences in the area during her absence. He caught the eyes of the older woman deeply and enquiringly searching his face through the morning meal.

Although a slight mist fell visibly beyond the windows, he decided to venture outside to understand his surroundings better. As he negotiated the graveled area in front of the house, he turned and looked back at where he had slept. He confirmed that the house was really no "house" at all but a reconstructed portion of an ancient castle. Some walls and ruins of the old fortress still stood to his right as he faced the door he had exited. He was surprised at how much of the medieval structure remained intact but many walls and turrets were broken. The covered, but uninhabitable for humans, portion of the older part of the castle had become, it appeared, a shelter for livestock and their food. It was the most unique barn that he could imagine. Never having been around a castle he regretted even more deeply that his lost foot prohibited exploratory climbing about the structure. He could not even ask about the history of the place for he probably would have been aware of it were he truly Schleiter.

Having let his vision sweep over the ancient but half-ruined edifice, he carefully climbed to a spot where he could see over an inner wall of the fortifications of antiquity. Turning his view further outward, he could survey the countryside around him. He saw that although a deep and dark forest encircled his location, the area immediately around the old fortress was bare of vegetation. Looking over the forest and into the valley below, he spied cultivated fields that incited his curiosity as to what crops flourished in this terrain and climate.

Turning to look toward the old but used ruins, he saw the man Weber, pail in hand, pause to look at him. As the moisture began to penetrate, he returned to the residence wing.

The pages of the calendar of May turned over into the late days of that month and then to June. For several weeks, Carl remained almost totally housebound except for a few opportunities when the weather afforded sitting alone in the sunshine. He felt that the mistress of the house and her two faithful retainers watched him but generally kept their silence. He returned the watchfulness and, as much as possible, the silence.

He saw relatively young men occasionally in, but mostly about, the castle and its grounds. They were rarely in the residence. They spoke a language that definitely was not German and sounded as though it must be French to the young Texas airman. He assumed that these were the French laborers. The countess had mentioned that without French workers they would not have been able to work the land. He did not understand why the erstwhile enemies of Germany would be working in the land of Hitler. Every situation that incited his curiosity was a danger if he attempted to satisfy that desire to know.

The countess often moved the caring for her long, radiant hair from the privacy of her room. Bringing out the brush and comb she permitted *Frau* Weber, Carl now knew as Annaliese, to stroke it with the brush and comb. This ritual usually occurred in the small and comfortably warm sitting room. This room opened into the great room. The older woman seemed to enjoy running the comb and brush down the hair's length. On one of these occasions she commented, "I told your father when you were so very small that you would be a beautiful lady with wonderfully lovely hair. Now, was I not right?" From this, Carl understood a little more that the older woman was an old family retainer with deep affection for the young lady. Carl found himself envious and strangely excited, warmed, and covetous of the older woman's chore as he watched the grooming.

Each Sunday the Webers left the residence very early to attend mass at the local Catholic Church. They were usually off before Carl rose from bed and returned by eight in the morning. The religious activities at the castle included the visit of a priest named Nimitz at least once a week. He not only visited with the Webers but also with the workers who Carl had come to know were indeed French.

It was the daily practice of the countess to absent herself to the library early each day. There she could be observed reading a Bible and then sitting quietly for a long period with her back to the door. Intrigued by this practice, Carl came to believe that she had some of the same spirit as Lydia Cameron, the ethereally godly girl he had known in college.

The day came for *Frau* Greider to make her coveted call at the castle door and four females and three males escorted her. *Herr Kreisleiter* Greider insured that he was in the group; the other males, husbands of two of the women, escorted their wives. Greider made the introductions as he presented his wife and a woman friend of hers to the "captain" and the countess. He then presented *Herr* and *Frau* Anton Schlenkmann, the town's mayor, *Herr* Rudolf Randorff, a local merchant and his wife Erika, and *Herr* Heinrich Hühn, editor of the regional newspaper. Carl grasped that the Randorff woman, greeted and embraced as Erika by the Countess Marlene, claimed childhood friendship with her hostess.

As coffee and tea were set before the group, Hühn turned to Carl and boasted, "You know, I was welcomed heartily when I was last in Berlin for meetings sponsored by Dr. Goebbels' ministry of information. The big shots certainly welcomed us. Party, party, party. I have never been to so many parties in one week before in my life. I do not believe I met you but you were pointed out to me as one who had connections in this area. I would not have known—I, uh, mean the terrible—I, uh, mean the great injuries you suffered because of your bravery—they changed you. I have read, though, that our doctors lead in the world in reparative surgery. They certainly have done a great job for you. The remaining scars you can explain are saber wounds from your university days when they are healed. That will certainly add prestige—a member of a university saber club." Carl almost smiled at this reference to university saber cuts.

It apparently made no difference to the newspaperman that Friedrich Schleiter had never been a university student much less a member of such a club. His supposed wife opened her mouth to set the record straight, "Friedrich was never at university and was not a member of any university club. In fact, he did not enter *gymnasium*." Carl thought, "Wow, she really cut her husband down to size in front of these people. If I were Friedrich I would be either mad or hurt, I do not know which. I do know that I would talk to her when we were in private."

Greider attempted to smooth the possible marital rift, "That just shows the ambition, diligence, and commitment to the Party that has allowed such a young man to rise so quickly. I have always said that book education is not everything by a long shot."

The sighting of Schleiter in Berlin by Hühn gave Carl only a brief start before he realized that if his "wife" was unaware of his sham identity he need not fear casual strangers.

Greider then presented an idea, "I think it would be good for you, Captain Schleiter, to present the awards to our *Hitler Jugend* at the ceremony. After all, you are a hero decorated by order of the *Führer* and you are married to the mistress of this castle. I also heard that you became a member of the *Jugend* at its start.

Randorff supported this motion, "I agree that is a wonderful idea. Greider and I talked about this several days before coming to the castle today. But we kind of like to keep things to ourselves and have told no one else about the awards ceremony."

Schlenkmann, the *bürgermeister* lauded, "You are a great example to our youth, Captain Schleiter, the young ones can see from your record how much they can achieve and how high they can rise in a short time. You are so young to have such glorious responsibilities in helping to solve the nationalities problem. All in the local party have heard of the famous Captain Friedrich Schleiter and his coordination of the movement of so many thousands to the eastern territories."

"What in the heck did all that mean?" Carl wondered to himself.

After conversation that covered many fronts, it always returned to the glory of the *Führer*, his inspired leadership, and the absolute direction he provided the nation. There were also remarks on the need to cleanse the blood of the nation of the lesser races and the retarded and mentally ill. The visitors vehemently agreed that those who had a family history of mental illness and retardation should be sterilized. Schlenkmann set forth the proposition, "As the *Führer* had said, we cannot permit the mixture of the races and so undo millions of years of evolutionary progress!"

Despite her authoritative and oft repeated claims to life-long friendship with her hostess, the *Frau* Erika Randorff remained coolly aloof to the countess. Her eyes, blue as the sky-tinted elements of Meissen china, steadily observant, studied the eddying pool of people. Their character changed and became as stone steady as those of a sphinx when they fixed on the Countess Marlene.

Marlene maintained as much silence as possible within the range of cool politeness and Carl noted that she had gone out of her way to look as plain and bulky as possible. After more than an hour of hungrily devouring the coffee, tea, and sweets set before them, the party, under the leadership of *Herr* Greider, departed. When Carl returned to the kitchen Marlene had already made her way there, and he found her talking energetically to *Frau* Weber, whose face was as flushed as the beets she was peeling.

Carl noticed that each day, six days a week, Hans rode off the castle grounds with a team of giant horses pulling a wagon. These animals were larger than any he had seen on farms in America. The only ones he had ever seen to match these had been some great horses drawing circus wagons in Houston. When he asked the destination of Hans, the countess explained to him that with the war Hans had many duties. She added that the laborers were indeed French prisoners of war released from prison camps following the campaign of 1940 with the provision that they work on German farms. Placed on their parole, if they attempted to escape and were caught they would be summarily executed.

In addition to supervising the labor of the Frenchmen, she explained, Hans went in to Littach with milk and other produce of the estate. He returned with needed staples such as salt, pepper, flour and other items. In addition, the older man continued his peacetime duties as forest master. The strange thing was that the wagon used by *Herr* Weber always carried up to a half load of hay. Thinking it safe to ask why the wagon always had hay on it, *Frau* Weber answered, "Oh, you know that Hans. He's too lazy to take the hay off so he just lets the horses do the extra work and pull the hay too," explained the man's wife.

"Not in my book," thought Carl. The answer made no sense at all. If he had ever known a man who was not afraid of work it was *Herr* Weber, whose only break from dawn-to-dusk work was meal times. Unsure of his ground, careful not to show ignorance where he should be knowledgeable, he held his peace.

In the clear fresh air of May and June Carl had come to appreciate the beauty of the castle's setting. Located high on the great hill it dominated the juncture as two valleys became one. Through each of the three valleys ran a paved road variably lined by a forest or by single trees separated by about ten yards from one another. The forests had sufficient trees whose leaves changed hues with the seasons to show a nature-created quilt of color. When the atmosphere was clear, the panorama of the glacier ladened peaks of the Alps dominated the southern horizon. He then asked Hans, "How far are we from those mountains? Are they in Germany or Switzerland?"

Hans quizzically and briefly replied, "Oh, they are Swiss and the distance is about sixty or seventy kilometers."

About two weeks later *Kreisleiter* Ernst Greider rang the bell from the iron gate at the outer wall and *Herr* Weber made his vehicle's entry possible by electric means. Upon his entry into the house, Greider informed the countess that it would be necessary to requisition her home for housing of a regional National Socialist Party conference. The uninvited guests would arrive in six days. Five rooms would be required and the countess would provide the morning and evening meals in her dining room. In the event that additional labor was required for cooking, table service, and housekeeping, the Party would provide it, as well as additional meat and staples. With a calm but frozen face, Marlene agreed, and after thought, said she would accept the additional house workers.

On this visit of Greider, Carl noted the countess offered no tea or coffee, indeed tendered nothing to the visitor. When the official had left, Carl, sitting in an adjacent small room overheard *Frau* Weber ask, "Why did you say we needed help? You know that we could handle that crowd with no help."

Her mistress then explained, "It may have aroused suspicions if we had not let him have an opportunity to put agents here. We certainly do not want to give him any reason or excuse to move people into the castle on a permanent basis. He can do it without reason, but I think it best not to give him concern. He just might put an agent in the house if he thinks we might be hiding something."

"Arouse suspicion? Suspicion of what? That she did not like her *Nazi* husband? No, that would not be reason. Then what? Obviously, there was an activity of which he knew nothing."

Maybe black-market activities or maybe even smuggling things into Germany? Yes, that could be it. Carl really hoped they were not caught. They all seemed like real nice people.

He would have liked to be useful but the injury to his leg prevented, so he usually remained in the library away from the others. In spite of their obvious distaste for him, even the two women and the man began to have moments of sympathy for this crippled young man. Increasingly the countess conjectured that he might have lost his manhood as well. His leg did not miraculously re-grow but in every other way his health and strength grew. His cheerful acceptance of separate beds in separate rooms joyfully continued to surprise her.

On the sixth day, the *Nazi* officials arrived for the conference. During dinner, the talk centered on the events and progress of the war as the state radio and the newspapers reported it.

Carl found himself acting as host to this group of his enemies with the countess at the other end of the long table. The meeting of Hitler and Mussolini, the Italian dictator, in Salzburg late in April, which promised increased cooperation between the two powers encouraged the dinner guests. They were further joyous in their Japanese allies sweep across southeastern Asia and the oilfields of Indonesia. One official commented, "The English and Americans must see that they have lost and sue for peace if they are possessed of any intelligence at all." Carl found it easy to maintain his silence without being offensive through an owlish demeanor combined with short answers to direct questions.

The optimistic talk of the war filled the discussion of the morning and evening meals but on one occasion the conversation turned to the future of the *SS* captain at the table. One of those at the table asked, "How long will it take for you to recuperate and join in the struggle?"

"A long time, I believe."

One "guest" presented the thought that he could be fitted with a false leg and return to desk duty in Berlin.

"But I have other injuries, burns and the like, as well." Casually it was pointed out that he could free a fit man for the eastern front where reports were that the army was continuing its summer offensive. "Yes, that is so if I were able. Surely the war will end this summer when the Bolsheviks are defeated. It is amazing how they continue to resist after their industrial centers have been captured."

One of the visitors affirmed, "There is no way that they can continue to resist with little war production and the U-boats choking off any hope of re-armament from Britain or America. The *Führer* has proven his military genius many times over when he has overruled the military minds of the General Staff."

"You are very silent, Captain, but you must know of the plans for the future. We understand that you have the good fortune to be close to our *Führer* almost every day. Do you not agree that the Allies' cause is dead, finished?" This interrogatory came from a block-like individual dressed in the uniform of the Party. Carl learned that he was one of the Party leaders from the city of Muhlheim.

Carl, with red tingeing his face, parried, "There's an old saying taught me by a wise old woman when I was not careful. She said, 'Be careful, boy, there's many a slip between the cup and the lip.' The Russians seem to have resisted far more than expected and there are stories that they were able to muster enough strength for a winter offensive and America is really harnessing its industrial might. We all know that they are the world's best at mass production. I believe that there is a lot of war to be fought yet."

The Muhlheimer leader would not desist, "Oh, the Americans! They are soft and they can only produce Ford jalopies like the T Model. Their machines do not compare to our Mercedes. Can anyone make a plane superior to Doctor Messerschmitt? Our scientists and engineers are conceded to be the best in the world. Besides there is an ocean for the Americans to cross with their 'mass production!' And what waits for them in that ocean? Our wonderful U-boats! And they must also deal with the Japanese who taught them a thing or two in Hawaii."

While this conversation transpired, Marlene watched Carl for what seemed a minute without diverting her attention to the others and their talk at the table. At the end of the meal when no one was near to hear, she stated, "The remarks you made were not like you, Captain Schleiter." As she brought to mind his official status "Has your experience made you wiser? For your sake I truly hope that it has." She then quickly moved away.

The Party conference ended and the uninvited "guests" left. One thing seemed strange to Carl following the departure of the Party convention "guests" He noted the placement of a "tea cozy" over the house's only telephone. This instrument was located in the kitchen as that was the room where its ring was most likely to be heard. Carl saw but did not ask why the phone needed insulation.

Following the departure of the "guests", Marlene informed him that she had told the Webers that she and the captain would join them again for meals at the small table in the kitchen. She explained, with her gaze fixed on Carl's face, "This would ease some of the burden on Liese. There is so much work to do. Caring for the animals and working as much of the fields as possible. For Liese this is a great house to keep orderly and clean, so I want to cut as much work as possible."

Her face remained calm and stolid when he replied, "That seems like a sensible idea. I am all for it."

During their first meal in the kitchen, Annaliese said that *Frau* Randorff had telephoned that day. Carl listened carefully to the ensuing conversation for any hints as to the identity and character of people he might be expected to know.

Marlene asked, "Did she want something specific? Or was it just a general call for conversation?" As she asked these questions, Carl observed her quickly scanning his face for a reaction.

Frau Weber responded, "No, she just wanted to express her sympathy again for the wounds that your husband incurred. She said that she would like to get together with you and just the two of you talk about the old times."

During a meal, Carl asked *Herr* Weber, "Is there anything that I can do to help with the work?" He continued that his contribution would be minimal because of the crutch-imposed limits.

The German stared at Carl in silence, his mouth frozen open as he prepared to deposit a large forkful of potatoes there, "You must really be bored, Captain Schleiter. I never thought to hear you volunteer for farm work using your hands. I'll think if there is anything that I can put you to."

Both of the women had stopped eating at this conversation and looked at Carl as though he was the oddest animal that had ever inhabited the planet. "Not in character," mused Carl to himself, "but I had better carry on the bored initiative," as he remembered Schleiter's mission in the city.

He continued, "Well, there are no Russians to fight and no Jews or Gypsies to relocate and, as the countess knows, I am not much of a reader. So I will do what I can." He was instantly puzzled because the complexion of the Weber woman turned pale at his remark.

Marlene quickly changed the subject to the expected visit of Father Nimitz to see the Webers. The Webers seemed pleased with the prospect of another visit and Carl listened carefully to determine as much about the relationship as possible without asking questions. Carl remembered that Nimitz was the parish priest and was close to the Webers. It had also become apparent that the Protestant countess and the Catholic priest liked one another. The Catholic cleric frequently visited the castle, saying, "*Frau* Annaliese; you are the best cook in Europe. No one can beat your strudels."

Often chatting and sharing refreshments with the residents in both the sitting room and at the table, he also engaged in extended and serious conversations with the other three castle residents. All insured they were well out of Carl's hearing on those occasions. Carl could understand that the priest might be counseling the Webers, but why the long conferences with the young Protestant woman?

The countess' information was borne out when the tall, heavyset priest arrived. She greeted him with graciousness, offering him both coffee and tea along with sweet bread on china whose thinness and delicacy astounded the Texan.

The curate, ostensibly on a pastoral visit, encouraged, "Countess, will you and your husband not remain and talk with us? Oh, these pastries are so . . so mouth watering! How do you do it, *Frau* Annaliese, with the shortages and all? Captain Schleiter, I trust that your recovery is going well. I have always thought of you as a vital young man and to see the impact of your injuries…it truly saddens me. What do you think the future holds for you? Will you reenter the war?"

In his time with Lydia, she had told him that while they did not know the future they knew Who held the future. Knowing that he could not say such a thought, he evaded, "I do not know. My abdominal and burn injuries are even more serious than they appear on the surface. But tell me of yourself." The American wanted the conversation to center on anything other than himself. At this point, the priest turned his attention to his hostess.

Marlene became freely involved in her conversation with him asking detailed questions as to the welfare of the people of the parish. She named names and was fully aware of whose baby was due or was ill, who was suffering from a broken arm, and whose son was in Russia.

The priest thanked her not only for her concern but also her ministry of food, clothing, and sympathy for his parishioners. He particularly thanked her for the purchase of prayer candles for mothers who were worried about their sons in the armed forces of Germany. The talk went on for some hours with a great deal of laughter springing out of the countess' small witticisms and puns. Carl had glimpsed only a slight bit of this side of her personality when she had talked with the hospital personnel. The question of the nature of the relationship between her and her departed husband rose like a gorge in his throat. He was startled at the emotion rising in him at that consideration.

The priest directed little conversation in his direction but Carl was aware of the penetrating eyes of one who knew human nature well, focused on him. Did this man, who was obviously very godly, have the gift of being able to look into other men's minds as Christ had read the thoughts of the scribes and Pharisees? While that thought should have been disturbing, it was not, for some reason unfathomable to the fraudulent *Nazi*. It was late when the priest mounted a bicycle and pedaled away down the driveway.

Frau Erika Randorff also made her desired periodic journeys to the castle on the high hill. The interaction between her and the countess fascinated Carl as he patiently observed them. By watching and listening attentively, he was able to confirm that the countess and the merchant's wife had played together as young children but the rise and rule of National Socialism had caused real warmth between them to cool. He learned much as *Frau* Randorff boasted, "My brother Heinz has written me that his *panzers* will seize their objectives in Moscow by the first of August."

Marlene then cautiously inquired, "Would you please tell me again why we are at war with the Russian people. I thought Hitler and Stalin had signed a non-aggression pact in 1939?"

"Oh, Marli, you know that the *Führer* has always hated the godless Bolsheviks! Bolshevism is a Jewish conspiracy to destroy our western culture. We are in a culture war and it seems only we Germans are willing to stand and fight for our European values and for the purity of the Aryan race. They tried to grind us down at Versailles but we are being led to new heights of greatness by our *Führer*."

The visitor's attention then turned to Carl, "I do not understand why you do not keep your woman better informed, Friedrich. Is she really so naive or is she against the *Reich*? You had better tell her to be careful or some good German will report her to the *Gestapo*. There are those who suspect that she belongs to that group of young traitors from Ulm because she refused to be part of the union of German maidens."

Carl attempted to pass it off with a smile, "I believe you have just told her. But we both know she would do nothing to betray the good of her country."

Now the countess shot a dart of a look at him at his riposte to her acquaintance.

"Well," continued the sister of the *panzer* leader, "I may not be the child of a count and a countess but I just know that soon Heinz will have a marshal's baton if the war will only last long enough. The Russians will probably surrender too soon, though. Then the English and the Americans will quit when they see that they can never beat us. So we will remain only among the better class."

A seven-year-old son and a six-year-old daughter occasionally accompanied the Randorff woman. They refused the pointed invitations to go outside and play, preferring to race through the large halls and rooms, grabbing furniture stinting their sliding and helping make their turns more abrupt.

Erika Randorff enthused, "Aren't they dears! Little Ludwig can hardly wait until he is old enough to carry a weapon for the *Führer*. He is such a good little National Socialist that he already knows the oath of the Party and all the ranks of the Party officers. Dear little Renate, she so wants to be a mother and have as many children as she can for the future of the German people. Now, dear, one mustn't touch the vase without asking Mutti. How long has this house had that old thing, Marli, I remember it from my childhood."

"Oh, let me think." came back the hostess, "I guess it's quite new. I believe my mother's father, or was it her grandfather, brought it to his wife from Paris. He found it in a store that sells old things, you know, antiques. It has not been here for centuries like some of the items on the tables. I doubt if it is more than two hundred and fifty years old. Yes, quite new, and probably was not terribly expensive when my ancestor, whoever he was, brought it as a token of his love for his wife."

"Well, I like modernity," commented the merchant's wife, "We live in the age of the New Order and I like the clean clear lines of the new designs in furniture, crystal, and, oh, everything. The old things and ways must make way for the new. The old beliefs must give way to our new faith in the *Führer* and the *Reich*. He must be our only loyalty. The *Reich* is the future for the world. I am so glad that my little Ludwig and Renate will be educated in this clear thinking and not be confused by all that grace and love your neighbor stuff of the old religion. You know, that 'do unto others' business, I say just 'do them in' if they can't take care of themselves. Clean and clear, no fuzzy thinking there!"

"I can not agree with you, Erika. You are an old friend and I would hate to lose your friendship. The old and tried ways have much to offer because generally they have stood the test of time. Besides, maybe new designs of furniture are not so strong or as powerful as advertised. The new ways of Napoleon appeared all powerful until that French conqueror went into Russia and then he faced the English and Prussian armies and, as it is said, met his Waterloo. No, I like the old things and the old ways."

After this conversation, Erika and her children soon left and her visits were much more widely separated.

The next morning Carl determined to visit *Herr* Weber in his labors. Moving across the graveled area, he made his way toward the semi-abandoned ruins of the citadel. As he neared, he caught sight of Hans moving about. Making his way to him, he greeted the outdoor man and asked if he could do anything. The answer came, "If you can milk three cows you could." Carl soon discovered that Hans milked sixteen cows each morning, taking most of the milk to town in the wagon. There the rail stationmaster placed it on a train to the city where it was processed and dispatched to the milk shops of the region.

Carl responded, somewhat to the surprise of the farmer, "I think I can handle that," without giving a reason for his confidence. Many times, he had handled the milking chores at home. Weber moved a three-legged stool beside a cow and gestured for the injured man to sit and fill the pail under the udder. With the help of Hans, Carl complied, and soon the slush of milk hitting milk as the container filled succeeded the sound of milk squirting into an empty bucket. Carl was even able to retrieve the milk from under the cow and place it a safe distance away. Seeing two other metal containers, he was able to pick up one by using only one crutch to complement his good leg. He persevered and was able to move this pail under the teats of another cow secured in a loose neck yoke. Depleting the udder of the second cow he moved on to the third and was able to look on three full buckets of milk by the time Weber returned.

Farmer Weber seemed able to say only, "Unbelievable! Crazy! I simply don't understand!" as he poured the buckets into a larger container saving only enough for the use of the house. When Carl asked what would be done with the surplus Hans Weber told him that it would be taken into the town along with eggs, potatoes, and vegetables. Surely an *SS* officer would likely be ignorant of the daily operations of the place. In any event, he felt good about being able to do some work and make a positive contribution.

For the first time the American was able to investigate up close the horses that pulled wagons and plows in Germany. Even now, he had trouble taking in their size; they were larger than he could imagine any horse could be. When he asked, Hans, a quizzical look on his features, told him the names of the cows and the horses. Moving further in and around the ruin, he discovered a pen holding five dogs. They were of the breed that he had known in Texas as German police dogs. These dogs were both larger and apparently more vicious than any he had experienced before. When asked, Weber said he released them at night to roam the grounds of the castle to provide security, not saying from whom or what they provided safety. Always able to make friends with dogs Carl talked soothingly to the animals and they slowly seemed to accept him. Eventually the Texan was able to reach into the cage and begin to scratch the ear of one, which immediately inspired jealousy in the others.

The outside man of the house looked upon this newly developed acceptance and friendship with very apparent shock and disbelief. "Will wonders ever end?" he mumbled, shaking his head repeatedly. From that day forward for the next month, Carl was a steady contributor to the chores around the castle. Often the young countess also joined the two men and did some of the most onerous duties such as mucking out the horse stalls and transferring the manure to the pile under the gutters and over a catch-pit in the German manner for fertilization. When Carl saw her dressed in midnight blue slacks and a buttoned shirt with her hair stowed on top of her head in two tight buns, her hands encased in gloves, he knew that he had never encountered anyone so intriguingly magnetic.

It was not only her alluring physical appearance that drew him. He never thought her the most beautiful girl physically that he had even seen. Her nose was probably not formed exactly right for her to be compared to Hedy Lamar. Her neck was not long and slender like that of the swan that once seemed the ideal of Gothic fables. Rather it contained the full and strong vitality of life displayed so often in the visible beat of her pulse there. The gaiety of her talk with the Webers, Father Nimitz, and the hospital personnel supplemented the vitality of her appearance. Not only was she winsome in personality but she also displayed strength and fearlessness in dealing with the *Nazi* official Greider. Yet she remained cold to him, her supposed husband. This was a blessing as it helped him avoid the temptation to take rights to which he had no claim. Her aloofness kept him from making unguarded statements revealing him as false. He remembered dancing in Sbisa to the old Texas Aggie swing tune of the late thirties, "rather be out on the highway thumbing a ride than have Miss Greta Garbo for my blushing bride." Increasingly he began to imagine what it would be like to have the Countess Marlene *von* Krönitz as his true bride.

The evening summer air became softer, warmer, and as comfortable as a cashmere sweater. Tired of being alone in the house one evening Carl decided to move outside and negotiate his way down the drive to the gate. The dogs were loose and rushed toward him with fierceness in their demeanor, but upon nearing *him*, they changed their whole being to warmth and friendliness. The two crutches and his one leg had to be placed apart as a tripod in order for him not to be bowled over by their joyous leaping and attempts to lather his face with their tongues. In the distance toward the ruins, he could hear but not see Marlene and Hans Weber urgently calling the animals. After a few moments of canine welcome to him, they departed as rapidly as they had come. Continuing down the steep grade to the gate with exertion, he found it securely closed and locked. The gate was strongly constructed. A padlock secured the iron-sliding bar that blocked any attempt to force open the gate.

The effort coming down the grade forewarned him he would be tested even more to return to his starting point. He began his move up the hill toward the ell of the old structure that lay on the far side of the graveled courtyard. Each time his leg moved forward, he had to bend his knee in order to clear his foot above the rising ground. He then had to thrust his body forward using the farm-developed strength of his arms and shoulders. Pearl-like beads of perspiration glistened, covering his forehead. Swinging and straining, he approached the gravel area. As his foot swung forward to land on the gravel, he faced directly toward the ruins. The shadows of the moon played a hopscotch game across the earth's surface. As the moon's shadow passed from the castle, its light revealed the silhouettes of seven or eight people near the castle wall.

This was a puzzle sufficiently strange to be called a mystery. In his experience and to his knowledge, very few visitors came to the castle. When he shouted "Halloo" to the party all but two quickly disappeared inside the castle walls.

At almost the same time, the countess came striding purposefully toward him. As he continued and approached the door of the residence she came to him and explained, "Some neighboring farmers wanted to come see one of the cows that Hans has been talking about each day when he sees them in town. Can I help you through the door?" She said no more. Later that evening he saw but could not hear a quiet conversation she had with Hans.

Carl's curiosity was intense. He knew instinctively and logically that the figures he saw were not neighboring farmers. How could they leave so quickly over the one gate or over the outer wall? They were there near the ruins and then they were not there. If they had been the French workers, she would have said so. No explanation that he could think of satisfied him.

The blue sky spreading a canopy over southern Germany carried his thoughts instantly and involuntarily to the deeper, sea-blue of the countess' eyes. Driven by that vision, he decided once again to venture outside in the early evening dark for the exercise and the entertainment of a short maneuver to the castle ruins. The air was soft and balmy as he swung his legs forward between the crutches and then moved the wooden aides ahead again. Although night had fallen, the clear skies permitted the moon and stars to light the way so he had no trouble negotiating over the castle yard. Encouraged by the simple joy of exercise he proceeded further than he had planned and circled toward the back of the ruined portion of the castle. The noise of the hooves of the horses and the crunching of the wagon wheel told him that Hans Weber had returned from his regular journey to town. Turning to retrace his steps, he thought that he heard voices from inside the ruins. He assumed that *Frau* Weber had come out of the house to see her husband.

As he rounded the castle wall to approach the place where he thought Hans would be, he had not taken a dozen steps when he was startled to see before him a tot with dark hair and, it seemed, dark eyes. In her arms she carried a doll with a fringed cap. Involuntarily he exclaimed with good lungs, "Hallo, what have we here?"

The little girl looked at him passively and directed her eyes from the top of his head to the ground. She issued a statement and a direct question from a child's honest curiosity, "You do not have a foot. What happened to your foot?"

Uncertain as to what to make of this pixie's sudden appearance he could only return a greeting and a question, "*Guten Abend,* little girl, how are you?"

The sound of the onrushing feet of Hans Weber, crying as he came, gave Carl pause. "There you are, Naomi. I told you to stay with me," cut short further discourse with the child. Even as he snatched her in his arms, Hans answered Carl's unspoken question, "This is our neighbor's daughter. She rode home from town with me to visit with the countess. Her mother will come for her very early in the morning before she goes to work at the machine works."

Carl had many questions he would have liked to ask, but Hans carried the girl at a much faster pace than Carl could manage over the uneven ground. When he did enter the residence wing, the Webers and the countess were in serious conversation. Before he could join the conversation, the countess swept the tyke into her arms and hurried upstairs. Carl found this incident more than puzzling. What was so serious about having a little girl spend the night with an adult she should admire? Why did it appear that they wanted to keep him away from Naomi?

The next morning when he arose, he asked about the little visitor, hoping that he might have the morning meal with her, but the lady of the castle quickly replied that her mother had come for her at first light. When he made his excursion out of the house, he made his way to the old ruins that also served as a barn. As he passed the wagon with a half load of hay, he noticed that the little cap of Naomi's doll lay abandoned on the hay.

Within a week of the Naomi episode, while he was in the barn, the door to the dog pen came open and the dogs rushed out. While Hans had observed the interaction of the crippled man with the animals, the countess, less familiar with Carl's affectionate understanding, cried in apprehension. It quickly was obvious that all was well between man and dogs as they ran from Marlene to Weber to Carl in great triangular orbits, tails wagging, tongues out, and eyes bright with the joy of companionship. It was obvious to Carl that one of the dogs was nursing pups and these, too, soon made their appearance. The four young canines came cowering to Carl as the closest human to the open door of their pen and rolled on their backs in front of him. Finding a seat on the tongue of a plow, he reached down to scratch the stomachs of two of the pups. The other two, aflame with jealousy, rolled to their feet and pushed themselves under the ministering fingers. The mother dog, proud of her offspring, galloped to the site and lavished her love with her tongue on both her pups and their new human friend.

For only a moment, the countess watched the interplay without a word or sound. Hans rounded up the dogs and returned them to their pen. All deference gone, Marlene instructed Carl, "Come into the house with me. I will talk to you and you will talk to me."

She then determinedly stepped off toward the entrance of the quarters. Carl had no recourse but to follow her,

When she entered the house, she marched directly to the small room that Carl had identified as an office. When Carl arrived within earshot, he called and she answered peremptorily, "Come in here!" When he entered the room she again commanded, "Sit down."

She had never addressed him in such fashion, had scarcely addressed him in any way. "Why this now," he puzzled to himself. "She sure is upset. Is she angry? Things seemed to be going well under the circumstances. What now?"

She filled out the answers to his questions directly and immediately. "You are not Friedrich Schleiter! I do not know who you are but you are not Friedrich Schleiter! Because of your injuries and surgeries, I did not expect you to look like the Friedrich I knew, but I did know his character. You are not Friedrich Schleiter! Who are you?"

CHAPTER 4

❀

June–July 1942
Revelations

Astonished and with a mixture of panic and relief, Carl confessed, "I am Carl Frederick Solms, Lieutenant, United States Army Air Corps." as though he were already a prisoner following the rules of the Geneva Convention, omitting only his serial number. As he answered, he stood and drew himself as upright as he could, considering the crutches.

Her next questions followed quickly from a tight and pale face, "Are you a commando? How did you assume my husband's identity? Are you or were you a spy? Did you desert from the *Wehrmacht* or the English?" Her questions were somewhat incoherent even to herself as she mentally and excitedly explored the possibilities, even the improbable ones.

Carl hastened to answer, "No, I am neither a British Commando nor an American Ranger. I am certainly neither a spy nor a deserter. As I said, I am a lieutenant in the American air corps. I was flying in an English bomber when anti-aircraft shot it down at night. I parachuted to the ground safely and eluded capture. I worked my way through the countryside seeking to get to Holland and from there I hoped to return to England.

"After I arrived in the city as I sought a way to cross the river I was apprehended by Captain Schleiter who was at the point of murdering me when flying debris from an English bomb killed him. I then put on his uniform and because he had written permission to come to Littach, so close to Switzerland, I changed my plan of escape."

He desperately wanted to convince her that he was not her husband's murderer. He suddenly realized that her opinion of him was important and he did not want to be considered such a creature. He did not want her to think of him as her husband's killer.

"I can not say your husband's death was an accident but it was the result of an act of war."

"But you speak German perfectly! How did you learn the language so well?"

"All four of my grandparents migrated to Texas from Germany and settled in an area comprised heavily of people of German heritage. My grandparents spoke only German in the home and, being farm families had little need to learn English well. Because both of my parents had been raised in German-speaking homes we also spoke German with only a few English words thrown in. The first language I learned was German with a Texas twang.

"On my first day of school I could not understand the teacher who spoke only in English. I understood and spoke only German. When I discovered my predicament, I was smart and tried to talk as little as possible and listen as much as I could. The teacher probably thought my silence indicated deep thoughts but I only wanted to avoid being teased. Many of my schoolmates were in the same boat and had a limited grasp of English. I was fixed on learning the language spoken by most Americans and tried to be in the company of schoolmates who spoke English only."

"But your pronunciation is perfect. You speak wonderful, educated German. Did you learn that in your education?" The countess asked the question in the cultured language of England as though to test the truth of his story.

His answer came not in the same Oxford mode but in the idiom of New Sendlingen, "That's because of *Tante* Anna, my father's cousin. My father's uncle did not go to America but stayed in Germany. His daughter became a widow when her husband was killed on the Somme in the First World War. She was a schoolteacher but suffered during the turbulent economic times in Germany in the twenties. When my parents learned of her troubles, they invited her to come to Texas and live with them. She had been too proud to ask but they valued family too much not to ask."

Satisfied, she returned to German, "Your parents must be good people!"

"They are very good people. They are good to my four sisters and me. They are good to their neighbors. They are good to their animals. My father is a good farmer and mother is a good farmer's wife. I worry about them. Although I have four sisters, I am the only son. They will have received word that I am missing in action. When I am not reported a prisoner of war they will fear that I am dead and I should be for I am sure that I was the only one from the bomber to escape alive.

"We called our cousin *tante* because she was more than ten years older than my oldest sister. *Tante* Anna, who loved the literature of her native land and the language in which it was written, guarded the purity of the German the three youngest children, and I am the youngest, my sisters are all older, had learned at home. She set aside daily time to cleanse our pronunciation of German and to teach us the richness of German literature from the legends of the *Valkyries,* celebrated in the operas of Wagner, to Goethe, from the Brothers Grimm to Heine. She taught us of the German heroes from Arminius who destroyed legions of Romans to the unifier of Germany, Count Otto von Bismarck.

"She loved to tell us of the land that she had known as a child and bride. We, and especially me, came to know German cities almost as well as we knew Houston and San Antonio. I learned to recognize the dialects of the regions of Germany. She filled my mind with the images of a park-like land."

"She would exclaim, 'For me Germany is so beautiful. The forests are mostly clear and clean like the park in Houston, not like those in your river bottom with all their underbrush and sticky vines. We knew not of poison ivy and little of, what is it, yes, red bugs and ticks and snakes. The leaves and, what do you call the leaves of pine trees, yes, needles on the ground are like a soft carpet. There walking together is a pastime for families and couples. Oh, the young people love to have packs on their backs and hike through the woods and onto the hills. My Ulrich and I loved to take a little food to eat and a small bottle of wine to drink by the river and watch the clear green water of the stream flowing on its northward way to the sea. I'm not going to say what else we did there, that is for my memory only.'"

"Oh, what she told you is so true. She must love her fatherland dearly," interjected the countess.

"She looked back with wonderful memories but when she became a citizen, our ways as Americans became her ways. While she wept over the war between the two peoples she loved, she despised Adolf Hitler and accepted the need for Germany to be cleansed. *Tante* Anna continued to correspond with well-educated people in Germany and received first hand reports on the *Nazi* program after 1933. Some of her fellow teachers were Jews and she heard of the increasing persecution of her friends because of their ancestry. She wept at the stories in the paper of *Kristallnacht.* Several of her friends were small merchants who lost their business and their livelihood by the assaults on their shops. More than anyone she taught us to despise Hitler and his *Nazi* thugs."

Carl continued by telling of his kinwoman's description of the land of her youth with enchantment in her eyes. "The geography surrounding her native town became almost as well known to us as the land on which we dwelt along the Guadalupe and Colorado rivers of Texas."

The castle mistress interrupted after the description of the *Tante* Anna's birth area to ask for more specifics. She then exclaimed, "That is only a few kilometers from my father's estate. I wonder if she knew of my father? He also had friends who lost their livelihood in Hundefurt."

"Hundefurt?"

"Oh, that is the small town near my father's estate, or what once was his estate, of Wendenhof in Hanover."

"You mean the province of Hanover?"

"It once was a duchy and the Duke of Hanover became King George the First of England early in the Eighteenth century. He was a distant relative of ours."

"Well, I have told how I came to be in the city's hospital and why I speak German well. More than I should have told the wife of an SS officer. My fate is totally in your hands. If you turn me in I will almost certainly be executed."

The Countess Marlene, now knowing that Schleiter's death had widowed her, watched intently as she listened to the tale, and learned and understood the details. At its conclusion, an abrupt question sprang forth from her lips, "Then you did not kill Friedrich?"

He, with as much urgency as was implicit in her query, came back with, "No! I promise you that he died just as I said." Although he did not regret the death of SS Captain Friedrich Schleiter and would have slain him if necessary to escape, he discovered that it was important to him that she know that he had not killed her husband.

Not a word passed as she seemed to consider the situation. Her unfocused eyes appeared to find some pattern on the wall fascinating. Remembering his college days of penny-ante poker, he admired her calm face that betrayed so little emotion. She would have been one of the best at the poker table. Not only because she could maintain her self-control but she was also, it seemed obvious to him, the smartest woman, if not person, he had ever encountered.

Finally she spoke. "What you have told me rings true as far as the character of Friedrich Schleiter is concerned. He was a vicious, self-centered bully and a coward to boot. I find it totally believable that if it were in his power to take a human life with no danger to himself he would." She then paused for another long interval. "His hero beyond even the great Friedrich of Prussia was another

Friedrich. He worshipped the one called "The Wonder of the World," really in Latin *Stupor Mundo*, another Friedrich the Second, but this of the Holy Roman Empire, one who used babies for experimentation. Cruelty lay in the depth of his mind. He was aptly named Friedrich.

"You might question as to why I married him if I had this view of him. Did I think this of him before we married? For sure!

"I feel a need to tell you the background of my family and my marriage—I should not call it my marriage. My father is Count Erich von Krönitz. As I said our land is in Hanover province between the cities of Hanover and Braunschweig. You told me that your cousin, the one you call *Tante* Anna, lived near there.

"This house we are in and the land and fields around it are the ancestral home of my mother. My parents met in the University of Tubingen while they were students. Her friends insured the young count-to-be and the young countess came to know one another as descendants of noble families. All who knew them tell me they loved each other quickly and deeply. I never knew my mother because she died when I was born.

"While he was in university, my father became a committed believer in Christ. He learned that it was not his membership in a culture or even a church that was important. He was determined that his highest loyalty and obedience would be to God in the tradition of Martin Luther and so many other German heroes. His thought was so clear, his logic so strong, the work of the Lord so visible in his life that I too came to love Jesus. My desire is not only to love Him but also to obey Him as my Lord and Master. I studied scripture to know Him and His will better. I digress.

"Father had entered the profession of law following university in 1911. He served the Kaiser and Germany loyally on the Western Front in the Great War. He became a judge before Hitler became chancellor and I know he was highly respected not only in Germany but also throughout Europe. The international legal community respected his writings and opinions. He despised the thugs of the National Socialist Workers Party, and even more, the criminal Hitler. He was forced to resign his position in law when, in 1934, he refused to sign the personal loyalty oath to the chancellor. He would not accept Hitler as dictator. From that moment, he was suspect to the *Nazis* and not only lost the position as judge but was in danger of being arrested and sent to a camp where the regime put those they believed opposed Hitler.

"Friedrich, on the other hand, was the son of a mill worker who was a minor Party official in the town of Hundefurt. From the beginning he was an enthusiastic *Nazi* for it gave him the right, the obligation, he thought, to bully those in disfavor. First, there were the Communists, or Bolsheviks as the *Nazis* called them. Then in 1935 it was the Jews' turn to receive the beatings and property destruction. You mentioned that your cousin hated what happened on *Kristallnacht*. He participated in that outrage with joy when he was only seventeen. He was so enthusiastic and energetic that he came to the attention of Heinrich Himmler who brought him to his personal staff two years later as a nineteen-year-old.

"He was envious of our status as nobility and was ambitious to rise to our social position. In addition he thought that I would be a real prize at the *Nazi* social affairs as a true blue-eyed Aryan who," as her face reddened slightly, "had a reputation of being beautiful. He wanted me not because he could love anyone other than himself but because I would be a wonderful ornament, a prize for his ego in 'his' home and at his side, and because he would no longer be a nothing in his own eyes but would be married into the nobility.

"He had no opportunity to court me because I would have nothing to do with him. He never attempted to cause me to love him and never truly proposed but threatened me through my father and demanded that I marry him. One day he called, and having four men waiting in his vehicle, demanded entrance into our home while my father was away. I believe that he picked that time on purpose. I will never forget that scene, as he stood just inside the door. He informed me that my father was considered a traitor by Himmler and was to be imprisoned and possibly executed for his disloyalty to the *Führer* and the nation. He said he could and would intercede only if I married him. Please understand, my father would have rather be executed than to have known that I married this scum in order to save a wonderful man's life. I agreed to marry Schleiter but only after he put everything he had said in writing. I knew that what he was doing, if revealed, would cause his fall from favor not because it was deemed wrong by the *Nazis* but because he agreed to save an 'enemy of the state.'

"I knew he would betray me as soon as convenient unless I had proof of his betrayal of the *Nazi* program. He agreed because he thought that he could get his hands on the letter when he was in our home. Then the fate of my father would be sealed. He convinced himself that he could get the letter by making me suffer. It is strange that his death and your replacement in his uniform saved my father from prison and possible death. My sadness is that he, uh, my father, thinks I willingly married Friedrich Schleiter.

"When the marriage occurred in a purely civil service my father was deeply hurt, yes, angry, and did not come to the wedding. Furthermore, he who loved me more than life, asked that I no longer live in the house in the north because he did not want the *Nazis* to have access to it. Therefore I came south to the castle with the Webers. They know all this history. They have detested the man who forced himself on me. You probably have sensed that hatred. Hans began to soften toward you when you milked the cows, clearly something totally out of character for Friedrich Schleiter.

"Friedrich Schleiter did every thing he could to humiliate me in our short married life together of less than a week. I will not, I can not relate how." Carl began to ache to wipe the tears forming in her eyes and glistening in streaks down her cheeks. "He returned to the headquarters of the *SS* just three weeks before you said he was killed and when he did I stayed here on the land I inherited from my mother.

"There, I have told you all. My father's fate is in your hands if you are a real deceiver. I have given you the truth, and if you are true, you have given me the truth. Now we both can live truthful lives as far as our relationship goes. And," she added with a rueful smile, "we each ask the other to trust. Now our relationship will be built on truth and trust."

Carl wanted to know more, so asked, "When did you begin to think I was false?"

"First, I was puzzled by what I thought was Friedrich's behavior. He was neither polite nor courteous to anyone less powerful or influential. I really could not believe that he would risk his life for lower-class children. You talked to the nurses and others in the hospital and gave them gifts of flowers. All the hospital personnel admired and loved you. Everything that you did, from your first greeting in the hospital to looking at a book written in English, a willingness to sit with good but humble people like the Webers, all screamed to me that this was not Friedrich. I could not accept that even a near encounter with death could change such a man.

"But finally the dogs. I thought that maybe a change had occurred in you, I mean in Friedrich. Oh, I get confused! I do not want to call Friedrich Schleiter my husband. I never thought of him as a true husband. He is—was more of a taker, a rapist, a lowborn criminal who had a hold over me! Anyway, the dogs hated him from the first moment they saw him. I know that they would have torn him to shreds if given the opportunity. I know that he hated them as much as they hated him as well. He would have kicked a puppy if he could; he would have crushed a little dog to death under his feet. I think they sensed that and they loathed him.

"But with you, they tolerated you from the moment that you came together more than anyone I have ever seen. Then I saw their love for you. Dogs know identity by smell more than by sight and they smelled that you were not Friedrich. They knew that you liked them and theirs. When I saw them licking your face and not chewing it off I knew, I knew! It almost caused me to faint when I saw a man to whom I could be married treat the little ones of Greta so tenderly. That could not, that could not be Friedrich, I knew! I doubt that even Jesus could change a man that much and you had said nothing of Him. No, you were a stranger."

At that moment Carl knew this woman drew him as no other had. She appeared totally unselfish and willing to make sacrifice for those she loved. He knew that she was as a magnet to him not only because she was a beautiful woman physically but also because she was a woman of depth, character, and faith. Beneath even his conscious thoughts, he knew that before him was the whole package of a lovely and good woman. Inwardly he cursed Friedrich Schleiter for what he had done to her and for failing to appreciate her and to seek to win her commitment. Then he thought of what a fool the *Nazi* had been. With care, selflessness, kindness, consideration and other virtues, he may have been able to win over this prize among women. He had chosen to take by force what he was not able to win in any other way. He had been thankful for the death of Hitler's man because it saved his own life but now he was more gratified because now she was free from a monster.

Because of his feelings for her and the desire within himself that she think well of him, he again took up the revelation of his life.

"I think you should know that when I was in college, or, as you say in Germany, university, that I met a girl named Lydia who had a faith in Christ like yours. Although we were never romantic, we spent much time together. We talked of many things but the most important was the role of Christ in Christianity. She taught me the true meaning of faith and the true meaning of what it is to be a Christian. It was through her that I committed to follow Him. I wish you could know her. You would be great together."

Marlene rose from her seat and announced, "There is something I, no, we, must do! Please follow me." She brushed by him and he had to note the trail of sweet and clean odor that followed her. His brain was reeling and he never knew how he managed the crutches in those moments but he soon found himself sitting at table in the kitchen with the Webers.

The young noble woman, now calm and assured as to what had to be done, took an explanatory detour before getting to her main purpose.

"Hans and *Tante* Liese," she began, addressing Carl, "are as dear to me as any humans I have known could be other than my father. I told you that Liese was as much of a mother as I have even known. She was born in this house when it belonged to my mother's father. It is more her home than it is mine. If not legally, it is hers in her heart. She and my mother were of an age and played in the castle and she has told me that they acted out their dream of secretly being princesses. Hans is the son of a farmer who tilled this land owned by my grandfather. That land is still worked by tenants, or was before the war. Before Hans became steward, he was the forest master of the area and has returned to that position because of the war. I tell you this because I trust them with my life and I am going to trust them with your life.

"Hans and *Tante* Liese, this man is an American flier named Carl Solms. He is neither my husband nor Friedrich Schleiter but a lieutenant in the American air force. He has told me that flying debris in an air raid killed Friedrich as he was preparing to kill—in cold blood—this man before you. He will continue to stay here because his false identity offers protection not only to us but also to my father. Now according to Lieutenant Solms this is how he came to be here under these circumstances."

The young Countess Marlene then recounted the events, with occasional fill-ins from Carl, as to how the American came to the situation, giving evidence of her acceptance of the truth of what Carl had related. When finished the four sat at the table and considered one another. Then Hans Weber rose, gave Carl a manly hug, excused himself, and left. Carl tried to puzzle out the meaning of this departure. He really did not think that he was going for the police but had no idea of why he left abruptly. Liese Weber sat a moment, then offered to make coffee, and left her chair and moved to the young countess named Marlene and gave thanks, tears staining her face as other tears marked the face of Marlene. "Thank you, dear Jesus, for finishing this nightmare. I will light candles to thank You and to prevent another bad dream from arising." She then fulfilled her promise for the coffee.

Both Marlene and Liese agreed that the revelation made all come clear. They had begun to accept the change in the character of the man they knew as Friedrich Schleiter but somehow it did not make sense. How could a person change so much in the nature of his being? The changed character they had observed in the man they mistakenly thought was Schlieter made the acceptance of the account of Carl Solms believable.

Hans soon returned with a block of wood well over a foot long, about eighteen inches high, and eight inches wide. He bent down and held it by Carl's shortened leg and said, "Yes, it will do." He then asked, "May I use the right boot in the wardrobe upstairs." He added with a beaming smile, "I don't think you will be using the boot for the right leg soon." The women's faces registered shock at his remark, but Carl smiled in agreement with Hans. Hans left immediately and returned shortly with the boot in hand.

"He likes you," commented the girl Marlene to Carl in the moments Hans was away.

Carl asked, "What's he doing? What will he do with the wood and the boot?"

Liese answered from the vicinity of the stove, "I do not know for sure but he is an expert wood carver and loves to make things. Maybe he is going to make a wooden boot."

The two women and the displaced American sat and asked dozens of questions; the women asked Carl and Carl asked the women. "Had Carl seen Indians?" asked *Frau* Weber. She also wanted to know of his boyhood on a Texas farm.

Under the two women's prodding to know more of his past, he described how he grew until his mid-teens as a country boy with the assumption that he would take his father's place on the cotton farm. He confessed that his parents and grand parents were of humble birth. They had farmed other peoples land before they came to Texas but now they were able to farm their own land. He continued, "I have four sisters, all older than me. Did I tell you that before?" as he looked at the younger woman. "My chores and work around the farm during my boyhood kept me busy. I nevertheless had time to go hunting in the woods of the bottomland of the river with my rifle and 410 shotgun. The lives of all the small animals stood in great peril."

The young countess exclaimed in amazement, "You had guns as a young boy? Astonishing!"

He related how he studied the ways of the furtive forest creatures and learned that being still in the absence of concealment often provided an escape from detection. "Several times I told my father, 'I would not have seen the rabbit if it had not run.' I learned a great deal during those hours in the forest. I learned measures of evasion that served me well several times during my flight through the German countryside.

"In addition, I had time for schooling through the New Sendlingen Independent School District. My father lacked commitment to my education beyond the elementary level. A simple farmer needed only the basics such as reading and arithmetic for his livelihood. Neighbors and kin informed him that the law said that his children had to go to school until the age of sixteen."

Carl described his first day of school, "I was the first to arrive. Being alone with the considerate teacher, she insured I avoided the harassments of my classmates because of my ignorance of the language she spoke. As other children entered the room babbling in English, I vowed, 'I will learn this English. I can do anything these others can do. I will listen and work hard to learn'. I learned and mastered the language of America."

Carl continued to describe how, as he matured, his world became more and more English speaking, not only in school but also through movies and the reading of everything he could obtain. He took advantage of every opportunity to learn the English used everywhere but in his home.

Tired of talking of himself, Carl wanted to know, "What is the personality of Count Erich von Krönitz? Is he formidable?"

"He is kind and gentle with those he loves but he does not brook injustice or fools easily. He is rather formidable, as you asked, because he is quiet, even austere, with strangers."

"What do the Americans think of the war?" both women questioned.

"Until the attack on Hawaii, the majority opposed our participation. After the Japanese attacked and Hitler declared war it seemed to have great support before I left."

"What do the Germans think of the war?" Carl inquired but received no answer but another question..

"Are there really many people of German heritage in the United States?" asked Marlene.

"Yes, I have read that more Germans have come to the states than any other nationality. In the eighteenth century, they settled in Pennsylvania and Virginia. There are many of German descent in the Midwest, by which I mean Minnesota and Wisconsin."

The questions and the conversation poured forth in a torrent until Carl asked about the condition of the Jews in Germany. The warm convivial setting instantly dissolved into cold silence until Herr Weber returned with an enigmatic smile although he lacked a Cheshire cat. Each of the women importuned him to tell them what he had been up to but he showed his declination by only continuing to smile.

Well after midnight they made their ways with laughter echoing through the house to their apartments and slept. Each was emotionally relieved but yet aware of the danger that lurked each day. The revelation of Carl's false identity and the death of Friedrich Schleiter increased the danger to each one. They all knew that the despicable Friedrich's presence had afforded a measure of protection because of his standing in the Party and particularly with the *Reich's* dictator.

It was the freedom from anger and hurt in her heart and mind that made Marlene's sleep innocent and deep following her prayers. Carl slept well because now he had a group with whom he did not have to deceive and whom he did not desire to deceive. Hans and Liese Weber closed their eyes to deep repose because they knew that the young woman they loved so deeply no longer faced a life bound to an evil man. They also were delighted that this castle, which their hearts owned, was no longer to be the lair of the *Nazi*. In addition, Hans had developed a reluctant liking to the man he had thought an *SS* officer.

Days rolled by. After more than a dozen of them, Hans came into the house to the table where Carl and the two women sat for the evening meal. Opening a package beneath the table that he had carried in his hand he drew it up and presented Carl with the boot he had asked for from the wardrobe. He said to the American, "Try it on!"

Liese almost cried at her man, "Hans! Don't be cruel!"

Hans said, "Let me show you," and pulled a rounded piece of wood that fit snugly into the boot but was itself hollow. The wood came to an elongated tapered point. Hans had carved, with the delicate skill of a Black Forest artist, a wooden false leg. Carl's leg fit snugly inside flexible wooden strips. These, in turn, remained attached to a larger block of wood that ended in a two to three inch peg. There were legging-like straps keeping the prosthetic secure against the leg. Hans showed him that he could insert the wooden aide inside the boot and secure it with a pin that was maintained in place with a much smaller pin. Hans had manufactured an artificial foot inside the boot that would move on a hinge. Hans explained, "This will take some getting used to and we will have to pad everything considerably with cloth to keep all tight and secure. Liese, get some soft old cloth and let Carl try it on so I can make any adjustments I need to."

Full of doubt, Carl permitted Hans to insert his shortened leg into the device and strap it securely tight. Producing the boot, he fit the substitute foot and ankle into the boot and placed the securing pin in place. With a command of "Try it!" Hans stepped to Carl's side as he attempted to rise. It was good that he did. Unused to walking with two feet much less with an improvised foot,

Carl found his balance precarious as he stood. He was supported by Hans but the pain of the wound at the end of his leg was intense. He persevered in taking five or six steps, supported by the older man. Liese Weber exclaimed at the pain reflected on Carl's visage, "We will have to toughen up that stump! One thing we have plenty of is salt. We will bathe it in warm salt water. My mother always did that for our wounds and it soon made them well."

Hans demonstrated how the artificial limb could be used outside the boot as a "peg-leg"as well as in it.

The facial cuts, both accidental from the collapsing building and deliberate by the doctors, had healed although they still radiated an ugly red. The older couple reassured their new friend that his complexion would improve although the scars would always be disfiguring. The fugitive American blessed the wounds and marks for they provided a mask of his true identity and allowed him to play the role of Friedrich Schleiter.

While the exchanges between the others were taking place, the young lady some called "Marli" sat quietly with manifestations of the proverbial wisdom of an owl. Her eyes followed the injured man with passive consideration only wincing when his face showed obvious pain. After Carl rested a few minutes, he said he wanted to try the boot once more but asked if they had more padding available. "In fact," he queried, "is there any soft rubber anywhere?"

Hans ruefully responded, "The war has called for all unused rubber to be turned in to the government. Right off I can not remember any." He looked to his wife for any ideas.

Liese suddenly rose to her feet and left through a door opening from the kitchen. She returned triumphantly, "I remember Eva, the maid, had rubber that she used for purposes I will not discuss. I saw them in her room after she left." She then hoisted a piece of rounded material that had the appearance of a sponge as though she had a great hunting trophy. With scissors and a few moments she had trimmed the stuff to a fit inside the wooden leg and said, "Try it again. See if this is any better."

Marli uttered her first words since the experimentation had begun, "Do you think you should? It pained you so the last time. Perhaps you should wait until the wound becomes more calloused."

In anxiety to be rid of the crutches Carl insisted, "No, I want to try it again, just a little at a time, but I want to build it up as soon as I can." With Hans' assistance after the rubber softened the leg extension, he rose and walked a little further than he had on the first attempt. Although his expression showed pain, he controlled his facial tension more than before.

Now Liese had drawn hot water and poured what seemed to be an overwhelming torrent of salt into the basin placed at the feet of the *ersatz SS* man. Kneeling she rolled the cloth of the trouser leg up to the knee and took the red stained limb in her hands. Telling Carl to relax his leg she then immersed it into the saline solution. She next lifted it, let the solution drain off, and then repeated the process again and again. Carl could not see immediate improvement in the wound but humored the sweet-natured Liese.

The day was now well on its way and again Hans Weber harnessed the large horses to the wagon half loaded with a great pile of hay and left the castle grounds on his way to the town. At noon Liese, Marlene, and Carl sat down for the mid-day meal. The women, it seemed to the man, were a little on edge as they usually were when Hans was away. Throughout the meal the women talked of repairs and chores to be accomplished. Carl noted the change in the younger woman. Color now animated her cheeks and the ice had disappeared from the blue of her eyes.

Liese turned the discourse to his background in Texas, asking if they called the farm a ranch. He replied, "No, my family only had a farm where we grew cotton and corn. We did not market cattle."

Liese, determined to keep the conversation on this subject, persevered, "How big was this farm?" When he described the size of his father's farm, although converting acres to the German measure required some time, the two women seemed surprised that it was so much. Annaliese again wanted to know his background and asked about his mother, also "Do you have brothers and sisters?" He described his family, again saying that he was the youngest of five children, and gave the situation of each of his siblings as well as his parents and grand parents. He again told of the ministry of his cousin in teaching him to speak the best German.

Marlene then became alert as she looked straight at him, "Now I understand. When we first talked in the hospital in the city, I thought that both your voice and word usage was different from that of Friedrich. The doctors told me, though, that you had had a blow to the larynx and your voice would be different forever. Of course, that did not explain the different words you used but that could be explained by your, I mean Friedrich's, exposure to the talk of Berlin."

Carl continued with his description of his background including his college education. He had to explain that in America the differentiation between college and university was minor but that his education had been practical and not classical in literature. At this time, Liese excused herself to attend to the cleaning after the meal while Carl and the girl he increasingly thought of as Marli continued their conversation in the library. There, she, the countess, asked if there was a "Lili Marlene" in Texas waiting under a lamp post for his return.

Upon this question, he felt obligated to tell more of his background. He recounted that while he had dated several girls, none were serious as pertaining to marriage. He felt perfectly free to describe Lydia and his relations with her.

The countess interjected, "Then you do have a girl waiting for you?"

He explained that during their junior year in college, his roommate, Bruce Wishart, had arranged a blind date for Carl with Lydia Cameron, the best friend of Bruce's hometown girl.

Carl described how Bruce had assured him, "I have dated, uh, I mean really that I have gone steady with Lois, since our junior year in high school. We both know Lydia well. Lois really wants me to find a date for her. She said Lydia deserves somebody better than me and you are the only one that could possibly fit that bill. I am not going to say that she has a great personality because that would be the kiss of death as far as you having her down. She is very slender with kind of short hair, but not very short. When Lois and I are with her, the conversation seems to get more serious. She is pretty but not a movie star type. If you agree to have her down only the guys who talk to her will even remember whom you dated but the smart ones will be impressed. I can't say she is a knockout in appearance."

He told of Lydia's clear and strong beliefs and commitment, of her love of literature, and her understanding heart. Carl explained the true situation that, although many would find it hard to accept, his relationship with Lydia and her affection for him always remained on a spiritual and intellectual plane.

At this point *Frau* Weber remembered chores to be finished in the kitchen.

Carl continued, "The two girls from west Texas arrived on the campus not by train but in the automobile of Lois' parents. Now if you want to talk to a rancher's son that would be Bruce Wishart. He is by far my best friend. We were assigned to room together our 'Fish,' or first year of college and remained roommates for all four years. When I entered the air corps, he stayed with the ground forces. His father owns a large ranch out in west Texas near a town called Lamesa. He is a good man, the best I have known, and I wish that you could know him. The last I knew of him was that he had been assigned somewhere in California for some kind of army language or intelligence training. For some reason I thought that his father has significant political influence which may have helped to get that assignment."

Carl now began to ask the questions that earlier might have revealed his fictitious identity.

"I have seen and heard strange sounds in the court near the old ruins. I do not know what, but it seems that something unusual is going on around the castle. I know that Hans comes in from his rounds of the forest late but what I hear is not the sound of the wagon. It is like people moving and murmuring. What kind of night visitors do you have? That little girl, what was her name, oh, yes, Naomi, you took her from my presence so quickly? You said that she was a neighbor's child but I have seen no neighbors around the residence. Just who are her parents and where do they live?"

As his questions became more probing, he could see the baroness become more ill at ease. He was particularly interested in the little Naomi and the cap of her doll. For this, Marlene had no explanation.

When he inquired about the daily trips to town by Hans, she insisted that as a forest master, Hans had to make a daily inspection of the forests in their region. He took the wagon down the fire lanes and through the woods to make sure that all was in order. The countess added that Hans came to the position as a grant by the Weimar government for his service in the Great War.

CHAPTER 5

❀

July 1942
Relations

She soon seemed tired of this conversation and left for the hinter parts of the house to talk to Liese. That strong-bodied woman soon came to Carl and said it was time for another salt bath for his leg. He had no option but to permit her to help him into the kitchen and once more to submerge his leg in the hot salt water. Time demonstrated the benefits of this treatment, as he noticed within a few days not only a healing over of the wound but also a deadening of the nerves in the extremity. Each day he was able to take more steps with the artificial leg and boot. The peg leg was more comfortable without the boot but the boot made him feel more whole and improved his spirits. His walks outside the castle, usually accompanied by the countess, increased in length.

While the lady was busy about the house and her own affairs, Carl increasingly anticipated these moments almost, it could be said, greedily. When she preceded him on the narrow walkway and the sun shone on her hair, it seemed every fifth to tenth strand was auburn. Occasionally she would toss her head so that her waist length tresses cascaded about, strangely bringing the thought of an iridescent waterfall to his mind. The shape of her body dispelled any notion of fat hiding under a billowing gray dress lingering from his first sight of her in the hospital.

Her small jokes and witticisms that would lose their punch in the retelling made him know that this woman loved life, and when appropriate, enjoyed moments that were not all seriousness. He learned that her quick mind could result in a quick and sometimes cutting tongue that she prayed to control. Every minute with her increased his enjoyment of her companionship. Increasingly he consciously counted her a close friend.

In early July, Greider requested the presence of Captain Schleiter and his wife, the countess, at the July duty-parade in town. He asked that the distinguished officer, who had risen through the ranks of the Hitler Youth, present the awards to local members of that group. The castle conspirators agreed that the invitation must be accepted but upon the advice of Hans, Carl would not wear his artificial limb. Hans said that the *Nazi* regime was calling up all who had military experience even through they had lost limbs or eyes. If Carl did not want to find himself in the service of the Third Reich, he had better appear as incapacitated as possible. Hans added, with a smile, that he would have been happy to have served under a captain with Carl's intelligence and character. "Yes, you would have been a fine officer for the Kaiser's army. It's too bad that your grandparents left but then you would still be too young for me."

Carl questioned if he would have been a member of the Hitler Youth after 1933 rather than a member of the Future Farmers of America. Hans assured him that he would have enrolled in the youth group named for Hitler because he and his family would have been suspect had he not. Carl thought it a strange world where decisions made long ago impact even the lives of the living. He remembered the ripple effect of a stone thrown into a pond and how it reaches out and out. His grandparents had migrated from Germany and the stone of that movement rippled in his return to that land not as an ardent German but as a soldier in the American army.

When Carl stated and asked Marlene, "We in America have heard of the Hitler Youth. Were you or any of your friends a member?"

She explained, "*Hitler Jugend* (Hitler Youth) was applied only to males and the term for girls over twelve years old was '*Bund deutscher Mädel*' (Association of German Maidens) usually shortened to '*BdM*'. Shortly after the National Socialists came to power, every German child and adolescent was required to be a member of the appropriate organization. There were groups for boys about twelve or younger, the *Jung Volk* [Young People] and for girls there was the *Jung Mädel* [Young Maidens] and different groups for those approaching maturity. In 1935 I was supposed to become a member of the *BdM* but my father refused to have me shaped in the *Nazi* mold and sent me out of the country to Switzerland to school."

"The Party gave him no problem at the time because he was both a distinguished jurist and from an ancient and titled family. It, however, gave me a record that was suspect and shortened my stay at university. All of my childhood friends became members of these organizations and most became warped totally into followers of the Party. You will certainly encounter some of them for they seek the aura of my titles and heritage. When I remind you who they are and mention that they are friends from my childhood please, please do no trust any one of them!"

During the second week of July, Hans harnessed the horses not to the hay wagon but to a lighter carriage that seemed a relic of days long passed. Carl once more outfitted himself in the uniform of the German officer. The countess appeared in a sky blue light wool dress that only enhanced her natural attractiveness and whose tint highlighted the cobalt of her eyes. Even Hans and Liese looked approvingly upon their young mistress and at each other with happy glances. There was ample room for all and the sun lifted the dew from the ground. The four were pulled back into the world's activities as the carriage rolled around the curves down the slope.

The well cared for horses did not take much longer to get the carriage to town than the automobile of Greider had taken to come to the castle. As they neared the square, the evidences of the day's planned event became ever more obvious. Throughout the town they saw the *Swastika* banners hung on posts and flying from upper windows. The town square blazed with red banners setting off a centered black, broken cross. The color seemed so strong that it tinged the faces of the spectators and participants as though red dye had been cast into the air. Large photographs of Adolf Hitler in a brown shirt festooned available walls.

Greider handled the introductions of those assembled to one another. Carl remembered *Herr* Schlenkmann, and *Herr* Randorff, and *Herr* Hühn. *Herr* Schlenkmann took the opportunity of the greeting to present him to *Stammführer* (Major) Vollmering. Carl learned that this officer was the leader of the youth in southwestern Germany. Randorff made the opening statement as Schlenkmann and then Vollmering followed. Then Greider called those receiving awards forward to receive their medals and badges from the hands of the young *SS* captain assisted by the countess, if necessary. *Herr* Schlenkmann noted the presence of *Herr* and *Frau* Hans Weber, reminding the audience of Hans' distinguished service to the Fatherland in the Great War of 1914 to 1918.

Carl was satisfied that Vollmering remained aloof prior to the ceremony and listened with close attention as the speaker condemned the assassination of Protector Reinhardt Heydrich of Bohemia and Moravia and commended the retribution upon the Czech village of Lidice. The *SS* major gave a glowing report of the war with the Russians and predicted the fall of the cities of Sebastopol, Leningrad, and Moscow before fall. Their allies, the Japanese, had conquered the Pacific and controlled the oil of the Dutch in the East Indies. "The war," he assured his listeners, "is nearing its end and the new thousand-year reign of the *Reich* is imminent."

The ability to restrain a smile, learned during his college days, was beneficial in these circumstances as the speaker extolled the youthful captain as a worthy example for these boys. The *Stammführer* continued that *Reichsfuhrer-SS* Himmler himself had asked that he look upon the well-being of this fine young National Socialist leader of the future. "And! And! And the *Führer* himself was to be informed of the health status of young Captain Schleiter." Upon this news of the personal interest of the genius of Germany, the boys broke forth into wild, exultant cheers. Their elders, both on the stand or simply spectators, joined the exuberant cries of the children.

Then the names of the boys to be honored were called, and as they came forward, Randorff whispered pertinent information to Carl for any remarks he might want to make to encourage the youth. As they came one by one, the boys, dressed in black shorts, brown shirts, with knee length stockings, reminded Carl of younger editions of himself. Nervous at his charade, he regretted the misdirection of these good-looking boys.

Upon completion of the ceremony, *Herr* and *Frau* Greider invited the entire honor party to their home for refreshments and fellowship. Knowing that they were obligated to attend, Countess Marlene and Carl, enabled by his crutches, followed along with the others the short distance to the home of the Local Party Leader. *Herr* Vollmering's first inquiry concerned the status of health of the young captain, justifying his question by, "As we said at the ceremony the highest authorities are interested and are curious as to when they will see you back in harness again?"

Carl was thankful for Hans' advice to leave his prosthetic behind and was delighted that he had shown limited mobility on the way to the house. He reinforced the impression by asking, "May I be granted permission to sit in your presence because I am very weak and fatigued?"

The official expressed regret and asked about his general health other than the loss of his foot. Remembering something he had heard in the American army from doctors, Carl responded, "Sometimes I must stay in bed immobilized. There are many days when my back acts up and I can hardly move. Some part of the collapsing building must have struck me in the back. The doctors found no vertebrae damage so it must be in the muscles." Carl then asked for permission to raise his injured leg, complaining of a rush of blood to its extremity. When both the guest and the hostess granted permission, Carl caught sight of Marli who seemed to have caught something in her throat, as she quickly coughed and turned away from him. It suddenly struck him that he increasingly thought of her not as "countess" or even "Marlene" but simply "Marli."

The conversation no longer centered on him but turned in whispers to the air raid of the British upon the city of Cologne. It had apparently been a massive raid on May 30 that had destroyed most of the central city, although by some quirk bombs had not destroyed the city's magnificent cathedral. "The British are just barbarians to seek to destroy the art and beauty of our dear nation. But we know that the *Führer* will make them pay," pronounced one of the women.

Then the *Stammführer* consoled those within hearing distance that, "I have heard that German scientists are developing weapons that would make the enemy regret the day that a bomb was dropped on the Fatherland."

Pleading extreme fatigue, Carl asked Greider, after a profuse expression of appreciation for being allowed to honor the youth and to assemble with such a distinguished group, if his party might be excused to return to the castle. Leave was quickly given, and with much less dissimulation than the request. The events of the day completely enthralled the local Party functionary. His face glowed at the recognition that his town and its people had received. As far as he was concerned it could not had been more of a success.

Enroute to the castle most of the party was silent other than a few chuckles that forced their way from the soft lips of the countess, "May I please sit? My leg is about to burst with a geyser of blood all over your beautiful carpet! And my back, I just do not know when it will fail me. Oh, thank you. Thank you. A real hero of the *Reich* thanks you." Then a string of almost smothered laughter burst forth. As Hans halted the carriage in front of the door to the housing wing, Marli turned and joyfully exclaimed, "Thank you, Hans. I was a silly girl when I last had such a merry good time as I did this day. God bless you and Liese."

As she dismounted the carriage, after Carl had reached the ground, he out of habit braced himself against one crutch and held out his hand to her. With the instincts of a lady, she took his hand and looking into his face murmured, "Thank you" and disappeared through the door. Carl wondered, "What livened her up? The events were okay but nothing to get high over. It's not like her to be so giddily happy." A phrase learned from a Hispanic buddy came to mind, "*Que pasa?*"

Almost as though to ease the stress of the deception committed about his physical well being the day before, Carl rose before breakfast, pulled on his wooden leg, inserted the leg in the artificial foot in the boot and secured it with the retaining pin. He found it more difficult to descend the stairs than to ascend with the boot. He had to hold the railing and move carefully but he did manage to get out of the house and to move around the grounds. He discovered that the treatment imposed by Liese seemed to be working. Now he could walk some distance before the discomfort forced him to rest. He was determined to push himself day and night as far as possible when opportunity afforded. His venture outside caused complimentary comments from Liese and Hans at the breakfast table and Carl expressed his appreciation to the pair for making it possible for him to walk without the crutches. He explained that in the house, the peg leg was more comfortable but on the gravel and in soft ground it was good to have the support of the sole of his boot.

He walked to the limit of his comfort once more that morning and twice that afternoon. With his increased mobility his assistance to Hans, who seemed to have so many duties, increased. When those chores had been finished each morning he normally went to the library and took a book from the shelf and read. He found it interesting to read the books in German and generally devoted himself to those that presented a theological view all the way from Luther to the Anabaptist writers. He discovered that he could not agree totally with any one of them but that he found something from each author that he thought was true. Once when reading a work of Philip Melancthon, Marlene entered and asked what he was reading. When he said "Melancthon" she asked what he thought of him and he honestly replied, "There is much I do not understand, there is much that I concur in, and there is some with which I definitely differ." From his concurrences and differences with the author came a significant discussion of matters of the Christian faith.

Seeing the two in a genial discussion Liese sought to increase the amiable atmosphere by serving coffee, tea, and sweets. Having heard in town complaints about the shortage of genuine tea and coffee and aware of the blockade imposed on Germany, the frequent service of those items puzzled Carl. When asked, Marlene replied, "I do not know. It just seems that Hans has his sources and I do not ask."

Carl increasingly found this girl, who he guessed was several years his junior, equal to Lydia in both intelligence and spirit. While Lydia had seemed ethereal, Marlene was bound to the earth in mind, spirit, and body. He remembered Lydia's intellect and commitment but in this countess there were those qualities and additionally the physical being. He found her increasingly intriguing. She seemed to be of the soil when she worked in the barn throwing hay to the cows and horses, feeding the hogs (or *schwein* as they were always named) and even mucking out the stables in her slacks and shirt costume. In the library, she was a well read, knowledgeable, and deep-thinking individual who considered what she read through the lens of scripture. Their conversations, occurring almost daily with refreshments served by Liese, were warm not with the heat of controversy but with the joy of freely shared convictions. Above all she was, to him, more pleasurable to gaze upon than any sea or mountain landscape.

She was like the statue of Saint Teresa, both spiritual and sensual, but she never permitted the latter to limit the former. One day when he was trying to satisfy his visual pleasure without staring and not really succeeding, she rose and went to the shelves. Finding what she looked for she turned and handed it to him saying, "Not all of us are pagan worshipers of Wotan and his disciple. This man tells what it truly means to be the slave of Christ. His name is Dietrich Bonhoeffer. Permit me to read an excerpt, '*when Christ calls a man, he bids him come and die.*'" She continued, "*Herr* Doctor Bonhoeffer has demonstrated his commitment to this thought by refusing to worship either Hitler or even the nation and is now confined. I wish that you would read this work and give me an opinion of an American mind. I have read that Americans are pre-eminently practical and not theoretical, I mean, you are supposed to be the world's pragmatists."

Through her talk now and previously, she had, without intent, spun a web of the delicate fibers of spirit, sweetness, logic, commitment, admiration, and yes, heart-aching love. Emotionally, he was a prey caught in the spider's web, and then without intent, trussed in the encircling fiber. While the predatory spider preyed and pulled the life juices from the victim, that was neither the desire of the countess nor the fate of the trapped by the invisible strands of love. Her character and personality unknowingly wove the fragile fibers that bound him.

His openness and small town friendliness had begun to ensnare her. The falling timber of the fiery crash of the building has crushed what once observers called a Roman nose. The repairing surgeon, Doctor Bacher, had skillfully reset it according to the identification card of Friedrich Schleiter but did not attempt to restore the aquiline one of Carl Solms. The scars, once livid, had settled into simple brown streaks across his face. A child seeing him in full light may have been alarmed but in adult society, where scars had been seen before, they could be accepted, maybe even honored if gained with just cause.

The Baroness *von Ritterbach und Krönitz* began to see the inner worth of the man she had thought to be her husband. There was his leg. He was a cripple. No woodcarving, no ingenious reconstruction of a lost foot, could restore his agility and strength. On the other hand, he expected treatment with the respect, courtesy, and equality with which he treated her. He seemed to see her as a woman who through no fault of her own had gotten herself into an ugly situation. He revealed not one indication of servility even though almost all other than the Webers were obsequious in the face of her lineage and potential wealth, as he believed himself a peer to the world.

Curious as to his attitude of equality, on one occasion she purposely informed him, "You know I had nothing to do with it but we are cousins, though not close, of the Battenberg family. You do know of them, do you not?"

Knowing that he should have been impressed by this disclosure but also seeing the twinkle in her eyes that showed teasing would be acceptable, he mouthed aloud the syllables, "'berg' now that's mountain or hill or something and 'batten' must be the family name. So—they are the 'Battens' who live on a hill. Yeah, in America we call those kind of folks 'hillbillies.'"

Marlene's unbridled laughter brought Liese in with alacrity to see if her charge was been attacked or what. Seeing the alarmed expression on the dear retainer's face, she settled in a gentle but continuing laughter, asking the woman, "Do you know how he described the royal family of his allied nation? He called them 'hillbillies'! I do not think he knows that many of King George's ancestors came from Germany. The family name was Battenburg until the last war when anything German became impolitic, Carl. They anglicized it and put the mountain before the family name and it became Mountbatten. Really, did you not know this? Oh, you are good to give me a laugh like that." Liese looked at Carl with total approval for his gift to her lady.

"I really didn't know but I thought I would kid a bit. I could tell that your relation to that family was a matter of which you could be proud if you wanted to and that the Battenbergs must be big people. Our schools in Texas, though, taught us that we should treat all with courtesy and only those who merit it by deed with deference. Our teachers said that if we worked in a gas station we should treat the school janitor the same way we would treat John D. Rockefeller. Of course that would probably never happen since a man who could accumulate so much money would draw awe." The little restraint left in their relationship began to melt following this conversation.

After his next walking jaunt, during which she accompanied him, they once more settled into the library for their valued discourse. Her demeanor, which was subdued and somewhat troubled, mystified Carl. His heart was exultant by the events of the walk for during it she had reached out her hand to grasp his as they cleared one rough spot and did not pull away once passed that area so they finished the tour hand-in-hand. Now troubled by her obvious blue mood, his mind raced through many unpleasant scenarios while he waited for her to speak. Was she going to tell him that there was no way that their relationship could mature? That sure made sense. Had Hans been arrested during a smuggling operation? Many indications of something going on beneath the surface around the castle and its grounds existed. Had she suddenly developed repugnance toward him? He lacked poetry in his soul but the thought crossed his mind that he had lost a leg and now he might lose his heart with this girl. "Speak, please speak!"

She spoke. "You have, I know, noticed some strange things about the castle and in the movements of Hans. I believe you have the right to know because your danger is increased through your association with us."

As she paused, he joyfully broke in, "You are smuggling items into or out of Germany in order to meet expenses!"

She smiled at the naivety of his guess and responded, "Well, yes, in a way we are. Our items are people, whom we smuggle out, not in. All this year there has been a drive to, as the officials say, 'relocate the parasite races to the eastern occupied territory.' What they mean, what they are doing is sending them to concentration camps where they die either from starvation, disease, of in a gas chamber. This is their 'final solution' for the Jewish question, the gypsies, homosexuals, and those who irritate by not agreeing with them through and through. This I know because Friedrich bragged about his role. The orders you found in his satchel were to accomplish this in the city. He told me, no, threatened me, that only my marriage to him had kept my father from the camps. I am involved because it is what I think Christ and all the church fathers would have us do for these people.

"Now Hans is involved for different reasons. At the Somme, he was badly wounded and unable to move between the lines. A comrade crawled forward through the wire and the bullets, oh, you should hear him describe it, and pulled him back foot by foot to German lines. Just as his comrade knelt up to lower Hans into the trench, a bullet hit him in the throat and he died within minutes. That man's name was Micah Goldberg, the son of a jeweler in Dresden. Hans is determined to repay him by saving as many Jewish lives as he can.

"We are all three involved in the rescue effort. As you know, Hans goes to town each day with the wagon. He takes any products of the land that need to go and he obtains the things we need and also fulfills his duties as forest master by traveling through the forest trails and firebreaks to check on the health of the woods. During some of those trips through the trees, he finds refugees and brings them back to the castle. There is a place under the hay where you can hide four adults or two adults and four children.

"You might ask, 'How does he know when and where he is to meet the refugees?' That is something, which he will not divulge even to Liese. All I know is that there is someone in town, who does not know about Hans, but signals him every day. Usually the signal says that no one is waiting for him. He knows the person who signals him but that person does not know who is receiving the information. It would be difficult for the *Gestapo* to find a member of the net work in Frankfurt or Hamburg and unravel the net from that end. Each member's knowledge only goes back up the network. Hans is really the key right now. He knows who provides him information. If he talked under torture, he might divulge who that person is. That person could be tortured to find out who gives them the information.

"We do take precautions and have little subtle alarms in the event that any member of the net work is in the custody of the police. Remember, Hans' contact does not know that he sends a message to Hans. He, or she, tells him whether there is someone to be picked up and which of about five places the pick-up is to be made. Hans will then be sure to check the forest in that area.

"I try to provide some security for Hans by going out on my bicycle to see if he is being followed. On the way back, he travels through the fire lanes, ostensibly to check the status of the trees of the forest. He travels as slowly as the horses permit. They often want to get home too fast when they leave town and start for the castle. He travels at a snail's pace but he never stops although he makes a show of looking at the trees. His passengers-to-be have been told to remain in hiding until Hans calls to them.

"When Hans arrives he conceals his face with a cloth mask and approaches the place of concealment. His passengers never see his face and he has them put on cloth hoods that keep them from seeing even the wagon, although they certainly can feel its motion and noise. Hans leads his customers by hand and assists them in mounting. Their hoods remain until they are ready to enter the escape route. They are to hear no voice after Hans' call and instructions to them nor see any face. Once on the open wagon bed Hans opens a well concealed door into the hay that is, as you have noticed and commented on, always there. Hans puts new hay on the wagon and arranges it in a different pattern daily. Hans then drives the horses leisurely, usually driving further through the trees as though continuing his examination, to the castle and into the old ruins.

"When I was a child I played the beautiful princess who needed to be rescued by a knight in shining armor in the ruins and in the towers. One day I discovered a door in the floor that opened into a very ancient dungeon of the castle. For some reason I told no one, although I later found that Hans knew of the hidden space and kept that to himself as well. He has told me that there is a tale that a medieval baron of the castle had a long escape tunnel dug. If he saw that the castle was going to fall to his enemies, at least he could escape although I hope he would take his family with him. On the other hand, it may have been a way to get food into the castle when it was surrounded. Anyway, there is a tunnel leading from the dungeon under the border with Switzerland that bypasses any border guards. We have beds and tables in the dungeon area so that we can hold refugees there until our friends in Switzerland are ready for them. When Hans goes to the ruins during the day, he takes food for any who are there. He tries to make sure that they have enough for two or three days in the event that visitors or some such prevent anyone from going down to the dungeon.

"The government of Switzerland has an understanding with Hitler's government that if any refugees fleeing Germany are apprehended in Switzerland they will be returned to Germany. The Swiss authorities do not look as hard for those in flight as does the *Gestapo*, but we do have to be careful. That is for sure!

"As much secrecy as is humanly possible is maintained. Our greatest fear is that once out of Germany some rescued person will accidentally blurt out the circumstances of the rescue into the ears of a *Nazi* agent. If we go on long enough it is bound to happen sooner or later. The less they know of the operation the safer we will be. We think not just of our own safety but also of those who are yet to come.

"Hans takes them through the tunnel across the border to Switzerland when we think it is safe. There they are welcomed fairly openly by fellow Jews and some others and are safe from the camps unless the Swiss authorities accidentally capture them. The Swiss Jews in appreciation for what we do always try to have some delicacies such as chocolate, coffee, and tea which they have saved, or hoarded if one prefers, from before the war to send back with Hans. I can neither tell you of the secret route from Switzerland that has been arranged nor the safe destination of the Jews because I do not know.

"Now it is decision time for you, Lieutenant Solms. It seems that you have three choices. First, you could report our activities to the authorities but I think that you are too smart for that for they would thank you nicely, then lead you into the yard and put a bullet in the back of your head. Your second possibility is to leave the castle and return to Berlin and attempt to survive the war as Friedrich Schleiter. That would seem to be unwise for even if you were not discovered you would probably be sent into action missing foot and all. The third course is the one I think you will and should take. You should let Hans escort you out of Germany into Switzerland so that you can return to your forces and even to America. That is the practical thing to do and we have said that Americans are the most practical of people. If you choose to reveal us, I ask that you tell us and give us time to flee ourselves. What will you do?"

When she finished her presentation, her face, calmly cold and impassive, concealed any of her inner thoughts; but her eyes fixed on his features as though trying to penetrate the depths of his mind. Neither she nor he moved for minutes as he considered what she had said. He had known within himself that something was going on that until now the three others kept from him. A regular escape operation on a rather substantial scale surprised him. He knew that his decision would shape him and his future as far as the mind could contemplate.

Finally he spoke, "You did not mention that there was a fourth way. I would like to continue here and help you in any way possible. The authorities do think I am an SS officer and would think that no such operation could go on under my nose. As an SS man I might be of some possible assistance. In addition, my tenure in the Air Corps was to be for the duration of the emergency plus six months. If I leave now I would be a quitter and as you asked yourself, 'What would God have me to do?' Your Bonhoeffer has answered that question, first for you, and now for me. He has written 'Through fellowship and communion with the incarnate Lord we recover our true humanity and at the same time are delivered from the individualism which is the consequence of sin.' In addition if I returned to America I would be discharged and not be able to fulfill what I set out to do. I want to see the Nazis defeated. If you and the Webers will have me I want to stay and work with you."

He failed to be explicit as to the most potent reason for staying but it was woven into the definite emphasis on the last "you" in his statement. The countess, however, did think she caught an emphasis on the pronoun.

As he finished his talk, his fixed eyes on the floor because he wanted to hide the emotion welling up in his throat. When he finally looked up at her, as she remained silent, moisture like light dew filled her eyes. Affection for this man surprised her as it flooded through her. She found a slight difficulty in standing. Her limbs felt weak and the room seemed to spin.

She finally stood and said that she must talk to Hans and Liese because all their necks were in this together. Without asking, he rose when she did and limped by her side toward the back of the house. After a few steps, he felt with heart-beating joy her hand slip into his. As they entered the kitchen, Liese was peeling potatoes. As she looked up, a gentle smile flitted across her face.

"Is Hans near?" the countess asked the older woman. Soon Carl sat at the table with the other three. Marlene explained that she had informed Carl of all that they had agreed upon and suggested the three options, as they saw them, facing him.

Other words poured forth in a rush, "But Lieutenant Solms would not accept any of them! He says he wants to stay and help with our efforts. Now, I may have thought of that…he . . he says that his playing the role of Friedrich could be of assistance to us and that if he leaves it will be the end of his struggle against the *Nazis* because they will send him out of the American air force. Now, do we keep him on? What do you think?"

The husband and wife searched one another's faces, and after Liese gave an almost imperceptible assenting nod, Hans exclaimed, "Yes." He then embraced the American once more and said that they would have to work out things that might improve their security. "But," he kept on, "first we must show you the little princess' underworld accommodations so it's to the old castle we go." Hans, Carl, and the "little princess" left the kitchen and began the walk to the ruins of the old castle. The young lady, concerned about the uneven ground, assisted the semi-invalid in maintaining his balance by holding his hand and arm.

When the group reached that part of the castle ruins that served as a barn and stable, Hans led them around a corner into a small area enclosed on three sides by ancient walls of stone and mortar. He made short shrift of the hay and stubble lying about on the floor with a broom, stored close by, and bent and lifted a huge iron trapdoor. Carl was bewildered at the apparent ease with which Hans swung the door upward but then he remembered that a girl twelve or less had also lifted the door when she first found it. When the door was open, stone steps were visible leading down the wall to another level. Then the reason for the ease of raising the door became obvious. A cantilever weight made it possible for a sturdy twelve-year-old girl to lift the trap. Hans turned and laid his hands on a lantern whose wick he ignited with a match that exploded like a small firecracker as it swiped across his trousers. Carl noticed their shadows dancing like witches on the walls of the chamber as they descended the rough steps.

There were no "guests" registered in these accommodations at the moment. Carl could empathize with those who entered this cavity as they fled from their homes and all with which they were familiar. Some of the tools of the dungeon yet hung, rusty and uncared for, trophies of another cruel era. This cavern repelled any seeping moisture, keeping all within dry. The ashes of fires raised Carl's curiosity as to why he had never smelled smoke in the air at the castle. Seeing him look at the fire evidence and searching for an explanation for the removal of the smoke, Hans told him that the smoke of the always-tiny fires vented and dispersed high up into and out of the great old tower.

Carl questioned Hans as to the length of stay of his "guests."

"Usually they come in one night, stay a night, and are on their way the third night. If there is a problem, unusual check points on the other side of the border, they may stay with us an extra night or two."

The whole operation fascinated Carl but he determined not to gain knowledge he did not need to know. The spread of the circle of knowledge might jeopardize the salvation of the lives of those he had begun to care for and those strangers passing through. He did find it safe to ask, "How do the fugitives know of this sanctuary and the whole, the, uh, this 'underground railway'?"

To this question Hans replied, "They don't. They are taken by someone to a place and given instructions as to how to get to the next refuge. It may be by Jews who have been able to assimilate or have in some manner gone underground and can survive. It may be by Germans whose conscience requires them to do something. Strangely, it may even be by Communists who have avoided detection. The instructions are oral. I believe that members of the organization secretly watch them enroute, and if there is danger, direct them to another point along the way. No one knows more than one point; no one knows the whole scheme. If the police arrest a group on the way to an objective point, the operator of the point must become a refugee. All the operators of the various points are told to stay out of sight of the refugees as much as possible, even to issuing directions only in writing.

"Those fleeing must be people of faith. They must trust their rescuers and the system. They go through places where anyone following them would be obvious to the observers watching them. No serious damage has resulted when legs of the route, but only legs, have been compromised in the past. The authorities have not had enough information for a general crackdown. Our greatest danger lies with a betrayer or a Gestapo undercover agent who goes all the way through the system and reports what he has experienced."

"But," persisted Carl, "Can not those fleeing get some sense of the wagon, the direction it goes and that this is a castle or part of a castle. Is not the countess in danger of being exposed?"

"Only a bit. As soon as we contact them, I tell them to put hoods on one another and the chamber inside the moving haystack is very tight. I follow the fire lanes through the forest. I do not go directly to the castle and it is difficult to sense direction change in the dark chamber under the hay. As soon as they are here, I tell them to stay inside the wagon until I check their hoods as they exit. Usually Liese or the countess has the door open to the chamber beneath and we can move them with their hoods on. From the beginning, they are told that they have a choice, they can choose to trust or they can choose the camps. This is where you can assist in security. I tell them to keep the hoods tight but there is no way I can be sure that they do. Could you sit in the back with a mask and see that the covers stay put?"

"For sure. Did little Naomi get out safely? She was wonderful. How did she lose her hood?"

"Yes, she reached Switzerland in right order, the little rascal. If she had been with us, you could be sure that she did not remove her hood and stayed where she belonged. I told her to stay with me in the walls of the castle and, lo, I hear you outside greeting her. I thought she had betrayed the whole thing. I must tell you, though, that our traffic has been slowing down because all have been relocated east by the *Nazis* or have managed to escape Germany or hide somewhere in this country. You can ride in the hay tomorrow and we will find out if we have any more guests for tomorrow night."

"Do you think it's smart to throw him into the operation so quickly, Hans?" queried Marli.

"Oh, this seems to be a quiet time and the sooner he knows the ropes the better. I'll be leaving around five, Captain Schleiter," continued Hans as though the matter was settled no matter the objections of the countess.

"Why 'Schleiter?' You know he is Lieutenant Solms."

"Just to stay in the habit. Our protection is in this man as 'Captain Schleiter.' So that is what we must call him often."

At three-quarters past four Carl had pulled himself onto the wagon and began a search for the concealed door of the hidden nook under the hay. Unable to discover its secret he felt like the village idiot when Hans came and casually reached into the hay and grabbed the edge that appeared and pulled the lid open. The chamber inside was small, so small that Carl could not visualize more than two or three in the space. His first thought was that, if he had to be concealed, his participation would reduce the number who could be hidden even further. He decided, however, that it was a decision for Hans to make. He slid down by bending his left knee and looked up at Hans. He heard the voice of Marli, "Go with God!", as the door closed. Then the wagon tilted slightly as Hans mounted to the bench and the motion began.

The trip to town passed without incident and he heard Hans discussing the shipment of the two containers of milk on the next train, the prospects for harvest, and a general condemnation of the enemies of the Reich. This conversation had begun with an exchange of "*Heil* Hitler" and ended the same way. Hans then maneuvered the wagon to another place and informed Carl in a muted voice that he was going into the "*Silver Swan*" for a beer, which was his general pattern.

When he returned, he reported in small low tones that they would have no guests that night and ordered the horses to move the vehicle. After they had passed into the forest about two hundred meters and turned off into a fire lane Hans halted their progress and opened the door of the covert and asked Carl to join him at the front of the wagon. Carl, though surprised by the offer, happily got out of the closed chamber. He then watched as Hans drove the horses though the wide lanes between the trees. Occasionally he stopped and threw hay off the wagon, "For the deer." They meandered through the fire lanes of the forest back to the castle and the women. Marli was waiting for them in the ruins while Liese Weber watched for their return through a kitchen window. As Carl turned to dismount from the high bench seat, he saw the younger woman holding out both arms to assist him in his descent. As his feet hit the ground, he found himself in the loose embrace of the woman for the first time. At this moment their eyes locked as she turned away with blood suffusing her face with a red glow.

Several days after Carl's initial venture out with Hans, the Horch sedan of Ernst Greider entered the castle grounds in mid-afternoon and stopped at the entrance to the residence. As Greider exited the car from the left rear door, an individual in civilian clothes came out of the right rear door. Marlene greeted the two men courteously at the door of the residence while Carl slipped out of his artificial leg and boot, insuring that these items were well out of sight in a closet. Entering the room where the others were standing in relative quiet, he returned the obligatory "*Heil* Hitler" that greeted him. Greider turned so that he could see both Carl and the man in civilian clothes. Greider then introduced, "Major Oelze, this is Captain Schleiter of the SS, the young officer I mentioned to you. Captain Schleiter and Countess Schleiter, I will let the major inform you of the reason of our visit. Captain Schleiter, Major Oelze is with the state security police." Even Carl now knew that this man was a *Gestapo* officer. Why had he come to the castle?

Carl and Marli immediately turned their full attention to this officer of the secret police who responded in a taut and decisive tone, "There have been several disappearances of some of those people who were to be relocated to the east from cities of the Reich. There appears to be a regular channel for their flight to international borders. At first, we suspected that they were going north to Denmark and then Sweden. We have had a break, though, that tells us the trail leads to Switzerland, not anywhere else. We have reason to believe that the route crosses into Switzerland very near to this location, that is, we believe that it lies within fifteen kilometers of this spot. We suspect that they are crossing overland near here although we do not see how that is possible because our border security is tight. It would be virtually impossible for anyone not authorized to cross the Bodensee or the Rhine. This area offers the only land route to Switzerland where you do not have to cross water.

"When informed of your presence in this area, I felt compelled to inform you as a matter of courtesy and respect of the ongoing operation we will have. If there is anything you, your wife, or your servants could do to aid in exposing the traitors to the *Führer* who aid these enemies of the state, I am sure you will do your duty for our beloved *Führer*. I am leaving Paul Ranck as my representative in Littach. He is one of the most efficient members of the security police. He has an uncanny nose for treason and smelled out cells in Vienna. There were many there who, if they were alive, would have wished that Paul Ranck had never lived."

As the two visitors turned on their heels and marched through the door to the Horch, Greider looked back over his shoulder and shrugged as Marli and Carl followed them out into the slight afternoon mist. As fast as they had come, they were gone and the misplaced American and the countess returned and called the Webers to a conference.

Marlene made the first comment, "Well, there is both good and bad in this news we have learned. The positive is that, thanks to my *ersatz SS* husband, this place does not appear, I repeat, appear, under suspicion. The bad, of course, is that the agent of the *Gestapo* will immediately detect any suspicious activities. Hans, should we continue and if so, how?"

Hans held forth, "One thing I must do. I must continue my trips to town just as I always have. We can have no obvious break in the pattern of our lives. Now, the picking up of riders is another matter, for the *Gestapo* may follow me or they may ask to ride with me. In the first case, if I could detect them, I would follow a route that those fleeing would not know. If they were riding with me, I would again not follow the prescribed route. How can we get them from the forest to the castle without detection? You may be sure that there will be many more *Gestapo* people, including women, on the lookout."

"We can not just leave those fleeing out in the woods waiting to be snatched up!" cried Marli passionately. "When they get here they are so close! This is their last station! If they are arrested here, the whole chain can be compromised for they have been through every step and some will talk whether voluntarily or by torture. We must think."

"How many possible routes back to the castle are there, Hans?" asked Carl.

"Eight, if you count the Oberkrontal road," answered the driver.

"Do you have a bicycle, Countess?"

"Of course."

"Have you ridden it in recent months or years?" continued Carl's interrogation.

"Everyday until I was ordered to your—I mean-ah-Friedrich's side by the SS. When the ground was soggy or there was snow, I follow the highway but at other times I managed to get into the woods. It was a great relief to my situation, you understand, exercise, fresh air, and the use of muscles." explained the lady of the castle.

Carl was unsure as to how to address the countess by name so he phrased his next utterance with care, "What do you two think of this plan, as far as it goes? First, Countess, you will ride your bicycle. Hans, it is true that you must continue your routine into town. Liese will watch as you leave to see if there is an obvious follower of the wagon as it leaves the grounds. When you leave, she will start taking the bedding in from the windows. She usually does about that time anyway. If she thinks you might possibly be followed she will start at the middle window upstairs which you can see from quite a distance. The countess will follow you on her bicycle as you leave. She will follow either on the route you leave on or on a route that will permit her to follow you later. She may even get ahead of the wagon and come back just to talk to you. If you have any acquaintances in town, it would not seem odd for you to visit, Countess. You might do that as well. Timing it right, she can check out the route both before you and behind you, Hans. She will continually check to see if you have anybody on your tail. I just wish that there were some way for me to get around. I will be going to town on the front seat with you regularly. That will give us two pairs of eyes to see if there is any checkpoint. I will consort with the security people to try to discover what they are asking and where they are looking. My *SS* uniform should provide cover for my interest in their companionship. We can watch and see if there is a better way to guard our operations. What do you think? What else is there that we can do?" As he finished Carl felt like he had given a lecture and worried that the others would think that he stepped beyond his role. It was immediately obvious that they did not.

The wagon excursions continued on a daily basis except for Sundays. Carl donned his uniform, being careful to take his crutches but leaving his wooden leg and prosthetic boot concealed under the driver's bench of the vehicle. The slow movement of the great horses and the wagon gave Carl time to converse in greater depth with the older man. While Hans did not seem willing to speak of his actions in the First World War, he was happy to speak of his family both now and in the past. He learned for the first time that the Webers had three sons, all serving in the armed forces of Germany. Two were on the eastern front in Russia, one a *Luftwaffe* pilot and the other a communications man. Hans and Liese had not heard from the one in communications since the previous January. The middle son, Conrad, was a driver in the *Wehrmacht* serving between France and western Germany. Hans explained that they served their fatherland and not Hitler. He said they learned to love Germany, the German people, and the old German culture both in their home and at school from the time they were on their mother's milk.

When asked if his sons knew the countess when they were young, Hans replied, "Our youngest is named Walther, but we call him 'Wali.' He is three years older than she is. You know that we have had to work hard, our position is not high, and our sons have always respected her position. Yes, they did play among the ruins of the castle when she and Count von Krönitz visited. He also would consult her in order to receive a woman's guidance. He came often to look out for her interest in the estate that she inherited. She was always the imaginary queen and the boys were her subjects. Even though younger, her personality and character were more important than the fact that she was of nobility. She was very smart and always knew what to do and was decisive about it."

"Oh, then she was a bossy little girl?" Carl wanted to know.

"Oh, no! no! Each the boys, even Rudi, seven years older, wanted to be her servant-warrior hero. She was such a sweet little thing, so good, so smart. They knew that she was of the nobility and should have authority. She also charmed everyone without intent. Schleiter was an idiot. He is probably the only person in her life that she hated. The hate came first for what he did to the Jews and others, then it grew because of what he did to her father and her relations with her father. Finally, her hatred increased because of the depraved way that he used her. She spent many hours on her knees struggling to keep hatred from ruling her. Evil! Evil! Evil! She remembered that our Jesus suffered for us. I think she told herself that her suffering was for another. I believe I may have liked you even more if you had killed him for that is what he deserved. I think my sons would have died for the little Marlene and it may be that some will die in keeping the Bolsheviks out of our land and away from her."

Carl considered that statement and asked himself, "Is it possible to separate the struggle for Germany from the defense of the *Nazis*. No," he decided, "practically it is not; but I respect this man. I think it is impossible to correct him or even to discuss the point."

He then turned the talk to his companion's family and past. He learned that Hans' father and his father's father and his father's grandfather had all both plowed and planted the land and carved wood. He also learned that the forebears of Hans' mother had served the castle and its owners for more than a century.

Now they turned out of the forest and followed the road into town where several male bystanders greeted Hans warmly until they identified his companion. While the words of greeting remained, warmth departed. Carl asked Hans which *gasthaus* he would recommend and Hans directed him to the *Silver Swan* located a few hundred yards further up the street. Bidding Hans "*auf Wiedersehen*" in an autocratic and superior manner, as befitted the reputation of Schleiter, Carl swung off to the public house on crutches. The stones of the street slowed his pace as his crutches did not find quick stability and it took him several minutes to reach his destination.

As he entered the dim interior of the tavern, his eyes took time to adjust before he was able to locate an unoccupied table. As he advanced to the table, he became aware of other customers scattered around the room. A couple of more than middle-aged farmers were sitting close to the tinted window. It would have provided a view of the street had it not been purposefully opaque. Then there were three men sitting back in the darkest corner of the room with clear glass steins of beer before them. Carl found his seat at the table in the center of the room, propped his crutches against the table, and ordered a small beer, that came quickly in a clear glass tankard. The beer was local and Carl had come to understand that many small German towns possessed their own brewery although there were regional and national brews as well. Carl had never developed a taste for beer but it was unthinkable to try to order iced tea or a Coca-Cola in this environment so in Germany he did as the Germans did and slowly sipped the beverage of Germany.

His appearance in the *SS* uniform drew obvious attention from not only the proprietor but also his five customers. He saw the others in the inn whispering about him, the newly arrived stranger. Quick glances on the part of the farmers and prolonged looks from the other three accompanied these *sotto voce* observations. Carl decided that if there were any *Gestapo* men in the *gasthaus* they would be the three in the corner. When the proprietor returned to his three-legged stool behind the counter Carl decided to engage him in conversation and, in a most unimaginative but normal way, addressed a remark about the great weather to him.

Fortunately, the stool-sitting individual was more interested in Carl than Carl was in him for he quickly left his perch and took a seat at the table. He followed up the short discourse on the beautiful summer day by adding that he had seen Carl as he had attended the presentations to the Hitler Youth and that he had great admiration for the heroes of the *Reich*. He expressed sympathy to Carl for the loss of his lower leg. His curiosity about those who were close to the *Führer* was soon evident by his indirect questions. He longed for all the crumbs of information that he was sure the *SS* officer could provide. Carl sensed that he wanted this information but was intimidated about asking openly about the routine and personalities of those close to the dictator. Because he lacked any knowledge of such matters, Carl was glad that he could pretend to be close-mouthed regarding state secrets and one who kept his knowledge to himself.

When the two farmers rose from their table to leave, Carl's interrogator left to settle accounts with them and to wipe away the moisture from their table. This gave the other three clear field to approach his table and greet him, "How's it going, Captain? Are you the man living at the castle? Yes, we have heard of you. You married a baroness, right? Not only a count's daughter but a countess in her own right, thanks to her mother and her mother's father. Yes, you have done well."

Carl was amazed at the familiarity not of knowledge but of manner. The rudeness of confronting him with his marriage struck hard against his own sense of privacy. Remembering the uncouthness of the man whose uniform he wore, he knew the course he must take. He leaned back, and while he responded not directly or orally, his whole manner shone with self-congratulations about this conquest of a noble woman. He did allow himself to say, "Yes, the *New Order* has brought about many changes. They have been good to those who truly love the Fatherland but we have made those who do not pay for their disloyalty, haven't we?" Carl disguised his disgust at the turn of the talk and attempted to act out the demeanor of an *SS* officer with few words. Although he had desired to be in conversation with these men, every word he said to them risked exposure.

Finally he pointed out, "Hans should be leaving in his wagon. Do you know Hans, the man from the castle? Well, I rode down with him just to get out of that place. It may have been built to keep enemies out but when you are in it you feel like it is keeping you in. If I only had the use of both legs, I would have walked to town to get away from the women. Hans comes to town almost every day. Would you mind if I joined you again tomorrow? Right now I had better check on the wagon, I would not want to go up to the castle with crutches!" Having drunk more than their capacity of the strong local beer, the three enthusiastically enjoined him to come again at every opportunity.

As the wagon reached the edges of the town, Carl told Hans what he had done but that he had made no discovery of the plans or methods of the hunters. Hans in turn said that he had learned that there were none fleeing Germany at the forest rendezvous. "But," he added, "there is always tomorrow."

CHAPTER 6

❀

August 1942
The Executions

The morning hours at the castle developed quickly into times of as much contentment as existing within the reach of a totalitarian government allowed. After breakfast of bread, cheese, boiled eggs, and coffee or tea the residents pitched in to accomplish the chores as Hans went to check the fields because "harvest time is soon upon us." He supervised the French prisoner-of-war laborers. Marli and Carl worked together in feeding the animals, mucking out the stables and pens, and making the minor repairs necessary. Marli referred to Carl as "our Texas cowboy" and laughingly said that he could not persuade her that cowboys of the nature of Tom Mix were not every day sights in New Sendlingen. She teased that his home town was really named "Cow City," "Bullburg" or even "Muleshoe. In retaliation, Carl practiced mock obeisance to "your Royal Highness" when he did not adopt the increasingly familiar "Marli" as her title. He loved to point out the name of the nearby city of "Stud Farm" for Stuttgart and other distinguished names like "Pigs Crossing" for Schweinfurt. What was the humor of Muleshoe compared to the "only one hill" of Nuremberg? In their laughter at their own humor, they pretended taking offense and on one occasion began to throw clods of dirt and worse material at one another when mucking out the stable as though they were little children.

After the chores and horseplay were over, they returned to the residence and washed thoroughly in the basin of warm water and strong lye soap provided by

y celebrated the completion of the tasks
Liese. After cleaning themselves e and *zweibach*, strips of slightly sweetened
with a mid-morning snack of shared this time with them for moments
twice-baked bread. Usually in the kitchen and around the house. Alone the
before departing for her to explore each other's interests and intellectual
two young people cont ompanion's mother was the Countess Theresa *von*
level. Carl learned th d owned holdings of land for centuries, and some of
Ritterbach. The fa ated in Switzerland some centuries earlier. The mar-
their land had ad thus joined two ancient families, one from the north
riage of her r nue had continued to come to Marlene from the outlying
and one fr ne had inherited from her mother.

Nazi re asked if her mother had been Catholic, Marlene smiled, "No, my
land mily is descended from Count Ulrich who fought the Catholics and
rttemberg a Lutheran state. Later they rather secretly accepted much
eachings of the Anabaptists. Many of those people were committed to
uidance of an "inner light" and did not want to be constrained by the
le. I know that many of the tenants of my ancestors' land moved to Penn's
olony in the seventeenth century. There are still people there called the 'Pennsylvania Dutch,' are there not? Really, they should be called 'Pennsylvania Germans' or 'Deutsch.' I think that my mother was not as structured in her beliefs
as my father. The discipline of the Bible controls him. There was, Liese tells me,
no religious obstacle to their marriage. Government records labeled both
'evangelicals.'"

She probed of his past. "Are your parents Catholic or Evangelical?"

"My parents are Lutheran but not great evangelizers."

"And your mother? Is she patient or quick tempered? What activities do you
think she enjoys most? Does she provide good meals? Which of your parents is
the stricter disciplinarian? Tell me about your sisters? Are they as smart as you?
Are they pretty? Your cousin Anna, did she go to university? Where? You made
her sound hard. Is she? Would she have liked to remarry? I think I like her
because you told me she despises the *Nazis* and Hitler."

She continued to enquire. "Would you tell me about your schooling? Were
your examinations for university difficult for you?"

"If you are asking or think that I had to take exams to go to my college you
are mistaken. The college had to admit any graduate of a high school who
requested admission," he revealed.

"But to enter this high school, I guess it is what we call *gymnasium,* didn't you have to take an exam for that," she queried?

"No. No. In America, almost all the states require attendance well into the high school years. I can believe that my father would have taken me from school had it not been for the compulsory attendance laws."

She pointed out, "In Germany there are two all-important examinations that determine the level of education that a child will receive. All German children get eight years of school and then take examinations. Those who do well on the examination continue to *gymnasium,* an advanced high school. The others learn a trade. Those attending *gymnasium* may qualify for university after three of four years if they pass their examinations. Those not qualifying become bookkeepers, clerks, and minor civil servants. Only the highest performing students attend school beyond *gymnasium.* You can see why you impressed me in attending university."

"But you certainly attended university, didn't you?"

"Yes, I attended Tuebingen for two years before the war started for us. The authorities required me to leave because my father bore the repute of 'politically unreliable.' I had not been a member of the Hitler youth movement and so must be punished. In addition, a woman at the university was considered unpatriotic because of Hitler's program of pushing motherhood and large families. Girls are encouraged to have as many children as possible to insure the future of the race."

When Carl mentioned that he had participated in sports she seemed eager to find out more, "What sports did you do?"

"I played football, basketball and ran track in high school but only played intramural sports in college."

Her next question revealed a misunderstanding, "Were you a forward, midfielder or defense in football?"

His attempt to define the difference between American football and German football gave them a chance to laugh and tease in pretended misunderstanding. Basketball was not new to her and track and field events were simply "athletics."

The talks also dug deeper into their beliefs and into those they admired intellectually and spiritually. In these areas he was not at a disadvantage despite his engineering weighted background. These occasions provided enjoyment to both as they told of the important things in their lives. Each saw that the other had the ability to laugh at his or her own quirks and eccentricities.

To Carl these were not only moments of glorious satisfaction but also of anguish. The pleasure of these occurrences had the dragging realization, like a sea anchor, of their two separate worlds. She was of noble birth and potential heir to two great estates from her parents. He was the descendant of immigrants who were in every sense commoners. His inheritance could or could not include one fifth of a two hundred-acre farm. What were forty acres compared to this mansion that was part of an ancient and historic castle? Often, when alone, he pondered his aching desire, his longing, his commitment to her. Something far deeper and wider than her physical attraction moved his emotion. He had discovered that her simple presence presented a paradox of peace and a pulse whose pounding seemed to threaten his ribcage. His spirit desired to merge with hers in worship and work for not just one but for many common goals. He remembered her every touch. These moments of conversation made him know that he loved her. Now he knew what the Greek language's words for love really meant. He recognized the physical nature of his feelings. Her being drew his as powerfully as a great magnet pulled metal. Her friendship, her companionship, her character caused him to hunger for it for the duration of his life. But if it were not for this physical and emotional love he would have wanted her to be his sister

Above all, he wanted to serve her, to protect her, to give himself for her. This was far more removed from a selfish desire than he could ever have imagined that he could feel before these precious periods. He knew that he would count every moment as joy if he could only sacrifice himself for her. He cared not that she might not know of his gift to her; he simply longed to surrender all to her.

Occasionally their eyes would lock and he would attempt to look into her inner being to see if there might be a scintilla of hope; but there was no sign. The eyes of the girl presented neither coldness nor great warmth beyond the pleasure of shared laughter and good conversation.

Occasionally Carl permitted himself the rending picture of her in some one else's arms, of some one else becoming more deeply aware of the recesses of her soul and spirit. When these moments came, he wanted to cry although all in his being told him that men do not cry even at the loss of their heart's highest desire.

After these mornings of reflective talk, the afternoons brought back the realities of the world and a nation at war. Carl thought that Germany seemed to be at war not only with her enemies beyond her frontiers but also with her own people. The danger that those residents of the land faced made the need of the castle group's efforts to save some German lives as clear as the sun on a cloudless day.

Hans and Carl worked outside with the livestock in the afternoon routine until they left for town after mid-day. Marlene also chose this time to get her exercise on her bicycle as she headed out to the many lanes, trails and roads through the forest. Liese was always in the window on the second floor to watch the departing figures. When the wagon reached the town center Carl made his way to the *Silver Swan* while Hans disposed of the farm products. In the inn Carl joined his *Gestapo* acquaintances if they were present.

On the fifth trip, a Thursday, Hans gave a signal that there were some fugitives from the *Nazis* waiting in the forest. Carl could see that Marlene had also picked up Hans' signal and knew that she would watch behind them. Hans followed the exact same routine as he prepared to leave the town. As the great pair of horses drew the wagon through the twilight, darkened further in the lane between the trees, Carl had difficulty responding to Hans who carried on the conversation as usual. Carl realized that he should also but his mind raced at the thought of this first experience of saving the lives of whomever awaited them. He was startled when a voice called from behind them, "How's it going?" and then he recognized Marlene as she passed them on the wide lane through the bare limbed trees of the forest and peddled ahead only to turn around about a hundred yards ahead of them and return.

"There are many police and *Gestapo* searching the forest. They must have been alerted somehow. Please be extra careful!" she reported. Then as she left them, she laughed as though she were a young schoolgirl flirting with a local hero-boy and had not a care beyond her own popularity. Carl turned to watch her as she disappeared down the division of the trees. The wheels of the wagon squeaked as it rolled along the packed dirt road. Occasionally Hans stopped the wagon and entered the tree line as though inspecting the condition of the vegetation. He did this to scout for police as well as to satisfy any unknown eyes. When he returned, sometimes with some leaves or branches of pine needles from a tree, he always seemed satisfied. After making several turns onto different trails, he stopped once more and again disappeared into the darkening shadows beyond the trees.

Five figures dressed in dark clothes followed him as he emerged from the shadows of the tree line. Three, judging by size, seemed to be adults while two appeared younger. Their heads covered with sacks, no determination could be made of their ages. Two looked to be less than ten, judging from their height.

With help from Hans assisted by Carl, they were quickly on the wagon and into the cubicle under the hay as the wheels once more rolled.

As the wagon made a turn to head toward the castle, they soon became aware of figures along the trail ahead of them. Both Hans and Carl recognized that they would have to pass through a checkpoint run by the *Gestapo* aided by local police. Carl at that moment became deadly cool and calm, as ready as he could be to use his wits to defuse any awkward situation.

Recognizing some of his acquaintances from the *Swan,* Carl sang out a hearty "Halloo!"

Those at the checkpoint responded with a friendly, "*Wie geht es Ihnen?*"

Hans kept silent and let Carl do the talking because of the latter's acquaintance with at least some of these men, his military rank, and his supposed membership in the *SS.* One of the local police held a needle pointed iron rod about seven feet in length. When he asked a *Gestapo* officer, "Shall I run the hay through?" Carl's heart fluttered and skipped a beat.

A Gestapo man answered, "*Nein! Nein!* This is *Sturmhauptführer* Schleiter of the *SS.* Nothing would slip by him. *Guten Abend, Hauptmann.*"

"*Sehr gut,*" Carl chose his words carefully, "Have there been reports of fugitives locally? We saw no criminals anywhere and we went far into the wood behind us."

"*Ja,* an informer has reported that some Jew pig-dogs are in the pipeline to get to Switzerland and should be in this area either now or very soon. There are search parties in the forest and they may flush them out. We are being doubly alert."

"It's good that you are. We must be careful with so many of our foes around," was Carl's declaration of the truth of the situation and continued, "We'll be on our way. When I am up for a long period my leg gives me all kinds of fits. So I need to get it up and rest it soon. May we proceed?" Carl complained of his injury to insure that there would be no support for a move to order him back to duty with the *SS.*

"*Bestimmt,* Captain. And may you have a good night."

As Hans urged the horses forward Carl thought his chest would explode as his coolness vanished and his heart thumped, thumped, thumped against his ribs. The whole earth seemed to whirl like a merry-go-round about him. In moments his heart settled into a normal rhythm but he felt a cold dampness over his entire body. That too disappeared by the time the team clopped into the castle grounds. At this point Carl left the vehicle as quickly as he could to remove the *SS* uniform for less identifiable clothing and to retrieve his prosthetic boot. Hans continued, bringing the wagon to a halt inside the ruins, and called the passengers to come from their hiding place as Carl rejoined the group.

Carl led the group hand-to-hand while Hans opened the trap door to the old dungeon. Lighting a lantern the older man ordered, "This way!" The five fugitives moved in unison to his bidding, and following Hans went swiftly below. Carl followed. As Hans prepared to pull the rope to close the trap door Msrlene joined them and also descended into the chamber.

Hans then said to Carl, "Let me show you the secret of *Schloss Altburg*. He then walked to a wall where ancient tools of torturers hung from iron hooks welded to a large iron plate that seemed to be about six feet high by five feet wide. Twisting and pulling a hook in the upper right hand corner of the plate it swung inward leaving a dark door opening through the wall. The old farmer continued. "Follow me and I will show you a miracle" as he stepped through the opening. Carl obeyed and found himself on a platform with an ominous black fissure sinking into the earth before him. As his eyes adjusted, he discovered a ladder descending into the pit. He also discovered a pulley through which ran a rope. At the end of the rope at the top of the shaft was a sling large enough to carry an adult.

"Good." said Hans, "We will show you the secret. Down at the bottom of this shaft is a centuries old corridor through the earth. We do not know for sure today if it was an escape route but we think it was. All we know is that we are the only living souls in the twentieth century who know of it. My mother's father was one who did and he took me into it and all the way to the land of the Swiss. It was a good way to get chocolate, cognac, and champagne without paying taxes. You see some were not above wanting to evade custom duties and so my father and I discovered that this dungeon, that only the curious little countess discovered, is connected to the tunnel which lies ten or fifteen meters below. The beautiful part is that the tunnel opens up into Switzerland at the other end. When the castle lord had the tunnel dug, there was little separation between this duchy and the Swiss. I personally think the master of the castle wanted an emergency escape route from it or a route through which to bring men and supplies if besieged. So if we can get our customers here we just about have the battle won. To me it is again fulfilling its purpose—to help those in peril to escape.

"Now our problem is to notify those on the Swiss side to be ready to greet our guests. We do this by turning a light on in the uppermost room in the residence. This light can be so focused that our co-workers in a very limited area can only see it across the border. We must be careful, for the Swiss government does not want Jewish émigrés to pass through their country. They definitely want to maintain their neutral status and not offend Hitler's regime. The countess has already asked Liese to light the signal. By the time we reach the meeting place, the others will be waiting. It will take more than a half hour for our émigrés to reach them. You may ask, 'Can they be trusted?' The answer is '*Bestimmt*.' There are only two there and they are half-mad Zionists and crazy enough to do anything. They have their own routes to get those we send them to Palestine, we believe, but don't know for sure."

Carl and Hans had opportunity to examine their clients closely for the first time. There appeared to be a family group of a mother and father, a son and daughter, and an old man who Carl and Hans assumed was the grandfather of the children. Hans cautioned all they were to ask no questions and that no names were to be given. All but the old man seemed confident that they could manage the descent on the ladder and the man of the family prepared to proceed down into the hole.

Then Carl saw the pulley and swing arrangement put into use. When Hans sought to position him over the abyss, the grandfather showed resistance but family members persuaded him to permit himself to be lowered into the darkness below. Hans grasped the handle of a manually operated, geared winch and slowly let it rotate as the sling and its contents sank into the black. When a voice came from the bottom of the shaft that all was well and the grandfather was safe Hans reeled the sling back up and the others began the long descent to safety.

Carl asked, "Although I would love to see your tunnel and meet the others, don't you think that it would be better for me to remain behind?"

Marli provided a definite answer, 'We would not let you go down. I usually remain back to guard against the possibility that the police might come. It would not be so serious a question if Hans were not here because he could be checking the forest or the fields. My absence at night would be more noteworthy. Your absence with your missing leg would be very difficult to explain. So we stay."

After closing the trap door, they moved back to the residence and found that Liese had a meal waiting for them on the table with a place also set for Hans. "We always do that in case we have surprise visitors to let them think that we expect Hans to return to the house at any moment."

As they ate their meal, the young countess remained silent although her face flushed and she displayed a smile that she seemed to find impossible to repress.

Liese, knowing her moods and with the license of a mother figure, asked her, "Why are you acting so pleased? You look like you are ready to go to the fair and have a good time. What gives?"

"Oh, I'm very happy! Five more have reached safety. I rejoice every time a group reaches safety. Now they are out of the reach of the secret police and relocation in Poland or wherever. Those children! We will probably never know their names and they will never know ours but God links us together. They are, you know, still His people, those who bless them God will bless, and those who curse them God will curse. Because they are still God's, no people should dare to persecute them. I do thank God that He has grafted us into that vine. I am happy. Maybe there are five marks on the scoreboard for us and maybe not. I don't care. We rescued five and did them good. That is enough to make me happy."

As she gave this little speech she approached Carl and placed the palms of her hands on his cheeks, holding his gaze straight into hers as though to insure that her message was clearly received and understood. In one sense, she failed because at the touch of her hands on his face, the only conscious thought was the sweet glory of her touch and the flood of joy it gave him. Conjecture about her feelings toward him filled his mind and flooded his emotions. She was certainly polite and gracious but also coolly correct, never touching him other than holding his hand. When her hand grasped his, he surmised that she only meant to steady him as he moved on his artificial leg. Sympathetic and caring he knew her to be; but he doubted that she returned the strong emotion he felt for her.

He compared the woman entering his hospital room in the city to this glowing girl flitting around the kitchen. "How could I have been so misled?" Now her smile and her eyes seemed bright enough to substitute for a lamp had there been no light in the room. The clothing designed to deceive had fulfilled its mission by impressing the observer as drab and common. Her loosened hair, no longer in the tight bun that pulled her face taut, permitted her face to settle into the softness of lovely womanhood early in maturity. The midnight blue split skirt clung closely to her hips and the glow of joy discounted the lack of cosmetics on her face. Every day that he was in her presence, she became more magnetic.

When she announced, "I am tired and exhausted. I'll leave you two alone to wait for Hans," and quickly left the room, a sense of hollowness came into his chest. Liese watched as Carl's softening eyes followed the mistress of the castle.

"There are moments in time that we should preserve. There are times when our hearts are so happy. Those are the times we should file away in our memory," the middle-aged woman said for the ears of the young man. Carl started. He had never thought that the woman had philosophy in her. He wondered at the cause of this remark. His wonderment at the expressed thoughts of *Frau* Weber ceased quickly with the entry of her husband who smiled broadly at his wife and said, "Well, the *Führer* has relocated some more of his smartest citizens out of the country. I learned the man we took out tonight was one who studied the basic physical composition of beings. His woman told me that he had received honors from all over the world for what he had discovered. I wonder where they will end up? In England? In America? In Palestine? Anywhere they go they will help their new land."

After eating a light meal, drinking a small glass of wine, and wishing Carl a good night, Hans led his wife from the room. Although there was excitement racing through his body, there was nothing for Carl to do but also to take himself to bed and there to toss fitfully over the events of the day.

The next day led on into day after day until the colors of the forest surrounding the castle began to show symptoms of the changing seasons. The departure of the green in the leaves allowed the underlying russet and red hues to reveal their own beauty.

Inside the living quarters, the routine of rising, working, and resting continued, as did the daily journeys to town. Few visitors came and Marli and Carl made sparing visits as they strove to act as though they were husband and wife albeit not a truly loving couple. Inquiries began to come from Berlin as to when, if ever, Captain Schleiter would be able to return to duty.

The efforts of the Berlin SS to discover the status of the young captain increased as both national party officials and members of the local government came to the castle to verify the recuperation of the bright star of Hitler's finest.

Ernst Greider appeared on behalf of the local party members to inquire as to the recovery. Seated in the great hall of the restored portion of the castle he observed, "Your color is much improved, Captain. It almost looks like you have been working the land. Do you think that you could sit at a desk and relieve a healthy worker in Berlin for action on the front?"

Marlene interjected quickly, "Not at the present, for sure. Friedrich's bathing in the sun has done wonders for his color but there are many days—and we don't know when they will strike—when he must remain in bed. You know many of his injuries are in his mind. His dreams must be dreadful for he screams out like a possessed spirit in the middle of the night. There are some things that he can do and needs to do to speed his recovery, I believe. We do encourage him to get out of the house as much as possible for his trips into town. It seems to relieve his mind of the buried memories of the fire coming into his face. But believe me; he would need two people to care for him in Berlin"

"Oh, we will keep watch on the situation," responded the local *Nazi* leader, "We know that he will want to serve the *Führer* and the *Reich* with all his ability. The authorities in Berlin would like to have him working again as soon as he can. In fact, there has been talk of sending an *SS* physician to examine him to see what could be done to get him back in harness. I will inform them of your information and suggest they send a doctor who can help with his trauma as well. This has been a most relaxing moment and thank you for receiving me."

As soon as the visitor left a miniature council of four was called together to consider the future actions of Carl. It was a fixed certainty that Carl must not go to Berlin where his exposure was almost certain. Many there knew the real Friedrich Schleiter well. There would be those who knew him much better than did Marlene, his supposed wife. In addition, any work for the *Nazis* would subject him to a charge of treason by the American army for no one in America knew of his true activities. Hans and Liese, Marlene and Carl all acknowledged that, if possible, he should not risk going to Berlin.

The question as to how they should address the American arose. When with others they had to refer to him as Friedrich or Captain Schleiter. Within the castle and its grounds the young woman had became increasingly formal as she addressed or referred to Carl. He was now always "Solms." or Lieutenant Solms. He thought this was humorously strange due to the danger they shared and the informality of most of their relationship. They agreed that they must be careful to call him by his German identity with others. The older couple followed her lead and did not permit themselves to become informal in their addresses no matter how intimate their physical contact might have been or might be. Carl began to see that this older couple was able to balance a close relationship with formality without any reservations on their part. While they referred to their young lady with great respect, they also demonstrated their close affection and devotion for and to her.

The recognition of their different roles and positions in life and society caused no alienation on their part. Although of noble blood of high rank, she remained the girl they had and would always care for. Carl found their discussion, in an oddly cool and stiff manner, of his situation and his person, as though he were an object, both interesting and somewhat amusing.

"In that Mr. Solms cannot permit himself to be taken to Berlin, possibly he should join some of the escapees and go to Switzerland and then seek repatriation to America," proposed Hans Weber.

"Absolutely not!" he countered. "It is strange and odd that while I am in grave danger I yet remain the countess' best protection. She married Friedrich Schleiter for the protection he afforded her father. If he were to disappear, the *Nazis* would hold her and the two of you responsible. Even if the police did not hold you all for his murder, they would find you guilty for not revealing my false identity. My disappearance as Captain Schleiter would bring danger to each of you. Besides, as we say in the States, I joined up for the duration of the national emergency plus six months. There is a war to be won against the *Nazi* forces." He was careful to put his struggle in terms that it was against Hitler and his party and not against Germany for he sensed that all three loved their people and their land. "And," he added, "why do you not call me Captain Schleiter or Friedrich all the time so that you do not make a slip?"

"I hate the sound of his name!" exclaimed the young widow who did not think of herself as a widow. "One thing I gloried in was that I was not forced to wear mourning clothes. But, yes, I, we will call you by your assumed *Nazi* name when in public."

"Another thing. Can we do this?" he asked, "Can I have the bed of an invalid set up down here on this floor? Can you keep some animal blood ready, Hans? If visitors come and we have time, we can soak bandages in it to put on my leg. I will make fewer trips into town and if I go outside, I will keep myself well covered. That should not be difficult with the colder weather coming on."

"*Ach. Ja!*" Liese almost shouted. "I have a mixture that will make your eyes look like you are death on legs! It will not hurt you but your eyes will be bloodshot all the time. You sure will not be the pretty boy," sliding a glance at her young mistress.

All agreed that the young American impostor had to risk the town trips to gain information from his supposed *SS* colleagues. When asked about his acting ability he responded that he had played a lamppost in a school play so successfully that a dog in the script had paid him a visit. The puzzled looks on the older couple's faces soon joined the little laughter of Marli.

So began a life of curtailed activities for Carl. At the first indication of visitors at the gate, the entire household stood prepared to rush him into bed. Carl "found" the strength to accompany Hans on trips to town occasionally. On those occasions, he was careful not only to use Liese's concoction that brought forth the red veins in his eyes and paled his complexion but also to move with such deliberation that onlookers feared that he might collapse before their eyes at any moment. He posed as the suffering and wounded soldier, anxious to be away from distaff domination, for the benefit of his supposed comrades in the *SS*. He let it be known that he suffered debilitating agony from some injury to his back. Talk concerning Carl's reporting for duty drifted away but his connections with the *SS* agents remained unchallenged.

This channel provided the disturbing news that a German agent in Switzerland had overheard a conversation in which a child, obviously Jewish, had blurted forth the news that her family had come out of Germany through a tunnel. The German secret police and all other forces assisting them were now searching for the location of a possible underground escape route. The *Nazi* authorities ordered scholars to examine medieval documents to discover extensive abandoned mines, while police searched for entrances to old mines and evidence of recent excavations. Carl also learned that the *SS* intelligence service gained some information that an escape route was located close to Littach. The patrolling of the forests and fields continued at an intense level.

Heinrich Hühn's newspaper reported several times the police capture of fugitive "enemies of the state" in neighboring towns, dealing with those enemies in the most severe manner. Hans glumly assured all that this meant that they had been put to death summarily. As the number of those fleeing from their lifelong homes decreased, Hans remarked, "The number of Jews with any chance to flee must be lessening quickly. The regime has re-located most to the east. In addition, many attempt to flee who are being caught. They really lost their opportunity to get to a better place before the war started. I told Micah's son that he should take his family out in thirty-seven but he wouldn't listen to me. He said his father was a good German who had fought heroically for his country in the Great War."

Marlene explained, "Micah shared danger with Hans. Remember when I told you that when Hans was wounded, Micah Goldberg pulled him to safety into the trenches at the Somme? Goldberg lost his life saving Hans."

Hans continued, his concern reflected on his face, "They have said that I cannot have contact with his family simply because they are Jewish; but I have tried to keep in touch. There has been no response since the end of thirty-nine and the start of the Polish campaign. I am afraid that Micah's family has been relocated to the eastern occupied lands." His glare at Carl reminded him that just his pose as the *SS* Schleiter carried images of evil.

The sun, declining in the southern sky, still warmed the earth under the pale blue of the late summer heavens across which occasional wooly lamb-like clouds slowly traveled. Cone-bearing trees seemed to watch, like tall proud sentinels wearing green uniforms, as their neighbors changed their dress into the reds and yellows of the approaching autumn. Carl was to make another venture into the town to discover any available information from the black uniforms of the *SS*. The rays flickered and flittered between the needles and colored leaves of trees and then crossed the wagon as it moved down the snaking slope of the castle road.

All was quiet and normal in town as Hans directed his vehicle toward the *Silver Swan* with Carl slouched down and trying to make himself appear as miserable as he could. Both he and Carl pretended that the latter needed great assistance to dismount. The streets contained children both playing and performing their chores. Women moved along the street as they gathered their daily provisions from the green grocer, the baker, and the butcher. They placed their purchases into sacks of dark twine woven into a broad net. Carl had noticed that the women of Littach shopped for food daily. These excursions to the market seemed to be as much social events as economic necessity as the housewives gathered in groups of two to six to discuss families, health, and friends but rarely politics. That province usually remained reserved for their men.

Hans assisted Carl from the wagon, helped him lean precariously against the vehicle, and then retrieved the crutches from beneath the seat. He offered solicitous care as Carl began a cautious journey to the door of the *gasthaus*. With the help of Hans, Carl gained a seat at a table surrounded by six chairs. There he waited for the innkeeper to draw a beaker of the local beer from the great keg and for Hans to bring the stein to him. When the latter was satisfied that his charge was comfortable and provided for, he asked to be excused to carry out his business, which was, of course, immediately granted.

Soon two men in the uniform of the *SS* appeared, accompanied by the one Carl remembered as the local *Gestapo* agent he had met earlier, Paul Ranck, who was less than average height compared to the other men around the village. The idle thought crossed Carl's mind that some woman had been faithful in her visits to food stores in order to satisfy his appetite. He certainly lacked leanness. One of the *SS* men Carl recognized as Rudi Gerlach, one of his earlier *gasthaus* acquaintances, and was not surprised to see Rudi direct the two others to the table where he sat.

Their posteriors had hardly touched the chair seats when Rudi leaned toward the false *SS* captain, and in a loud whisper, informed, "We are going to have good hunting tonight! Some kikes are in the woods near where the road splits off to Kislingen. Soon we will cleanse the *Reich* of some more vermin! We have them surrounded and they have surrendered but we will have our own 'final solution!' You must come with us and report to the *Reichsführer* Himmler! Join us! You must report this to Berlin! This will be a feather in all of our caps."

Carl found himself more than assisted in his rising from his seat as the two SS men reached under his armpits and lifted him upright. Rudi reached for his crutches and thrust them upon him although he hardly needed them as they half carried; half escorted him out of the *Swan*. Carl sensed himself swept away on a torrent that would end in a cataclysmically tragic event. Later he would remember little of the activities that resulted in his being seated in the front seat of a military truck. Never physically unconscious, his awareness returned when he saw Marli approaching on her bicycle.

His companions identified her within seconds and yelled, "Let the countess also join us." Before either Carl or she could react, the bicycle and its rider were deposited in the back of the vehicle and the group was on its way to where the Kislingen road turned off. The sight of military vehicles hurrying from the town center was not a usual event in this corner of the *Reich* but the young American fugitive noted, even in his hypnotic like state, that the people of the town studiously avoided seeing the activity.

Later Carl described his condition at this moment as that like the rabbit in the river bottom that was frozen by the eyes of the snake slithering and sliding through the weeds. Although he was not the prey, the horror he suspected at hand petrified him. He sat immobile as the vehicle passed by fields now cleared for the winter and into the forest to the junction of the Kislingen road.

Several other conveyances, some clearly military and police vehicles and some not, waited, almost wedged between the roadside trees. Their driver stopped the truck without clearing it from the road. The noise and motion of men descending from its bed followed immediately. The cab's door beside Carl opened quickly. Again they half-lifted, half-helped Carl from his seat. His crutches appeared from the back of the vehicle even as the escort propelled Marli toward him. Their undesired companions encouraged both Carl and Marlene into the trees. The two had no option but to go forward.

In the growing darkness, they approached a group of dimly lit figures. Four pitifully clothed individuals appeared surrounded by guards bearing lethal-looking machine pistols. The four were, Carl surmised, mother and father and two children. It was clear to both Carl and Marlene the police and Gestapo had apprehended the group they expected that night.

The father begged for his family even though not fathoming the fate that awaited. He begged only to leave Germany. He beseeched that they not be sent to a camp. While Carl had his ever-present *SS* side arm, it was more a symbol of position than a weapon. He could only lean against his crutches and watch the tragedy unfold. Time was counted in seconds as the *Gestapo* and *SS* spoke at a staccato pace.

Then the *Gestapo* agent Paul Ranck screamed, "There will be no camp for you, Jewish swine!" The machine pistols then rip-sawed the evening calm. Even as the echoes of the gunfire faded into the forest, the lives of the family four slipped into eternity as their bodies twitched and then were still on the ground.

"Leave them and get out of here!" Ranck commanded all but three of the uniformed men who he motioned to stay. Although in a shocked condition, Carl again gained the cab of the truck with assistance but only after Marlene mounted, tears glistening against the softness of her cheeks, and slid into the center of the wide seat. Even the police driver maintained silence as they road along the forest lane.

Other than the deaths of his crewmates on the British bomber and of Friedrich Schleiter, Carl had never seen human death first hand before. The latter had seemed both accidental and providential. It was totally different in some unexplainable way from the death of the game he had killed on his hunts and even the farm death of a hog on the first cold morning of the fall. He had seen chickens' heads taken off but somehow that too was different. The boy from the farm had never become hardened to the violent death of humans. Friends had died in accidents but he had not been a spectator. The bombs they had dropped on the city had caused women and children to die but he had been isolated. The suddenness of the deaths of the other members of the Wellington's crew, as horrible as it was, did not permit the lingering images to stalk his mind.

His mind turned to Marli as he condemned himself for his self-centeredness. She too had experienced in sight and sound the horrendous act and she had not been prepared as his military trainers had tried but failed to prepare him. He cast a glance in the dimness of the night light as she sat in the moving truck, eyes distantly fixed, the tracks of a few tears tracing down her cheeks. Carl felt slight shudders rack her body as she sat in a stiff and frozen posture.

Even the driver seemed disturbed by what they had all witnessed as he announced "I will take you to the castle" forgetting that neither Carl nor the countess had been taken to town in the truck. When the transport arrived before the castle Marlene strode stiffly and purposefully into the building, casting a look neither to the right nor to the left, while Carl asked the driver to lift off the bicycle.

Carl struggled to gain control both of his emotions and his crutches and belatedly followed the countess into the hall. Liese met him and demanded as he entered, "What's wrong? What happened? Where is Hans? Why did you return in the military truck?"

Carl calmed her most urgent fears, "Hans is fine as far as we know." He continued and told her of the atrocity that he and Marli witnessed. He then added, "The countess is torn apart emotionally. It may be that you could comfort her. Will you try, please?" Wordlessly, Liese rose and went to seek the young lady she loved dearly. She returned a few moments later and reported, "She would not talk with me and asked me to leave her alone. She is in the library and she weeps. But come, can you eat something?" As Carl followed, his eyes caught the sight of the mistress of the castle, shoulders heaving and cheeks flooded with tears, kneeling in prayer.

He did not see her again for more than two days.

Liese informed Carl that the lady of the castle stayed in a morose mood in her room with watery eyes. The next day as the three others were sharing a meal the young countess appeared at the door and quickly and silently took a seat at the table. As Carl left, she followed and softly called his given name, "Carl, may I talk to you?"

Carl stood silently as she somberly approached. Finally at an arms length separation she spoke, "I have wronged you in my thoughts, that is, I have thought ill of your actions without real cause, and I owe you an apology and an explanation. When I came to my senses, I realized that I had been wrong in my thoughts-no, more in my feelings. When I quit being emotional, I realized that I had given safe haven to the raw emotions that cried out to me that you should have done something."

When he attempted to interrupt, she quickly continued. "No, let me finish!

"When we let them die like cattle in the slaughterhouse; when we just watched the butchery! My heart, my whole being screamed, 'How could Germans do that?' We can be good people. My father is a good man. The Webers are good people. Your people are of German blood and are good people. I do not understand how good people who love their children, oh, all children, as much as we do just sit and let them be mowed down like that. What have we in Germany become? What will the Lord require of us?

"My first thoughts, no, really emotions, were that you had the authority of the uniform of an *SS* captain and felt like you could have tried to stop it all. I was so frustrated at being able to do nothing! My guilt was that of one who watches and does nothing. I hated the feeling. I wanted an object for my frustration and you were it.

"But when I started to think and not just feel I knew that there was nothing that you could have done, absolutely nothing, to save that dear family and that if you had tried both you and I would lie beside them. Please forgive me!" With these last words, she lifted her lips to place a quick kiss upon his cheek.

Carl lightly touched her upper arm and agreed, "Oh, don't say that you're sorry—you are right—I should have done something. No apology is called for as far as I am concerned. The deaths tore us all up but I have thought about my actions and there should have been something I could have done—that there was something I could have done to save that family without endangering you. I feel guilt and uselessness on my part. I excuse myself in my thoughts that there was nothing I could do. If there was, I have not thought of it. Oh, God, I do not know! I should have done something, but what?"

After standing for a while, eyes gazing but not fixed on the top of her head while she stared as though at a distant object through a window, he gave direction, "Let's talk to the Webers." Marlene agreed that it would be good to talk to the older couple and led the way to the couple's quarters and once again, the four gathered around the kitchen table.

Carl questioned first, "What went wrong? How did the *Gestapo* get so specific on where the refugees would be? Has there been an informer? Should we ourselves consider fleeing?"

Hans broke, "I will not fly from my own country! I have fought for the Fatherland and will continue to fight for her in the best way that I can by trying to make this land good. But we need to know what the *Nazis* knew and how they knew it."

All agreeing to the need to find out what was known of their activities the group reached the conclusion that Carl should venture once more into the *Silver Swan* to nose about and see what he could discover about the knowledge that the police had of their activities, if any.

As the meeting adjourned, Hans encouraged them, "There is a new place that I just discovered right on the road where fugitives can be secured. It is under a bridge where the builders left a small compartment of stone and concrete at the west end. The hole is large enough to conceal two men at the most. When I was a child I went there when I wanted to be alone or hide. I was never discovered and I never told anyone about it. You should like it, Solms. I called it the 'hole in the wall' although it is not a hole and there is no wall as such. Once I read about a group of robbers in your west called the 'hole in the wall gang.' But be careful in Littach."

❀

September 1942
Conspirators

The meeting was a council, not an ordinary council, but a conspiratorial council. The council met to conspire against evil. It was a small meeting, only four were present. There was a German middle-aged man, a veteran of the trenches of the last Great War, the war to end all wars. There was also his wife, strong and good in the fashion of a mother. Then there was the young countess, alienated from her father but determined to follow his footsteps of faith. Finally, there was the oddest of all, an American posing as a captain of the *Schutzstaffeln*, the *SS*. The group gathering occurred around the meal table and the discussion was deadly serious. The delicious odors of past preparations of foods in the kitchen added to the seemingly inconsistencies of the gathering. The wise middle aged man, Hans, cautioned, "It was a close call. How did the *Gestapo* know that the family was coming and where they would be? Has a leak developed with our contacts? We must know before we can allow the countess to be endangered again."

Carl agreed quickly with respectful familiarity, "You are absolutely right. We must gain some information but how do we go about that?"

Marli proposed, "The *Gestapo* and *SS* have seemed very open with you, Carl. Do you think you could get Greider or even Ranck to give at least a hint of how they were so sure of capturing the fleeing family? Is it possible, no, all things are possible, but is it feasible to try to get them to share some little bit of talk with you to give us a hint, that is, if you want to risk it?"

"Well, I am willing to give it a try although I will have to be lucky." he responded and continued, "I'll go in the evening when I hope that several will be in the bar."

"Be careful, Carl. They may know more than they have indicated and may , be laying a trap of some kind. Watch every word you say, please," cautioned Marli, with nods from Hans and Liese.

"But I must be natural or else I will seem strange. It seems to me that Captain Schleiter was something of a loudmouth around men. My buddies always said that I talked a lot but never said anything. That might be my redemption at this point," the American responded with a smile, pleased that she seemed to care about his fate. Later he would remember that their fate also rested with him.

"Remember," reminded Hans, "we were shocked by and silent about the outrage we witnessed in the wood. Ranck is an alert fellow and he could well smell a rat. Be prepared for him to try to trip you up in some devilish way."

Marli added to this with, "Hans is right. The devil can give him cunning. I, uh, we want you to go in God and in his wisdom. I will be in prayer all the time you are in the town."

Joining in the cautioning, Hans added, "Be careful about using Ami sayings and folk wisdom. Also, watch out that you are not intentionally surprised. Remember, you, as Friedrich Schleiter, know no English. It would be wise not to respond to any address in English. It would be easier to explain not responding than it would be to explain how you might have understood. That Ranck is a crafty fellow. If you can wear your gloves without rousing suspicions, I would advise it. Even then, please keep a handkerchief out and pick up things with it."

"If you are worried about fingerprints, and I guess Schleiter's prints would be on file, I don't think we need to have that concern. My hands were burned and scarred in fire. I really believe my current fingerprints are illegible. But are there other identifications that I need to be concerned about?" countered Carl.

"There may be one," picked up Hans. "I have heard that the SS tattooed each member's blood type under their left arm pit and I am sure that you do not have any number there. Be alert to any reason that you are asked to remove your shirt. It would probably mean that someone suspects something.'"

Carl mused to himself, "Again it seems that the fire did me a favor. It is strange how things work out. Had I not been trapped in the fire I would probably have been caught trying to get out of the country. I would not have met Marli and the Webers. Not only my hands were burned but my body was also. If I had had tattoos, they would be difficult to see under the scars. Back at college, Lydia talked of the ways of God being beyond our understanding. God may have heard my prayer when I landed after the plane was lost but He has granted more than I could ask for. I cannot hope for Marli but I will always be thankful that He brought her into my life."

The group knew that it was the practice of Ranck and some of his companions, as well as sympathizers such as the *Nazi Kreisleiter* Ernst Greider to gather in the *Silver Swan* at the late afternoon of each day for several beers, a few sentimental war ballads, and a somewhat guarded discussion of the state of the war. Carl went to the pre-war sedan because they had decided to forego the wagon. He sat in the passenger seat so that Marli could drive. Nervous and tense silence ruled in the car as the young aristocratic woman guided the vehicle through the curves descending from the *schloss*.

Untrained undercover operatives as they were, anxiety arched over them like the branches of the trees with their reddish orange leaves extending over the road. The density of the covering branches dimmed the light in the car bringing the face of Marlene into soft focus. Once again Carl thought, "She is so beautiful. I could sit and look at her all my life and never tire. I am so afraid for her." Once on more level terrain and with the fading rays of the sun striking their faces Carl's spirit rose, and it seemed to him, that of his companion did as well as she donated a wry smile for his benefit.

All was normal on the streets of the town as they neared the *Silver Swan*. Carl noted and indicated to Marli the vehicle of *Gestapo* officer Paul Ranck parked in the court of the inn. Boldly Marli maneuvered the old Mercedes to park by the *Gestapo* car and with serenity came around to aid Carl in dismounting.

Helmut Siege, one of the two butchers in the town, observed with sympathy the slow and tortuous trek of the young man in uniform as the young countess supported him. He recognized the couple for who they were as the town was proud that their Countess Marlene von Ritterbach had brought one who was so involved with the leadership of their nation to their community. The "tsk, tsk" of regret quietly left the meat man's lips as he considered the obvious damage that had been done to this youthful hero of the *Reich* by the fire as a result of his great heroism. Anyone should see that months and maybe years would pass before this man could contemplate any return to duty; he even had to lean on his wife and could barely mount the slight steps to the entrance. Such a pity!

As the pair entered the chamber, it took seconds for their eyes to become accustomed to its murkiness. When the pupils of their eyes opened, they were able to locate the mufti-clothed Ranck seated with the *Kreisleiter* Ernst Greider and *SS* Lieutenant Matthias Schönemann. Ernst Greider introduced the last man to the countess and the well-known captain of the *Schutzstaffeln,* her supposed husband. Greider then emphatically gestured for Carl to join them at the table for four while Schönemann trucklingly greeted, *"Wie geht es Ihnen,* my Captain?" which caused Carl to wonder if he had any cause to call him "my Captain." Nothing in all he had learned of Friedrich Schleiter indicated any contact with this Schönemann.

With the soft but strong assistance of Marli amid considerable shuffling and grimacing Carl gained his way to the table.

The three previously seated at the table watched with curious fascination as Marli aided Carl, patting first his shoulder and then his check, as she arranged his position with them. Finally, satisfied that her man had settled both comfortably and safely; having avoided spoiling his uniform with spills, she obtained a beer for him and excused herself for a "bit of shopping for some new dresses."

"Oh, things have really changed with you two, no? We all thought that her eyes could not see you but now she is not only your wife but also your lover. Did you bring her to the line or did her warm heart accomplish what you could not?" was the question posed by Greider.

The American evaded the question with an"Oh, things just worked out," as he carefully picked up his large glass of beer with his loosely gloved hand.

"She, or something, has really changed you. You really used to enjoy telling us of the whores in Hamburg; although I did not think the *Führer* approved of things like that," pressed Greider as Carl shot a sharp glace toward Ranck, whose hawk-eyes were expressionlessly fixed on him. "By the way, the *Nazi* official continued, "I notice that you are wearing gloves even though the weather is not cold. Why is that?"

Carl answered the last question with truth, "The burns on my hand and on my body are definitely not healed and are very unsightly. I wear the loose gloves that my woman gave me so that I would not offend the sensibilities of others. Would you like to see my wounds?" He made a motion to remove a glove.

"*Ach. Nein*! Thank you for being considerate. Your face is becoming, how shall we say, more healed day by day. Berlin has instructed me to inform them when you will be able to return to your duties. I will stay in touch so that you are back in harness as soon as possible."

Carl was glad that thought had been given to this eventuality. Hans and Marli had both told him that wounds and loss of limbs did not bar a return to military service, particularly for those considered able officers. They could replace a whole-bodied desk soldier for field duty. His continued posturing as though severely restricted in movement kept him from returning to duty in *SS* headquarters in Berlin.

The demeanor of *Gestapo* operatives was intended to disconcert the general populace. It meant to intimidate by manner. Because they wanted to be thought all knowing, they constantly intimated they knew the content of all conversations.

Throughout the chatter, Carl maintained his silence as the others engaged in small talk about the activities of the townspeople. Fortunately, Friedrich Schleiter had spent little time in the town. No one could expect him to be familiar with the personalities of its citizens. With the arrival of Heinrich Hühn, the conversation veered to a wider arena of the war effort and the crimes of Winston Churchill and that "Jew Franklin D. Rosenfeld." From that reference, the talk slid into a condemnation of Jews and the incident of the execution of the Jewish family. Carl withstood his great curiosity and listened as the talk progressed. His was not the only inquisitive mind. He heard Hühn ask how the authorities were so sure of the situation with the Jews in the forest.

"Why?" exclaimed Greider, "Do you want to print the story in your rag of a paper and reveal state intelligence secrets? We do have our sources, you know, both in this country and outside our borders."

"Ernst!" excitedly asserted the newsman, "You know my loyalty to the *Führer* and the Fatherland!" Calming his voice to a discernable whisper, he continued, "You know I knew of the operations in Poland and Russia and not a word came from me. Certainly, this was a small operation compared to the others with which I have been entrusted with knowledge. I just like to know the whole story so that I will not make false forecasts."

While this conversation developed, Carl noted that Ranck attended each move, each sound with great notice. Not a word issued from his lips but Carl knew that little was escaping consideration and so decided to play his role to the hilt.

"What do you say, Paul. Should we tell the good editor how word of the Jews came out? You were in charge. You did a great job and Himmler himself will hear of it. If you want to tell, it will be official. How did you learn of their presence and how did you accomplish it? Come, tell us!" Carl pronounced with assumed authority.

The folds of flesh around Ranck's eyes widened and he threw a glance around the room, vacant except for the five gathered around the table with even the bartender absent to the supply room. Possibly, Captain Schleiter's high political connections intimidated him or he was uncontrollably obedient to a higher rank, even though not the *Gestapo,* so obeyed the SS captain.

"In this particular case we just happened onto them. Our people do patrol the woods, you know. But in another case it was like this," he reported. "An *Abwehr* man in Switzerland happened to be eating in an outdoor cafe and heard a very young girl tell a friend that they had come out of Germany when they met good people in the trees and had been taken out on an underground railroad and escaped underground. We were able to determine in Switzerland the identity of the family and while they were safe from us, we traced back to their origin and began to interrogate all who knew them. You may be sure that the questioning demanded answers and we accepted no evasion.

"We discovered that there was a well-concealed system to guide them out of country. It bears similitude to what the Americans called their 'underground railroad' before their civil war. That is probably what the kid was talking about, not a real underground road. She may have heard her parents talking. It is a well-organized system and no one knew the identity of the next person in the chain of stations. We have still not been able to find the traitors at other stations. If we can find the last group of Jew lovers, we can roll the whole scheme up from the bottom end. It is sure that we are still looking for caves or tunnels in the area in the off chance that there may be a real underground escape route. There are no geological reports of natural caves or of mining so we are looking for evidence of digging, you know, fresh dirt and so on."

"Did not the girl or those in the chain give other clues?" queried Ernst Greider.

"Oh, as I said, the cells of the chain were not connected in the sense that they knew each other. The Jews were just sent to a rendezvous location where they were picked up. There apparently are signals that others give so that Jews will be waiting at the designated spot; the signalers do not know to whom they are signaling or the spot where the rendezvous will occur. The girl's mother was heard to say that the girl loved to make a good story better and that there was really no cave. Our agent was unable to hear more because the family left the restaurant immediately after the conversation."

"But, Captain Schleiter, I am surprised that you listen so closely. You seemed squeamish when we took care of that pack of Jew dogs. But now you seem interested and approving of the work we have done, no?"

"My wife had never witnessed anything like that and I was concerned about her distress. She has led a protected life, not exposed to the harsher facts of the real world."

Ranck pursued, "And just when do you think you will be able to leave her? If there were not orders from Berlin, we would have had her and her companions in for questioning before now. I understand that you have intervened on her and her father's behalf. He certainly would have been made available for interviews if we in the *Geheime Staatspolizei* had been free to do what we thought best but no. Our Berlin people forbid any action against him but I think our time will come. It will be good when you can get back to duty, no?"

"*Bestimmt*! What came over me when I went into the fire to save those kids, I do not know. But for that I may have been promoted, even given a district in the east."

"Exactly how long do you think, do the doctors think, you will be laid up with your injuries?"

To this query Carl replied, "I have not been able to see a doctor since I left the hospital in the city. Then they told me it would be well more than a year before my burns would be healed enough for me to do even part of a day's work. As you can probably guess the burns under my jacket are still wrapped and are quite painful."

It was at this time that Marli returned bearing packages, fulfilling her role as the wife who loved to shop and spend money. Her first words were, "You should see the lovely dress I found, I do believe that it must have come from a Parisian designer. The material feels like silk, but we know that cannot be. And I found a lovely loose shirt for you. I know it would normally be quite too big for you but with your dressings I think it will be fine. Will your regulations permit you to wear it? And did you have a good talk with your friends?"

As she helped him lift himself from his seat she turned to the others and invited, "Please, I wish you and your ladies to come to the castle for tea. Please tell your ladies they are welcome in our home. Oh. Come two weeks from tonight if it pleases you. I just think I will give a little *soiree* that evening. Put it on your calendars and be sure to tell your ladies. I know how men are about social things."

This bid to visit gave each married man some news to take home that significantly increased the welcome of at least two at their supper table that evening.

Once more alone in their vehicle Carl quizzed Marli, "Why did you invite those people to your home?"

Her reply perfectly satisfied him, "Earlier we discussed that we must avoid suspicion. What better way is there than to have society with them and let them roam over the castle. Certainly Ranck's eyes will probe into every cavity and corner but he will see nothing suspicious for there is nothing to see."

He told her of their surprise at the attentive care that she had given him but failed to mention the masculine intimations that he had "brought her to heel." He had been sensually thrilled by the touch of her hands and wished it to happen again but also did not want her to think that he took pride as a male. The ride to the castle occurred with a warm and satisfied feeling as he recounted the remarks of the others and his conclusion that they were not in immediate danger. They agreed that they must take care in the future. To his question as to whether they could or should communicate the *Nazi's* entry into the channels of escape she answered that she did not have the answer to either question for she knew nothing more than he knew.

Again, the group of four gathered around the kitchen table and discussed the events of the day. Upon hearing of the invitation for tea to the *Nazis* and their wives Hans and Liese agreed that while it was a good idea they should be careful that their guests left no "mice" behind. When asked what they meant by this Hans replied that he and his wife were aware of cases when the *Gestapo* left listening devices in people's homes and offices after visiting. For several reasons they agreed that there would be one room where the guests would not be allowed to go.

Marli asked, "Hans, do you have a list of the books that the *Nazis* have censored, the ones that Germans are forbidden to read? If you do not, where can we get one? The only reason that Friedrich didn't object to their being here was that he never read and was uninterested in books. But we had better remove any that we have and put them in a secure place before our guests are all over the residence."

On Thursday of that week, Marli and the Webers were delighted to open the door of the chateau and their sincerest hospitality to Father Nimitz. The immediate departure of Liese to the kitchen and her return with tea in the best of the heirloom silver and china proved the warm welcome that greeted the churchman. He, in turn, seeing the two youngest of the five sitting on a settee and their bodies separated by only inches began a close observation. In his mind, he knew that something had changed so he began questioning gently and as obliquely as he could imagine. He tried to make the queries as probing as possible without offending. Because he was the least acquainted with

Friedrich Schleiter, he thought his safest and most obvious approach was toward him.

When asked by Nimitz as to his recovery from the serious injuries he had incurred, the American's glance toward the young countess and Hans as if seeking aid in framing his answers, puzzled the cleric. Hans came to the SS officer's aid by saying "Quite well, really. But please understand that we don't want to show him off fully just yet."

Marli's declaration, "Father, you are a good man and you will keep this conversation confined to ourselves, will you not?" did not significantly relieve Carl's consternation at the revelation of Hans.

Carl, whose every sense told him of the danger they were all in every day of their lives in Hitler's Germany and screamed that no one outside their circle of four should be trusted, could only be passive in this instance. Immediately the priest directed a question toward him, "Did you feel God's presence or even a need for God when your life was in peril, Captain?"

"A question that I might expect from a religious man and a question that I would want to know," thought Carl, who could answer truthfully without evasion, "It seemed that I really had no time for thought or sensing. In the fire things just happened and they happened quickly. In the hospital I had to deal with an entirely new situation and accommodate myself to it."

The priest persevered, "You are not a member of the Church, are you? But are you a Christian? I hope this experience will help you see things as they really are and that you may be a citizen of God's kingdom."

"This guy is a bulldog," Carl thought to himself and assumed that the word "Church" meant the Catholic Church. Even then, a still small voice inside him whispered, "Do not ever deny Me even at the peril of your mortal life," and answered, "No, I am not . . I do not belong to the Catholic Church but I do belong to Christ, I acknowledge Him as my Lord."

"That is not the answer I expected from what I had been told," astonishment flushing the father's face as he flicked a glance toward first the Webers and then to the countess. "but it gives me the deepest of joy to hear it. Who has been most influential in your Christian life?"

"A very spiritual young lady I knew years ago." Carl determined that was as far as he would go in that direction and decided to take the offense to get the questioning away from himself, "Why did you become a priest, if you do not mind telling me? To me that is a great sacrifice to make, living a life of celibacy among other things, that is."

To this the priest replied, "No, it is not a sacrifice, it is a gift that is given that I, we, may serve Him more fully. I became a priest because I saw the beautiful work of the church through the centuries. Oh, I know of the carnality and the sophistry that has permeated this body of Christ at times but I personally am convinced that the church has done far more good than evil. I am convinced that it is the rock upon which Christ intended to build his kingdom. You do surprise me to the point of being shocked by your answers and questions. They are so different from what I expected."

Before the joint interrogation could continue Liese interjected question after question concerning the status of other members of the parish: "Has *Frau* Hünsinger had her baby? How large was it? What of the Vörster's son missing on the eastern front? Has there been any word of him? When will the bishop come again?" The protection from grilling that was being extended to him surprised Carl. At the same time he sensed a certain trust that the other three had for the curate.

After the priest answered Liese's quizzing, Marli stepped in to extend an invitation to the church father to the tea they were to have in ten days time, naming the other invited guests. Nimitz accepted readily but with a puzzled look. When their guest stated that he must leave, the entire group followed him to the entry hall. "*auf Wiedersehen*," was his German goodbye. His hearty handshake to Carl extended into a hug accompanied with a broad smile. The embrace brought pain, both physically to his scarred sides and emotionally as Carl remembered the embraces that he had received from his sentimental family folk back home.

Marli and Liese filled the mornings in the days between the priest's visit and the day for the tea with not only preparation of small delicacies but also cleaning the silver and the fine porcelain of Marli's inheritance. Marli explained that she definitely wanted to convince their visitors that they desired to be friendly as well as that they had nothing to hide. The late afternoons of the shortening days still allowed time for the two young people who had been thrown together to take short walks and longer talks. Occasionally Carl would hobble along on his crutches but usually he extended his capacity to move with the artificial limb created by Hans because it left his hands free and ungloved. He always hoped for just a slight touch.

The conversations began with depth and grew deeper as each plumbed the views of the world of the other. Carl was increasingly grateful to Lydia Cameron whose questions had focused his mind. Her encouragement of his thinking about why he lived had caused him to seek something beyond the gaining of pleasure and the avoidance of pain. He had come to abhor the darkness of being without purpose. The great "Why?" question had spread like a prairie fire into many lesser "why" questions.

At the beginning of one excursion into the woodland Marli had asked, "Why do you think that democratic equality took hold in America but it has never really been accepted in Germany?"

He was prepared with an answer, for his thoughts had occasionally been on that subject. "I think we owe it to a German, Doctor Martin Luther. His great doctrine of the priesthood of the believer essentially holds that there is no hierarchy in the kingdom of God. If there is no social strata in God's world, why should there be in the world of men? My professor taught that the first King James of England foresaw this when he said, 'If there be no bishops there will be no king.' Where there are no bishops there will be no counts or countesses, I regret to tell you. And there will certainly be no *Führer* undermining the written word of either constitution or scripture."

"But what kept Germans and Europeans from believing and acting on that same teaching?" she countered.

"There were too many tares and weeds in Europe, and I hate to call your class such, but the idea was planted in virgin soil in the area where the United States developed. We had neither nobility nor royalty and little aristocracy at first. In Europe the people always had to overcome the feeling that the true law required such social class divisions."

"So you say that the American concept of social and political equality was imported from a German's work even though he himself never accepted the consequence of his idea?" she repeated for confirmation and continued, "It would be strange if, after this war you Americans brought the idea back to the land of Luther."

It was not the joy of exploring one another's thoughts that made these little promenades a pleasure for him. The thrill that transited his whole being at her touch and the slight shivering chill that transfused his inward parts when the occasion required her to steady the half-invalid were moments of transport for the young Texan. The emotion engendered by these incidents inevitably caused his silence for moments as he regained his tranquility from the heart beat that seemed ready to burst his chest. He feared that these evidences must tell her of the passion that possessed him. He would not have used the word "passion," no matter its accuracy, for its very use seemed to sully the chasteness of this lady who embodied all that was beautiful inwardly and outwardly. When soft needles from a tree brushed her cheeks he was jealous and wished his hands could stroke her face as softly as did the needles. He envied the drops of moisture that the leaves left on the silky surface of the soft skin of her face during their walks in the woods.

While he remained adoringly deferential, recognizing the social and economic gulf that separated them, she was not oblivious to the softness, the tenderness of his eyes as she on many occasions saw him watching her. She found, to her surprise, that these silent expressions of devotion pleased her. She was increasingly aware of the degree he drew her to him. The scars left by the fire and the surgeon's knife were healing but she also found herself looking beyond the outward appearance. He surely had demonstrated courage and depth of thinking. His mind, while not honed to the keen edge of a European intellectual, was quick and sure in practical matters. She liked him. She liked him quite a bit, she decided.

The Countess Marlene *von* Ritterbach Schleiter, after consideration decided that a couple of pictures of Adolf Hitler should be pulled from the closet shelf along with the red and white banner with its twisted cross of the Nationalist Socialist regime for display. She explained the two reasons that she had for this augmentation. She wanted to protect the role played by Carl of an *SS* officer who dominated the castle. The castle group definitely should not raise suspicions by appearing to be far out of the mainstream of German society. As she explained her reasons for hanging the picture and flag of the dictator she continued, "We should not be too obvious. It might be like protesting too much but our guests should see them. Besides, outward show does not reveal the inward heart."

With the preparations for the guests, the little strolls, and their joint efforts in keeping the farming activities productive the time passed quickly. Suddenly it was the day of the reception. *Frau* Erika Randorff insured that she preceded her husband to be the first to enter the home of her childhood playmate as she gushed, "How wonderful it is to be in this house once more. It seemed quite large when we were children but now it does not seem so magnificent. I have made *Herr* Randorff promise me a house twice this size when we have won the war. We should all be quite as wealthy as the English then because our Fatherland's empire will be far greater than theirs. My husband is making sure that he has friends in high places so that his investment opportunities will be unlimited. When I visited Schaffshausen this year, I found just the site for our chateau after the war. It is on a hill overlooking the Rhine where you can see the waters of that beautiful stream of the Fatherland glistening in the sunlight by day and in moonlight by night. Am I not right, Herr Randorff? Here, please take these." as she thrust a nice bouquet of flowers into Marli's hands.

As Carl shuffled forward on his crutches, the merchant's wife turned her considerable attention toward him, "Oh, Friedrich, how glad I am to see you. But I do wish that I found you looking and feeling better. I know that you are anxious to get back in harness before all the glory is gone and the Russkies give up. But I do congratulate you on the conquest I have heard that you have made," she proclaimed with a side-glance in the direction of her one-time friend, the twice-over heiress to the great names and estates of Krönitz and Ritterbach, who was engaged in a rather mundane conversation with the mercantile prince of the town. "How did you manage that? You see, I have known your wife a long time and she was never one quick to change. She was always a headstrong and stubborn little twit. You managed it! How did you do it? I was never able to get her to recant any feeling."

Before he could think, Carl responded with a maxim that his father had often presented to him, "Oh, I have been told that a soft bit makes for a docile horse."

She jumped in quickly, "Oh, your familiarity with horses does surprise me."

The arrival of the obsequious Heinrich Hühn rescued Carl from having to hold further discourse with Marli's old acquaintance. Carl was sure that the countess would no longer call her "friend". Then came young Lieutenant Matthias Schönemann accompanied by a happy-faced female named Margarete Pann who seemed too old to be called a girl and too young to be deemed a woman but with the possibility of being a lady either now or in the future.

The priest, Father Nimitz, became the next arrival and Marli, the Webers, and even young Margarete Pann greeted him warmly. Marli's welcome was encapsulated in her first words, "Father Nimitz, you are most welcome into my home! It is perfectly wonderful that you can be here. At the appropriate time before we have our refreshments I wonder if you would thank our Lord for them."

At the entry of the priest, the other guests withdrew from his proximity and engaged in their own conversations in the salon with an occasional cold serpents' stare in his direction. The priest seemed oblivious of their open hostility, and after warmly greeting Carl and recognizing the Webers as they carried out their role as servants, moved on to the other group. As soon as he approached, even the subdued murmur of the detached group grew silent. The voluble merchant's wife boorishly confronted the guest of her hostess, "Well, here we have one who loves his church and his Christ more than he loves our nation and our *Führer.*"

The man of God responded, "In love there is neither more nor less. I love the people of Germany, the German nation. I love their warmth and their commitment. I love their holidays that have spread throughout the world. I love the music both of the folk and of the great symphonies and operas. As a 'father' who loves his children but does not love all their actions so I love my church children and the extended family of the German folk. But you are, in a way, correct. If I am forced to choose between my God and my country, I will with tears on my face choose my God, for He must be obeyed because He is God."

"Of course." he continued even as the little group seemed to want to get away from him, "This is not original with me but traces back to the earliest days of the church with Peter and Paul and on down through the halls of history even to those who protested the actions of the church, John Hus and Martin Luther."

Erika Randorff persisted, "Oh, I for one have given up the self-proclaimed Jewish savior and will put my trust in our Aryan German savior, our beloved *Führer*, Adolph Hitler. Each time I remember the cinema *Triumph of the Will* chills go down my back as he descends from the clouds into Nürnberg and even more so at the great rally at the plaza. *Heil* Hitler!"

Then, in a whisper to *Herr* Hühn, she communicated that her words would be shocking and not worthy of a lady, but as a modern woman she did not care. "When I see our glorious ruler among the crowds with the women and children worshipping him, sometimes I nearly wet my pants." The woman's crudeness, although uttered only to immediate bystanders, brought about several reactions. Hands flew to lips. The males present, to hide their smiles, turned their faces away. The expression of at least two of the hearers consigned the woman who anticipated the riches of the thousand-year Reich to the realm of the carnal.

Marli redirected her thoughts and asked Hans, who had arrived with a tray of delicacies, to help "Friedrich" to a chair until the remainder of the guests arrived.

Checking her mental list she knew that Ludwig and Erika Randorff, Ernst and Ursula Greider, Heinrich and Maria Hühn, Matthias Schönemann with his lady friend Margarete Pann, and, of course, Father Nimitz, were in attendance. Only three were missing, the mayor of the town, *Herr* Otto Schlenkmann and his wife Maria and the *Gestapo* operative Paul Ranck. Even as she recognized that the three were missing, the absentee list narrowed to one as Hans, acting in the forced role of butler, announced the arrival of the Schlenkmanns.

After moments of undistinguished chatter, Carl observed Liese indicating that she would like a private word with her mistress. As they moved to a spot near him he heard the older woman say, "Ranck has arrived and is looking around the court and buildings,"

"Oh," responded the hostess, "Hans, would you please go out to welcome Ranck. It seems that he may need something as he is looking about the grounds. Please welcome him heartily to our house and offer any help if he needs something. He may have car trouble or need something else."

Before Hans could leave, the man from *Gestapo* stood at the door dressed in the uniform of his organization. Handing Hans his cap, he strode as a dark angel into the room to the careful greetings of the others. Circling around the crowd, he accepted the proffered hands of those there with a hand limp in its grip but with restless, penetrating eyes that seemed to probe every feature of each face and cavity of the room. His gaze stopped and settled on the features of the husband of his hostess. Approaching Carl he stated, "It is good to see that your health is improving and that you are able to be involved in this *soiree*. Berlin directs me to insure that you regain your strength as soon as possible and to report to both the headquarters of the *SS* and the *Gestapo* as to your condition. Have you seen a doctor locally?"

"Oh, I am improving but it is very slow sledding. There is much pain in my leg and bleeding also. Each day I must have two hours of bed rest in the daytime in addition to a good eight hours at night. I am strongly of the opinion that it will be some time before I will be of more use than hindrance to anyone."

"That is hard to hear. Your abilities are needed so that others can go to the east. Even here you may have seen or heard things that are not right. I feel that I am an artist in searching out traitors and slackers and my nose tells me that there is some monkey business going on in this area, maybe even this estate. Is your wife loyal to the *Führer*? Berlin has informed me that the countess' father refused to serve the *Reich* as a judge and is thought not to be loyal to the *Führer*. And what of these retainers, the Webers? Are they secure?"

Carl, whose palms had become moist, was saved from further interrogation by the approach of *Kreisleiter* Ernst Greider and Ursula Greider, who softly confessed, "Friedrich, I took the liberty of inviting *Frau* Field Marshal Rudel to your *soiree* and I see that she and the Field Marshal are here now. I had no idea that we would be honored and privileged to have the marshal with us!"

Marlene, as did all others, heard this pronouncement and followed the direction of the gaze of all toward the entry to her home. As the new couple entered, decorations dangling from the Field Marshal's robust chest, she greeted them with the graciousness of culture. Her warmth was returned by the Field Marshal, "How is it going, Countess. Do you know my wife, Ulla? Please forgive our intrusion into your gathering. I only arrived last evening and my wife told me that she had been urged to attend by *Frau* Greider. I seized the opportunity to ask of my old friend, your father. Is he, uh, well? You know that we had great times when we were young ones. I know that he resigned as a judge and that was no surprise to me. He was always one who walked a straight line."

"I have not been able to talk with him for some time but at the last report he was well and overseeing his land."

"Oh, yes. I did hear that there was some estrangement as a result of your marriage." The Marshal cast a flicker of a glance at the one in the *SS* captain's uniform.

"That's enough of old times," interrupted the wife of the Party *Kreisleiter.* "What news do you have of the victories in the east? We have heard of the intensity of the struggle for the victory in the Crimea. Were you in that sector?"

"No, I was elsewhere. You should know that much remains to be done although Sebastopol has fallen and we have taken tens of thousands Russian prisoners. Many of us expected this to be over last year but more and more we realize that Russia is a huge land, greater than many could have imagined. The geography classes most certainly told us of the distances but until one actually experiences them, it is hard to visualize with reality. It is a land whose people love it as they would love their mother. We refer to our country as 'the Father-land' while the Russkies call their land 'Mother Russia.' Are you a psychologist of the social order? No? I did not think so but I am looking for an explanation of what the difference in the peoples might say about their whole outlook on life, if the phrases have any psychological significance. Why do such horribly led and inadequately supplied people fight to suicidal deaths? They seem to be willing to die for Mother Russia but not for Marxist-Leninism."

"Uncommitted," mused Ursula Greider. "Defeatist!" was the unspoken reaction of her *Nazi* leader husband.

"A man who wants to be honest," was the inward opinion of Carl although he also noted that neither the *Führer's* name nor role was mentioned.

The military leader then turned his full attention to the young man in the uniform of an SS captain and observed, "You displayed great heroism when you saved the children. My wife told me what you did and I congratulate you but I am sorry to see you so disabled. Your injuries certainly prevent you from combat. How complete can your recovery be?"

"My recovery is going very slowly but I hope that someday I will be able to regain some mobility." Then observing Ranck's rapt attention to their private conversation and thinking that it would be good to keep a pose of patriotism he continued, "I will be glad when I can return to duty and relieve some lucky individual who may serve under your command in the east. But there is yet bleeding and great pain from the amputation and other surgeries, not to mention the injuries from the collapsing building and fire."

"Ah, the poor devil you release from a desk may not thank you after he serves a few weeks pushing toward the Volga at Stalingrad. You can be thankful that you are not serving as a company or even battalion officer in that God forsaken place. But I understand that you do not need to worry for Himmler counts you as his eyes and ears in the secret places."

"Oh, yes," intruded Paul Ranck, "That's one thing I do not understand. Here we have a trusted subordinate of the internal security chief *Reichsführer-SS* Himmler and we know there is an outlet for Jews from the *Reich* in this *kreis*. Yet our captain has made no effort to contact his Berlin headquarters to obtain assistance in plugging the hole of the escapers. One call from him to *Reichsführer* Himmler would probably bring scores of men to aid our efforts."

"You make me think even more highly of our young captain, *Herr* Ranck. What you tell me shows that he has a balanced view of the needs of our war. So a few paltry Jews get under the fence. That certainly does not hurt our war footing. The Jewish men we could use in the front lines but few are allowed in the forces. In addition, I did think that the policy was just to rid the *Reich* of the Jews and like kind. I thought our government used Adolf Eichmann to try to get the British to take them into Palestine before the war just to get them out of our country. Or is it that the *Gestapo* wants to eradicate them from the face of the earth? I hope that the camps being opened in the east are not killing camps," responded the Field Marshal.

Turning his back to the others von Rudel gently seized Carl's elbow and directed him into an adjacent alcove where their conversation would not be overheard. After what seemed a quick check of the room, he observed, "Your bearing surprises me greatly. I came under the impression that you were a good-for-nothing lackey of someone in high authority. I pride myself in my judgment of men and although we have not spoken twenty words to one another, I feel that there is something to you that I did not expect. I honor your wife's father and deeply respect his opinion. Because he resented his daughter's marriage to you, I was ready to accept you for the worst. Would you please tell me how you won such a great girl whom I have known since she was a baby?"

Guardedly Carl decided that he had to answer this important man and that he had better tell the truth of Marli's marriage to Friedrich Schleiter.

"I may have changed some in our marriage. You see, I really wanted her and so told her that because of her father's resistance to the *Führer* I could see to it that he went to one of the camps or I could insure that he would remain free. She believed me and married me much to the distress of her father." Carl had chosen to use the word "wanted" rather than "loved" because he could not visualize love being so selfish.

"Hmmm," responded the general, "I agree with the *Gestapo* ferret Ranck in regard to the situation here. But I know I differ with him because I find this country air refreshing and very pleasing. Forgive me, but I read you as a man who could never place one he loved in the position you have placed the countess. I will tell her father that his worries in relation to his daughter are less than he thought, although his hurt is so deep that he will not listen to me. I have some other questions. Would you come over by the little window with me?"

After positioning himself strategically with his back to the wall so that he could observe anyone near the door or entering the room he first protected his actions with the words that he "did not want the eavesdroppers to hear their conversation" and then he carefully probed, "What do you know of the attitude in Berlin? Does the confidence remain high? Berlin promised new tank models that can deal with the Russian T-34's. Those machines were a great shock to us. No one gave the Russians credit for the ability to build such weapons. They are definitely superior to our Mark IV's. Is there any pessimism in Berlin? We have now gone through a second summer campaign and the Russians are stronger rather than weaker. We have heard that they have moved a great deal of industry behind the Urals. What gives in Berlin?"

Pleased by the personal flattery from the great military man Carl continued to be cautious in any response although he felt the sincerity in the marshal's remarks. "I left Berlin last March and have been isolated here for six months so I have really lost touch." He continued with a filling remark that he thought was safe, "We did expect final victory this summer and I am sure that the *Führer* and all the others are disappointed that it will have to go into a winter campaign. Where do you think we will go from here?"

"All I can say is that we need petroleum products and that the Rumanian fields are insufficient for all our needs so where can we find petroleum other than beyond the Caucasian Mountains? We are now driving on Stalingrad and expect it to fall shortly, opening the way to the southeast. Ah! Here comes your lovely young woman. Please instruct her to be careful around that ferret Ranck. I know of him and he is dangerous. Good evening, Countess, I have just told your husband that I will try to build some bridges for you with your father. I am both surprised and pleased by your young man. I thank you for your most gracious reception of my wife and me in such an unexpected fashion. Now we had better join the others before they imagine a conspiracy."

As they left the room Carl noted that a significant amount of wine and *schnapps* had passed through the throats of the guests and all seemed gay and congenial except for one. As he scanned the group, he could not spot Paul Ranck. But after shuffling outside the entrance to the residence with the departing Field Marshal and *Frau* von Rudel, he discerned the figure of Ranck. The Gestapo agent was in aggressive conversation with a French prisoner named Dresser just at the edge of light. Ranck broke off their conversation when he made out the intent gaze of not only Carl but also Marshal Rudel. Hastening toward them he explained, "I inquired about the internal situation in France and am happy to learn that the French were content with their government of President Petain."

Shortly after midnight all the guests and their vehicles had departed the castle grounds and Hans and Liese had quickly overseen the clean up of the residence by the French who were rewarded with gifts of wine and the remaining delicacies.

The four gathered over coffee to discuss the evening after Hans secured the doors of the residence. All deemed it a success in that it went as far as it could in diverting suspicion. After Carl disclosed the thrust of his talk with Rudel Marli confirmed, "My father and the Field Marshal were indeed close chums at their pre-university academy."

When Carl told of the "confession" that "Schleiter" had made concerning their union, her eyes softened in appreciation at the effort to restore her relations with her father. She also gave a favorable interpretation of the general's character, "My father always said Marshal von Rudel had probably compromised the principles of his early years through his commitment as a soldier. 'Paul has become too fixed on man's authority and forgetful of God's.'"

As the conversation turned to Ranck, their voices, without conscious intent, lowered. Carl related the noun "ferret" that the general had used for a *Gestapo* representative. They all agreed that it was good imagery for the small statured man with darting eyes and mincing steps. Ferrets would seek out rodents and thus the general's use of the word was safe. The little members of the weasel family were bloodthirsty with a love for killing for the sake of killing. The little creatures were incessantly probing and searching for victims. All four conspirators had heard his remarks concerning his suspicious unease about what was occurring not only in the county but even in the castle. Carl told of seeing him in earnest conversation with Dresser and renewed the caution to watch their words around the French prisoners.

Carl had become acquainted with these prisoners taken a little over two years previously in the German *blitz* through France. Hans had introduced them one by one. None of the group possessed any outstanding physical features. Only one was much taller than Carl. The first, described by Hans as the leader of the group, was Alois Ducite, a city magistrate of Lyon, who had risen to the rank of sergeant before being taken. The second was Antoine Armond, formerly employed as a pastry chef in the city of Limoges and who was loud in his disappointment at having been assigned to the French infantry. "If I had only been assigned to a rear headquarters, befitting my art in the kitchen, I would not have been captured and would now be preparing delicious French pastries. There is nothing like *petit fours* served on our fine Limoges Haviland."

Francois Chalvet, powerfully stocky even at a height above Carl's, was ready at all times to let listeners know that he was one of those workers of the world who would soon "unite to cast off their chains of exploitation." He delighted in telling, "How I have made the capitalists pay for their profits from the grinding sweat of my co-workers at the Renault automobile factory." Without a book, he was able to recite long passages from *Das Kapital* and the *Communist Manifesto* even as he gestured wildly with his muscled hands folded into firm fists.

Rene Dresser, thin and wiry with height just inches short of six feet, felt free to express both his support of the regime in Vichy as well as past pogroms against the Jews, declaring that nothing could ever convince him that Captain Albert Dreyfuss was not a traitor to France but the Jewish moneyed interests had rescued him. This level of vehemence against Jews in other countries in Europe surprised Carl. He knew that some bias existed at home but nothing like he was experiencing in Europe as he thought of his friends Ira "Apple" Adlerstein and Nathan Wilkovitz back in Aggieland as well as the other ingredients in the melting pot, the "Bohemian" Elo Frnka and "Mexican" Albert "Frito" Gonzales. His friends may have been from different religious and cultural backgrounds but they were all committed and patriotic Americans who succeeded by no conspiracy but by their own efforts. Each of them he had accepted as fellow Aggies, fellow Texans, and fellow Americans whose right it was to observe their culture and their faith as they pleased. The minor cultural differences were recognized, and more importantly, appreciated. The ideals of his faith and his education allowed no room for hatred.

The fifth Frenchman was Louis Boudreaux, a strapping six footer perpetually smiling, who had been taken from a farm in the south of France and whose whole attitude displayed joy at the privilege of letting his sinewy shoulders hoist large bundles of hay or anything else that needed lifting into the wagon.

These parolees had been assigned shelter in a cottage at the foot of the castle hill with a stove for cooking and heating provided. Hans, a correct soldier in the past, had maintained the rank structure by making the French Sergeant Ducite responsible for the cleanliness of the living quarters and the feeding of the trustee-prisoners.

Three nights after the tea and about three hours after darkness when all in the castle were asleep Carl wakened to a knock on the door on the lower level of the living quarters. Going to the window with the light of the front door illuminating the court he saw Hans in grave conversation with Sergeant Ducite. He then saw the two leave the court into the darkness toward the gate of the castle. Curious as to what was transpiring he made his way down the steps only to discover Marli also awake and standing at the door. Neither was aware of the cause of the disturbance. Deciding to remain awake to determine what transpired they settled where both ends of the residence were visible to wait for the return of Hans and quietly talked about the situation. Carl found this time, in fact any time that he could sit and look at the young woman, a pleasant period.

After an hour they became aware that Hans had quietly entered the rear of the residence. Approaching him they discovered that two other individuals accompanied him. He noted that they were blindfolded. Carl immediately recognized their clothing as uniforms, ragged and bedraggled, of the British Royal Air Force.

"What gives?" asked the mistress of the castle.

"Oh," answered the somewhat agitated Hans. "Alois the Frenchman found these two Englanders near their hut early this evening. The others did not see them and he decided to bring them to the castle because he did not know what else to do. He said he would like to help them escape but did not want to get in trouble with the authorities. He brought them here so that I could do whatever

I wanted to do with them. Of course he thinks he knows that an *SS* captain is here so he can say that he turned them over to the military through me."

Marli broke in, "The first thing we are going to do is to take the blindfolds off and then get some food into their stomachs. They are starved." Carl was glad that he had used the false foot and seemed healthy and that he had gone to the door in a robe. Having said that she was going to feed the men Marlene began to open cabinets and pull our bread, meat and potatoes. She placed them in the still warm stove where beds of coals were always in residence. The English looked on in resigned curiosity as they assumed they had been apprehended. Even without a bid or invitation, the two men had seated themselves at the table, elbows on the surface and their heads in their hands. Even while the food was on the stove for heating, she had set glasses of milk, plates and eating utensils before them.

"Will Alois tell the other prisoners?" Carl asked.

"He said that he would not because he really does not want to get involved. He is afraid of the others from two different sides. If he failed to turn them in and Dresser found out, he might tell the authorities. If he did turn them in and the English win the war he might be shot as a traitor when the war is over or the Commies might even kill him before then. No, he has washed his hands of the whole affair and turned it over to me. But what do we do now?"

Confident that the downed airmen understood none of their German because they continued to be disconsolate, the planning continued.

"Could this be a ruse and a trap?" asked Carl. "They did not come through the normal channel but then they are not Jews but British airmen. Hans, tell me more of our friends in Switzerland. How determined are they? What I really mean is how cold blooded are they? If these two turn out to be planted can we ask them to make sure they never speak again?"

"That is for sure. Our friends are angry to the point of hatred. I believe they would welcome the opportunity to rid the world of some of the Gestapo, the tormentors of their people, their loved ones and friends."

"First we must get them into the old dungeon and let them rest. We then need to get them into other clothes so they will not be so conspicuous when they get into Switzerland. And, Carl, we must insure that they do not know that you are supposed to be an *SS* officer and are really an American. If they get into Switzerland or even England and tell someone an SS officer or an American rescued them, there could be big trouble. So no English for you, no uniform for you and with your leg it would be good to stay out of sight if possible," directed Marli insuring that she assigned no military rank to Carl.

Having seen only a relatively humble kitchen because of the blackness of the moonless but not cloudless night the two were once more blindfolded and led out to the old castle ruins where they were guided into the depths of the vacated dungeon. After several days to regain their strength and to be fitted with new clothes they were blindfolded for their journey through the tunnel to the waiting Jewish network across the border. They were never to know the identity of their rescuers.

Thus the foursome in the castle got back in the refugee-saving business. As the flow of Jews ebbed, the flow of downed airmen, first British, Canadians, Australians and then, in increasing numbers, Americans, began.

All agreed that this procedure had worked well indeed and they would follow it in the future in so far as possible. Carl with his missing foot was to remain out of sight except for his duties in watching the routes. These precautions were unnecessary because months passed before they assisted more clients. When they did, their customers followed other instructions as the route became more organized.

Those of the castle often observed the indefatigable representative of the *Gestapo*, Paul Ranck, on the land belonging to Countess von Ritterbach. He made no secret of his quest for the hole in the German border that he knew existed. Sometimes accompanied by members of the local *polezei*, he most often poked and pried alone. No place seemed safe from his mincing movements and furtive eyes, as, like the tiny predator the general had likened him to, he searched for his prey. No place was safe from his continual search, although he hesitated to intrude into the living area of the castle. Whenever his hands, eyes, and feet searched the unrestored areas of the *Schloss*, he did not fail to call on those who lived in the restored wing as though on a friendly visit. These visits always seemed to excite his interest in a new room of the mansion with particular attention paid to the library where he slid his hands over the shelving as he remarked on their beautiful craftsmanship. Both Marli and Carl recognized that he was searching for what was not there, a secret passage or room behind the books.

During his visits to the residence, he often encountered Father Nimitz, which set his inquisitive suspicions on fire. This in turn resulted with open and accusing searches of the good priest's church and parsonage as he insisted that, "I know the secrecy that has been practiced by the Papists for centuries. I only wish that the great Bismarck had succeeded in eradicating that infamous institution from the Fatherland in his war of cultures." He questioned Marlene and Carl as to why, in that they were not Catholic, the priest found their company so compatible. The suspicious policeman could not accept the truth that they found fencing over theological doctrine interesting if not intriguing. They all concealed the fact that Carl participated freely and eagerly in these discussions because it did not fit into the character of the late Captain Schleiter. The tolerance of an *SS* officer puzzled the *Gestapo* man. The fact that the officer not only tolerated spiritual discourse but also showed a keen interest greatly perplexed the churchman more than the *Gestapo* representative, who did not know of that interest.

Despite his wanderings and rummaging around Ranck could find no hideaway, no warren, not even a burrow that would hide a human. Often seen in his company was the former French but Fascist banker Dresser. Even when Ranck was not around, the pushing and pulling of wall and panels, the lifting and prying of the Frenchman incited the curiosity of his fellow prisoners. The unrelenting effort to gain favor with his German captors eventually brought a result that he could not anticipate. In his meanderings, he encountered a downed flyer who was searching for the rendezvous point and rather than aiding him, he held him for Ranck. Two days later Carl observed but did not hear the conversation between an agitated Alois and Hans in which Alois reported, "Sir, our friend Dresser has fallen from a tree and has broken his neck and is dead. We know that he was close to and working with the *Gestapo* man and are afraid to report his death for fear that we will be suspected of causing it. What should we do, please."

As Hans later reported this conversation, he said that he told the man in charge of the French, "You are right not to report the death. There would not be much understanding at the death of a collaborator. You must report that Dresser bragged about how he was fooling the Germans and that he was giving them help so that he would have more freedom to try to get to either France or Switzerland. Bring the body here and leave it in the cow stalls. I assure you that Dresser will disappear and not be found in Germany."

That night as the other four French brought the corpse of their former fellow the only clue as to what happened to cause the broken neck was the smile and knowing eyes of the French Marxist Chalvet, which displayed no trace of sorrow. Hans then asked Carl, "Will you assist in getting this load down into the mine shaft?"

The two men, with the assistance of a rope and pulley, lowered the body into the mineshaft and under the border into the neutrality of Switzerland. Days later, a Zurich newspaper reported that a fall from a cliff had apparently killed a French prisoner of war in his apparent attempt to escape through Switzerland to France after he lost his sense of direction.

A smoldering Ranck appeared in the graveled court of the castle and loudly banged at the entrance to the living quarters three days after Dresser's disappearance. Ranck greeted the smiling Liese as she opened the door with a snarl and peremptory questions, "Where is the captain? Where is the countess? Tell them to come at once! I will see them immediately! The *Gestapo* will have answers! Get the two of them here at once."

When the two arrived, Ranck challenged, "I am going to get you. I am going to get you both. I do not know what you are doing or how you are doing it but my nose tells me that everything is rotten here. Our agents report that escapees are crossing into Switzerland in this sector. My guts tell me you are operating an escape route and getting fugitives across the border. Believe me, I am going to have you and this place watched every minute of the day. I am going to contact Berlin and insure that you, Captain, will go there for interrogation."

Carl had time to think how the words Ranck chose fit the situation.

Ranck continued, spittle both spraying from his mouth and moistening his chin, "You may be Himmler's pet, Schleiter, but we will make sure that you have not been turned against the *Reich* by this woman! And every bone in my body tells me that you, Countess, are a traitor to the *Führer*. You are a true whelp of that Jew loving father of yours! But believe me I will have my day."

Finally he stopped the cascade flowing from his mouth as through a petcock and turned on his heals to abandon not only the house but also their company. Although he slammed the door as he left Marli marched right behind him and opened the door as though in defiance. Carl joined her to watch as the *Gestapo* agent seated himself in the car and directed the driver to leave.

CHAPTER 8

⚜

October–December 1942
The Evasion

Only when Ranck was well gone did Marlene and Carl feel free to break their silence with one another. Carl spoke first, "I am not surprised at his suspicions but I am at his agitation. I fear saying that he lost control because I never want to underestimate an opponent. He is not sure of my true identity but if he can get me to Berlin, where there would be men who have nothing to fear from me, my charade would not last long. There certainly are those in the *Schutzstaffeln* headquarters who would be intimately acquainted with Captain Schleiter including a possible if not probable mistress."

Marli agreed, "Yes, there would be those there who might have known Friedrich even better than I did. But there may be another problem. The *Abwehr* is the political rival, if not enemy, of the *Gestapo*. On one side you are endangered by Kaltenbrunner's *Gestapo* discovering your true identity and on the other side you are threatened by the *Abwehr* of Canaris who would like nothing more than to expose a protégé of Himmler as false. Admiral Canaris is of the old school, and in his heart, despises the whole *Nazi* gang and the Friedrich Schleiters most of all. My father has known him for some time and has some respect for him."

"I can just imagine some situations where I am asked if I remember the time that we did this or that and I respond, 'Yes.' Then I am asked or expected to expand on the details. Or it may be that some wrong remembrance occurred with my questioner and someone else remembers that Schleiter was not there.

Or someone coming up to me and greeting me profusely as though we were the best of chums and either my silence or conversation gives me away. I really believe that if I get to Berlin I am a dead man and you and the Webers would probably be executed as well."

"Then you must flee! Go to Switzerland! Go now! The way is open and Ranck will never give you up now. I think he wants to get you if for no other reason than pride in his 'nose.' He will be another Inspector Javert, relentless in his pursuit. Please escape today or tomorrow!" begged Marli.

"I will go only if you and the Webers, and maybe even the French go, too. If I disappear now after what he said they will know that you have concealed a turncoat or a deserter or even think that I was a spy. It would be your death warrant, for the *Nazis* are without either mercy or justice. Besides with my lost leg, this is the best way that I can help bring about the defeat of Hitler and his group. By seeing to it that able-bodied airman have a chance to get back in the battle I still remain in the fight. No, I stay unless you go, and the Webers of course."

His concern for her and the Webers and his commitment to the cause of defeating the *Nazis* and their policies moved Marli enough that moisture dimmed her eyes. As she turned her face away he continued, "Another one you have to think about is your father. How long do you think he would last without being under the wings of *SS Sturmhaptführer* Schleiter?" even though he thought that the wings were those of a vulture. "In fact your flight would insure that your father was in a camp in quickstep time."

The danger that he now realized they mutually faced emboldened him to become more familiar with the young countess, "Countess, we are stuck. We cannot flee because of the danger it would bring to others and we are in real danger here. This I promise, if I am revealed as an imposter, I will do all in my power to protect you. We must get it into our minds, even to the subconscious level if we can, that you and the Webers never knew that I was not Captain Friedrich Schleiter. Certainly, you were not there when the hospital people identified me as Friedrich Schleiter. They told you that I was your husband. You told me that your married time with him was only for less than a week. I do not know what the result would be if you told them what you told me. That is, you never looked at his, uh, anatomy. You can say it was modesty and the shortness of the relationship that contributed to your confusion."

The countess of the von Krönitz and von Ritterbach families, maturing rapidly beyond her age, could find no fault in what he said. She hoped that some other solution might appear, so she wanted to talk Hans and Annaliese, more experienced and as much involved as they were. After all Annaliese, she again remembered, had been as much of a mother as she had known since her youngest days.

When they presented the situation, as they understood it, and their own conclusions, Hans agreed that the situation was serious. He estimated, "There really is no question that Ranck will succeed in having you ordered to report to *Schutzstaffel* headquarters in Berlin. It could come as an order to have a medical evaluation or for any other number of reasons but it will come. The security, the restrictions under which you go, will depend on how well he communicates his suspicions. You are correct; your peril also makes our situation dangerous."

"If I only had not come here, if I had given myself up as a downed airman, none of you would be in danger. Letting myself be mistaken for Schleiter was stupid," Carl condemned his own actions.

"Don't be a *dumkopf*," responded Hans, expressing his growing friendship and sense of acceptance and equality. After all, he was a farmer and forester and this was a farmer's son. "Our operation, what with the suspicion that the countess is under, would probably have been discovered before this had it not been for your presence as Friedrich Schleiter here in the castle. The count would, at the least, be in a camp. But what's done is done. We must deal with the situation as it is. We can not afford to be paralyzed like a rabbit hypnotized by a snake."

With all the thought that each put into the problem there was no solution that they could see that would remove the danger to them and to Marli's father, the honorable Count Erich von Krönitz.

Marlene then asked, "Can we pray? He will hear as he has heard Carl's prayers to this point. What a miracle it was that he ended in Friedrich's uniform. It was God's protection that he was saved from the fire. God kept me from knowing that he was not Friedrich immediately and automatically exposing hin. God has given us great affection for each other. We have much for which to be thankful. Will you pray with me?"

They all, with hands clasped, and with fervent hearts, quietly lifted their voices for protection. As Carl and Marli left the room their hands locked together. Carl sensed that sharing the common danger may have caused Marli to clasp his hand but...was it too much to ask that it meant more? As he caught a quick view of her countenance, he felt a riptide surge of emotion. This flood carried with it a current of hate toward the viciousness of the *Nazis*. Love desiring to lift this innocence at his side to an unknown but safe destiny floated on the powerful current carrying him.

Had Carl Solms been asked if he loved the Countess Marlene von Ritterback *und* von Krönitz he would have hesitated before he responded with a "yes." That "yes" would have had a great reservation for he knew in his heart that she was far above him not only in the treasures of this world but also in character. His love caused him to be willing to fight for and to die for this lady. Like a medieval knight his romantic love had no hope of fulfillment. He had no real hope of achieving physical fulfillment of that love, their union in marriage. He knew and acknowledged that he was content simply to serve.

That night as the countess, now of Ritterbach but destined also to be the Countess of Krönitz, let her head rest on the pillow her thoughts turned to Carl Solms of New Sendlingen, Texas. She recognized that her first rejection of the man she thought was Friedrich Schleiter had turned to a bland and neutral acceptance of this American, who might not be a real cowboy just as he maintained. At the time of the execution of the Jewish family, that acceptance had turned into a momentary rejection but had risen to a plateau of liking through the way that he had handled both the situation and her emotional reaction. Now she knew that her affection had grown beyond liking and it pleased her to think that his had also and to consider just how far her feelings might go in the future.

The wise Annaliese cautioned Carl, "Because we will be watched so closely, I think it best that you never walk outside without using your crutches. You should also have someone with you so that any spy might think that you are in danger of falling. Maybe the countess will accompany you. The more we can keep from the *Gestapo* the better."

Carl readily agreed that it would be wise, and good, to have the one he felt free to call "Marli" be an "aid" to his walks. Marlene fulfilled his wish and agreed to walk with him to steady him over the rough places.

The stormy feelings and apprehensions of that day faded in the light of the glorious day that followed. The sun seemed to grow in brightness, although its endurance seemed to weaken because the days were growing shorter. Now its strength brought forth the bright vividness of the colored leaves as well as the rich green of the pine needles. After breakfast and the finishing of chores, Marli asked, "Carl, oh, I really must be careful that I don't call you Carl in company, but anyway would you like to go with me a little in the woods this wonderful day." He responded in the affirmative with alacrity.

Following his instantaneous affirmative response, they set a course to and through the open forest, which dimmed the brightness of the sun. While their feet and the crutches sank slightly into the soft carpet of pine needles and fallen leaves the going was firm enough under the cone-bearing canopy of branches. Marli remarked, "You know, Hans knows every tree in this great forest. If one becomes damaged, he recognizes it the next time he sees it. If you look at each tree closely, you will see that it has identifying letters and numbers. When I was young I thought that there were an infinite number of trees in these woods but knew that Hans, the forest master, knew each of them. It pleased me to think that if a mere human could have such knowledge does not the great Master of all forests know every leaf, every needle that falls from His trees. It is wonderful that we are His trees, no, more than trees because we are in His image. Not one of these trees looks like Hans or is in any way like him other than they too are straight and true."

"That's right," affirmed Carl. "Although I never had this kind of forest to inspire my thoughts. Back home the woods in the river bottoms are a tangle of thorny vines, wild grapevines, poison ivy, and underbrush. You rarely walk for pleasure in them. But your thought was true and we both know that He tells us that not a sparrow or hair falls without His knowledge, and I assume, permission."

"That is reassuring in our situation." as she picked up the conversation. "But, to change the subject, how do you really think this war is going to turn out? Can the *Nazis* be defeated? It seems like Satan himself is guiding the *Nazi* leaders. I just trust that God is not aiding Hitler although many Germans, even those who accept Him, are sure that He is."

The Texan responded at once, "The Allies will win. I do not believe that either Hitler or the Japanese really appreciate the emotional reaction and determination that the attack on Pearl Harbor in Hawaii caused in the American people. From what I saw we Americans know that we are in a war without mercy. We once believed that there was too much propaganda. In the First War we were told that German soldiers bayoneted Belgian children only to find out that was not true. We discovered that was false and so will not trust many reports. Then we thought we knew, but now we know that we know. We know that we were attacked and that we did not go to war until we were attacked. It is strange how now I feel we have been under-propagandized. Few Americans really had any idea of the depth and width, of the cruelty, of the persecution of peoples by the German government."

Carl had to pause to think of ways to separate Marli and the Germans like Hans and Annaliese from the rest but in honesty could not. So he continued, "I am afraid that many good people will suffer terribly for the crimes of their leaders. I guess it is a kind of corporate guilt where populations must bear responsibility for the leaders they tolerate. I am afraid, Marli, that Germans are going to suffer a great deal from this war, far more than they have suffered so far. But what would you like to do after the war?"

Smiling piquantly, she turned to face him saying with no hesitation, "I want to go to America. I want to see New York and the Empire State Building and your capital city of Washington and Chicago where all the gangsters live and to hear the jazz music of New Orleans. I want to see the marvels of God's creation in America. I want to see the Grand Canyon, the Niagara Falls, the great beauty of the Half Dome at Yosemite, and the marvels of geology at Yellowstone. I want to see the great rolling plains where the Indians once rode. I want to see the Alamo where men died for liberty. Oh, yes, even here in Germany we remember the Alamo. I want to see the monuments to Washington, Lincoln, Jefferson, and liberty. There is too much to see and I doubt that I will have time to see all that I want to see. But what of you, what do you want to do if we survive?"

Carl hesitated before answering. The joyous anticipation that lit her eyes as she listed the things she ached to see in his native land caused him to take a deep breath. Her face glowed as wisps of dark brown hair curved about her eye and trailed over her full red lips.

"I want to work with aircraft, really with rockets. There is a man who has built rockets named Robert Goddard. I would love to learn what he has discovered about that propulsion system. I want to get married and live a nice peaceful life with many children. Maybe there is a contradiction, you know, peaceful and lots of children. What I mean is that I am tired of this danger and the killing always around us. I want to do research in rocket propulsion in an American university."

"That is interesting. My father has a friend whose son is involved in the same sort of thing. They are kind of Hitler fans because the regime has supported the rocket research program liberally. Possibly some day you will meet him if Ranck doesn't have us executed first."

The mention of Ranck's name flashed across Carl's consciousness like the flashing of a warning light on an instrument panel. "Do you think we are being watched?" he asked of Marli. "Ranck said that he would put someone out to watch the castle and its grounds."

At this moment, Udo the oldest and largest male dog came bounding up to them with every swish of tail showing the joy of his heart at having this particular human companionship.

"It is a good thing that you are not Friedrich Schleiter or else you might be less the other leg or at least an arm. Oh, my, forgive me, that was cruel."

"Please do not be sorry. I must accept the loss of my leg and a sense of humor will help. I had rather laugh than cry and I really want to be accepted as I am." Carl assured his companion but added soundlessly to himself, "Especially accepted by you."

The presence of the dog reminded Marli, "I meant to tell you that Hans has released the dogs day and night. Ranck is not the only one who can be on the alert and we have the dogs to guard the grounds. They are very protective of their territory. Our only worry is that Ranck will order them shot so that his agents can spy on us." On that dark note she directed, "Let's go back."

Annaliese watched through a window with a sweet but sly smile as the couple returned. She detected an air of increased concern on the part of the girl for the young man with the crutches. She remembered her feelings of nurturing when she began to love Hans and she felt warm and thankful for the remembrance. But she also asked, "What will come of this? They come from such different backgrounds. So many events can abort their affections. Both death and the war itself can kill their chance for love. I will light a candle at church!"

A cunning woodsman, Hans had always made it a practice to insure that no one ever followed him in his rounds as the forest master. In one of these rounds a short time later, he was thankful that he had established this practice for he discovered an American flier searching for the rendezvous of which he had been told. He took him to the road where a small bridge provided concealment and signaled him to remain quiet with hand and mouth gestures accompanying a strong "SSSSH." Hans handed over a small flask of wine, sausage, and bread present in his *rucksack*. Returning to the castle he informed the countess and Carl that like all young couples they needed to get out for some "social life." He then informed them of his discovery of the downed airman. He instructed them to stop on top of the bridge and quickly get the pilot out of sight in the trunk of the vehicle and return to the castle.

Every member of the little group knew their inherent danger. However, each also knew that they could not abandon the lone airman to die from the elements or surrender to the *Nazis*. Concern for the well-being of one lone airman was not the only consideration for taking the risk. Every capture of a fugitive endangered them as each would face severe questioning, if not torture, and might reveal sufficient to endanger them. In addition, the plan that Marli and Carl contemplated was so blatant and challenging that it might throw the stalkers off guard.

With the decision made, the Countess Marlene von Ritterbach *und* Krönitz telephoned her childhood friend Erika Randorff to ask if she and husband would be at home to receive a return call from the countess and her husband. The startled merchant's wife was well aware that her onetime friend had come under the watch of the *Gestapo's* Ranck. The request to call pleased her that the baroness remembered the old times and would be a guest in her fine home furnished in the latest modern design. After quickly conferring with her husband and weighing the advantages and disadvantages, the friend of the past set a time for the Schleiters to be at her door. After all, the countess came from the highest nobility. In the New Order Friedrich Schleiter seemed more than just a junior officer in the elite *Nazi Schutzstaffeln*. Everyone knew that Captain Schleiter was, or had been, an aide to *Reichsführer-Schutzstaffeln* [National Leader of Security Forces] Heinrich Himmler who was also *Chef der Deutschen Polezei im Reichsministerium des innerns* [Chief of German Police in the National Ministry of the Interior]. A person with such possible connections must not be offended socially.

When there were still two hours of the rays left in the day's sinking sun Marli and Carl entered the automobile that Hans had driven to the front door. Carl was resplendent in the black dress uniform of the *Schutzstaffeln*, his breast glowing with the red, black and gold of the decorations and awards that Captain Schleiter had earned.

The best that the National Socialist movement and the Teutonic penchant for uniforms could do, however, paled when the Countess Marlene von Ritterback stepped into the slanted rays of the evening sun. Her hair cascaded beyond the midpoint of her back, concealing the bareness of the back of her gown. It shimmered in the evening's reddish beams, moving in tiny waves with the slightest evening breeze and seemed to catch every ray of the decling sun and send it back,. Both gown and lipstick, so carefully saved and hoarded with other cosmetics since her father's return from Paris when peace reigned, rested in harmonious purpose to enhance beauty. Transference of the color of the calf length dress to her face replaced unneeded rouge as they tinted the smooth surface. Her whole being turned the work of the Parisian designer into a masterpiece that no human artist could match.

When, standing with her Hans in the court, Liese beheld the little one that she had loved and nurtured step into the light, her hands involuntarily flew to her face as though to say, "What has God wrought?" Her loved-filled heart sang a *Te Deum* as she thought, "So beautiful! So good!" A silent prayer of commitment followed, "Go with God!" as she handed a bouquet of flowers from the castle garden to her young mistress.

Hans, the fetcher of the automobile, at first stood expressionless as he beheld the beauty created when man worked with nature and followed the natural laws of proportion and color. Love flooded the heart of the hero of the trenches of a previous war and he had to turn his back to veil the tears starting in his eyes. The love he felt for his young mistress was so palpable that he was sure that she and the two others must feel it. In masculine fashion, however, all he could do was approach the man in the uniform and whisper, "Take care."

With the countess at the controls, the gravel ground together beneath the tires of the old Mercedes as it moved with increasing speed across the court, down the twisting drive and through the opened gate. Acting as though they had left too early to drive directly to town they slowly drove a roundabout way that happened to take them over the bridge described by Hans. A visual search from the slow moving sedan, when every sense, including instinct, keyed to detect danger, revealed none, they continued on their way to Littach and the Randorffs' house.

As they entered the residence, Marlene carefully placed the bouquet into the hands of *Frau* Randorff. The hostess needed to first secure her countenance before involuntarily exclaiming, "My God, you are beautiful!" as her nervous hands disarranged the flowers.

The Randorff children peremptorily bid the guests welcome and were quickly dismissed to their rooms as the hostess explained, "The must do their school work because we insist they get good marks. They are so smart and must be first in their class." Their hosts had brought forth their finest Moselle wine from the cellar and now directed the guests to seats. It was not long before the conversation turned carefully to the progress of the war.

Carl took a seat, with the assistance of Marli, within easy speaking distance from their host while Erika Randorff led her old friend to the other side of the room.

Randorff opened the talk between the two men carefully, "I was certainly expecting far too much but I had hoped that the Russians would have surrendered by this fall. Now it looks like our boys will have to suffer through another winter until victory comes in the spring."

Carl, remembering the account of Field Marshal Rudel temporized, "Yes, the Russians have defended their land much more than we expected." To himself he thought, "You are a lot more pessimistic, even defeatist, than you are letting on to this supposed officer in the *SS*. I don't believe you probably have the insight to see that victory is becoming more and more threatened but no one in this land dare admit it openly."

News had reached the people of Germany that events had forced General Erwin Rommel to withdraw from the gates of Cairo by mid-November. The *Nazi* news services had put him on the verge of capturing Cairo and sweeping as one jaw of a great pincer movement into the oil rich lands to the east. Airwaves and newsprint proclaimed the need to shorten the supply lines of the *Afrika Corps* as the reason for the withdrawal. Further news that American and British forces had landed within a week after the beginning of the withdrawal in the western regions of northern Africa compounded the situation.

Having had little recent news from his homeland the *ersatz SS* captain then directed the conversation in a direction of more immediate interest, "Will America be able to produce the fifty thousand warplanes their president called for in 1940? Many of our industrialists say it is not possible. What do your friends say?"

The merchant had difficulty keeping his eyes off Marli but was nevertheless able to insist, "Never! Never! Never! The Yankees do not care enough about their nation and are too soft and undisciplined to organize the way a nation must do for war. I use the term "nation" advisedly for they are a polyglot and mongrelized collection. Besides how will they ever get the necessary fuel and weaponry for their planes, no matter how many they produce, across the ocean when our U-boats are sinking every other ship and maybe next year every ship that attempts to cross the Atlantic. America will be only a minor factor in this war. They are isolated and should have maintained their policy of isolation like Lindbergh and others told them."

Carl wanted to say something that would support his false identity but could not give approval or vocal support to Hitler's cause. He thought he could honestly say, "There has been great success in Poland, Scandinavia, Greece, and Africa. What will stop the successes now?" To himself he added, "The Russian, British, and American armed forces."

The men turned their attention to the women as Erika asked her friend from the past, "Have you sought medical help for your barrenness? Here you are married to a young and apparently virile young *SS* officer but have no children. It is our duty to the Fatherland to bear as many pureblooded offspring as we can, but you and the captain have none. What is wrong?"

Carl started to say, "My injuries...," before Marlene stated her position clearly. "I do want to have children but I want them when I want them. I am not a brood mare to breed for the interest of the race. I have always said that I will bear children by the man I choose whether he be Jewish, French, Spanish, or...or American. If God permits, my womb will produce children when I am ready and not before! I am, Erika, neither sow nor cow to be bred at command. But I do thank you for your concern."

"Did the pause before she added 'American' have significance?" Carl pondered. The thought came to him, "She did seem to add 'American' deliberately. But wasn't that just another jibe at the German woman because the *Nazis* proclaimed to the world that the American 'melting pot' was only a polyglot race?"

Randorff remembered, it seemed something that he wanted to show the countess that required a seat close to her so that his hands could hold the photo album and his eyes could see far down her low cut dress. Marli understood and suddenly developed an overwhelming interest in a painting on the wall across the room that she just had to examine more closely. Erika knew that she and Marlene had discussed the work in the past but her resentment was not directed at her husband but at this "friend" in her parlor who had metamorphosed into loveliness.

After Marli had taken her seat well away from her previous location Carl reopened with, "Do you ever see Paul Ranck, Randorff? He was quite irate at the castle and I would like to apologize if we gave offense. We certainly meant none, and, really, are ignorant of what we might have done. Would you please tell him this and that we apologize." At the same time he gave a signal, that he thought was like that of a husband, to Marli that he was concerned with his leg.

She, like a wife attentive to her husband's wishes and needs, instantly arose, "Thank you so much for receiving us on such short notice. We have felt ourselves limited to the castle because of Friedrich's leg but we finally just wanted to put on our best and get out. I fear that Friedrich is having trouble with his leg once more. I trust you will excuse us?"

Excused they were, for even the hint of trouble with a representative of the *Gestapo* cancelled the comfort of their company.

After they departed Erika Randorff questioned, "I wonder if anyone is watching them," as she parted the edge of the window blind to see if she could identify the presence of the security police.

Not only because it was the era's correct social doctrine but also because he totally controlled the family assets, Ludwig Randorff could not restrain a little joke. He was sure of his position as head of the house. "I would volunteer for the job of watching your old friend because, you know, I am a loyal Party man. That girl looks to me like she is all woman. I can see why he made her marry him. You watch the cripple and I will watch the cripple's wife. That way we can both help the *Gestapo*."

While Erika Randorff had little control of her situation in marriage, she expressed herself by a glare, and turning, sped to the second floor.

Marli again piloted their vehicle slowly through the darkened town as they made a relatively unobtrusive show of pointing out the homes of acquaintances and appearing to slow to look at certain features. At one point, just beyond the edge of the buildings at a dark spot behind small trees, the car stopped. It seemed that the young *SS* captain had to relieve the pressure on his bladder, and with some difficulty dismounted the vehicle to urinate in the shadows by the side of the road. This proved no embarrassment to either him or his German companion for she drove the car on down the road where after no more than three minutes she returned.

When he again had taken his seat by his "wife" he reported, "There was no sign that we are being followed and I think I was there long enough."

Marli asked, "That was a good idea; but where did you learn to do that?"

"From reading nature books and western novels. I have read that when animals' instincts or senses tell them they might have someone on their trail they will double back just to check. I think that in English its called 'back trailing.' In the western stories I have read of men doing it as well. If some one had come along, my body functions would have provided an explanation. I guess you have always known it but I have learned that it is not unusual for men to relieve themselves like that in Germany. They could be arrested for indecent exposure in the United States."

"Very interesting, Very interesting," responded the lady, desiring to change the subject although not knowing exactly how for the moment.

It would have been easy for another car to follow them for their automobile traveled at a very leisurely pace. Carl thought it appropriate that he sit as close to his "wife" as he could just, of course, to maintain the picture of a young couple out for a romantic drive. Like Ludwig Randorff, he too was happy to be with this beautiful woman.

Marli stopped the car when they were on the designated bridge, quickly got out, put on a long but light coat, and going halfway under the structure, called in English to the pilot to come out. By the time the fugitive staggered up to the road, she had the trunk of the car open and half thrust him in as he struggled to bend into the small compartment. Carl, who remained seated in the vehicle, insured that his uniform was well covered. It seemed reasonable to both that a young lady would want to protect her finest dress with a light coat so Marli kept the coat on all the way to the castle. When all was secure, the car resumed its former speed. At the gate of the castle, Marli dismounted to ring the bell for Hans to open the entrance. As she did, Carl searched the shadows to see if they had a "friend" there watching the castle. It seemed that a shadow moved, but it was impossible to be sure.

When they arrived at the entrance to the residence Marli halted the car, and making a good show of it, helped her invalid "husband" through the entrance. Returning to the Mercedes, she drove into the shadows of the castle ruins. There Hans directed the pilot through the opening in the floor and into the dungeon. Marli comforted him and assured him that all was well in the English she had learned from the age of five. His response let her know that she now had a second young American in her care. She was also aware that she must caution Carl that he could not speak to this, his compatriot, because of security. She rightly guessed that he would be anxious to get a report from the states.

As quickly as possible she walked, with the dog Udo convoying her, to the residence where a light had come on in an upstairs bedroom as though Carl had gone there. Once he had opened and then secured the front gate, Hans extinguished his light. Other than the crunch of their feet on the graveled court and the lantern in Marli's hand, quietness and darkness prevailed. In the light of the shuttered kitchen, the young ones reported on the night events and all four made plans. The return of the young people with no apparent difficulty filled Hans and Annaliese with joy and they listened with satisfaction to an abbreviated report of the evening at the Randorffs.

Marli informed, "Carl, the flier is an American aviator. I can tell by his accent although it is not like yours. He did say, 'Thanks for the ride in the 'cah,' No, I don't know what state he is from! I didn't want to take time to get a full report from America!"

Carl reluctantly agreed, "Well, I guess you are all correct in saying that I should have no contact with him. There is no telling who it might get to if word reached America that a one legged Texas boy was operating in the land of the *Führer*. But, man, I would like to talk to him and find out how things are at home. You are right, total secrecy is our best protection but I sure wish he could get word to my folks that I am alive, at least."

He continued, "Since we are going to be so secretive I think only one person at a time should ever go to the old ruins and equipment storage area. Ranck certainly has men watching and we cannot have a flow of traffic to a barn. Someone will eventually have to take give food to the guy. We can let some time pass so he can regain some strength before we give him clothing for blending in with the Swiss. We also must make the proper arrangements made for his reception at the other end of the tunnel. Hans and Annaliese, you are the most frequent visitors to the ruins usually so you should be the ones who take food and such to him. You each often carry bundles when you go out while the countess usually only carries tools like rakes and shovels if anything. The countess will have to go out once to explain to him in English what is going on, without breaching our security."

Carl debated with himself as to whether he should attempt to have his parents informed that he was alive and well. He decided that it was not worth the risk. The spread of the knowledge of their little group made compromise by loose tongues more probable. He asked Marli, "Please find out what's going on in America and England. How are we doing against the Japs? Does he think there will be an invasion of the continent soon? I do not know how you can reassure him so that he will give you more than name, rank and serial number. If he is very cautious he might think this was a trick to get him to talk." He ended his request by telling her, "I'll see what kind of psychologist you are and if you would be a good replacement for Mata Hari."

After her conversation with the American Marli reported that he had indeed been on his guard and reported his name as Stanley Louis Schmidt. His surname prompted a remark from the German woman, "Do all Americans have German names?" He further identified his home as being in a small town with a strange Indian name she could not remember south of Boston. He took convincing that those aiding him were not with the German armed forces. The countess reported to Carl, "He said the American forces on Bataan and Corregidor have surrendered but that the Americans have attacked the island of Guadalcanal in the southern Pacific. He also told me there had been two major naval battles in the Pacific and in one the Japanese fleet had been repulsed from its attack on Midway Island. He said the war effort was in full stride and the American people remained angry and determined to see it through to a finish. He also wanted to know when he could get to a neutral country and then back to his unit."

In three days Stan Schmidt was in Switzerland and in two more weeks he was back in England flying a P-38 twin-engined fighter.

Peace and quiet reigned at the castle in the last days of September and into the first weeks of October. The residents of the castle felt rather than saw the presence of those watching their moves. Hans continued in his duties in the forests and insured the remaining four French prisoners got on with the harvest. Carl continued to exercise and to build up his ability to walk using the prosthetic leg. Round and round he walked for an hour then two hours and eventually three hours in the interior of the residence. When outside he made sure he moved on his crutches for the benefit of prying eyes.

The four in the residence were increasingly aware that Ranck was applying pressure in hopes that one would break. The great fear was that either or both of the Webers would be arrested to be taken in for "questioning." On the surface, nothing happened. They could not know that Ranck sought authority from *Gestapo* headquarters to arrest the one he believed was a traitorous Captain Schleiter. His instinct was not a sufficient warrant to risk the political fight that was sure to follow the arrest of the *aide-de-camp* of Heinrich Himmler. Even in a totalitarian state, the false arrest of a favored one could bring strong repercussions. Where the omniscience of the regime was vital, even small mistakes became dangerous when the people could see them.

The walks of Carl on his crutches with the steadying assistance of Marli continued both for their own entertainment and to demonstrate that Ranck's tactics did not intimidate them. The mind and thought of his companion never disappointed Carl. He knew he was practically minded, educated and capable in facing day-to-day contingencies, but he realized that he lacked knowledge of the wisdom recorded in the literature and history of the world. This woman possessed a great deal of both knowledge and wisdom. Forced, for the protection of one she loved deeply, into a revolting marriage she nevertheless not only maintained her sanity but with it her sense of humor. Her childhood world with its values and ideals of justice, honor, decency, culture, and grace had ended with the ascension to power of Adolf Hitler in 1933. Not only she and the Webers were in danger of constant arbitrary arrest, trial, and condemnation to prison or execution but her distinguished, wise, and good father was in more danger because he had refused to be a toady to the regime's judicial system.

From her description, Carl knew that the most debased and depraved people in Germany had gained control of all the power that government can have. Yet she was able to live, and not only to live, but also to sing, and not only to sing but also to laugh. Day by day, he realized that she lived out the idea of commitment. It was not the commitment of "I will give myself to this cause" but the commitment of her whole world into the hands of God. She did not only sing the words of the hymns she knew but she knew that her God was indeed a mighty fortress. She knew that whatever befell her and hers, all was well with her soul. Her peace made his devotion grow apace. His need to protect made his sense of impotence grow.

Many suffered in this war of Hitler's. After one walk, as the trees shone in their brightest mixture of green, gold and red, Marli and he returned to discover Annaliese sobbing. She sat at the kitchen table, a letter before her, and a disconsolate Hans holding her hand.

Marli cried, "What's the matter? What news is there?"

Hans simply handed the paper over to her, which she read more quickly than Carl thought possible. Looking up at Carl, tears rapidly filling the blue pools of her eyes, she breathed, "Rudi is dead. The letter says he fell in action on the eastern front. It says that he died a brave hero's death in the defense of the Fatherland and that he had been awarded medals for his bravery and that additional medals will be forthcoming."

Marli's voice uttered the thoughts that filled her mind as she leaned, her head on his chest, against the American, "Rudi was so good to me. He was seven years older and was always so kind and understanding with a little girl. He made me toys out of wood and things he found around the grounds. He seemed to love doing it and I loved it. He was an artist with wood, even better than his father was. I still have, or had, some things he made for me. Some are here and others are in our house at Wendenhof."

Involuntarily Carl found his arms come around the grieving girl as she sobbed. Then she suddenly spun away and rushed to kneel by her *amah*. In his heart-wrenching grief, which was as deep as Annaliese's, Hans did not sob but sat with a still face, tears like rivulets coursing over the swell of his cheeks although not a sound came from his lips. When Hans finally raised his gaze to look at him Carl knew that he wanted those eyes to tell another man of the tearing within him. He in turn willed his eyes to tell Hans that his whole heart went out to him at this moment. He sensed that the other man caught the message of the eyes.

Wanting desperately to serve, to comfort, Carl could think of nothing to do but to pour cups of the coffee that had been prepared for his and Marli's return from their walk. He set the three cups before his friends and quietly left the room. As he left he considered the value of medals; "A medal is a poor substitute for a hand in your hand, a head on your breast, a whispered word of love from a son to his mother. A nation's honor to a man is not equal to a woman's love for a man. 'Killed in defense of the Fatherland!' After Hitler and his forces invaded Russia they have the gall to say that Rudi was 'killed in the defense of the Fatherland.'"

Then Carl considered, "Is my situation different from that of Rudi, and of Conrad and of Wali? Mama has cause to grieve just like Annaliese. Her shoulders also shake with sobs. There is no comfort Papa can give to her. 'Missing in Action' until a year is up and then 'Presumed Dead.' Well, Mama has some room for hope while Annaliese can only pray that a mistake has been made. I have escaped three times. I can say that I truly believe that I fought for the defense of my home and I pray that our leaders have not deceived us, as Hitler and his gang have fooled the Germans."

Carl stayed alert to their own peril because that was all he could do. He noted that the other three, even Annaliese, seemed realists. Maybe it was the cultural memory of wars past that inoculated them slightly. War is about soldiers killing and destroying and war is about soldiers being killed and destroyed. The only evidence that Carl saw of Annaliese's grief was that she went to church more often. From what he knew of her, he suspected that she went to pray for her son's soul and to light candles for him.

Annaliese was alert enough on these church visits to take count of those watching the castle and its grounds. Each time she returned she reported to Hans and Carl any changes in the set-up of Ranck's men. It seemed that the number of the watchers was increasing and drawing closer to the grounds. Large horn-shaped devices were set up on the perimeter of the grounds with their open end facing toward the buildings. "Listening devices," murmured Hans.

"Ranck is getting serious," added Carl. "Can anyone think of anything that we should be doing?"

"No," replied Hans, "It could be that the *Gestapo* is trying to panic us. What I believe is that what Ranck says is correct. He has no real proof and if he falsely accuses one of Himmler's own without higher authority, he could be in big trouble. So just keep cool. I have checked the dungeon to see if as little evidence of use as possible is there. I even caught many spiders and bugs that I found in dark places and put them in the dungeon. I hope the spiders do their duty and set up housekeeping quickly with many webs. If the police discover the tunnel, our story must be that we did not know of its existence. That probably won't do but we will have to stick to that story under the severest questioning."

Hans could not bring himself to expand further on what he meant by the "severest questioning" although he thought it might be wise to prepare the others for the worst.

All agreed they must prepare their statements in the event that the worst happened. The great sausages called *wurst* and bread called *brot* that would resist spoiling were placed in their *rucksacks.* Each packed a piece of hand luggage ready for flight. Carl's bag included a place for his prosthetic boot. While all this went on behind the walls of the castle, observers from the outside observed only the continuance of daily routine.

Carl suggested, "Let's suppose that Ranck and his people make a search of every room in the house. What hints or clues could he find that might tip his hand that we are not what we are pretending to be?"

Marli immediately answered, "Carl, you and I have tried to show signs of affection for one another like a loving couple. The *Gestapo* has remarked that 'you have finally brought your wife to heel.' Do you not think it would seem strange to searchers that your clothes are all in one room and mine in another? I am not suggesting that we share a room but maybe you should move your clothes and other things into my room. If you need anything I could bring it out to you or if I am not in my room you could feel free to go in and get what you need."

Carl wondered how she knew what the Gestapo had said about "bringing her to heel."

"That is a very good suggestion," Annaliese encouraged. "Your room does need some men things in it. Also you had better check the reading material you have there because you know Friedrich would not allow you to have those authors that Hitler forbids Germans to read."

Hans added, "I know that you have always liked to read late into the night but I know another thing about our building. Do we have permission to go up to your room? Carl, do you want to make it up the stairs?"

Carl was not about to miss the opportunity to absorb more of the atmosphere of Marli's presence and gladly agreed to her assistance in climbing the stairs. As he entered Marli's room with the others he felt rewarded for his effort. It was not only the sweet odor in the air but the feeling of how the room reflected her personality. The decades old walls lining even older exterior battlements in Spartan like starkness represented the world of men and military. Overlaying that impression, he observed, Marli had created in her quarters a sense of intelligent womanliness.

All was not puffy pink but any observer would note that this is the room of a happily feminine female. The titles of the books told of an intelligent being who rested in this chamber.

Carl noted that the bed with its posts was clothed with down comforters like all the beds he had seen in Germany. Childhood and adolescent keepsakes hung not only from the walls but also from the borders of the mirror. Taking note of some wooden toys Carl wondered if they had been the work of Rudi. Marli followed his gaze and answered his unspoken question, "Rudi made that little boat for me when I was about eight years old. He gave me this little wooden doll with absolutely no clothes on it and told me, 'Marli, you should be ashamed letting your baby be without clothes.' So I immediately found some scraps of cloth and made clothing for my little Wolfgang."

Her own mention of the name of the dead member of the *Wehrmacht* was enough to cause immediate tears in Marli's eyes and she turned, embraced Annaliese, and whispered, "I'm sorry, little *mutti*, I didn't think."

Annaliese put her arms around her childhood charge, tears streaking her cheeks, and rendered comfort herself. "I know, my Marli child, it hurts. I am a country woman who has seen the cycle of life. We are born. We live. Some longer than others. We die. Then it is Christ's work to care for us. I have asked the Blessed Virgin to ask her Son to care for my Rudi. She will have a heart of compassion for she saw her Son die and she knows my sorrow. Now it is we who live who must continue to struggle in this life. Now that she too has lost Rudi and is a widow, Maria and her two little ones will suffer more and longer than this old woman so I dread her future."

Hans, eyes moist, interrupted with his direction to, "Look, here is the space in the wall for you to drop any book that you should not be reading. It will drop all the way to the basement and lie behind the panel there. Of course you should not have many books here for time to get rid of them may be short. Is there anything else here we should check after we bring the captain's clothes from the other room." Carl noted that when Hans gave him a rank it was always the same as that of Schleiter although he had once informed him that he was only a lieutenant. He thought it was probably for security reasons but wondered if Hans did not have a need to make him equal to the despicable SS officer.

Each promised to continue to look for anything that might betray them and then continued with an only slightly modified routine.

In the evening in addition to both idle chatter and serious conversation, the four developed a habit of playing a variety of games. In the games where partnerships were required, Annaliese saw to it that the younger couple was a team with the excuse that God would not let her oppose her husband even in a game. Her joy overflowed as she observed the two young people earnestly discussing books and as the countess instructed the Texan in philosophy and the theology of Christianity. When their talk centered on Christian doctrine they did so with one reading from a German language Bible and the other from an English Bible. Annaliese noted that as time went on not only did their heads draw closer together but also their bodies followed the lead of their heads. The relation between the two young people gave her both joy and concern for she knew that they were all engaged in a most dangerous undertaking.

Within a fortnight of their consideration of what safeguards they could take to preserve their safety, the bell at the gate rang and Paul Ranck demanded through the speaking box, "*Heil Hitler!* Open the gate and control the dogs or they will be shot! I have come for them for the *Führer's* use. Open the gate at once and leash the dogs!"

As Hans called the animals and put them in their kennel area, Annaliese pressed the button that allowed the electrically controlled gates to open. Marli and Carl watched as a small caravan of the Mercedes of Ranck, a small open truck with four enlisted *SS* passengers, and an enclosed van for the dogs drove onto the courtyard.

Carl thought that only another man could understand the anguish on Hans' face until he saw Marli's tears and knew that they were from empathy. Hans feared the dogs were in immediate danger if they attacked these interlopers. Speaking and acting with love he led first the male Udo and then the female Greta followed by the other dogs into the enclosed vehicle. He counseled the dogs to be obedient and to do well at whatever they were called to do saying, "If you do evil it is not your fault. If men do evil they have a choice but you do not. So learn, obey, and live."

As the loading was finished, Ranck addressed Carl, "I want to speak to you if you will grant me some time. Where can we talk in private?"

Pointing with a crutch from the larger room where they had moved Carl directed the *SS* operative into the little room off the library. Before the internal security man entered the room, he took the opportunity to circle around half the room with his eyes focused on the books displayed. Ranck finished this little parade with a punctuation of "Humph!"

When he arrived in the room, Carl settled in a soft chair and motioned for the *Gestapo* man to do the same if he desired. Ranck chose to remain nervously pacing in the confinement of the room. At the same time his eyes seemed to be darting and probing into every nook that he could see even as he began, "You know that my nose tells me you are false, Captain. My suspicions and my instincts tell me something is wrong. You know that I am one who says what he thinks but if I am wrong about you there could be big trouble for me. I may have already gone too far in talking to you this way but you would probably have found out anyway. I have notified some officials in Berlin of my doubts about you. Those in the *Abwehr* wanted to know everything I have on you. Some in the *SS* with the same contacts that I have were also interested in my suspicions. Those officers are mostly above me in rank although some are at the same level. I have scared the piss out of them for they know that Captain Friedrich Schleiter has the protection of *Reichsführer-SS* Himmler. They say that the *Führer* himself knows you and has a great liking for you.

"What I am saying is that were it my decision alone you would be arrested immediately. The little charades that you, the countess and her *putzfrau* are playing does not fool me one minute. I believe that anyone in Berlin who knows you, particularly Himmler would agree with my suspicions. I have asked permission to escort you to Berlin for 'consultations.' So, if you are who you say you are you will have some wonderful reunions in Berlin. If you are not and know the way out to Switzerland, you had better take it immediately. Do you have anything to say?"

Carl was ever thankful that his mind did not fail at this time. He quickly realized that he must put on a bold front and act the part of Captain Friedrich Schleiter, "Wonderful! I am tired of this country life and it will be good to get back into harness once more."

Remembering the hotel clerk's willingness to provide a prostitute in the city, he thought it safe to add, "There are also several women there who will respect me more than you do, Ranck. I must say, though, that your diligence will not escape the attention of powerful people in the regime's headquarters." Carl was proud of himself for adding the last statement, which was neither exactly a threat nor a promise of a good word in high places. Watching Ranck, he saw his eyes flick as momentary doubt flashed across his features. Like lightning though, that hesitation went as fast as it had come.

Without another word, the *Gestapo* man left the room. Outside he paused to express guileful appreciation for the dogs, "In the name of the *Führer* and the greater *Reich* I thank you for the gift of these animals. *Heil Hitler!*"

The four noted that as the three-vehicle caravan passed through the gate it stopped to permit two uniformed *SS* debark to stand watch. Carl immediately told the others what Ranck had said and added, "It looks like he is going to make sure I don't follow the option to flee."

Although each of the four was glad that their tunnel secret remained secure, they knew that Ranck had entered a course from which he could not turn. Carl expressed what each realized, "Something is going to break in our situation. I cannot go to Berlin and I cannot use the tunnel alone. Again, we must remember that if I flee you all will probably die. If we all flee, which we still can, Marli's father and possibly your sons would bear the brunt of our defection. We must think of something else."

After several hours, no one could come up with a solution to the quandary facing them.

Finally, in the evening, Carl announced, "I will try to buy time if Ranck gets permission to bring me to Berlin. In addition, Hans, will you help me hide the false foot you made me in some piece of luggage. Can you make a false bottom in one of the suitcases? The thing is large and difficult to hide but I would like to have it in the event of emergency. And, Liese, could you pack some foodstuff and drink that will not perish for me to take.

The others said as one, "There must be some other way. The *Gestapo* is sure to discover your double identity and treat you as a spy. Then they will come looking for us."

Carl answered their protests with a question, "Is there another way that offers any hope for Marli's father? I will call upon God to save me as he did from Schleiter. He has always had a cleft in the rock for me and I trust Him once more. In any event, it will give us time. But please make preparation for my going so that if Ranck and his men come I will be ready." Annaliese and Hans, seeing his fixed determination, complied with his instructions. After discovering that placing the false foot in a false bottom of his bag was not possible, Hans carefully wrapped it in a light blanket and clothing. Liese also carefully wrapped and packed cheese, sausage and hard bread.

For three days all was quiet and the routine of the castle continued although each resident felt the strain for each knew that change must occur. Carl searched the Psalms and was comforted that he was not the first to flee and know that his only refuge was his God.

It was the evening of the fourth day that Ranck once again demanded admission to the castle. This time he arrived alone in his car. After the prescribed, "Heil Hitler," he marched arrogantly into the foyer of the residence. There he commanded, looking at Carl, "Pack your things. We are going to Berlin to settle this affair. We leave immediately. Do you need help? How much time do you need to pack?"

Carl surprised Ranck by saying, "I am ready to go right now. I have been looking forward to this and have my bag all packed and here in the hallway. But where are your guards? I thought that you would escort me with an armed guard."

Ranck explained the absence of guards, "I have been told to bring you to the headquarters of the *SS* with as little attention as possible. I can use no handcuffs or fetters of any kind on you. They do not want the reputation of the *SS* or of you sullied in the event that I am wrong. They believe that I am wrong but they may want you to return to duty in any event."

Even Ranck had to half smile at the next report, "They asked me if I needed guards to handle a one legged man. I, of course, answered that I could handle you even if you had two legs. I will take your crutches when we are on the train. That should keep you stationary. Now say your goodbyes and get in the car in the front seat."

Hans first placed Carl's bag in the car and then turned, and with deep affection showing through his eyes, firmly grasped the Texan's hand in his woodworker's grasp. A motherly embrace followed from Annaliese who guarded the balance of the young man on crutches.

Then Marli seized the moment to display warmth in order to maintain the role of a submissive wife whose love had grown. This need to role-play allowed her to give vent to that impulse that was so strangely moving within her. She moved softly into the span of Carl's arms and embraced him as she kissed him with genuine passion. As she stepped away from the one who was supposedly her husband she was shocked at the reality of her feelings for this American. She could not stem the flow of her tears and in her heart committed him to the God of her father. Then Carl was in the car with Paul Ranck at the wheel and they were away.

Darkness soon concealed the trees and hillsides that passed by the windows of the automobile. Only then did the *Gestapo* agent explain, "We will drive to Rottweil, leave the car and travel to Berlin on the express. We should be in Berlin tomorrow morning."

Carl thought it safe to ask, "I am not very familiar with the towns in this area. How long will it take to get to Rottweil?"

The answer was, "A little more than an hour. I wanted to get away from Littach because I wanted no one to see us leave and ask questions that might be embarrassing at a later time."

The German was precisely correct in that it took a little more than an hour to reach the rail station in Rottweil. After parking his car, Ranck required Carl to accompany him to the ticket window. With no subtlety Ranck demanded, "*Heil Hitler!* I will have two tickets on a sleeper car for representatives of the Gestapo and the *SS*. Here are the orders and identification for both myself and Captain Schleiter." The best-laid plan began to unravel.

"Heil Hitler, but please forgive me, *Herr* Ranck. The authorities have delayed the train overnight and attached two additional baggage cars to it. The train will have not only the two additional cars but will also have a car for the guards of the materiel. You will find that they have room for you in the *Bahnhof* Hotel across the *platz*. Your train will leave at a quarter to nine in the morning. *Heil Hitler!*

After some glaring and grumbling Ranck, accepting the fact that the war effort of the *Reich* did not march to his music, drove to the hotel. After the *heiling* of the *Führer* the two travelers were provided with a room with two beds. Ranck insisted on one room. Carl smiled at the solicitous attitude that Ranck showed toward him and deducted that his companion was not serene in his suspicions. After a modest meal, the two retired for the night with Ranck in possession of Carl's crutches.

Ranck had them fed and at the rail station well before the time for the train to depart. Until they entered the rail car, Ranck paced up and down the platform in bursts of nervous energy. When they were able to board, Ranck located a compartment and pulled out a sign from his brief case that announced that the national security police reserved the compartment. He again required Carl to surrender his crutches with the remark, "Taking your crutches is probably better than having you in handcuffs."

The agent stood, looked out the window, sat, stood again, sat on the opposite side of the compartment, and stood again. After some time had passed, Ranck announced that he wanted to see if he could find out what was in the cars attached to the train and to see if he knew any of the guards. After an hour of watching the fall countryside slide by the windows, Carl became aware of a scurrying and shouting outside the compartment. Hearing shouts of "enemy aircraft, enemy aircraft" he pressed as close as he could to the window just in time to see an airplane bearing the red, white and blue target symbol of the Royal Air Force. He recognized that the airplane had two engines as it banked away from the train in a great curving arc. Even as he looked, he saw spurts of pine needles, grass and dirt paralleling the train from the impact of the machine gun bullets of the warplane that followed on the tail of the other. He then saw another of the attacking craft, then another, bank in the same course as the first.

Then he thought that the planes carried weapons other than machine guns when there was a tremendous detonation from the rear of the train. The blast seemed to lift his car as though a leaf caught in the wind, turned it on its side, and slammed it into the ground.

CHAPTER 9

❀

January 1943
Fulfillment

.

The energy released by the explosion at the rear of the train, combined with its forward motion, caused the remaining cars, not utterly destroyed by the explosion, to slide along the ground. Helpless in his quarter-rotating chamber, Carl saw the forward motion of the train cause the grass of the ground to slide by immediately outside the window. Although it only took seconds, it seemed like minutes before the motion came to a total halt. Although dazed and bleeding Carl realized the door of the compartment leading to the passageway had flown open. There was sufficient light for him to locate his bag and open it.

He noted that a scarf for protection against the November cold was on top and he used it to slow the flow of blood from a deep cut above his hairline. Digging deeper into the bag he found the boot with the artificial foot. Sitting on the window, which was pressed against the turf, he managed to fasten the foot device and the boot securely to his leg. He then threw his bag through the open door and into the hallway. He used the armrests of the seats as a ladder to climb from the compartment into the passageway. Pushing his bag ahead of him, he crawled to the end of the rail car and managed to work his way through the open carriage door to what had been the right side of the train but now was uppermost.

Suspecting the wheels might be too hot to touch, he managed to lower himself using the rods and brake lines under the rail car. His appreciation of the skill of the Black Forest wood carver increased as he was able to put weight on his amputated leg although the artificial foot provided little flexibility. When he reached the ground, he saw that others were following his path of escape.

He moved to a position that allowed those following him to place their foot on his shoulder. He could then assist them in the small leap to the ground. The only problem that arose was when an old woman, certainly someone's grandmother, stood with both feet on his shoulders, her long dress falling over his face blinding him. At the same time, she demanded that he lean down so she could dismount without jumping. With his artificial foot, this was impossible. The efforts of others finally rescued him as they commanded, "We are here, *Oma*, we have you. Let go of the captain and we will get you down." With much wailing and expression of fear that surely at least a leg would be broken she was lowered to safety. Without a word of appreciation to any of her helpers, she stalked off condemning all of the *Führer's* enemies to the deepest fires of Hades for their attack on a poor old grandmother peacefully riding a train.

Seeing a village about a quarter of a mile away, Carl headed toward it. Negotiating his way carefully over the uneven surface he found that again he was leading a trail of survivors to the hamlet even as groups of villagers were making their way toward the destroyed train.

Once at the village he entered a *gasthaus* and found the proprietor was still there. He identified himself, "*Heil* Hitler, I am Captain Friedrich Schleiter of the *Schutzstaffeln*. Is there a phone anywhere here?"

"*Heil* Hitler, yes, Captain, and the county office has been notified of the disaster. Aid and transportation should be here shortly. How many injured are there?"

"The stupid question that is always asked at times like this," Carl thought to himself, "How should anyone involved in this mess know how many injured there are. You probably should have a better idea of that than any of us do." But he answered softly, "I don't know but there must be many in the cars behind the one I was in."

Three quarters of an hour passed before ambulances and trucks arrived to carry the wounded and the dead. With each of the passing moments, the pain Carl had belatedly begun to feel grew sharper. By the time a man with a red cross on his sleeve approached, he could not stand straight and to stand at all brought great pain in his abdomen.

Carl once more found himself being evacuated to a German hospital only this time he was conscious of the movement. Due to the small capacity of the local hospital, the medical people placed him on the floor. There he discovered that he could not stretch out straight on his back but had to lie in a semi-fetal position to reduce the pain in his midsection. The two overworked doctors first saw to the needs of those more seriously injured. It was only after the arrival of two other doctors from neighboring communities another hour later that he was seen. The doctor who checked him was unsure but did not doubt that he was in great pain. It was interesting that this doctor had no time for the national greeting, *Heil* Hitler.

He informed Carl, "I can not tell the nature of your injury. The worst would be a ruptured internal organ that could be debilitating. On the other hand, you may have bruised or strained muscles. In any event, there is nothing that we can do to help you recover except give you rest and we do not have room for that. Is there a place where you can be provided for with rest and care? Time will tell how serious your injuries are."

Carl, deciding not to tell anyone how important a man Captain Friedrich Schleiter was, asked, "Is there any news of Paul Ranck? He was my traveling companion but he went to the rear of the train moments before the air attack." He did not think it necessary to add any more details.

"I am afraid that your friend will not be found among the living. The explosion was so great that it destroyed all the cars behind yours. It seems that fighters attacked the train. That is the first time we have seen them here. We are far from England but these were two-engine craft and they must have a longer range. Anyway they certainly made a mess and caused quite a bit of damage."

Carl provided, "Could you please notify someone at *Schloss Altburg* near Littach of the attack and the fact that I seem to be injured although not too seriously. The person to contact is my wife, the Countess von Ritterbach. I would also like to have any further news of Paul Ranck with whom, as I said earlier, I was traveling.

The doctor, knowing that he was treating an *SS* captain, and the husband of a baroness, assented, "Certainly, Captain, you will be informed when any definite word is received."

The physician took immediate action, calling to a nearby policeman, "This *SS* captain wants immediate notification of the status of one…What was the name again, Captain?"

"Ranck," Carl could only whisper due to the pain of forcing air over his larynx, "Paul Ranck."

The medic relayed, "Paul Ranck. The name is Paul Ranck. Was he in your custody, Captain."

"No! No! He was of the *Geheime Staatspolizei*. We traveled together to Berlin," Carl groaned.

Carl had to wait on the floor of the hallway of the hospital for three days amid talk of his heroism and leadership before Marli arrived with the car. The day before she arrived, the police notified him that they had indeed made a positive identification of Paul Ranck and had found his identity documents that showed he was an agent of the *Gestapo*. With the word of Ranck's death the words of a Psalm flew unbidden into Carl's thought, "The Lord is my rock, and my fortress, and my deliverer."

When Marli arrived the next day, Carl was tenderly carried to the car and placed in the back seat. Fortunately, his need to remain in a curled position made it easier for him to be comfortable. Not entirely trusting the injured man's judgment, the medical people gave a full report to his "wife." The doctors prescribed, "Your husband must be on strict bed rest for a minimum of three weeks. If the pain has not subsided or if at any time it increases to a marked degree, you must take him to a large military hospital for further care. Here are the locations of such hospitals in the south of Germany. We believe that he only received severe bruises in being thrown around during the wreck. But he seems like a good man who really cared about his traveling companion so take care of him."

When they were well clear of the hospital town Carl told Marli, "Ranck died when the bombs and munitions exploded. He had my crutches with him so I will have to get new ones but Hans' foot worked beautifully."

With this news, Marli pulled the car to the side of the road and wept tears of thanksgiving for the providential salvation.

"I know that I should not give thanks for the death of anyone but if he had not died you would have, my father would have, and probably Hans and Annaliese and I would have also. A war action removed him and his threat and I cannot say that I regret it. We did not kill him. Indeed, it would have been of no use for us to murder him. Now we can tell Hans and Annaliese of our deliverance."

The slightest bump in the drive back to the castle brought a shooting pain within Carl but he was so happy that he took the pain to his heart in appreciation of the rescue it brought to mind.

Marli, who had wiped her tears away, reported, "We told the guards at the gate about the attack and the explosion but we did not know what had happened with Ranck so could tell them nothing. They only knew that he was leaving on official business and that you went with him. Apparently, Ranck has kept them in the dark about his suspicions about you but not our house. He told them that they were watching the castle for your protection although he never said from whom they were protecting you. They were just to report every activity they observed on the castle grounds. I will stop and tell them that we were informed that their leader is dead."

After more than two hours, driving over the curving road that led to Littach, they arrive at the gate and Marli was true to her word. When the guards heard that Ranck was dead they looked at one another, and then one asked, "What should we do now, Captain. We were assigned to a special detail to Ranck. If he is gone, to whom do we answer? You are an *SS* captain, can you give us instructions. We don't want to desert our post without orders."

"Report back to your permanent unit and inform your commander that Captain Friedrich Schleiter relieved you of your post. Tell him that although I was seriously hurt, I trust the care I will be given by my wife and her servants."

After these instructions were given by the man on the back seat, Marli drove up the hill to the castle grounds where Hans and Annaliese waited, having been alerted by the ringing of the gate bell. With great care Hans and Marli assisted Carl into the home. Brooking no discussion, Marli directed that Carl stay downstairs. She further directed Hans to set up a cot with a firm mattress for the invalid. After quickly accomplishing this and determining that Carl was up to it they discussed the new situation. Only a wait and see policy made any sense because no one had any idea if the strict surveillance would continue in the absence of Ranck.

Carl's restriction to bed allowed much time for reading and discussion with Marli under the approving eye of Annaliese. Marli probed into the mind and values of the stricken man.

"When you were about thirteen or fourteen what did you want to be when you were an adult, Carl?"

"Well, before I was thirteen I think I wanted to be a cowboy or Indian, but really couldn't make up my mind. I liked Ken Maynard and Tex Ritter. Ken Maynard was a little guy and guess I liked Tex Ritter because, obviously, he was a Texan. After that, I thought it would be great to be a football coach and come up with new and revolutionary plays. Then when I went to college, I thought I would be an airplane designer. The closest I could get to that at the time was to study mechanical engineering. Wouldn't you know that the year I graduated the college began to offer a major in aeronautical engineering?"

"But what were your personal desires and goals? Did you want to get married? Did you think you wanted to be a father? You told me of Lydia but did you have other girl friends?"

"Sure, but I guess it would be better to call then friends who were girls. Honestly, I believe that some of them wanted to get serious but I did not. Lydia was the first girl who seemed to like to talk about serious things. Before that, the girls only wanted to talk of parties, clothes, and other people. Lydia liked to talk about ideas and, I guess, what might be called philosophy."

"Did you read books of philosophy? Have you read the classical philosophers beginning with Socrates?"

"No, I really can't say that I have."

"What of the medieval period. Did you study any of the thinkers of that period either in school or on your own?"

"Give me some names to think about but I think the answer is going to be 'no.'"

"Well, there is Anselm of Canterbury and Peter Abelard, now there is an interesting story, and the Muslim Averroes and, oh, Thomas Aquinas."

"Nope. Sorry, lady, but I guess I am an ignoramus," he insincerely apologized.

"And the more modern students of ideas such as Nietzsche, Kant, and Kierkegaard?"

"I have only heard their names and know that they lived and wrote. I cannot tell you one thought that came from them or one book any of them wrote. I guess I am just a dumb old farm boy of a Texas Aggie sorely lacking in knowledge of philosophy. But I did use an elective to take a course in European history from a professor named Meadows. He said he was a robe and sword historian and I think he meant that he taught little about thought. He believed in what he called the 'wave theory' of history. By that, he meant that there are great waves of historical movements that sweep all before them and carry individuals who ride them to greatness. His favorite example was Napoleon whom he said caught the wave of nationalism and rode it until it encountered the same wave going in opposite directions from Russia and Spain."

"And what do you think of your President Roosevelt?"

"Uh, what shall I say? I guess I believe that there is good and bad in his policies. The good is that he may have prevented a revolution in America. It could have been a Communist one or it could have been a Fascist one like here in Germany. The people were desperate during the Depression and wanted economic help. The bad is that he centralized more and more power in the national government in Washington. I think his policies have diminished the sense of individual responsibility among Americans. But again the professor said that this also is a wave that will roll over anything that gets in its way."

Disappointed in the shallowness of his reading knowledge, she continued to find that his commitment to the best values impressive.

"Who are your favorite figures from the Old Testament?"

"Well, any of the great figures who believed God. I guess David because he showed repeatedly that he did believe God. First as a boy he fought Goliath because he believed God would give the giant over to him, then he refused to murder King Saul because God had said that he, David, would be king and he trusted God's word. After all, God did describe David as 'a man after my own heart.' I can't choose more wisely then God."

"Carl, what qualities do you look for in a friend?"

"Hmm, let me think. What did Bruce, Gary, and Steve have in common? They were all my friends. They were all three loyal and honest. While they were no geniuses, they were all intelligent and did not have to worry about grades. They were serious but not too serious. I guess, in a way, while they were competitive they were not impressed with themselves. But, as I think, it seems that they all had a really serious side. They seemed to want to commit themselves to something. It seems to boil down to that I like people who are serious about their integrity but have a good sense of humor."

Another time she asked about the members of his immediate family and laughed at his imitations, with obvious affection for his targets, of his family members.

"Now, Papa is a really good man but he makes me smile when he tells me a thousand times over, 'Corl, see dat tree?'

'Yes, Papa.'

'What ist doose grueen tings ahn it?'

'Leaves, Papa.'

'Are dey dollar bills, Corl?"

'No, Papa.'

'Den remember, money don't gwown trees!'"

Occasional Marli's peals of laughter echoed through the house as Liese looked at her husband with an involuntary but most welcome smile on her face.

Although a European aristocrat whose families claimed great estates, Marli questioned whether he was richer than she was in the real wealth of living. He described so many things of his life before the war. The great family Christmases with grandparents and cousins, the high school football games with cheerleaders cavorting before the stands, and the pranks played on other cadets in college. All these descriptions carried a great joy of living in their telling. His favorites that brought not just a smile to her lips and laughter to her usually serious eyes outlined the hunting for raccoons and opossums.

"Gus Eberhardt and I were out hunting 'coons' one night when we were about sophomores in high school in the river bottom...."

"Wait," she interjected, "I thought raccoons were land creatures and not water animals. I don't think I understand what you mean by the river bottom."

He laughed, "The 'bottom' is not the bottom of the river but the woods that followed along the stream outlining the lowest part of the shallow river valley. Anyway, Gus and I were hunting and our dogs chased a coon up into a little bitty old tree. The tree had lots of leaves on it but it was not big at all. Well, we grabbed that tree and shook it as hard as we could. Out jumped a coon and it ran lickety-split with our dogs right on his tail. Before we could move or anything, another coon jumped out of the tree and ran into some brush not far away and we did not see him come out. We could not see him in the brush but old Gus said, 'Listen, Carl, you get on the other side of the brush pile and I will go in and drive him out and then you shoot him, okay. But be careful and do not shoot me, okay?'

"I said, 'Okay, you go in and chase him out and when he gets away from the pile I'll blast him.'

Gus was in the brush pile a couple of minutes when I heard him scream, 'Oh, no! Oh! No! Oh, dammit! I've been shot.'

"I said, 'What do you mean you've been shot? I haven't shot and I didn't hear you shoot.'

"'If I get upwind of you you'll know that I've been spray-shot by a danged big ole polecat and you had better look out cause it looks like he's coming your way.'

"That stink was still on Gus when we went to school two days later on Monday."

"But, Carl, I don't understand. What is a polecat? I never heard of a cat that had a spray weapon."

"A polecat is a skunk. Don't you have skunks in German forests?"

For some reason she laughed until her sides hurt at this and many other descriptions of the carbide lights bound to his head and the little eyes that revealed the presence of the prey. The reality of the great freedom that he had known as he matured, she compared to the organized life of adolescence in Germany even before Hitler.

The countess indulged her curiosity during the days of enforced inactivity with the young man whose experience of life was so different from any she had known or knew of.

"What was your university, or as you say, your college life like?

"A&M is all male and all military. It is an authoritarian environment with the senior cadets at the top of the student body. At the bottom are the first year students, or 'Fish.' They must run errands for the second, third and fourth year students, and have a regular regimen of activities they must perform. The sophomores, or second year students, really give the Fish a hard time. The student body is organized in military units. A 'Senior Court' enforces discipline and deals with honor violations and the such. There is no representative government like other American schools."

"But what do you do for companionship with girls? You did mention Lydia, you know."

"Oh, girls come to campus on weekends by car, train, and bus. They come for the football games and the dances as well as to see their boyfriends, if they have one. I told you this was the way I met Lydia. It was what is called a 'blind date.' That is a date where neither has met or seen the other. Many weekends big bands come to the campus and huge dances would be held in the dining hall. That building, Sbisa Hall, could seat over five thousand. When the chairs and tables were moved it made it a magnificent dance floor."

"The atmosphere was austere but we did have a great deal of fun with one another. We played tricks and shared experiences. In many ways, the stress we all encountered did not make us hate our days in college but bound us closer to it and to our friends there. Of course, my special friend that I told you about before was Bruce Wishart. He was as close as any brother I could have. We shared a small room for four years and really learned about each other.

"Tricks we played on each other? You want to know of our pranks? The simplest was 'drowning out.' All this involved was throwing a bucket of water on someone in the middle of the night they were sound asleep. There were meaner tricks like putting a goat in someone's room when they were gone for a weekend.

"My college was a poor boys' school. It did not have a lot of prestige throughout America except maybe in farming. In Texas, however, many mothers wanted their sons to wear the uniform. With the threat of war it became somewhat patriotic to go to A&M."

She discerned an uncomplaining spirit in the presence of pain that he could not conceal when he changed position ever so slightly. For a week, she worried about his inability to eat and she thought she saw his weight drop. Then it seemed that he grew stronger each day as the pain faded. Sitting with his back propped against pillows became the normal position for both reading and talking with Marli.

Carl, in turn, sought to know the young countess better. When asked, she was glad to tell him of her favorite writers and thinkers and explain briefly what they believed. When he asked, "What were you like when you were an eleven or twelve year old? Did you like dolls? What did you do for fun?"

"Let's see, that would have been the year before Hitler came to power. If we were at Wendenhof I did not have any children for playmates so I would ride, horses that is. My father had a wonderful stable and loved to ride and taught me to love it and sit well also. Of course, the horses are all gone for the war now. I think the first time I ever saw Friedrich Schleiter was when I was riding. He tried to stop me. I do not know if I was frightened or just a snob, I really was a haughty little kid up there, but I went right by him as fast as I could.

"When we were here at Altburg I played with Liese's boys and with Erika. Of course, because I was the highest ranking in the social order I always had to be the main character. The boys teased me and said either I would grow out of being a little snob or my father would get it out of me. How I do regret what I was in those days!"

"Did your father ever know or meet Hitler, that is did he ever have a chance to talk to him?"

"No, he said that he never spoke a word to him and never wanted to speak to him. He was able to observe him at close range at the Olympic Games in Berlin in 1936. My father really believes that Hitler is criminally insane because of his behavior at the Olympics. He once demonstrated to me the rocking motion that Hitler made while seated in the stands. He said that he had seen that same behavior in paranoid criminals in the courtroom many times. He fears Hitler because he believes that he is diabolically clever and possesses a powerful presence. My father is austere, some would say even cold, but he is highly moral with a deep sense of justice. He abhors those church leaders who compromise their faith for the hyper-nationalism of Hitler."

Father Nimitz did not delay when told by Annaliese of the explosion of the train and the injury to Captain Schleiter but came to the castle as soon as he could, and upon gaining permission to see the injured man, approached him. With a broad smile he complimented, "You are a hard man to kill, for that I am very glad. I would have missed you and our little talks. I believe that the countess would have missed you, also, and I know that Annaliese and Hans would have mourned. As we see, you are alive, although maybe not so well. There will be a candle for you in our little church. What of the attack? I guess it must have been an English bomber. Someone said machine gun fire hit the explosives in the baggage cars. Do you know what kind of planes attacked the train?"

Carl answered the interrogation, "We were attacked by twin-engined fighters with English markings. They obviously have a long range and probably had wing tanks to increase their reach, which turned out to be quite impressive. They certainly were armed with machineguns. I do not know if bombs or machine gun fire started the explosion. I would guess that they were American made P-38 Lightnings although the English probably were flying them."

"You do know your enemy aircraft. I didn't know that you were interested in such things. I am quite surprised," remarked the good padre.

"Uh oh," Carl remembered. "I talked too much about that. Keep your mouth shut, Solms. What you say is more likely to get you exposed than what you don't say."

In the middle of his second week of convalescence after the sun's light had dimmed and while he animatedly conversed with Marli, Hans handed him an official looking envelope.

Fearing some news that would endanger all those in the castle he carefully and with hesitation slit the envelope. Having been shown the letter by her husband on his way through the kitchen Annaliese had joined Marli and Hans for the opening. Like the sun coming from behind a storm cloud so the smile came upon the countenance of Carl as he read the contents. Without any other word, he handed the pages to Marli, "Please read it to Hans and Annaliese."

Complying, some of the words that stuck in Marli's mind were, "You are hereby placed on extended convalescence leave by the personal authority of the *Führer* and at the request of *Reichsführer-Schutzstaffeln* Heinrich Himmler. You are to return to duty only when you know that you are fully recuperated. Because of the reports of evaders escaping the Reich in your area, when you are recovered you will assume the duties of Security Chief of the region. Your orders are enclosed."

The directive gave more information with an exhortation to assist in Party affairs in the whole of Swabia. Attached to the orders Himmler had taken time to write a personal note

"The *Führer* and I are aware of your contribution to the sacred cause of the purification of German blood. He commented on the total zealousness with which you have rooted out the contaminants of our Aryan genetic heritage.

We are pleased that the German gods have seen fit to preserve your life two times. On you is the stamp of providence and you will find my orders directing you to continue your search for the Jews, Gypsies, and other pollutants of this Aryan nation. As a young man you must guard yourself for you represent the hope of the German people. I trust that I will have your complete loyalty in the future.

I must warn you, however, to be careful in your actions and statements. You have powerful enemies here. Your father-in-law has powerful friends who have an extremely low opinion of you. One has been reported as saying that the Baron von Krönitz would rather have his daughter a widow than your wife. We have not been able to verify that report as to its veracity or to whom he may have made the statement. Many of the count's friends have close connections to the *Abwehr* and its director, Admiral Wilhelm Canaris.

On the other side is Ernst Kaltenbrunner of the R.S.H.A. He wants my position. He will seek to destroy anyone like you who he thinks loyal to me. I believe that he is more dangerous to us than Canaris and I know his agents are watching you closely.

Heil Hitler!

s/Heinrich Himmler
Reichsführer—

"Well, my friends, what do you think of that? I am not only delivered but am honored by Himmler. That part about continuing to search may give us more room to operate. But this we know, unless this is some kind of trap, we are pretty safe for the immediate future."

"Oh, this is wonderful. This is too wonderful!" asserted Marli as she bent over to throw her arms around his neck and kiss him on the cheek.

"Indeed it is wonderful," concurred Hans. "It seems a miracle. My lady," he continued to the countess, "Do I have your permission to fetch a bottle of the good Rhine wine that is well hidden in the cellar?"

"Yes! Yes! We will have a party! Annaliese, what do we have ready that will be good with the wine." The jubilation went into the evening.

Later that night Carl took time to consider the warning about those, who being Himmler's enemies, were also his enemies.

The breakfast tray brought by Marli in the morning carried a decoration of an evergreen vine around the rim with a single blossom in the center. The evergreen encircled the cup of coffee and three slices of dark bread with butter and preserves standing ready on the tray. A beautiful silver napkin ring lay atop a folded and pressed linen napkin embroidered with the monogram, "MRK."

"Oh, my," exclaimed the patient, "Is not this the fancy do! Is there meaning to all this decoration?"

"Yes, it means that we are having trouble getting real coffee and this is half real and half imitation. It is not too bad this way, but we may come to a time when we have no real coffee."

"But what of the napkin with the letters and the ivy and the flower?"

"Oh, ho! It is hard to get anything by you! I chose to have Ritterbach in my monogram along with my first name as well as Krönitz. It stands for Marlene Ritterbach Krönitz. If I put the 'vons' in I would run out of breath."

"But what of the flower and the wreath?" Carl doggedly asked.

"That, oh that, I tried to get fancy and artistic but it is silly. The lone flower is you surrounded by the evergreen, which means that you will always be surrounded by lov..., life." Marli responded as a tinge of charming crimson crept across her cheeks.

She then turned and hastened into the kitchen to return not only with a tray for herself but also accompanied by Hans and Annaliese, and, settling in a chair with the tray balanced, she began.

"We three think it would be good to talk about the new situation. Hans has seen no evidence of men spying on the castle. You seem to have a ticket to go wherever you want, at least in the county. When you are well again, we believe that you should cement your standing by acting as if you are searching for traitors and Jews. The townspeople suspect that there is at least one *SD* agent in town because a teacher was arrested and taken away. It seems some of the people heard him say that he did not think Hitler was so great. He was a good and learned language teacher."

"*SD*," Carl interrupted, "What is that? Part of the Gestapo?"

"No, for the regular German it is worse. They are the secret security police. They do not wear uniforms and people cannot identify them in any way. They are your neighbors, friends, acquaintances, even your children. Some of the agents serve because they really believe in the *Nazi* cause, some serve for money, and some serve to save themselves or their loved ones from the camps. The *Sicherheitsdienst* is not above using Jews to expose those not totally devoted to Hitler. Almost for sure there is at least one in Littach," explained Hans.

Marli added, "It might be possible for you to find out who the agent is so that the good people of Littach might be warned." Carl questioned to himself if she meant that all the people of Littach were "good"? He decided that she meant those who would say something derogatory about the national leaders and the Party.

Carl cheated on the medical order that called for three weeks strict bed rest because his pain rapidly faded after one week. Carefully he negotiated his way about the house and was again thankful for the skill that the Black Forest born Hans had with wood. Over the months, Hans had divulged that his father had been a highly skilled wood carver. While the son had accepted the opportunity to become responsible for the forest, "I was taught to love wood and in the forest I can love the stuff from the beginning." Yet he maintained much of his father's skill with his hands and tools.

Hans told Carl that he loved the smell of wood and that he could differentiate between the odor of each variety of tree and its wood. "My father taught me that when I had a piece of wood in my hands I had to love it. A tree or part of a tree had to die for me to have the chance to work it. I always asked the wood for forgiveness as I spoke to it, 'I know this shaping is painful to you but I promise that you will be beautiful when I am through. We know that you would have died someday anyway but when I am finished you will be so lovely that men will want to protect you and keep you forever.' Then the wood would say 'That's okay, Papa, just remember it hurts more when you cut across the grain.'"

The new crutches Hans presented as Carl began to feel the need to move quickly demonstrated the artistry that a son had learned and inherited from his father. The woodsman humbly offered extremely serviceable crutches that bore the beginning of a master carver's decorations. In the evening while Marli and Carl talked, Hans took the crutches into the kitchen where he and Annaliese would share the day's events. There his little sharp-bladed knife would add to the finely etched decoration of the supports. With the passage of time, the decoration included not only the trees of a forest but also the outline of Castle Altburg and its great hill. Then the figures of a man and a woman walking hand in hand, eyes focused on one another, emerged under the magical knife wielded by Hans. Each time there was an interval in the use of the aids Carl looked forward to seeing what the craftsman had added.

Carl appreciated both the fine work done on the crutches and the quick mobility they provided. It took minutes to secure his severed leg boot in order to escape bedpans and necessity often did not afford that time. He did feel free to use the crutches less often as he again exercised and inured himself to the discomfort of the boot. Almost three weeks to the day following the aerial attack on the train, he asked Marli, "Would you walk with me for a little? I am anxious to go outside."

With a voice that reflected more joy than a simple assent she delightedly responded, "Of course I will go with you! You may need my support at times. You must dress warmly for we have snow falling and you must take care not to slip and fall. Let me get our wraps and we will be off."

Carl examined the promise that she would "go with you." How far would she go? There was no way that a member of the highest German nobility would go to America with him. He wanted desperately to think that, but disciplined himself not to have that dream.

Their little walks began again as November phased into December, but grew longer when the weather permitted. They renewed their visits to Littach town where doors opened more generously to them. Wherever they walked, an arm of the countess always linked under his arm in the event he "might need her support at times." Himmler had made sure that the Party apparatus in the county knew that there was a new man in charge of security in that part of the country. Now Carl came to be even more in favor not only with the local authorities but with the townspeople, not a stranger from the north to be honorably tolerated. The obvious favor he possessed with *Reichsführer-SS* Himmler made him one whose good will should be curried.

It was a week after Carl had first regained his mobility that Marli approached Carl and reported, "We have received an invitation to a *soiree* at the home of Ernst and Ursula Greider.

"They say Major Erwin Foltermann will be the honored guest. He is the chief of the district *Gestapo* and says he has never made your acquaintance. Ursula said that he particularly requested that you and I be invited. I think we simply have to go. It would be suspicious if we declined."

Carl cautiously responded, "Could it be a trap? Think. Did Friedrich ever have a chance to meet him? You would know that better than I would."

"He stayed in this area for less than a week. I am sure he did not meet him then. I do not know if they met in Berlin. It certainly is a possibility," responded Marli. To which he added, "There is nothing to do but go and be careful in what we say. I got along with you for weeks when everyone thought I was Captain Schleiter. Maybe I can get by him for one night."

While Carl dressed in the black uniform of the *SS* with a red and black swastika armband on the left sleeve of his jacket Marli put on a seasonable black gown that swept the floor as she walked. Her waist long dark brown hair, topped with a jeweled tiara, rippled and glistened. As she entered the upstairs hall from her room he involuntarily exclaimed, "God in heaven, you are beautiful!"

Pleasure flooded her features as she acknowledged, "Thank you. Do you really think so? What would your mother in New Sendlingen, Texas, think about such a woman as me?"

"She would love you as the whole world would love you if the whole world could only know you."

She took up the discourse, "I am not concerned about the whole world loving me but there are a few who I dearly want to love me. I want my father to love me but I think I have separated myself from that love. Carl, he is such a good man, so straight and true. You are much like him in your character although you do not have the learning in philosophy and the law of man and God that he does. I am not saying that you are not intelligent but that he has had the benefit of being educated as a baron of Germany in Europe's finest universities."

The Texan thought, "There it is. Never have I wanted anything so much in my life compared to the desire to have her as mine forever and to hold her. She is the daughter of a European baron and is a baroness in her own right. I am a refugee from a cotton farm on the prairie of south Texas. Like she said, her father is a graduate of the greatest universities in Europe. My father never entered high school. No, don't let your heart be broken with dashed hopes."

With neither saying another word, he offered his arm, which she held tightly against her side as they descended the stairs. Even through the multiple layers of cloth the softness of her body permeated his senses and caused his inward groaning to grow more profound.

By the order of Heinrich Himmler, the car and driver previously assigned to Paul Ranck were now at the call of the new security chief. As they left the castle residence, the car was waiting with the back door opened and manned by the driver. Carl had never learned the driver's name in his encounters with Ranck and now, after a perfunctory *Heil* Hitler, took the opportunity to say, "I am sorry that I have not had the opportunity of hearing your name but I believe that you must know who I am. Would you please tell me your name?

"*Heil* Hitler, sir, I am Corporal Ludwig Pfefferkorn of the 56th Brigade. I have been assigned as your driver."

"I can see that you have, Corporal. I would like you to meet my wife, the Baroness von Ritterbach, whom I doubt you have met. You might be called upon to drive her from time to time. Ranck was unmarried, was he not?"

"Yes, indeed, he was unmarried," answered Pfefferkorn, struggling to keep his eyes straight ahead and off the form and features of the goddess-like woman.

As they entered the home of the Greiders, both the host and hostess greeted them with great generosity but with some surprise. "Oh, you are walking on your own now, Captain Schleiter. Did you get an artificial limb?"

Carl did not tell the whole truth but only a part, "Yes, I was fitted with a prosthetic leg. I would not call it totally comfortable but it gives me far more freedom of movement than did the crutches."

To this their hostess responded, "You certainly move well. Whoever did the work knew what he was doing."

Carl wondered if the blue eyes of *Frau* Greider did not take on more of a shade of green when she turned to talk to Marli. It must have been something in the coloration of the room and its furnishings for as he looked at the men and women even brown eyes seemed to become a little like emeralds; although the eyes of the men only had the jade look when they were observing him. Strangely, the reverse was true of the women in the group. *Frau* Ursula Greider took Marli by the hand and led her and Carl to the table where there was a fine layout of *hors d'oeuvres.* The hostess then insured the placement of tapered glasses of wine in her guests' hands. She explained, "Major Foltermann has not yet arrived but he will be here shortly. He told me that, with my permission, he would be late.

"He said again that he is anxious to meet you, Captain Schleiter, as you will be working closely together here. Will you excuse me now while I mix with our other guests?"

Both Marli and Carl were glad to have a quiet moment to move to an isolated spot. Carl asked, "Well, what do you think?"

"I do not sense anything that seems dangerous. All seems very normal but here comes Erika. I have seen her moving from group to group and now she comes our way. Be careful. She may have been a friend once but I do not trust her now."

"Marli, my dear friend. You do look luscious tonight. You are very cruel because you are making all the men's eyes pop out of their heads. That may be a crime against the war effort. We do not have enough men for the Russian front and you cause German men to lose their eyes! You are not doing your bit to provide soldiers and mothers for the future of our *Reich*. Of course I am just teasing and joking." declared the merchant's wife. With hardly a pause she continued, "Oh, look we have a new arrival."

Carl and Marli did look and discovered that the new arrival must be the *SS* Major Foltermann. Like Carl, he was clad in the uniform of that organization but with the rank of major.

Marli's old friend Erika maintained her control of the conversation; "Ursula is bringing him over here. I will be very interested in what he has to say and I appreciate Ursula bringing him to me.

"Good evening, Major. We are so glad to have you in Littach. We really don't see you very often."

Ursula Greider broke in to introduce the major to Marli and then Carl to the major: "Major Foltermann, may I present our highest representative of the nobility, the Baroness Marlene von Ritterbach Schleiter. Captain Schleiter, it gives me pleasure to present you to Major Erwin Foltermann, or have you met before?"

Carl maintained his silence, waiting to take his lead from the senior officer but hoping that Foltermann had never met Schleiter. Foltermann denied, "I have never had the pleasure of meeting the renowned young captain. He is conscientious in moving excess people to the eastern territories. That is why I requested this affair of Greider. I thought it was the best way to meet you, captain. I do understand that you have had some close calls so the gods must be looking out for you.'

Carl decided that boldness might be the most cautious approach. Taking the senior officer by the elbow he guided him away form Erika Randorff and posed a question, "Have you been in Berlin, major, it seems that I may have seen you there because your face is very familiar. Of course, you are right. I have been through some hard things and sometimes my mind forgets. I know that I am not as sharp as I once was." There, that provided him a little out in the event that Schleiter had had a conversation that should have been unforgettable.

Foltermann's reply brought relief, "No, I have not been at headquarters for years and I am sure that we have never met. It is good that we have now because we will almost be working in harness together. We are so close to the neutral Swiss that this area might be a good escape route for anyone trying to leave the *Reich*."

Wanting to act as he imagined a real *SS* operative would in such cases, Carl requested, "You will keep me informed about any activities in your sector. It is sure that I will let you know of anything I discover. By the way, would you have time to give me some hints on how to carry out my responsibility for this area's security? I know how to round people up and put them on trains to the east but I have never had security duty before. I would be glad to drive over and see your operation and get your instruction."

Flattered by the request Foltermann agreed, "It would be a pleasure and an honor to be able to help an aide to our *Reichsführer* Himmler. Captain, you do me great honor." He then submitted to temptation and turned to the captain's lady, "I hope that occasion might permit you to bring this lovely lady over to my headquarters. She would certainly turn the heads of my men. I risk a great deal in asking you to let her accompany you for her appearance will ruin my unit's efficiency for days if not weeks. All day my men will dream of you, baroness. Captain Schleiter, I congratulate you on your capture of such a beautiful wife. Now I must circulate. Even in the *Reich* there yet remains politics."

"It is good to know you, Major Foltermann, and I look forward to working with you. We would like to know you better and hear of your family. Until we meet again."

Marli murmured, "Why don't we circulate, too. If its politics maybe we can pick up some political intelligence. Oh, there is Field Marshal Ulla von Rudel talking with the Schlenkmanns. Shall we see if their conversation is open?"

Carl agreed, "Yes, it would be good to see the Field Marshal's wife again. He seemed a good man and I would like to know how he is doing in the east."

Slowly they edged over closer to the three-person conversation, attempting to make eye contact all the way to see if they might be included in the talk. As they did Carl, alert to the constant threat of a misstep, noted that Erika Randorff maintained a short distance behind them. When Ulla von Rudel looked their way she immediately welcomed, "Friedrich, Marlene, do come join us," extending her hand to Marli. Continuing she informed them that, "We were just talking of you, Friedrich; you have now closely encountered death again but survived again. Poor Paul Ranck, such a man, so diligent and aware. The two of you must have been going to an important meeting regarding the security of our Swiss border. Now you alone are responsible for that safety. You will be having contact with the Swiss officials. The Swiss have been cooperative with the *Führer* and have not caused any trouble. They do not want the Jews in Switzerland any more than we want them in Germany. But if they help, you had better bring our little lady here some chocolate."

"That is a thought but I do not know how the war has impacted their imports. It is hard to see how something could get into Switzerland when we and Italy completely surround them." commented Carl, "But we will see."

Carl and Marli lingered and talked with several others before leaving. As the evening had progressed Carl had often thought, "These people are the enemies of my country. They are my enemies. I act as their friend, and had circumstances been different, I could have been a friend. But they have been contaminated with ideas that are foreign to what I have learned. So we are enemies. But not Marli, no, she was . .vaccinated.. was . . inoculated with the teaching of Christ. While she lived in a corrupt culture she remained uncorrupted by the grace of God."

Pfefferkorn, who would prove faithful in his duties, pulled his vehicle to the front of the house when he spotted them coming out and had a rear door open when they reached the car.

Marli entered first. She slid half way across the seat and signaled Carl to enter by the same door.

Her position on the seat meant that only their clothing separated their bodies Carl noted with some wonderment and subdued pleasure. As the car pulled away from the curb, he sat with his hands on his knees. Suddenly he felt her hand on his as she said, "It was a nice evening, was it not, Friedrich?"

The false *SS* captain now regretfully understood that they continued to play the loving couple game for the benefit of Pfefferkorn but had no trouble agreeing that, "Yes, it was a very nice evening, darling. You were the star of the occasion and I was the envy of every man there." Thinking further he continued, "It was wonderful!" To himself he added, "I wish that we could have this kind of evening and many other such evenings together forever."

Marli then discussed the gowns of the other women in universally complimentary terms.

Carl expressed different views, "Erika's dress was nice but Ursula's obviously tried to conceal the unconcealable and *Frau* Field Marshal Rudel, well, she looked like a Field Marshal.

"Friedrich, you're terrible," smiled the lady as Carl was able to see another smile on the face of their driver.

"You indeed were the most beautiful."

With a slight laugh, Marli said, "Thank you. That means a great deal to me," as she continued with her hand resting over his on his knee. He turned his hand over as to hold her hand in a soft, affectionate grasp. He continued to hold it all the way to the castle and she let it lay in his like a sleeping, warm, little dove. As the car took the turn on the way to the castle her head swung until it touched his shoulder and there she permitted it to remain for a second longer than necessary.

Carl enjoyed the drive and regretted the end as Pfefferkorn made a wide circling turn to position them right at the door of the residence and had the rear door open before Carl could manage to get his wounded leg out.

Lights dimly lit the interior of the house and it became quickly obvious that Annaliese acted out her role as substitute mother as she waited up for her charge and her "date." "Well, how was it?" the elder woman wanted to know. "Did all go well? Were there any tricks?"

Marli assured her, "Everything was fine. It seemed that 'curry' was the spice of the evening. Not that it was on the food or anything. It was all over their approach to Captain Friedrich Schleiter, the fair-haired boy of Himmler. We should all be ashamed of associating with one who connects with such people as Himmler and Hitler. Yes, almost all wanted to curry the favor of the new security chief and, why, they even complimented me on my dress."

Carl permitted himself a little Texas talk, "Whoa, there," and then switched back to German for the understanding of the Webers. "The countess was the hit of the affair. It was not her dress that brought praise but her own beauty. She made that gown more beautiful than it really is. I thought I might have to draw my pistol to keep the men away. I think nine out of ten of the women would like to have drawn it to shoot her. In all it went exceedingly well and I had a good time."

"As did I," added Marli with a blush tinting her cheeks.

After a short discussion to include relations with Major Foltermann, they bid one another goodnight and went their three separate ways.

Carl and Hans decided that a wise course called for Carl to play his role to the fullest. Pfefferkorn was at the castle soon after daylight to drive Carl into Littach to the little office that Ranck had established at the city hall. Carl found that the office was small not only in physical dimensions but also in men. He discovered that the entire staff consisted of Pfefferkorn and himself. Pfefferkorn explained, "Ranck called upon the local police and SS units from the state capital or Stuttgart for help when more manpower was needed. It is a fact that the *Reich* cannot afford the manpower to have able-bodied men sit and wait. Please forgive me for the reference to able bodied, sir, but your injury could well be the reason you have been assigned here."

"That is good, Pfefferkorn, there is no offense taken," Carl assured the driver. "But how do the two of us know what's occurring in this area? It is quite large for two men, you know."

"We are an intelligence point that receives information from many sources, SS units, patriotic citizens, Berlin, and others. Speaking of Berlin, we believe that the *SD* has no less than five agents in the town. At least one of them is a woman because of all the reports we get on what women say in their private meetings, toilets, and so forth. Another has a little reputation, we gather, for being against the regime, not so much as to make him or her suspect in that we have not picked them up. Maybe in the past he, or she, had some slight connection to a Marxist party."

"Are there files kept here?" Carl asked.

"Yes, indeed, sir, these drawers contain the files. I believe that there is one for every person in and around Littach. They are kept locked at all times other than when documents are removed for use. When the document is removed, the file is again locked. Let me show you, sir, that we have a pressure release mine that is set when we leave the office for a quarter hour or more. Let me show you how to disarm the mine. See here, sir, you just insert this little pin and all is safe. If we leave the office at night, for instance, we pull the pin out. I assure you, sir, that Ranck came up with this idea and that no one other than him and me are aware of this precaution. It would mean the life of an unauthorized snoop."

Carl thought to himself. "I'm glad no child or innocent person tried to open the file." He asked. "You say there is a file on everyone in town. Is there one on you? No? Is there then one on me? Oh, yes, I guess it is quite a thick one, no? Right. I know what would be the case in Berlin but here do regulations permit me to look at my own file?"

When told that he could look at the file that discussed him, Carl pretended to lose interest but said, "Maybe some day I will look at them. It is fun reading what people have to say about you, right?"

From the office, Carl walked down to the *Silver Swan* to greet the proprietor and any patrons that he knew. Sure enough, he spotted several of the security police sitting in the warmth of the tavern. In the semi-darkness, he saw one rise and march to him and he recognized Lieutenant Matthias Schoenemann, the young lieutenant he had met in previous ventures into the *gasthaus*. The lieutenant saluted and greeted, "*Heil* Hitler, Lieutenant Schoenemann reporting sir."

"Relax, Matthias. I see you and some of the fellows are having a beer. May I join you?"

"Of course sir. We would be honored."

After less than an hour of superficial, even inane, talk Carl excused himself, contacted Pfefferkorn, and returned to the castle. There he reported to the others what had transpired and expressed doubt that there was anything significant in his file and felt little need to read it. Both Hans and Annaliese agreed that the schoolmaster fit the description of one of the secret agents that moved among the citizens. Neither had any conviction as to who the woman was who would secretly betray her friends and neighbors to the secret police.

Carl went to the office and read reports to a degree that would satisfy Pfefferkorn and any others that he was paying attention to his assignment. The files showed that there had been organizations that moved Jews out of the country surreptitiously through such vehicles as milk trucks and false rail passes. There were also reports of betrayals and confessions under torture that pointed to the movement of refugees, to include downed airmen, to and through the area of Littach. This leak in the wall brought strong orders directed at Paul Ranck to stop this traffic.

On the other hand, the increasingly cold weather and snow made walks rare but encouraged sitting by an open flame in one of the fireplaces of the castle. The coal-fueled fire in the sitting room blazed minimally and the lights were dim as the group sat in the afternoons and evenings. Father Nimitz, who seemed to appreciate the conversation particularly with Marli, increasingly joined them. He seemed to joke with her in a way that indicated that something in the joke was serious. "When do you think you will be ready to come into the church, young lady?" Another question from the blue, "Will you or any of your friends be going to Italy soon?" He followed, "Remember I gave you a map of places to visit where there are wonderful monasteries that will take in wayfarers and ask no questions. You do not even have to be Catholic." Finally, he would comment, "You are so spiritually-minded that you seem destined to be a bride of Christ."

At the last comment Annaliese interjected, "Not this warm little bunny. She has too much love to give a man to become a dried-up sister. He may be a man of God, my little lady, and I may be a member of the Church and he may make me say a million Hail Mary's for penance but don't you listen to him."

"Don't worry, Tante Annaliese, you should know that I have drunk too much from the minds of Luther, Melancthon, Calvin and other Protestant thinkers to turn now. Besides, what would my father say? I have hurt him too much."

The young couple renewed their walks together usually in the afternoon with the winter sun but also some mornings. The Countess Marlene inherited the German fondness for slow walks in the freshness of clear air and did not find it difficult to inveigle her young American to accompany her. She continued to find it wise to put her arm between his arm and body ostensibly to keep him from slipping.

They walked and they talked as they walked, never tiring of exploring one another's world of home, school, history, culture, and endless parade of other topics. Carl learned that this region of Germany derived it names from the "*Suevi*," one of the tribes participating in the Germanic incursions in the late Roman Empire. This tribe settled as neighbors of the "Allemani." The Romans began to call the entire area east of the Rhine the land of the Allemani.

She learned of the incursion of the American settlers into the lands of the Indians and the long period of time when whites fought the darker-skinned people for possession of the land. She learned of the legends of the Alamo, of Goliad, and of San Jacinto; that Texas derived its name from an Indian tribe called *Tejas*, meaning friendly. He told her of the discovery of great pools of oil under the earth's surface in many regions of the state.

They agreed that the history of her people could be described as old, rich, often tragic, and cultured. They also agreed that America and Texas embodied the qualities of youth, vibrancy, untapped wealth, and fluidity in that it had changed and continued to change in its racial and ethnic composition.

Although Carl enjoyed any conversation with the mistress of the castle, he really would have preferred describing to her the beauty of her face. Often drops of water from melting snow dropping off branches or falling from the air fell on her forehead, cheeks and nose. It seemed to him at these times that no priceless pearl lying on creamy satin in its open box could compare with the beauty of these moist beads on her blemish-free skin.

The talks often took on a much more personal aspect as when she asked, "If you have a goal or if you really want something, Carl, how hard will you work to achieve it?"

He did not parry, "I think that I am pretty determined. My friends say it is my German heritage to be hardheaded. I wanted to finish high school, I finished. I wanted to graduate from college, I graduated. I wanted to fly, I learned to fly. I wanted to escape capture when our plane was lost, I still am not captured."

"Carl, I really believe that soft bonds that are invisible to you bind you. I am no fool. Annaliese and Hans are not dumb heads and they know it," pointed out the Baroness Marlene as she stopped and turned to confront him face to face.

"What are you talking about?" parried the red-faced Carl. "Oh, there are bonds that keep me wanting to help downed pilots to escape and to keep you and Hans and Annaliese safe. Are those the ones you are talking about?"

"Don't pretend to be an idiot and a coward! I know that you can be bold and brave in all areas except one. Why are you afraid to be emotionally hurt? Our whole world knows that you love me and I really do not think that the word "love" is strong enough. You reveal to our world, to me, your adoration for me. It is in your eyes as you look at me, in your voice as you speak to me, it is in your hands as they reach out to me. Everyone knows it from Field Marshal Rudel to the French workers. Many tell me how wonderful it must be to be loved with such a love. But you will not speak!"

Shaken and silent for seconds, Carl finally uttered, "But you are a countess and I am a farm boy. You are rich. You will inherit two great estates while my inheritance might be twenty acres of Texas farmland. You are really well educated while I am only trained to design machinery and fly airplanes. You are whole and beautiful while I am scarred and maimed. You can trace your ancestors as nobility for century upon century. My ancestors were hardly better than peasants and I can only go back to my grandparents in my lineage. No, I can never hope!"

"Carlein, you may be frightened by what faces us but I will not be frightened. You fail to mention the one great thing that not only unites us but also makes us equals. Our Lord, the only legitimate dictator, has ordered us to be one in Him. More, he has raised us to the position of His children. We are equal. In fact, in the area of spiritual growth and commitment you are my superior. I was raised, as you say with so many benefits of contact with the great thinkers of the faith but you have seized every momentary opportunity to advance in the knowledge and strength of Christ. You have truly believed God, not just believed in Him."

She continued without pause, "See those peaks in the Alps there, the snow and glaciers glistening in the sun. I believe that if I asked you to climb over them you would do it at once. I am going to ask you to do something that is not so dangerous and hopefully not so fatiguing. We have pretended to be husband and wife for months in every way but sharing our bodies in bed. Now will you make me your true wife and marry me?"

He was embarrassed by the moisture that formed in his eyes and wanted desperately to hide them from this dream in a dress and objected with the obstacle that he saw no way of overcoming. "Beloved one, you failed to mention that as far as the German law goes you and I are now married and so we really can't get married again. Or do you mean after the war if America wins and we survive?"

"I am ready for you there!" she burst forth. "Do you remember that Father Nimitz mentioned a map showing the location of monasteries in Italy? Why do you think he had given us such a map? Do you really think that we might travel to that Roman land at the height of this war? We never said anything but we knew that he suspected some of our activities. The Catholic Church would have disciplined him if he had become involved and forbid it. He is a disciplined man, obedient to his church but he is also a good man, and so gave us information to help the fleeing Jews. The monasteries will give sanctuary to all who come their way, no questions asked.

"I have taken it upon myself to talk to him and explain without too much detail that Friedrich is dead and that you are really not my husband. I also asked him if he could secretly marry us and not violate his duties to the Catholic Church. He said he could under the circumstances.

"Carl, I love you dearly. Of all the men I have known and ever hope to know you are the one I want to spend my life with whether it be in Germany or Texas or as a missionary in the South Seas. If God grants me the joy of motherhood it is you I want to be the father of my children. It is your strength that I want to count on. I want to lean on your strength in times of trouble. It is your sly humor that I will need to get us over those little rough spots every relationship has. Carl, be brave in this area! Marry me!"

Dumbfounded, Carl hesitated between sitting on a log to regain his senses and taking her in his arms and agreeing to be her husband. Hesitation only came because it seemed that the forest was rotating and circling about them. He knew that rarely do gifts dreamed for come true like this and that he would have what he wanted more than anything he had ever thought possible. Yes! He would marry this wonderful woman and his joy would be overwhelming. Indeed, it already overwhelmed him.

No real decision was necessary as he took her in his arms and felt the freedom to claim her lips as his own. During their embrace, he looked upon her face, and somehow, saw the joy she felt even as she closed her eyes in a state of bliss.

While his actions screamed assent to her offer, his own lips finally said the words, "This is beyond my wildest dreams, my darling Marli. I cannot believe that someone like you would have me. The next best thing is that I would grow a new leg. If God can bring us together all things are possible. Let us go in and talk. We should tell Hans and Annaliese. I wish we could shout to the world. Oh, that Mama and Papa could know!"

As they turned toward the residence, the thought seemed to strike both minds that they had forgotten a very important Person, simultaneously stopped, and together said. "Let's give thanks to our great and good God for His blessings and bringing us together." They spoke with one voice and union of commitment.

When Hans came into the residence at the request of the radiant couple relayed through Annaliese and the four were all together Marli made the announcement, "Carl and I are really going to be husband and wife. We have just agreed to get married and Father Nimitz will marry us. Will you be the witnesses to our wedding here in my home? We know that our marriage will not be official under the law of the state but it will be by God. It will not be a sacrament recognized by the Catholic Church but in the eyes of God, dear ones, we will become one. Hans, would you please ask the good priest to come. If he can come, let it be tomorrow or, if not, the next day. Anyway find out when he can come and marry us. You need to go in person because we can not be sure of the security of the phone lines." Addressing Annaliese she bubbled, "Little Mutti, you can not know how happy I am!"

The beaming and mixed features of the older woman belied the statement of Marli. She moved as quickly as she could to take her in her arms. A joyous smile curved her mouth while tears washed her cheeks. Holding the one who had been her charge since babyhood, the one whom she could dress in pretty dresses and the frills of femininity she whispered, "My little angel, what joy! What a blessing to see you joined to a really good man." Then, tears flowing more profusely, Annaliese felt impelled to add, "How I wish my Rudi could witness your joy. He loved you so. He would be thrilled at our joy. May God bless him!"

Marli agreed and added with great longing, "I wish my father could be here too. Do you think he would like Carl? When the war is over I hope he will love him as much as I do."

Hans mounted his bicycle and was off to inform their good friend and spiritual shepherd before Annaliese ended her statement. Within an hour he was back and reported, "The Father said he would be here tomorrow at two in the afternoon and he added that he expected me 'to dig up two of the best bottles' that I have hidden away. He added that he expected a great feast from the hands of Annaliese Weber."

Even before he returned, however, the two women turned to an important issue of a wedding: what would the bride wear? Carl watched in wonderment at the serious talk of the two females as they considered what must have been a weighty matter for them. Finally, Marli asked, "What of my mother's wedding dress? I saw it come out of storage when I was young. Could it still be packed away? Would it fit?"

"Yes," Annaliese assured, "I know just where it's packed. You are taller than your mother, and I think, bigger in the bosom but with a little work this afternoon and tonight I think I can make it do."

Carl broke into the conversation to state without equivocation, "I will not be married in a *Nazi* uniform nor will I wear anything of Friedrich Schleiter's. What can we do about that? Wrap a sheet about me?"

Annaliese rose to the occasion, "We have some of Rudi's clothing in our apartment, I believe there is a nice dress suit there. You seem to be of almost the same size and shape. Would you let our Rudi be your best man through his suit even though he is with the angels? If all is right with you, Countess, will you let Hans stand in for your father and give you in marriage? It is all right. Good. Now let me get the dress and the suit and we will see. It looks like the needle and machine will be busy soon."

When Hans returned he saw neither his wife nor the bride-to-be as they were in a room pulling, pinning and pressing the almost forgotten wedding gown. Having been stored carefully it maintained its pristine virginal whiteness.

Carl had been shut in another room with instructions to get into the suit of the best man who could not be there. It was, because of Annaliese's sewing fingers, as good a fit as anything he had taken from the rack of a clothing store. As for footwear Carl's refusal to wear anything that had touched the body of SS officer Schleiter, posed a problem but again they found that Rudi's shoe, although larger than Carl's foot required, made him presentable. Carl also thought it providential that he would stand using the crutches, now ever more intricate in their fine carving, because of his relationship with their crafter.

Subdued excitement filled the residence throughout the afternoon and into the evening meal. While joy reigned supreme in the hearts of all four there was little laughter and much restraint. Suddenly Marli was shy as she looked at her food but could not keep her eyes from glancing up to look at the man she was to marry. Carl also tried to keep his vision on his plate but his hunger to behold his loved one forced him to look up also and when he did and their eyes met she would turn red and return to look again at the mostly untouched food.

After the evening meal, they were able to be alone in the dimly lit sitting room where finally Marli felt free to rest her head on his shoulder. He in turn knew the joy of putting his arms around her and drawing her so close that he felt the warmth of her body even through their heavy winter clothing. He experienced the unfettered joy of caressing her face in all its soft beauty with his lips. Then they also talked of the probabilities and possibilities of their life together. Knowing that they could not know or expect much about life in the future they were content that they had the present, but they agreed that, whatever the world's condition, they wanted children.

When Annaliese approached, she shooed Carl to his room saying that Marli must try on her mother's altered dress and that he could not see her wearing it. When she saw the fit was perfect, she issued her final order to her former charge, "Now it is time for bed for you, young one," as she again clasped her to her breast and wept for the joy of the moment. She continued, "Tomorrow is a big day for us all, so calm your excitement and get a good rest."

When Carl appeared downstairs the next morning he asked, "Where is Marlene? We should talk about plans."

"Plans! Shmans! You can not see your bride before she walks into the room with Hans!" exploded Annaliese. "Your only plan is to be in the library at the side of Father Nimitz at three in the afternoon. You have the rest of your life to plan and carry out plans. But today my little Marli is going to marry you!"

Carl stood at the Catholic priest's side at five minutes to three watching with rapt attention the entry to the library. Annaliese prepared a record of music by Felix Mendelssohn for the record player while proclaiming, "I don't care if this man was Jewish. We shall have his music for it is not Jewish. It is human and it is German. It is very beautiful and Mendelssohn was German. I have saved it from the brutes and will hide it once more after today."

At the first notes of the music Carl saw Hans come around the corner of the entry to the room and then a flash of white and then the luminous white of his bride's dress of satin that shone like the pure white of the snow of the Alpine peaks. His palms moistened and his breath shortened as he beheld her beauty. Combs secured her hair piled on top of her head. They also held a pure white veil that covered her face in softness. Annaliese had given her wedding present by her labor. His consciousness of that moment removed awareness of the ceremony as it occurred and future memory of it. Words falling like petals from a Texas crepe myrtle tree flashed into his hearing but they could not compete with the vision of his bride. Suddenly it was over and he heard the priest tell him to kiss his bride. Steadying himself with one crutch and with the help of his wife, he was able to embrace her as the other crutch fell to the floor with a clatter.

After the ceremony, Annaliese ordered them into the great dining room where she had again set out a bounty far too great for five people. They sat at a shortened table with Carl at the head as befitted a host. Annaliese had placed the new Mrs. Solms at the opposite end of the table as the hostess. Father Nimitz sat at the right hand of Marli while the Webers flanked Carl.

Carl saw the interest that his new identity sparked in the churchman who could hardly restrain his questions as to Carl's background, America, and Carl's religious convictions. The priest's curiosity once more called forth a discussion about things spiritual. Carl was open, and several times expressed his appreciation for Father Nimitz's service which went beyond the wedding ceremony where the father had joined Marli and himself as wife and husband. The five sat long and talked much until Annaliese excused herself only to return with first one tray loaded with the best food she could concoct and then with yet another similarly burdened.

Finally the priest said, "I must leave if I can rise and walk. We rise early for the morning mass and then there are confessions. After what you have eaten and imbibed today, Hans Weber, I am certain that you will have much of which to repent, if only because your stomach tells you to. So I will bid you good night and," looking first at Marli and then Carl, "may God bless you and make you fruitful in spirit and in body."

The four remained seated after his departure and discussed what was to them miracles that had brought them together.

A loud banging, far more violent than a simple knock, at the kitchen door at the rear of the house suddenly interrupted their laughter and joyous talk.

Carl, not yet accustomed to being in authority, suggested to his bride, "You should get out of sight and change your dress as soon as you can." Without pause, he told Hans, who stood prepared, "See what that is, please, but wait until Marli is gone." He then looked and gave thanks to God that they had lowered the heavy shutters covering the windows.

Hans moved deliberately to the kitchen and shouted, "One moment please, who is there? One moment please." Carl struggled to stand, and with Annaliese, stood at the passageway to the kitchen where he could both observe Marli's flight up the stairs and the situation with Hans at the same time.

❀

CHAPTER 10

January–November 1943
The Fruition

When Marli, in her wedding gown, disappeared, Carl signaled by a nod and hand motion for the older man to open the door where the loud banging continued unabated. Throwing back the several bolts securing the thick wooden door Hans lowered the arm of the door latch. The door flew open from an outside push. The three in the kitchen saw a figure dressed in the flight clothes of the Royal Air Force, his face streaked with dirt, beseeching in English, "Let me in! Please! I need help! Will you help me?"

Hans, unable to answer in English, attempted to signal the intruder to be calm by putting his hands forward with palms down. Pushing his hands downward toward the floor he tried to settle the man down while reinforcing with words in German, "Settle down. Settle down." Hans's hand motions and demeanor reestablished some calm and he motioned to a chair. When seated the man said in English, "I was told that I could find help here. You will help me, will you not? I am flight lieutenant John Crieger of the Royal Canadian Air Force. I was shot down five days ago. I know I am not far from Switzerland and I have been told that you can help me cross the border."

As Annaliese quickly sat some food before the man and as Hans seemed on the verge of offering assurance, Carl motioned for Hans to come to him. Carl whispered, as the older man approached, "Would you get my pistol from upstairs?"

Every instinct of alertness within Carl vibrated at the thought of the sudden clamoring at the door. Like prey sensing the presence of a predator, his senses and his mind searched for signs of security or peril. From his mind flooded questions to his consciousness, "What would have induced me to make such noise and attract attention to myself when I fled?" Another question, "How did he know of this house? We have made every effort to keep those we helped from knowing where they were. Why is his face dirty? I thought it best to look as normal as I could."

Then Carl's eyes searched for hints of peril, "Why is he so clean—while at the same time having a dirty face? How did his face become soiled when his clothing is clean? I had better remain as an *SS* officer in charge of security for this area. At least until I am sure, that is."

By this time, Hans had returned with the Walther pistol and had placed it in Carl's hand.

Marli followed Hans into the room. Pointing the barrel at the target he growled in his most vicious sounding German, "You have been misinformed and have come to the wrong place. I am Captain Friedrich Schleiter of the *Schutzstaffeln*. You may have heard of us as the *SS*. You will tell us where you received aid and information about this house so our security police can, shall we say "reward" them for pointing you in my direction. But first, shall we go through the formalities?"

When the intruder failed to respond to German, Carl instructed Marli to interpret. When she finished Carl drew a small note pad and a pencil from his pocket. Carl then interrogated "Your full name?" Marli jotted the information down. "Your rank?" More scribbling. "Your service number?" "Where were you shot down?" No answer. "How many were in your crew?' No answer "You had better answer if you want to live. I have already shot one flier in the city."

Carl possessed personal knowledge that Schleiter's character had permitted him to shoot a downed flier if providence in the form of a British bomb had not intervened. Schleiter's dossier in Berlin may well have painted a true picture of his cruel and ruthless nature. Carl, in the face of this probable impostor, had to maintain that image. The threat, more of an exaggeration than an outright lie, had an effect. The complexion of the uninvited guest blanched a bit it seemed to Carl. When the "Canadian" refused to answer further Carl asked, "Weber, will you take this pistol and escort our guest outside. I think he is going to try to escape. I am going to have to shoot him unless he can give us more information about who sent him here and helped him. Here take the gun while I work these crutches."

Once outside, Carl moved about fifteen paces onto the gravel of the courtyard and again took the weapon from Hans. He then ordered, "Kom," which sound means the same in German and English. When the "guest" moved to within about ten feet of him Carl ordered "Halt," another trans-language word. When the self-identified Crieger stopped, Carl moved around him and as Crieger tried to turn around so that he could see Carl the latter ordered, "Nein."

Carl then had Marli, who had followed the group out, interpret. He seemed to pronounce sentence, Marli, her hand to her mouth in shock, complied as she repeated her husband's message, "My husband says, 'You are trying to escape the *Reich*! If you cooperate, you will go to the war prisoners' camp. If not you will be shot while trying to escape. You are trying to escape, are you not? Now, tell us how you came to this place. Who has helped you get this far?' He says he will count to five and if you have not begun to help then…. .ein ..one!….zwei . .two . ."

The man who called himself Crieger then shouted in German, "No! No! I am *Gestapo* on a security check. We had suspicions and we thought to check this place out. I can prove what I am saying if you will let me reach into my boot and get a flare out. I do not have a weapon. Please do not shoot! Please!"

Shock again shook Marli as she watched. Her new husband ordered, "You can, but be careful. Move slow! You speak German but that proves nothing. There are many German-speaking people in Canada. Go slow, *schweinhund*!"

As quickly as slowness would permit the flare came out and the lighting strip pulled. The flare had hit the ground no more than thirty seconds before a black sedan raced onto the gravel through the now open gate. The driver put heavy weight on the brake pedal but the car continued to move forward as it rolled over the round bits of stone. It eventually came to a complete halt slightly beyond where the castle group stood with the impostor.

Carl, exasperation in his voice, demanded, "What do you think you're doing?" before any of the passengers vacated the car to explain. He then continued, "This man first said that he is an English flier seeking to escape, and then he said he was *Gestapo*. Just who the hell is he?"

One of the new arrivals with the insignia of a sergeant reported, "Heil Hitler, Good evening, sir. I am sergeant Eberhardt of the *SS*. We were sent on this operation by the Stuttgart office because of a report of a former agent in this area that suspicious things were occurring about this castle."

Carl took the offensive, "*Heil Hitler,* sergeant does *Reichsführer* Himmler know of this operation? Does he know that someone is questioning my integrity and commitment to the *Führer?*

"No, Captain, it seems that the operation was ordered by Doctor Kaltenbrunner, Director of *Sicherheitsdienst.* We only obeyed our orders. Would you have shot our comrade Crieger had he really been a British flyer? I believe that you convinced him that you would."

Carl evaded, "See this leg. It came from a bombing raid. Do you think I sympathize with those British rats who attack my German comrades? Are you going to report that I threatened him? Report ahead and see what happens to you. I considered him an escapee when he came to the door."

"We had better go, Captain Schleiter, *Heil* Hitler." Eberhardt and his group seemed in a hurry to get into the car including one whose face slowly regained its color.

After an obligatory but perfunctory "*Heil*" Carl stood with the others as the automobile curved its way through the gates and down the hill. When Carl turned, he saw the other three looking at him in some perplexity. Marli, face showing white even in the moon light, pointed out with a quiver in her voice, "You really did not answer his question. Please tell me, would you have shot him?"

Annaliese and Hans gave strict attention to Carl's answer, "Not under the circumstances that existed but if I believed that his death would have protected you or that his life threatened you, if I thought that I knew I could make you safer by his death, yes, he would now be dead. I have learned that this is not a game with laws or rules that never change. Warring parties change the rules of war and international conduct to suit their interests. Really, the only question that I want to answer is what is it that God wants me to do. I made a vow before Him to protect you. The world, everyone, should know that I will keep that oath to the utmost of my ability."

Silently the group turned and returned to the residence, wrapped in their own thoughts, knowing that sleep would not come easily.

As they entered the kitchen Annaliese, almost as a routine, asked, "Does anyone want coffee?"

No one wanted the coffee but Hans said, "I think I will have some wine. I think I need some wine to settle me down." Marli and Annaliese agreed that wine would be good and relaxing after their moments of tension.

After taking a sip of wine Marli mused aloud, "Well, this is one way of having an exciting wedding night but not exactly what I expected or would have ordered. I guess life has its surprises all the time. It looks like life with my husband will have surprises. But tell me, Carl, what made you know that he was an impostor?" Hans and Annaliese seconded the question by simple head nods.

Carl first gave all the rational reasons he suspected something was amiss including the fact that the stranger held his fork like a continental European and not the American way when he ate the food Annaliese set before him. Above all, he added, "I believe that God warned me. From the first moment I saw him something inside me screamed to be careful and to look at him closely. I do not ever remember being so focused and alert. Then, as we say back home I wanted to 'smoke him out.' Additionally I wanted to act quickly before any suspicions were confirmed in the event that he was not who he said he was. I regret having shocked you, Marli, but again, as we said in marble games back home, we are 'playing keepers.'"

The three Germans looked at one another, shrugged their shoulders, and moved into the house.

Before their heartbeats settled from the excitement, Carl's began to accelerate again as the reality that this was their wedding night gained dominance in his thoughts.

Almost before finishing a small glass of wine, Annaliese announced abruptly, "Hans and I are tired. This has been a long twenty-four hours for me, so please excuse us. Come, Hans," Hans, just reaching for the wine bottle to refill his glass, looked at his wife in wonderment until she caught his eyes and he understood. In embarrassment he said to the young couple, "Well, I guess you have things to do, uh...I mean you have many things to . . Excuse me, good night."

That night Marlene von Ritterbach *und* Krönitz Solms cried tears of regret over the absence of her father's sharing in her otherwise total joy. The white silk negligee and other silk garments that her father had brought for her trousseau years before when he returned from a trip to Paris, carefully drawn from their storage space, emphasized this mixture of joy and regret. She had kept the note that he had placed in the box and now re-read the words, "My princess daughter, I hope the man who beholds you in these garments is worthy of you. I pray daily that your husband deserves you and is able to tame your willful tongue. May he be your shepherd to lead you in the straight and narrow way of Christ. As you and he become one in spirit, body, and commitment may your union be fruitful in both spirit and flesh. I adore you, darling. Your father."

Overwhelmed at this reminder and one-way contact with her father the bride had to sit for moments to attempt to communicate in spirit and heart to heart over the great distance with her absent father, "Father, he is leading me in the good way and will lead me more and more, I know. Father, please know that the one you despised never beheld these garments and would never, ever, have seen them. I would have burned them first. Oh, how I wish you could have shared my wedding day. I wish you could know Carl. I know that he loves God and me as much as you do. If I weep a bit it is because I miss you and am so happy in the love you had for me. One day I hope that we can share that love again but this time it is with Carl. Now I am a wife and my man waits. Good night, Father."

Annaliese slept well that night. After all, she had not had more than three hours of sleep out of the last thirty-six hours what with her altering dresses and suits as well as preparing a wedding meal. Being aware that her young mistress would probably not rise early, she knew she could sleep later as well. If Hans insisted on being up at his regular dawn hour and wanted to eat, he could get a slice of bread with butter and jam; she needed rest. They would go to mass and confession tomorrow but not today and the good father could just whistle if he disapproved. She entered the kitchen in mid-morning and began to prepare for the descent down the stairs of the newly weds. First, she set the table for two and used the finest Nymphenburg china flanked by linen napkins preserved from the time of Marlene's grandfather, Count General August von Ritterbach, hero of Sedan, and the finest candelabra in the house. She thought she had time to mix, knead, and roll the dough to make the circular rolls, sweetened with precious sugar and cinnamon, that she knew were her Marli's favorite. The coffee could be ready if not in a minute then in three to be mellowed with thick cream. As she worked, she could not restrain the bounce in her aging legs nor control the smile that lit her face.

She knew the countess when she was little, she had known the countess as an adolescent, and she knew the now mature countess. She had learned to read the little girl, the adolescent, and she knew the mood swings of this young lady. Annaliese knew her charge possessed a tongue that could cut the unwary. She knew also that the same tongue could soothe and comfort the wounded. Marli she knew to be volatile but not erratic; her affection once given was constant. She was serious minded while filled with joy. Liese knew that each day during the last four months Marli had fallen more deeply in love with the American.

In her heart, Annaliese also realized that Carl would provide and protect her Marlene. Strong willed, even proud, intolerant of many things, the young wife would need love and strong guidance. Not bothered by the semi-theological question as to whether God has one certain man for one certain woman, she simply knew that Carl met realized and unrealized needs of the girl she loved. She waited and watched.

When the waiting was over, she felt joy move her heart as she beheld the countenance of the bride. The girl had been radiant the day before as she entered the chamber to be wed. Now beams of bliss shone forth from her eyes, her lips, her cheeks, even her hands in some magical way. As she moved slowly down the stairs, body against body with her husband, the beams that seemed to radiate from her eyes were matched by those her motherly *bonne* directed toward her and her bridegroom.

Carl, again wearing the boots with the prosthetic, looked upon the table and Annaliese with satisfaction but he looked upon his wife with exhilarated adoration. Annaliese presented the German style breakfast and departed, closing the door to the kitchen. Had she had the effrontery to listen at the door, which she definitely did not, she would have had difficulty in discerning either voice, lowered to barely more than a whisper.

Day rolled into another day and then another and both Marli and Carl realized that they had things to accomplish. After two days, Carl started returning to the little *Gestapo* office for some time each day, reading and mailing reports, then cruising the roads in the car, "just to keep an eye out." His contact with *Unterscharführer* Ludwig Pfefferkorn became more frequent and their relationship more informal.

The evening that Marli invited Corporal Pfefferkorn, "Would you please stay for dinner?" the bonds grew stronger and bound more closely even though the young man at first demurred. Marli refused to accept his declination of the invitation and the non-commissioned officer found himself at the table of the noblewoman. He found himself much at ease in the presence of his commander's quick and beautiful young wife. The time spent with his commander and the captain's wife, who was only a few years older than he was, became an event that he anticipated. The invitation to eat and talk with the castle group became more frequent with the passage of time.

Faces around Littach grew grim with the alarming news from the eastern front in early January as German forces adjusted their lines in the region of the mountains of the Caucasus. The ordering of national mourning for three days beginning February 3, 1943, meant that expressions grew even more grim. The capture of the entire German Sixth Army and its commander, Field Marshal Friedrich Paulus, by Russian forces at Stalingrad resulted in this period of grieving.

Now the *Nazi* forces were in retreat both in Africa and in Russia. As the citizens of Littach and its surrounding regions increasingly realized that Germany would lose the war, both grumbling and arrests for defeatism increased. First, an informer reported the carpenter Eichenburg who disappeared, according to his wife, after a midnight knock on the door of their apartment. Then a waiter in the *Gastatte Storch* quietly said to customers that maybe now people would see that Hitler was neither all-powerful nor all-wise. Within a week, he failed to report for work. A check of his room by the proprietor of the *gastatte* only showed a bed that had been slept in and nightclothes lying on a chair. Orders came to Carl to take the names of anyone who asked about the fate of the waiter. As directed, he told the residents of Littach who asked with hesitation that the man had "been taken in for questioning."

Everyone accepted the presence of agents of the *SD*, the most secret of security police charged with keeping everyone in Germany "in line," amongst them. No neighbor could be trusted not to reveal a "seditious" remark, no matter how innocent the intent of the remark.

As war roared around the world, life for those in the castle continued to be calm and blissful within their cocoon. The newly married couple continued their talks well into the evening, and when weather permitted, their talks combined with their walks among the trees. Carl discovered that his beloved Marlene struggled to control her words, which could be as caustic as acid, when discussing other females she knew. Carl actually questioned, "Does Marlene feel betrayed in her subconscious that her mother died and left her motherless?"

Hans continued to work to save downed airmen from capture although it was evident that this side of the rescue work troubled him. One late afternoon while Carl helped with some heavy work in the ruins, Hans confided, "You know, Carl, that it was one thing to help fellow Germans, yes, they were Jewish but they gave us some of our greatest German culture, to flee. As you know, a Jew saved my life in the last war. It is another thing to help those who are out and out enemies of Germany to escape. I love my land but not this government. I will fight for Germany but I would fight against this government. When does a government become one with the land? When does a government totally unite with the people? What am I to do if I see the Russians, or the French, or the English, and, yes, the Americans in these hills? I want neither any of them nor Hitler and his gang in Germany. I tell myself that they must come in order to insure that Hitler goes. But I feel bad."

The occasions when Hans helped downed airmen became less frequent but then increased as ever-growing numbers of Allied planes flooded German skies. The Allied planes were met by the ground and air forces of the *Luftwaffe*. Early in their contact with those helping them escape, the downed airmen learned of their rendezvous point near Littach. The day before the airmen were to be met, a woman in Littach watched a truck on its daily drive through the town. The garb of the driver informed the woman of the approach of downed fliers and place of contact. When the truck came through, the driver always honked the horn as he approached the center of the town. One short blast of the horn indicated that one flier required rescue, two short sounds meant two downed airmen, three very short told of three, and one long blast informed that more then three were enroute. The woman then relayed to those at the castle the information through the color and placement of her wash on the clothesline.

The woman had no idea who received her signal nor what it meant. She helped because the regime had taken her husband to the camps. Essentially widowed, she washed other people's clothes and every day placed the laundry on the drying line. On the days when the damp clothes would freeze, she would put out washcloths. The whole town admired her for her diligence in seeing that her clothesline never emptied in daytime.

Every day one of the members of the castle household, usually Carl, watched for a signal on the line. When a signal was on the clothesline, either he or Hans would check the area surrounding the rendezvous point. Carl would visit the site under the guise of making a security check while Hans would be doing his duty as forester. Carl told Marli, "If the police are present about the only thing I can think of to warn the fugitives is to fire my weapon into the woods and say that I thought I saw a fugitive."

Carl presented a problem that he had to Marli, "I do not want you to meet the fugitives. It might be too dangerous and I sure don't want anything to happen to you."

"We've settled that long ago. You are in more danger than I am. If word came back that some *SS* person was aiding people to escape it would not take long for them to determine your guilt. No, I will meet the fleeing ones in the car," was the young wife's response.

"No, please do it my way," came back Carl. The newly weds settled their first little married disagreement by compromise. On some occasions, Carl would go alone, on others Marli would go alone and on still others both would go.

Hans would be asked to meet the fugitives only when either Carl or Marli could not.

The days of spring arrived and by May the trees that had lost their leaves were beginning to bud once more. In the middle of the month, Carl arrived at the residence in the evening and called out in excitement, "Marli! Marli! I have some news!"

When she met him midway through the house he continued, "General von Arnim has surrendered in Tunisia. All the German and Italian forces there have given up!"

Carl was surprised at the fervor of her embrace. His news kept him smiling when away from observation and encouraged him, but he did not expect this usually controlled young woman, his wife, to get emotional about it. "Hey, sweet one, this does not mean that the war is over or that the defeat of Hitler's forces is assured," he whispered into her ear brought so near to his by her clasp.

She replied softly, "I have news for you also. I am sure that you are going to be a father."

News from Africa became instantly of secondary importance. News from the front in Russia faded to personal insignificance. Suddenly the knowledge that the Ruhr industrial complex of Germany collapsed in ruins or burned in flames reaching high into the sky as Allied bombers pounded the region day and night shrunk into secondary significance.

"Carl, move or say something. Don't you want our child?" asked Marli petulantly as Carl stood and looked at her. "I guess you won't love me when I am big and fat and my hips get stretched out of their joints. Oh," as the smile of joy turned to tears of frustration at his silence, "I'm just going to be another German *hausfrau to* you."

The best utterance the overly detailed mind of Carl could think of at this historic family moment in the face of his wife's semi-hysteria came out as, "You don't look pregnant." He then continued, "What, uh, when, uh, are you sure? When is the baby due?"

When met by her stony silence and cold glare, he recognized her fears, "My marvelous Marli, that is not true and you really know it. This is the best news of my life other than your agreement to marry me.

"What could make me prouder and more delighted than to see you carrying our child? My love will be doubled for there will be two to love. In addition, I know you. You are discipline personified and, after the little one comes, will have yourself back in shape in the shake of a lamb's tale."

He then took her in his arms so that their hearts beat against one another and let his lips explore her face, saying all the while "I love you and will always love you. You are more beautiful at this moment than you have ever been. My love for you is not based on your looks because if we grow old together, as the saying is, our looks will fade as our faces and bodies sag. But I love you because not only are you beautiful but because of the spirit and character that you possess which will be the same when we are aged old people of seventy. I believe I will love you more then than ever. The question is, whether you will still adore me when I lose my gorgeous unscarred complexion and must walk with a cane?"

She ceased her weeping as the tears turned to almost giggling laughter, "Of course, you ninny. You know how I like to let my fingers run over your features. It is as if they are on a roller coaster at a fair. Up and down the scars they go. Moreover, you shall have skates before a cane.

"But to answer the question, the baby is due in November according to my calculations. I hope that is a good month. He will have to go through winter and I must remember to keep him warm. Carl, are you feeling well? Now you look just a little pale," she added with a laugh.

"I guess I am. It is kind of a shock. I never faced fatherhood before. But then I guess you have never faced motherhood before. Do not misunderstand. I am thrilled but overwhelmed. As a boy, you wonder what it is like to be a father and now I am going to find out. Really what I want to do is to be thankful."

The young pair knelt and thanked God for this development in their lives and asked His sovereign protection spiritually and physically of the one developing in Marli's womb.

Now they knew that their responsibility extended to another who had not been there before. As the noose of defeat drew closer to the German homeland and the *Nazi* elements of German society grew more desperate this concern for their child increased proportionately.

Less than two months after the surrender of the German forces in Africa, the Allies continued their offensive across the Mediterranean into Sicily and occupied that island by August 17, 1943. During the same period the army of the Soviet Union, which increasingly seemed an unstoppable force, won a victory over a giant German counterattack at the city of Kursk and continued an implacable drive to the west.

Annaliese, always more ebullient than Hans, burst into tears of joy when she heard of her little Marli's expectancy, saying, "There is much knitting to do.

This house is big and drafty and the baby will be so little. Warm clothes will be needed."

Hans, as pleased as his wife and baffled at the same time, asked, "Is there a crib that you want to use, Baroness." He had a hard time shedding his deference to the young but noble lady.

Marli's answer, "No, I believe the baby bed that I used is at my father's," brought a smile of service to the older man's countenance as he envisioned carving the finest little sleeping space for the baby that the Black Forest had ever seen.

Annaliese replied, "Conrad writes that he is well but is kept very busy and is always tired" when Carl asked what they had heard from their sons. "He is always preparing planes to fly. It seems that the American and English keep sending planes over every day and every night and the German planes sustain a lot of damage. Both the men who fly and the men who care for the planes are exhausted. There is little rest for the men who keep the planes fit to fly."

Carl agreed that the air war must be intensifying, "We now have about one airman or group of airmen seeking refuge each week where we once had about one a month. That might mean that there are more planes over Germany or else the *flak* is getting very good."

"Maria has written that the bombing of Bad Mühlingen has been terrible. The town is almost destroyed and everyone spends night and day in the shelters. There are planes at night, hundreds of them, hundreds more planes in the day. She said that at night the planes are English and during the day American. Thousands, men, women, and children, have been killed and thousands have been injured. It is horrible!" reported the older mother.

"I am glad that we are in this peaceful corner cuddled close to Switzerland so that Marli and the baby are safe, at least from the bombing raids."

As the Russians continued their drive to the west and the Allied forces landed not only in Sicily but also on the Italian peninsula, Carl began to think about possible future exigencies and asked, "Hans, could you set some fuel for the automobile aside in containers? It may be that at some time we will need to make a trip for some emergency…"

Hans concurred, "Yes, that would be a good idea and I will skimp up what I can. We get a very limited amount for the car and the farm but I think maybe I can save and hide about five liters a week."

The calm that prevailed at Littach permitted the social life of teas and parties to continue although on a reduced scale. In June Carl delivered a note to Marli received at his office inviting the Baroness Marlene von Krönitz Schleiter to a "tea" at the home of *Frau* Maria Schlenkmann. When she read the invitation Marli broke into tears, shocking her man who asked with a hint of panic, "What's the matter, my treasure? Do you think it's a trap?"

"Oh, they just want to shame me! Just look at me! I am fat and getting fatter every day. They are all going to think to themselves, 'Isn't that a pity! She was trim and neat but now look at her belly!' I have no clothes that will cover my belly but those old tents I wore to spite Friedrich."

"I didn't know that you are still sorry that you are pregnant and I thought you were now happy about us having a child," only increased both the wailing and the gushers of tears until Annaliese sped into the room. Her soothing words and application of female logic incomprehensible to Carl brought about an end to the sobs. Marli rushed over to Carl and wrapped her arms around his neck, her meteoric manner turning into squeals of delight at her love for her husband and her great joy in her expectancy.

"I guess it is ironic justice. I hated Friedrich Schleiter for forcing me into marriage. I wanted revenge. We should not seek vengeance. I know that. It is strange, funny strange, that the clothes I wore for spite are now my garments of love. Don't you think, Carl, that God really has a sense of humor?"

Carl sat dumbfounded as the two women, having assured him that all was more then well in their joy, left the room with Annaliese's arm about Marli's waist.

When Marli returned from the social dressed in a glorious maternity dress fashioned by the crafty fingers of Liese, both Carl and Liese were anxious for an account. She immediately said, "I did enjoy it. Everyone made over me. Erika told me that she was glad that I had become a good German and was fulfilling the *Fuehrer's* command to German women to have children. Not that I enjoyed hearing that. I let her know it too. She really can get under my skin. She always did even as children. She also asked how I felt about the war in the east and in Italy. I told her that I had learned to leave that to the men—that that was not a concern of women. Will God forgive me for that lie? Do you know Elizabeth Vogelsang, Carl? Her husband was a brilliant young professor of literature at the university until the *Wehrmacht* called him to duty as an officer.

"Some months ago she received notification that her handsome love had been killed on the eastern front. Well, she gave Hitler and his gang what for. She called him an ignoramus who did not care about the tragedies he had brought about. She even asked me how I could bring a child into this world and particularly into a land ruled by such a maniac. Ulla von Rudel finally got her to quiet down and the rest of the affair went quite well—very charming. You would hardly have known that we were in a great struggle."

Carl thrilled to the feel of the movement of their child in Marli's abdomen. Several times each evening he would take the opportunity to let his hand rest on her stomach just to experience the joy of the unseen but obviously very real child within his love. As he let his hand feel the turning of the child, his eyes beheld the mother and his love extended into new directions. Heretofore his love had focused on his wife's character and beauty. Now it grew into another commitment that he recognized but could not describe.

Marli did not need the injunctions of Annaliese to continue her walks with her husband and pushed him to accompany her on relatively long jaunts about the estate during the summer months and into the fall. They talked of their child and the future that waited. Neither could prophesy the future. They agreed that the months that Hitler would rule were limited but were uncertain if a peace would be negotiated. It is true that the *Nazi* propaganda machine of Doctor Paul Joseph Goebbels made sure that Germans were aware of the Allied commitment to unconditional surrender of the Axis nations. Could and would the Americans and the Russians be divided into making separate peace terms with the *Nazi* regime? That was no more unthinkable than the peace pact dividing Poland that the Russians had signed with Hitler in 1939. If the German forces succeeded in throwing the invasion of the continent from England back into the sea, would the people of America and Britain say enough is enough and come to terms with Germans?

Both Carl and Marli recognized that they could be treated as traitors if the German people were not convinced of the depravity of Hitler's programs. This required the total defeat of the *Nazi* forces and the revelation of atrocities so that no future Hitler could say that they lost the war only because traitorous forces betrayed Germany from within. If Germany were totally defeated who would provide the occupying forces? Russia? Great Britain? France? The United States?

All who spoke openly of the obvious evidence of the declining fortunes of the Axis endangered not only themselves but also their hearers. Hearing but not reporting made the hearer an accessory to treason. The threat, like a miasma, hung in the air, not to be spoken of. The danger lurked but could not be seen in the anonymous agents of the *SD*. Townspeople disappeared. Men and women were here yesterday but are absent today. While the baker might remark to his wife, "You know Otto Kladde, the butcher, has not opened his shop in three days. I saw *Frau* Kladde there yesterday and she really looked bad, all pale and shaking. I thought it best not to ask about her man."

His wife may have replied in hushed tones, "Oh, I was in the shop the other day buying some cutlets and he was saying that he did not think the war was going good and that maybe there should be a change in government. He said that when people lost confidence in the hand on the tiller that maybe the pilot should be relieved. There were several women in the shop at the time." The butcher had indeed vanished.

Carl had heard much of George Washington's Farewell Address to the nation urging America to remain free from foreign entanglements. Would Americans consent to having their men remain overseas or would they require their government to return to isolation? These great questions of men and nations influenced their own lives and they considered the possibilities of what would require them to remain in Germany. Would the future permit Carl's return to America? Would the authorities, whoever they were, permit Marli and the child to go to America? These questions they could not answer but they could control the name of their child. So they discussed the possibilities.

Marli began by favoring Carl Erich in the event the baby was a boy. Carl demurred because he was afraid of being egotistical, "No, please don't put my name on the child. I really would like to honor your father. You have told me what a wonderful and Godly man he is, who lives his life with truth and honesty. I would like to name our first-born son Eric Albert for your father. "Eric" because Americans would have a hard time understanding why it was spelled "Erich."

She agreed, "That makes me very happy, Carl. It pleases me. You are right in the way you described him and any child should be proud to bear his name. But what if it's a girl? Should we name her for your mother? What is your mother's name, by the way? You have always just called her 'Mama.'"

"Her name is Minnie and I will not stick that name on any girl. It is really made fun of in American movies and comics, you know 'Minnie the moocher,' 'Minnie Mouse' goes with 'Mickey Mouse,' and there is also Minihaha of Hiawatha. No, no Minnie. I love your mother's name of Teresa. What do you say to Teresa Anne?" So the little baby gained a name four months before its expected birth.. The life in the castle developed its own rhythm with an occasional exclamation point of the rescue of a downed flyer.

The quiet calm around Littach with few apprehensions or even sightings of downed airmen caused the state and national authorities to seem to desire, as it were, "let sleeping dogs lie." That is until orders came for Carl to seize the widow Vogelsang for questioning about "seditious statements against the *Reich* and the *Führer*." It was alleged, a secret informant had reported to the *Sicherheitzdienst* that amidst a group of women Elizabeth Vogelsang had attacked the nation's leader in word and manner. She was to be seized secretly and brought to Stuttgart for questioning. The orders required the greatest secrecy possible in the apprehension and movement of the woman. Pfefferkorn expressed his curiosity as to who could have reported the woman and seemed genuinely intrigued by the problem even as he carried out the orders without further word from his officer.

As Carl read the order, he remembered Marli's description of the events at the social affair at the home of *Burgermeister* and *Frau* Schlenkmann. He remembered also the provoking questions and pushing of Marli's girlhood friend Erika. The initials of the informant, "ER", gave him no pause as he remembered Erika Randorff's studied listening to as many conversations as possible. He longed to shout to all to be careful of the merchant's wife but reality forced him to limit his caution to Marli, Hans, Annaliese and Father Nimitz.

The priest's visits to the castle had increased since the marriage as he felt more as if he belonged as a trusted fellow conspirator. Timing his visits carefully to arrive just as Annaliese placed the food on the table, he also enjoyed conversation with the four. Hans and Annaliese confined their talk to the people of the parish and activities within the church. Marli and Carl felt free to discuss their views of Christian doctrine, which differed from the vicar's. The priest would occasionally inform them that he had heard that unexpected guests had knocked at the door of such and such monastery in Italy.

Carl warned, "Please be careful in any conversations you have with anyone, even your most trusted acquaintance. My headquarters in Stuttgart has informed us officially that the *Sicherheitsdienst* has informers in the town. I do not know who they are. Any one of them may have expressed opposition to the regime in the past. Some are zealous *Nazis* and some have been threatened by their past actions and words. I believe that the last give documented statements or actions about their friends. That is, they must turn in a certain number every month with the details of when and where the accused made the statement. In order to save themselves or their families they will lead acquaintances into criticizing Hitler or the war and then report them.

"As security chief of this area I never get the names of the informers. The report is that so and so made such and such a statement at such and such time at such and such place. I, as the local chief of security, then call the accused in and confront him with the details of his actions. I then must take appropriate action that can range from a summary trial and execution to a reprimand. So far I have been able to only warn the accused to watch their tongues or they would face further action."

Marli continued on the subject, "It is truly suffocating to have to watch every word you say for fear that some misspoken or misunderstood statement will be reported. I have my suspicions about at least one informer. That person seems to be the common contact with all those who disappeared. That includes others who Carl has investigated on orders from Stuttgart. Let me just say to watch yourself around Erika Randorff."

Carl confirmed her suspicions of her childhood friend. As though on cue, Annaliese reported after answering the telephone at that moment that *Frau* Randorff desired to speak to the countess.

When Marli returned from her phone conversation she said, "My 'friend' Erika wants us to come over for a little social event and asked for a date that would be convenient to us. I wanted to tell her that no date would be convenient. I do not see what I saw in her when we were girls! I think she checked in her brains at the door of adulthood and became a blind follower.

"But then, I thought second thoughts and told her we would come over at mid-week. Is that alright, Carl?"

"Sure," he replied, "It will be interesting to see if she plays any little games with us. We should be careful of any little traps she might want to set for us. These little bunnies don't want to get snapped up by the copperhead," and went on to explain that a copperhead was a venomous snake back home that fed on the little cottontail rabbits.

At mid-week Marli again dressed herself in the dress that Carl had first seen her in when she came to the hospital in the city. Although it still covered her like a tent now the coloring of her face and maternal configurations of her body created a sense of the fulfillment of womanhood. The material was still the soft light wool. She also let her hair flow down her back and she cosmetically concealed some blemishes in her complexion that only she believed existed.

The evening was clear and the Alpine peaks sent the vision of their pristine white slopes through the clean air over the border into Germany as Marli and Carl entered the Pfefferkorn chauffeured car. Pfefferkorn delivered them to the door of the merchant's residence and hastened to open the door of the automobile and assist the two of them. Their hostess' greeting made the bile boil into their blood even as broad smiles revealed the whiteness like ice cycles descending from a glacier. "Oh, my dear Marli, how glad I am to see you. Friedrich, I only a few weeks ago told Marli how pleased I was that she had gotten in line with the nation and will produce a warrior for the future of the *Reich*. I always said that she really would be sensible and understand our needs as a people to face a world of lesser races. I was frightened that she might be a member or sympathizer of that traitorous White Rose (*Weisse Rose*) gang from Ulm that dares criticize the *Führer* and the Party."

Restraining herself both as to the real name of the father of the child within her and as to a cutting reply to her erstwhile friend, Marli simply responded, "Yes, we have a child and I trust that he will be as good a man as his father."

"*Mein Gott*, now that is a change! I can remember when you could not seem to stand the sight of Friedrich." Then Randorff leaned close to Marli's ear and whispered so as to be heard, "Did his performance in bed bring you into line like a good German woman?"

At this comment Marli spun, holding Carl's arm as though for support but more to restrain him, and coldly left the presence of their hostess. In their movement around the room they were happy to see the gracious *Frau* Field Marshall von Rudel who encouraged, "Please do not let *Frau* Randorff upset you. Her words do not do credit to even a *bourgeoisie* wife of a merchant. Her father should have insured that she was finished culturally before he married her to the affluent merchant Randorff."

That woman had more to investigate and soon was in their presence and their conversation again, "My dear Friedrich," she presumed to address Marli's man, "Are you really being diligent in rooting out seditious and treasonous talk? I have heard that you are getting reports of traitorous speech by several townspeople and have done nothing other than having them in for a talk. Do you offer tea and cakes to them when they come in? A friend of mine in Berlin has informed me that you would have been called there were it not for *Reichsführer-SS* Himmler. There is an administrator there who, I am told, waits for any slip on your part. Be warned. There are those who watch you closely all the time. My friend says that this great person still believes the reports of the great patriot Paul Ranck. I trust you have not changed your commitment to the *New Order* just to have more warmth in your marriage bed, if that is the reason for your change in diligence."

Carl answered with equanimity, "Don't you think that you go too far in probing into the relations within a marriage. Who is this friend in Berlin? I would really like to know so that someone from the SS office can reassure him concerning my performance of duty. You do know, do you not, that reports of fugitives fleeing the country in this area have dropped. Where there once were ten reported sightings there are only one or two now. Does your friend know that?" Carl did not bother to add that he did not consider it necessary to forward every report of a sighting to Berlin. He also made a mental note to screen any reports that did come in more carefully as to source.

Their hostess then turned again to Marli, "What in the world prompts you to let your hair be so undisciplined. It certainly is not in style anywhere in the world and I am sure that the *Führer* would not approve of such a mane. You must have a visit to the *friseur/*"

"No, Erika, my husband likes my hair this way, my father encouraged me to let it grow because he agrees that a woman's hair is her glory and I like my hair long. It would be difficult to wipe the Savior's feet with hair five inches long. What others think is of little interest to me but I do appreciate your concern. I trust that you will not write to Hitler to tell him of my outlandish hair!"

"Savior! Savior!" growled the hostess, "You had better learn, girl, that Germany has only one savior and that is our *Führer,* Adolf Hitler. We are through with the Jews and their Old Testament and the so-called king of the Jews. There will be no more turning the other cheek for Germany. We will take what we need to rule the world. Nature made it our destiny to rule over the lesser races and peoples. The sooner everyone learns that the better off they will be!"

Hearing the tirade, Carl thought that their hostess must have doubts as the Russians continued their push to the west, the British and Americans in Italy, and the air raids on Germany increasing in their implacable tempo. He remembered the saying he had heard and seen verified about rats. As the rodents realize they are cornered and as the circle closes in their desperation increases geometrically. This was the predicament of the *Nazi* leaders of Germany. The thought of the wrath inevitably to fall on this beautiful land and its old and beautiful cities turned his anger to sadness. The rain of bombs and shells would fall on the just and the unjust equally.

Marli said as they left the merchant's house, "I am glad to be out of there. What ever made me put up with her as a companion. I know, I was young but I still should have been more discriminating. Maybe it was because I knew I tended to being a snob and wanted to prove to myself that I wasn't."

Both Carl and Marli had used the way of William the Silent as he led the Netherlands against the Spanish Empire. This ancestor of the Countess Marlene spoke so eloquently he said little that could harm him or his cause. Not literally silent but his words committed neither him nor his government to a policy. Like her ancestor, Marlene and Carl talked gaily, even giddily, about the evening as long as they knew that Pfefferkorn could hear. Dresses and sweet cakes filled their conversation as well as their stomachs. Carl, playing with fire, quietly teased Marli so that no one else could hear that now he understood why she was getting such a big stomach. He then laid his hand gently and unobtrusively on that rounded surface to know again the thrill of feeling the life of their child.

Marli later declared emphatically to Carl and Annaliese that she wanted her child, like herself, to be born in *Schloss* Altburg. Annaliese, worried about her charge, encouraged, "The little hospital in town is good and in case of emergency you would be taken care of more quickly."

The reaction was both decisive and imperious, "No, at least my first born will come to light in the house of its forebears. All of my mother's people were born here. I will hear nothing more. The child will come forth in the bed where conceived."

Running his finger through her hair, Carl calmed all with a smile and quipped, "If the countess will not go to the doctor then the doctor will come to the countess. As the date nears, I will insure that Pfefferkorn stays close to a phone and that the doctor stays available. I will also make sure that everything that might be needed is available here."

This Carl did. Two weeks and a day after All Saints Day, which Carl knew as Halloween, Marli announced just as they prepared to rise from bed, "I think its time. Go tell Annaliese and you had better call the doctor and tell Pfefferkorn to get him."

Carl concentrated on keeping his racing heart from affecting his facial expression or his behavior. So many memories of the ridicule of expectant fathers flooded his memory that while he was deeply excited and concerned about this birthing business he did not want to appear ridiculous to anyone. He forced himself to swing on his crutches in measured rhythm to the quarters of Hans and Annaliese to inform them of the developments.

Hans crushed his attempt to display composure, "I believe you forgot something, Captain. Or did you mean to put on a shirt and sweater and leave your trousers in your room?" With a big grin he also added, "I don't think my Anna would admire your under shorts."

Continuing his pose of aplomb, Carl calmly went to the phone and made the two phone calls necessary to bring the doctor to the house. He then swayed his body between the crutches to their room and finished dressing.

Marli's labor continued through the day under the attention of both Dr. Heinz Richter and the faithful and concerned Annaliese. Carl and Pfefferkorn waited in the kitchen with the silent Hans. While the corporal wolfed down the noon meal set before him by Hans, Carl only managed to get a few bites through his stress-tightened throat. October 24, 1943, faded into the evening dusk as the son of the countess and the "cowboy" saw the light of the last rays of the day's sun. Carl forced restraint upon himself while waiting to see the ones he had loved for so many months and whom he would love for so many years if God permitted. When he first saw Marli as he entered he saw the little red face lying between his mother's arms, the top of his head just touching her upper arm as her eyes caressed him. Looking up at Carl, she said with a broad and knowing smile, "Look at what we have produced through German-American cooperation."

The maternally hovering and practical Annaliese asked, "What is the little thing to be called? You know he must have a name."

Both Carl and Marli, waiting until the doctor's back was turned, indicated with gestures that they did not want to talk of that in his presence.

The doctor reported to Carl, "Captain, the birth was neither difficult nor easy. Both your wife and the child came through well. We will need a name for the birth records at the county office."

Assuming his most authoritative mien, Carl pre-empted further discussion, "I will register him at the office when I am next in town. We thank you for your good work, *Herr* doctor. Other patients must have need of you. I trust that no one suffered needlessly due to the time that you gave to us. Thank you very much." Following Carl's nod to her, Annaliese discreetly guided the doctor out of the house and into the car.

As soon as the elderly doctor was out of hearing range Carl announced, "Dear Hans and Annaliese, we have decided to name our son Eric Albert in hopes that he will develop into a man like Marlene's father. We want to have his birth registered by Father Nimitz, not as a member of the Catholic Church, but simply registered to establish Carl Frederick Solms of New Sendlingen, Texas, as his father and the Countess Marlene von Ritterbach Solms as his mother. Obviously we do not want to have Friedrich Schleiter listed as his father. If the doctor files a birth registration as he might be required to do I will find a reason to search the records tomorrow and every day until I find it, I will then find an opportunity to destroy it."

Under the guise of determining the Aryan purity of certain members of the community Carl quickly did his search of records and was able to find and destroy the certificate of birth filed by the doctor as well as prevent any forwarding of the news of the birth to state and national offices.

No evidence would exist for the birth of a son to Friedrich Schleiter and Countess Marlene von Ritterbach. Well concealed under a figure of Mary and the Christ child in the beautiful church in the fields outside Littach was a certificate signed by one Father Ewald Nimitz and witnessed by Hans and Annaliese Weber. The certificate of birth stated that on October 24, 1943, Erich Albert Solms was born to Lieutenant Carl Frederick Solms, United States Army Air Corps and his wife, the Countess Marlene von Ritterback und von Krönitz Solms.

Carl's heart filled with a satisfaction defying description during the weeks that followed as he viewed their son at Marli's breast. In the quiet of the evenings, he considered the miracle of it all from his dropping into the land of the enemy to his union with a wise and beautiful noble lady of that land. In a way, they had become one flesh in the consummation of their marriage but now they united even more in the form of their child and the future generations of their descendants. When these moments came to him he lifted up his heart in a prayerful but silent paean for all that had come to him. Even the loss of his foot had worked to good.

The night of the birth Hans with a smile had produced from a storage area a wooden crib for the baby Erich that he identified as, "This is the bed which I have prepared for you, Countess. I took the liberty to select the wood and place on it what I thought were appropriate carvings pleasing to you." The delicate and intricate carving of the highly varnished but unpainted resting place for their son astonished Carl. One solid end displayed in carved relief the castle overlooking the village with the church spire rising above it. The other carving at the other end showed a man, a woman and four children walking toward the sun on the horizon

While their child filled the residence with joy and optimism for the future, an increasing mood of dark despond began to fill Littach. Despite the efforts of the authorized news, the people of the town learned from the Swiss sources that were so near that the enemies of the *Reich* advanced on all fronts in the east and in Italy. Even Pfefferkorn repeated, "Men from the eastern front, some of them horribly wounded, are saying that things are not going at all well there. They say that the Russians just keep coming in waves and are not getting weaker but stronger. Everything, their tactics, leadership, weapons, seems to be getting better. They say the Bolsheviks have crossed the Desna River and are pushing on toward the Dnieper River. They think that the Russians may even have also breached that great river by now. And the soldiers wounded in Italy report that the Allies have crossed the Sangro River and are slowly pushing north through the mountains."

Even the *Nazi* radio and newspapers reported the naming of the commanders of the allied expeditionary forces in December with General Dwight D. Eisenhower in overall command of the might of the western allies in all of Europe. Earlier the Germans learned that the American Army General Carl A. "Tooey" Spaatz would command the American Eighth Strategic Air Force. The German population found the name of this man who would largely be responsible for the American air attack, "Sparrow", something of an irony. They knew that the flights of the American bombers over the Fatherland would hardly be comprised of sparrows. Carl Solms remembered and found the biblical verse that "not a sparrow falls to the ground" encouraging.

Unending reports of "withdrawals for tactical purposes" and the "reorganization of the eastern front in preparation for a new offensive" became increasingly difficult to accept by those dwelling in Littach. Reports drifted in by word of mouth and over the air from nearby Switzerland that the German soldiers, although resisting valiantly, could not cope with the ever-increasing power of the Russians' numbers and material. Orders, instructions, and demands to flush out doubters and traitors flooded to Carl and the others in the police station. He assumed that these commands were also reaching the hidden agents of the SD. Erika Randorff confirmed this assumption as she frenetically stalked through the town, engaging in conversation anyone who would take time for her. Carl also noted that she not only attempted to engage others in conversation but also continued as an acute listener to conversations in which she had no part.

On one occasion, the French prisoner Francois Chalvet held his hand to his throat as though choking and then removed it in a cutting motion as he smiled broadly at Carl in his *SS* uniform. Hans reported that Alois Ducite had told him, "Chalvet is saying that the days of the *bourgeoisie* are about over and that the workers of the world will soon have their day. He has said, 'The first one I want to see on the gibbet is that *SS* captain at the residence.'" Ducite continued, "Chalvet says that Schleiter is a devil because he is most dangerous to the victory of Marxism in that he is kind to the workers and has even won the heart of the woman. He says that the captain is a wolf dressed in wool and that there will be a struggle after the Fascists are beaten and capitalists like him are the most dangerous. He said the SS officer will have to be liquidated for the cause."

At the other extremity, Pfefferkorn's manners communicated greater appreciation for and trust of his officer with the passing weeks. Following the news of the disasters of the German forces in Russia, he asked, "Do you think that the *Führer* can really find a miracle to stop the invasion of the Fatherland? Every day the war drains away more and more soldiers by the hundreds and thousands; the bombers are destroying our cities and factories; Dönitz no longer brags about the sinking of ships by the U-boats. Where will it all end?

"I am not dumb and I know that if the Allies create a second front in France that it really will be all over. I would never talk like this to anyone else. There are spies everywhere and *Frau* Randorff is one of them but I trust you for some reason. Maybe it is because your wife trusts you and I believe she is like the old and good nobility that were aware of their duties. Only a good man could gain the love that she has for you. The strange thing is that from what I expected, you were not a good man at all. I guess the love of a good woman made the change in you. You will excuse me for talking so openly. Surely you could have me shot for what I have said to you."

Carl acknowledged the openness of his aide, "You are a good man, Pfefferkorn. I know that you love Germany. You would give your life for your Fatherland. I do not know how we will all come out of this but my wife says that there is One who does and that we must trust Him. You are right, the love of the countess has changed me. If you continue to obey me, I will do everything I can to get us all out of this mess the whole world is in. Does your family need help? You have told me so little about them."

"My parents are dead. My father died in an industrial accident when I was three years old and my mother died of cancer in 1938 so I joined the SS to have something like a family with brothers. At first, I loved the comradeship of the military, the sharing of a common cause with other young men. I was proud to belong to the organization because it seemed the most committed to the nation's rights and cause. I knew the *Führer* solved many of the social and economic problems such as unemployment and inflation. Now I have begun to question the cost."

Thinking it prudent not to push the conversation, the fraudulent leader assured, "What you have said is safe with me and I don't think the days are as dark as you say. All will be made right in the end."

"Thank you, sir. I do not know why I trust you but I really do," the assistant and driver confided.

Within days Corporal Pfefferkorn reported, "Stuttgart headquarters called and said that Major Erwin Foltermann is concerned about reports of downed

Allied airmen who are trying to get to the vicinity of Littach. Many captured allied airmen think they have a route of escape near this town. He wants to come and consult with you and check the programs and procedures in place to seal off the Swiss border. They said Berlin is highly upset over these reports.

"Thank you, Pfefferkorn. He is welcome to come and check but you know that we have had no success in capturing any around here. The security police haven't reported any apprehensions since Ranck dealt with the Jewish family."

"You are right, sir, but my nose tells me something is going on around here. It surprises me that you are so little concerned about it. You go out on your motor patrols at night but nothing ever comes of it. The countess seems to have had a big impact on you and your views, from what I have heard. I am not terribly concerned for two reasons. First, as I have said, I think the war is lost and I think you agree with me. Why else have you not reported me and had me, at the least, sent to the eastern front? I also doubt the escape of a few fliers is going to impact the war very much. The more I think about it the more I think that you are not true. Maybe that is why I admire you and have a deep affection for you. You are a good man and if you ever need me, I stand ready to serve you, no questions asked. I now depend on my own judgments and not on what I read or people tell me. Sir, I serve you with pleasure!"

"Thank you, Ludwig." Carl for the first time addressed him familiarly, "I too believe you to be a good and true man who is loyal to the Fatherland."

At the appointed moment, the major arrived from Stuttgart to make his inspection and inquiries. As he toured along the Swiss border, he excused Carl from dismounting the vehicle during his walks along the boundary. Finally, he informed Carl, "The observation posts are located perfectly. The whole border is under the observation of at least two posts. You have also done a great job with the trip wire alarms. For me, I cannot see how the scheduling of foot patrols could be improved. The dogs have gained few indications of anyone in the area who does not belong there. I do not think a mouse could sneak across in your area. However, I would like to talk to the local police and a few other local people."

Carl heard the police chief report to the major, "All is as calm as the night Christ was born around here. We have had only one sighting of anyone in flight in the last six months. If the *Führer* needs rest from the bombing, Littach would be better than Berchtesgaden. Its so quiet here its boring."

"Maybe you should have a break from the boredom by moving to the eastern front!" the *Gestapo* officer retorted. Then to Carl, "Let's go!"

In the local security force office he ordered, "Schleiter, you remain here while I just walk around town for a bit."

As he walked through the door Carl imagined that he, Carl, received a strange glance from Pfefferkorn.

Within two hours, the Gestapo officer returned and growled, "There is something rotten around here. On the surface, your procedures look admirable but I have heard in town that many suspicious things are going on. Fugitives have been apprehended in Bonndorf and in Donaueschingen and in other towns to the north but here there have been no apprehensions. What do you say to that, Captain? How can you explain that, Captain? They have been caught in Neustadt and in Lorrach and in Waldshut but no, not one has ever been caught in Littach! What possible explanation can there be to that? More of those captured said they were headed to Littach than any other place in this area but none has ever been caught here in this quiet little hamlet. Please, please explain this curiosity to me, Captain Schleiter! My sources tell me your whole devotion to our cause has changed. Ranck reported his suspicions about you but his death and your connections in Berlin prevented a real investigation of his suspicions. Yes, indeed, there are queer things happening and I want answers.

❀

December 1943–July 1944
Invasion

"Sir, are you questioning my diligence? Or are you questioning my ability? Or are you questioning my devotion to the *Führer?*" counterattacked Carl. "If you are unsure of my commitment, please check my dossier with *Reichsführer* Himmler. Please be aware that the loss of a foot may change more than the physical! It is difficult to be so sure of one's self when you are crippled by the loss of a foot," Carl dissembled and then returned to the offensive. "If your sources are so sure of themselves you may ask them if they have detected any fugitive strangers in Littach. Have you checked with the local police to see if they are concerned about the security in my area? I will tell you that I suspect that one of your informants is jealous of my wife, the countess, even if they were childhood playmates. You see, I do know what is going on in this town and I think I know the identity of most of the *SD* agents."

Thinking as rapidly as he could Carl decided that silence was best from this point. "Maybe," he considered, "it is best for Foltermann to look elsewhere for fault. After all, it could be the police who were to blame. It could even be the *SD* agents because they were known for their own self-seeking. Some good citizen may be doing a good job in receiving and hiding the fugitives. I know at least one woman is not loyal to the *Nazis*. I must not accuse anyone else for that is a sign of guilt. Let Foltermann figure it out himself."

As Foltermann fixed his eyes upon him as though trying to look inside his mind, Carl decided to take another step. "Shall we call Berlin and report this situation to *Herr* Himmler? After all if we have a bad situation in this region and have no answers as to why, possibly the *SS* and the *Gestapo* could send some help."

Foltermann, voice tense, reacted, "I don't need help to know what's going on in my area of responsibility! There will be no phone call and no report to *Herr* Himmler by either you or me! You will hear from me again and I will find out what the explanation to this curiosity is!

"Is my car outside? It had better be because I have better things to do than this banter. Goodbye, Captain Schleiter! *Heil* Hitler!"

As Foltermann stalked out of the station, leaving Carl leaning on his crutches, the latter happened to glance at Pfefferkorn's face. The knowing look and small smile stirred the inner part of Carl's mind. As soon as the room cleared, he turned to the corporal and queried, "Well, what's on your mind, Pfefferkorn. You look like the cat that swallowed the bird. Give it to me and tell me what you think is amusing!"

"Oh, I agree with the major. There is something strange about Littach. There is evidence of those trying to get out of Germany all around us. There are captures over there and captures over there but there are no captures here. I still do not know why but you go out in the car to 'patrol' because you never find anything. Yes, you are a strange man but at the same time you seem a very good man, sir. I would never tell anyone my suspicions but I would warn you to be careful.

"I followed Major Foltermann at a discreet distance when he left for his walk around town and he went straight to your wife's friend *Frau* Randorff. He appeared to be calm and satisfied when he entered but was flushed and rushed back to the office after his hour or so talk to the woman. I really believe that she is a snitch who informed against you and her old playmate the countess.

"It makes me angry that the prying bitch could bring suspicion on you and I don't care what you have done or what you are doing. You have treated me like a brother and have been the first family I have known. I never thought that I would be on first name terms with a countess who I really believe has strong affection for me. Sir, your wife is so...so...German...so good...so strong, so mother-like, sir. She is what the old books say a wife and mother should be, sir. Sir, I love your wife as if she was the dearest sister that ever existed. She loves you as a wife should love her husband. Sir, I really like you but please believe me that I hope that no harm ever comes to you because I know that it would hurt her so much. You and she have my highest loyalty. But I must warn you that I know officially that you are being watched almost all the time so please be careful in your activities."

At first stunned into silence, Carl could only respond after he collected his thoughts. "Thank you, Ludwig. You are certainly right about the Countess Marlene. She has every good quality a lady should have. When she cares her heart flows over with an unrestrained love that will last as long as she lives."

Carl, smiling, then added, "I am glad that you described your love as fraternal such as a brother has for a sister otherwise I might be forced to have you posted to the eastern front. But I understand. Even if I did not love her as a wife, I know that I would love her with the deepest love a man can have for a sister. However, I love her as a man loves a woman." Carl continued with a stray and idle thought followed by a question, "Do you know that the ancient Greeks had three words for 'love' but those who speak the Germanic languages seem to have only one? I wonder why that is?"

Pfefferkorn then took over, "Sir, please warn her that she may think that the Randorff woman is her old friend but she hates the countess. I heard her say that she would bring the proud prig to her knees when she got enough information on her to convince the authorities that she was not loyal. *Frau* Randorff said that when they played as children your wife always insisted on being the princess or queen because she was really noble. *Frau* Randorff tells the women of Littach that your wife would say to her, 'I am of the real nobility but you are only a commoner, Erika, so I get to play the princess.'"

"*Frau* Randorff even inferred that she would invent some conversations quoting seditious statements by the countess but she has been foiled because your wife stays at the castle and rarely visits with the town folk. No one would believe that she was supposed to have said something against the *Führer* when she has not talked at all. To *Frau* Randorff she is Countess Mum."

"Thank you, Pfefferkorn, for the caution. We will keep it in mind. Now let us go and see what the good Annaliese has found for our evening meal. You will again eat with us as I tell the countess of your deep but brotherly devotion."

"Sir, please don't say a word. She might despise me for having even the kind of love and respect I have."

With a nod of understanding, the captain and corporal secured the office and departed for the residence.

Soon thereafter Hans reported, "I picked up an American who claims to be a general in the American air force and finally got him into the dungeon beneath the ruins. He rants and raves almost as much as the *Führer*. He demands to know what is going on, how the operation works, who is in charge? All that kind of stuff. He's like a stallion kicking in a Dresden shop."

After consulting with Marli and Hans, Carl thought it wise to take some preventive action so went to the concealed chamber. The downed officer's star on his collar convinced Carl that he was a brigadier general. Carl decided to let himself be identified because, he reasoned, maybe this man's high rank can help facilitate our operation.

The American officer was shocked to see a man who appeared as some kind of German officer, enter his place of concealment, render a salute, and hear the words, "Lieutenant Carl Solms, United States Army Air Corps, at your service, sir!"

The only words that came to the senior officer were, "What the hell?"

As quickly as he could and as fully as time permitted Carl explained his experiences since being shot down. He also explained what the quartet in the castle had done and continued to do to help escapees from Germany.

Without a great deal of what he thought would be unnecessary explaining his reason, he then made a request. "Sir, when, I guess if, you get back to England, I request that all fliers be briefed to say, in the event they were both shot down and captured, that they had been told to avoid this area. They might say that intelligence sources had reported that the SS officer responsible for security in this vicinity demonstrated that he would execute captured pilots summarily. However, the crews should understand that they should come this way if directed by others, primarily Germans, if they evade capture at first. I would appreciate some testimony that I am a mean so-and-so in order to build up my position. I still request that no pilots be told of our operation prior to flights into the continent."

"I will see if I can do that if and when I return to England. I must say that you are a bold son-of-a-bitch. It is strange how you got here where you are probably doing more good than if you were flying a plane. By the way, the krauts will check you out in some way. They may well try to sneak a plant on you. You know, have a German in an allied flying suit show up to see what happens."

"That has been tried once before, but I agree, they might try again. You understand that no one in Germany knows exactly how the route works from start to finish."

"Well, wilco to your request, Lieutenant Solms," and then with a smile questioning, "Or should I say, Captain Schleiter?"

"Could I ask, sir, who are you? I mean, what is your name? That is, who am I talking to?" Carl asked.

"Oh, sure, I am General David McDowell and that's all I am going to tell you. You know, you could be something other than what you claim."

Carl thought his contact with General David McDowell ended forever as he watched him clamber down the ladder to the tunnel and, turning upward, render an Air Corps salute.

As the December of 1943 turned into January of 1944 the Allied air armadas swept across the European skies in ever-increasing numbers and devastation. The German *Luftwaffe* struggled to stem the destruction of Germany's cities and industries. Fighter planes as well as anti-aircraft guns insured that the escape route through the tunnel continued to be used at lest on a weekly basis. The day activities of the residents of the castle continued. Sometimes visitors called on the young noble woman. Among these, of course, was her old "friend." Erika Randorff assiduously sought the Countess Marlene's views on the state of the war and the German leadership.

"You do know that it is only a matter of time before the *Führer* brings about another miracle like the great Friedrich did in the "Miracle of 1759" when the Czar died and the French and their allies were defeated. That was a time when everything seemed dark and lost but the gods and German character came through under the command of a genius. Don't you think that the *Führer* is a genius in military strategy, Marlene?"

"He has done much more than any of his enemies expected, that's for sure," Marli evaded.

"Not only that, but he also did wonderful things for our people before the Poles picked a fight and attacked us so suddenly in thirty-nine. Then the stupid French and high and mighty English had to stick their noses into our business, our fight. Things would have been good if they had stayed out, no?" pressed the merchant's wife.

"And the dirty Jews! Just see how our nation has been cleansed of that contamination! No good German can disagree with that. Our beloved *Führer* provided the people the opportunity to rid our nation of that scum, don't you agree?"

In response the only safe answer that came to mind was, "He did do what you have said."

Marlene, understanding on her own and cautioned by Carl, refused to talk of anything but the cold weather, the prospects of the crops on her estate, and her wonderful little baby who she was more than delighted to bring out from the nursery where she herself had once slept. The frustration of an old friend was palpable.

Another and more welcome caller was Ulla von Rudel. Although her husband was highly ranked within the *Wehrmacht,* she was pleased to be warmly welcomed into the home of one of the most ancient of the German nobility. She openly stated as she prepared to sip her tea, "I am honored to be received by you. You come from such an ancient line. I understand your family traces its roots back to the Saxon chiefs that withstood Charlemagne and they have served Germans of all tribes faithfully for a millennium. The Field Marshal's family only goes back to the wars with Napoleon and mine, oh, my, my father made his fortune in making paint for the inside and outside of houses. Your bearing, no, more your graciousness, shows me the value of your background. I am happy to be able to come into your home but, even more, you give me great pleasure with your company and conversation. Of course, I owe much to my husband who has had such a distinguished career."

Marli received the compliment with poise and replied, "You are most kind to represent me that way but I know that you know that you would be welcome into any salon in the nation. Your husband's bravery, skill and fame are honored by all who know him or even know of him. From all reports that I read he has acquitted himself well and honorably in all the fields where he has served and most particularly in the campaign in France in 1940."

"Yes, Marshall Rudel is a good and brave man who knows his business. The military life has been his existence as it was his father's and grandfather's before him. He has studied it on his own and under the best military minds of the century. You should see his library on the science of war. Now he is so frustrated. He and the other generals know what should have been done but that corporal in control thinks he knows more because, ha, he is a 'genius.' Now my husband knows that if the Allies are successful in landing in France the war is irretrievably lost. If we face a front in France as well as the ones in Russia and Italy we must sue for peace and hope that the other side will withdraw their demand for unconditional surrender."

"*Frau* von Rudel, you must be careful how you talk," cautioned Marli. "There are SD agents in town. You would not know if I were one—which I definitely am not. You must be careful with your tongue or else your husband might suffer."

"I have no fear of your being a secret agent of the *Nazis,* dear Countess," reacted the soldier's wife, "You do not come into town enough to be an agent of the *SD.* You bear the heritage of nobility and goodness. Everyone knows that. It is the talk of Littach. Your good character seems to have changed a man that all thought to be beyond good. Yes, we all believe even he has you to thank for the fact that he is well thought of in the community. All, that is, except those who are as he once was. But I must be going. It is good to be able to confide with you."

Marli aided the lady with her coat and saw her not only to the door of the residence but accompanied her to her automobile through the feathery snow of the January afternoon. The hostess of the castle watched wistfully as the vehicle disappeared. She too had enjoyed the break in the routine and conversation with an educated woman. She considered whether she had held herself too aloof from the society of Littach and if this might not bring more suspicion on all of those in the castle. She knew that she had pride in her family and heritage since childhood. She questioned herself, "Is the reason I don't spend time in town because of security or is it because I have little desire to contact the common folk there?"

When her husband arrived that night she mentioned "Do you think that not having much contact with the townspeople might lead them to suspicion about us? I think that I might have, as they say, a little *soiree* and invite Rudi Gerlach and his wife, the Hühns, the Randorffs, Erika would know that something was wrong if she couldn't come, and the Greiders. Is Major Foltermann married? No, well I'll invite him anyway along with *Frau* Field Marshal von Rudel."

Hans asked, "Would it be correct to use the Frenchies again to help in the kitchen and to keep the glasses full. The way the war is going, I feel a little nervous with the French in the house. You know that this one Armond was a pastry chef before the war. I think he would welcome the opportunity to keep his skill with the oven. The other three could keep glasses and plates full."

Carl was the first to respond, "That is a fine idea. They would probably welcome the break from the fields but do we have suitable clothes for them for such a service?"

Liese answered, "You leave the costumes to me. We are going to have a great time."

Carl agreed that the French could again serve indoors for the occasion so long as they simply offered the French prisoners an opportunity to help. The French quickly agreed to serve on a voluntary basis and understood they would earn a reward of food and drink that would be saved especially for them. So the invitees gathered with delight at the castle residence of the young countess.

Elena Hühn was unable to curtsy enough to satisfy her sense of unworthiness to be admitted to this place of this noble lady. As the guests arrived the Gerlach couple engaged Ernst Greider, "Soon the great miracle weapons that our scientists are developing will be in action and then we will see what for! I hear that we have developed a super fast plane with an entirely different propulsion system that will stand the Ami and English aircraft on their heads! And Rommel says that if the enemy dares to attempt an invasion they will never set foot on the continent. No, I say that no German should worry. We have the best generals, the best weapons, the best scientists and designers, the best soldiers, and, above all, the best *Führer* any nation has ever had. The enemy should look and see what he has done in taking a broken down and demoralized people buried in their shame and made them the masters of Europe and tomorrow we will master the world. The Bolsheviks may be pushing toward Germany but we have seen how quickly that can change when we remember the Miracle of 1759 and the great battles of Tannenberg and the Masurian Lakes. In the last war a few Germans routed huge Russian armies. Yes, indeed, I think the tide will turn if it has not turned already."

Greider contributed to the optimism, "I understand that the *Führer* has taken much more of the control over the army in France and will throw our panzers at them when the enemy is the weakest even if they do manage to get a foothold, no, a toehold on the beach. There they will be sitting geese. He is going to wait until the bait is taken and then snap the trap on them. Yes, it is sure that we will win. We must win. We are superior in all ways. It is in our blood. Germans are the children of destiny from before the Roman Empire."

Frau Field Marshal von Rudel quietly ventured, "My husband cautions that we must not think that the Russians can not fight and are not well armed. He told me that their new tanks are the equal of ours and they have them in increasing numbers. While he had never been up against either the Americans or the British, he says those who have are in awe of their air power and artillery. In Africa nothing could move on the ground during the daylight hours without the probability of destruction. In addition, their logisitical support is awesome. When an Allied plane is destroyed it is replaced by two more. When a cannon shell is fired there are five more waiting and twenty more on the way to the front. They bring meals with candy and turkey from the middle of America. A friend of my husband said that American fighter planes are now escorting their bombers into the deepest parts of our country. It is going to be a tough war to win according to the field marshal."

The slate-blue eyes of Erika Randorff had quickly swept over the small gathering even as she had entered with her merchant husband. Then her eyes quickly followed over the group to the wife of the field marshal and the other invitees. *Gestapo* Major Erwin Foltermann finally arrived at the castle door to complete the invited group. Removed from the main group as he talked with Mayor Otto Schlenkman, Carl thought he saw a glance of shared secrets between the secret policeman and the merchant's wife. This impression was reinforced as he detected the two move away in private talk with glances flitting first to the marshal's wife, then to him, and finally to Marli. As he covertly watched it seemed that involuntary and instinctive motions to others in the room were made by the woman or the Gestapo officer. As the woman and man talked she seemed to become increasingly agitated, her voice carried across the room, "I tell you there is something fishy here!"

When she uttered these words, the major turned and found other groups, leaving the woman red-faced through frustration, anger and embarrassment. Understanding only that the conduct of the merchant's wife was ill mannered the *Frau* Field Marshall approached her in order to soothe her. Erika, continuing to smolder like a human Vesuvius, erupted, "And what do you want? It is those like you who have made things so difficult for the *Führer*. Everyone knows that the *Wehrmacht* is not loyal to him. Your kind is so proud of their military skills but it was our *Führer* who showed them how to defeat all of Europe. When they were running things they couldn't even beat the poor frogs of France in 1914. Now in Russia they have fought the *Führer* more than they have the Bolsheviks. But when he is victorious there will be things to put right and the good, common people of Germany will finally have their say."

With hardly a pause she took off in another direction, "I say that there is treason in Littach and I have my suspicions just who those traitors are! They are not of the common people but they come from the high and mighty. But they will be found out and dealt with by the harshest means. You just wait and see! Sometimes I have more respect for the Bolsheviks because they do stand for something no matter how odious it is. I have said my say! Come, Ludwig! We are probably not welcome here anymore."

Amidst the silence of the assembly the Randorffs were promptly handed their winter wraps by Pfefferkorn, who had volunteered to assist as a quasi-doorman for the occasion, and departed as the *SS* corporal closed the door decisively behind them. Even after the abrupt departure the silence continued for seconds until the Gestapo Major Foltermann raised a glass and shouted, "To the *Führer*. *Heil* Hitler!"

This was echoed by a voluminous return of "*Heil* Hitler!" as glasses were raised on high. The hostess and her husband found it unnecessary to join in the shout but did silently let their lips move as though they too joined in. Carl, near Marli, seemed to feel his crutch slip on the floor just as the glasses were lifted and seemed appreciative of the support his wife supplied in the emergency. She threw both arms around him while continuing to hold a glass in one hand. They hoped that all would see that under the circumstances they could not salute the leader of Germany.

After the toasts Foltermann approached Carl and Marli saying, "That was a most unfortunate outburst. I hardly knew the woman when she approached me," he lied, "and said that Littach contained a cell of traitors that the police should clean out. She made charges against specific individuals," as he cast a look at Carl, "but admitted she had no proof. I told her that every check I could think of to make had shown no cause for suspicion other than the lack of apprehension of fugitives in this vicinity. Now I begin to hear of summary executions in the area. Really, those, any such executions, should be reported as 'captures'. The records must be accurate.

"It is strange that the woman was so adamant. She wanted us to use the direst tools of interrogation and demanded that we get answers. I told her I have discovered that some in the room had extremely close connections with those in the very highest authority. I also said that she herself must be careful of who she accused. And how goes it with you, Captain, are you still keeping things so very quiet in your sector?"

Carl was certain that the last question was a hinted accusation and not a commendation but he replied, "We have patrols out night and day but they don't seem to come up with anything. I myself go out often but find no living fugitives in the area," permitting himself a knowing but enigmatic smile.

"That is indeed strange for their raids are increasing in size day by day and our boys in the *Luftwaffe* are bringing more and more down. Of course we get most of those bailing out of their planes immediately when they hit the ground but some manage to evade our fellows. It is odd that they seem to avoid your sector but we will see. Then again you do have a reputation that I must consider. But remember the record keepers. I must be leaving now for it's a slow trip back to my quarters without using my headlights. Good night and please give my thanks to the countess."

Frau Field Marshal Rudel remained to be the final guest to leave. She declined earnest and repeated invitations to stay over night because vehicles could not use their headlights since edicts had suppressed their use. Germans now recognized the ability of Allied warplanes to penetrate the entire Fatherland. As the invitation was made by his wife, Carl looked up to see the French prisoner-of-war Chalvet's eyes fixed upon him with simmering hatred. Seeing that Carl watched him, he raised his hand as though to adjust his scarf but as he removed his hand he made a motion as though slitting his throat.

The marshal's wife, after voicing increasing despondency about the conduct of the war, declined the invitation to stay and take breakfast at the residence. As she left Marli once more admonished, "My dear Ulla, please watch your tongue for we know, not believe, but know, that the town is increasingly filled with *SD* agents. Think of your husband if not of yourself. It would not take much for Hitler to believe the worst of a Wehrmacht officer what with their reluctance to support him wholeheartedly in his rise."

"Oh, bother, I will be careful. I promise you I will watch my lips. You are dear to worry over the Field Marshal and me." and with that remark made her departure.

Carl noted that Chalvet could overhear the interchange and as he passed the *ersatz SS* officer Carl thought he could hear the hummed strains of the *Internationale* quietly stemming from Chalvet's throat.

Coincidentally, the flow of fugitives faded at this point in the war. Both Carl and Hans remarked about it to one another but neither could discover the reason for sure. Hans thought the police and army united were becoming more effective while Carl hopefully guessed that it meant that fewer Allied planes were being destroyed.

Because of the slackening in the flow, Carl found it strange when once again two figures appeared at the rear door of the residence seeking, "Can you hide us here? We were told that some one in this place can hide us, feed us, and help us get to Switzerland."

Remembering the malevolence of Erika Randorff and the suspicions of Major Foltermann, Carl ordered, through the English of Marli, even as he drew his weapon, "Get on the ground and put your arms behind you! Who told you of this place? Some Germans? We will now thank you for their names so that we may deal with them expeditiously. Oh, no! Comrades in England? Please make up your mind—you have already said too much to be protected. The *Gestapo* will know how to deal with liars!"

Then to Marli he commented, "If the *Gestapo* did not want these swine for questioning, I would end their miserable lives right now like the others but we have been directed to take prisoners for interrogation. Hans, tie their arms tight. I do not care if it does give a little pain. They should have more. Tighter, Hans, tighter."

"Marli, phone the office and tell them we finally got something for them to pick up. Hurry, please."

Even as the events occurred in rapid-fire succession Carl wondered, "Am I making a mistake? These men may have made it here on their own without contact with those upstream from us to direct them and to send the proper signals. If I am wrong I am sending the two of them to the prison camp at best. I just cannot take that chance for if I am right it would mean death to all of us—a rather permanent condition. I had better play it real safe and stick to the program set up before I ever got here."

The swift arrival of police began to reassure Carl that he had made the right decision for it seemed that the only way that the reaction could be so prompt was that the station was forewarned. A telephone call from Foltermann confirmed Carl's action the next morning as he was congratulated, "*Wunderbar!* Schleiter, *Wunderbar,* You performed as expected on our little test with the *ersatz* fugitives. Please do not be put out with us for the little game. We were ordered to do so by authorities of the *Sicherheitsdienst.* It seems one of their agents has reported suspicions about activities in the castle. We had to check it out. I am concerned about some of your remarks. You will not take it upon yourself to deal in the final manner with your captures. We do want them in the prisoner chain for interrogation if nothing else. But a good job."

"No offense taken," responded Carl, "There is nothing to hide here and those in the highest authority are well aware of my commitment to the cause. You need not say that you are sorry for what you have to do. What you have to do you have to do. That has been my thought all my life."

"Well, I just want to be right with you. By the way, I think that *Reichführer* Himmler may visit your area. At least we have been instructed to make extra security sweeps for some very highly positioned person from the SS who may visit someplace around here. So let us be in good order."

Realizing the closeness of Friedrich Schleiter and the head of the *Schutzstaffeln,* Carl reacted joyfully as though the news gave the best information that he could receive, "Oh, please let me know when he is coming as soon as you can. You know that he has favored me in many ways and I would like to thank him. In fact, we would love to entertain him in our home. At the minimum he should dine with us."

"I know that you would like to have some private time and conversations with the *Reichsführer* but I do not think it will work out. He is a very busy man, you know, and has so many responsibilities. There are many reasons that you should…can not have private conversations with him." parried the major fearful of what this favored captain might report.

The forces hostile to Hitler advanced inexorably. To the east in Russia they were as a meat grinder against the men of the *Wehrmacht* across the plains of the Ukraine. They first isolated the Crimea and then forced a surrender. Finland once more sued for peace with the Soviet Union, their great bear of a neighbor. Like a blood infection the forces of America and the British Empire pushed north up the leg in the boot-shaped peninsula called Italy, coming ever closer to Rome.

At the meal one evening in March, Annaliese read a letter from their second son, Conrad, "Again my job and duties have changed. Now we have few planes to maintain so I have been transferred to a rail transportation unit and it is not easy. The enemy air forces are very active and we get very little rest. With a great deal of hard work and long hours, most at night, we do manage to get supplies through to our men on the coast. The good news is that I have been promised that I will be given a short leave before the end of the month. I am very anxious to see the little Count Eric. How is the Countess Marlene adjusting to motherhood? Under the circumstances it must be terribly hard on her."

Liese paused to explain, "Conrad has not been told of your husband's true identity and he knows what we all thought of Captain Schleiter. He thinks that you were forced to bear the child of someone you despised. Should we set him straight when he comes home on leave?"

"No!" came the instant rejection of the idea. "We'll just let him think that Schleiter has changed and that I have changed. He will have to be satisfied to see the love that surrounds our child even if he has difficulty understanding all about it."

When Conrad arrived, Hans' face hid joy within him as he observed his wife tearfully embrace this second-born who was now their older surviving child. The deaths of comrades on the western front in the war years following 1914 caused him to be both fatalistic and self-controlled. Like steady bursts from a machine gun, his heart throbbed and rang within his breast at the vision of one son safely home, no matter for how brief a time, while his face showed no emotion. Carl noted the height of the son exceeded that of the father by about three inches. Both father and son had the same blocky build. The young soldier wore the insignia of a *Luftwaffe* sergeant.

"You have heard us speak of *Sturmhauptführer* Friedrich Schleiter, Conrad, who was married to our sweet countess? Sir, this is our son Conrad returned from the service of the Fatherland. My son, it seems that the countess is now happily married. And, Conrad, this young man is *Sturmmann* Pfefferkorn, the driver for Captain Schleiter."

Carl noted that Hans never said directly that he was Schleiter but the cool look that the *Luftwaffe* sergeant shot his way told him that Friedrich Schleiter was not appreciated by one member of the Weber family.

In short order the party was in the vehicle, both of the mother's hands clasping the closest one of her son's while the father looked on in silent contentment. Carl, in the front with Pfefferkorn, heard the chronic mother's lament, "You are too thin. Have they fed you nothing? Just wait, I will feed you beef and pork and noodles and cabbage and top it off with some strudel that I have waiting for you."

"That sounds wonderful but I really want to talk with you." rejoined the son while Carl sensed, but did not see, the eyes of Conrad flitting from him and back to the father and then back to his nape. Other than the normal expected expressions of joy at the reunion and the news that the sergeant could only be spared from his duties for five days the journey to the castle was uneventful.

As soon as the returning son got out of the automobile he was again engulfed in the arms of a female, only this time the arms belonged to the young noblewoman of the castle. Despite their difference in social rank the two had enjoyed hours of play together during her childhood. The association had created those bonds that should exist between brother and sister.

"Conrad, it is wonderful to see you! And you are safe. You have not been injured, no?" In her enthusiasm the Countess Marlene dropped into a colloquial speech pattern. "Your mother told me what to do to have our evening meal ready when you arrived and all you need to do is to wash off the dust of your journey and come and enjoy your mother's cooking. All I did was to see that it did not get overcooked and prepare the table for a very wonderful homecoming." Then turning her attention to Pfefferkorn, she invited, "Ludwig, you will stay and celebrate with us, please. I imagine that Hans will bring out several bottles of the fine old wine he has hidden away!"

"Oh, no, Countess. You really should not honor me by calling me by my Christian name! It's not proper for I am only a low-born enlisted soldier but I thank you for your invitation and your condescension. The boys at the barracks are waiting to give me their money and their rations in a game of *skat*," the driver dissembled with a look at her that both was totally proper but went beyond gratitude.

"Oh, well, there is certainly more than enough for six but we will make Conrad eat so much that he will be ill and cannot leave us for his duties. If he has to leave, we will try to make his trousers too tight to fit. And, Corporal Pfefferkorn, do not *schnapp* your companions under the table before you take all that they have, you wicked fellow," Marli teased.

At the table that evening Carl thought it would be in the part for him to ask, "How are things in northern France, Conrad? Does it seems that the Allies will try to invade soon?"

"Actually things have heated up, Captain. The underground has really begun to increase activity and it is worth your life to try to negotiate the roads. The hunter planes are everywhere and the planes of the *Luftwaffe* seems to have passed from existence. We struggled to keep them in the air but it proved impossible. And recently there have been more attacks from both American and English twin engine bombers. I have seen formations of the big heavy bombers but we are bothered more by low level attacks. Those light bombers are more accurate and they are faster and come at us over the hills and trees. Like the hunter-fighters, they have been attacking railroad traffic but in addition they have bombed rail yards and bridges. Nevertheless we have been able to haul much material for the defense of the beaches, although much is done under darkness.

"You know, I have seen England! On a clear day you can look across the water and see the white cliffs on the other side. So often it looks so peaceful, the water birds drifting in the wind, the little white waves breaking on the shore and the clouds floating by high up in the sky. But it will be so hellish when they come to Calais that not even a mouse will be able to get ashore. Field Marshall Rommel has seen to it that millions of mines have been planted on the beaches and anti-tank traps are everywhere. Our infantry and artillery positions have been surrounded with concrete and are almost immune to attack by air or artillery. Rommel swears that we will not let them have enough land to get their feet dry."

"Are the plans fixed on Calais as the landing spot then?" questioned Carl.

"Oh, not at all! It seems reasonable that they will land there. First, it is only twenty miles over the channel which means their ship can have a quick turn-around. Second, it would be the shortest flight time for their planes which seems so important to them. And finally, it provides the shortest and most direct route into the Fatherland. Also I have heard that there will be yet another reason that I cannot talk about. But let's not talk about war. Countess Marlene, I am glad to see you apparently happy in your marriage. You know that from our days as children I have the deepest and humblest affection for you."

The young wife blushed, "Yes, things have developed miraculously well for me. My husband is everything I could ask for in a man. He truly loves me and is so very kind."

"From what I have heard that is most surprising but then I had never met the captain prior to this visit." As he spoke he eyed the senior officer to see if he had overstepped himself but all seemed well. "Sir, I was prepared to dislike you but my opinion has been shaken. Your personality certainly seems different form what I had been led to expect if you will forgive me. Sir, I think it would be an honor to serve under your command." The last was almost an impossibility but Conrad thought it might be wise to ameliorate the familiarity of his remarks to this *SS* officer who was known to have influence beyond his rank.

"Those are kind words, Conrad. I assume that I can properly call you by your Christian name because if you are almost a brother to the Countess Marlene then you are almost a brother-in-law to me. So a certain familiarity is acceptable. But what do you hear of your brother Wali?"

"The last I heard was from you, mother. You wrote that he was to be posted to the Eastern Front and that was not good news to me. The Russkies take few prisoners and I am afraid that fewer still will survive their camps. They are hard fighters, I hear, and the cold is abominable. Don't cry, Mutti, he's a tough and wily little nut that I think will make it somehow. But how do things go here?"

As Carl and Marli prepared for bed their conversation centered on the table talk of the evening. Carl asked, surprisingly for the first time, "Does Conrad know of the tunnel?"

Marli answer was equally surprising, "No, I discovered it by myself and told no one although, as I told you, I later discovered that Hans knew about it all along but did not want his sons to know of it when they were young. He said that he feared that might get hurt in it and also that they might use it for some no good purpose. But what do you think of the preparations for the invasion?"

"I am sure that they are very thorough and his reports really frighten me. I do not want to go through life as Friedrich Schleiter and will probably be discovered if there is a stalemate. From what he said about the air activity I believe that the date of the invasion is not far off."

The days of Conrad's leave and help with the chores about the castle passed too quickly for parents and son and again motherly tears were shed as he boarded the train.

The next week Carl received an order that he was to report to Kislingen for a meeting with the *Reichführer* Himmler. In route, with Pfefferkorn at the wheel, he wondered how this meeting would turn out. How well did Himmler really know him? What areas of discussion might be dangerous? Who did he know at the headquarters of the *SS* that he might be expected to ask about? The best course would be to say the least but to be effusive in his gratitude for what the *Reichsführer* had done for him. He was glad that his background had instilled in him the ability to hold his tongue but nevertheless he had Marli apply just enough face powder to give his complexion a realistic pasty tinge. He was also glad that Schleiter seemed to be one to flatter, even to lie, to gain favor.

Having been informed that they would meet at the Security Office in Kislingen, he instructed Pfefferkorn to drive there. The car stopped in front of an unmarked building with several men in civilian clothes apparently loitering on the five steps that led to the interior. These men observed an officer in the uniform of the *Schutzstaffeln* but missing an ankle and foot that forced him to awkwardly wield crutches up the steps. Out of respect for one who may have given a member of his body for the Fatherland, one of the guards held the door open and the captain struggled into the building.

A *"Heil Hitler"* by one in the uniform of an *SS* major greeted Carl as he entered the building. Following the appropriate *Nazi* greeting came the standard inquiry, "How's it going with you, Friedrich? Not so good from your appearance and from what I hear. You have really been through it, haven't you? You look like you just got out of your deathbed. Whatever possessed you to enter that building? The *Reichführer* needs men like you to stay healthy and hale. Besides the little ladies will be able to escape your clutches now that you are a cripple. The secretaries in the office are getting downright plump from their lack of exercise running from you.

"Oh, we did have great times bedding the Berlin bitches when you were whole. I never reached your record of five different ones in a week, though. I would not have believed you if I had not used agents to verify your daily report. Perhaps I could compete with you now that your face isn't so beautiful. I imagine that the pickings are not as great in that village, though. And of course you are married and must watch your P's and Q's. The *Führer* doesn't approve of open free-love, now does he? Besides I heard that her family has connections with Canaris and the *Abwehr* would like nothing better than to get something on one of the *Reichsführer's* favorites. But he is waiting for you. Come!"

Like a wounded animal Carl shuffled on his crutches a short but darkened distance down the hallway to the door opened for him by the major and entered an anteroom where three uniformed SS men were stationed. A high ranking non-commissioned officer was typing at a desk while the other two scrutinized the newcomer thoroughly as the major preceded Carl into an inner office. Carl took a seat near the desk of the enlisted aide where a stack of blank paper embossed with Himmler's name and title lay. When all the others in the office save for Carl and Pfefferkorn answered a call into the inner office Carl seized the opportunity to slip some of the stationery into his brief case as a "souvenir." When the enlisted aide and the others returned, his eyes fixed on a smallish, mustached man who turned his bespectacled eyes upon him. A fervent *"Heil Hitler"* exploded from the lips of the major accompanied by the upward jerk of the right arm in the *Nazi* salute. Carl's *"Heil"* seemed like a weak echo, as a slipping crutch required recapturing by his right hand. The return greeting seemed most perfunctory to Carl as the infamous Heinrich Himmler approached.

"Friedrich! Friedrich! How I have missed you and your fervor! I have no one that I can depend on to carry out the purposes of the Party like you. Oh, Telge here comes close but you did exceed him. What a wonderful job you did in the undesirable race relocation program wherever you went. Would you like something to drink after your drive? You do not look at all well. *Schnapps?* Wine? Coffee? Tea? Otto makes sure we have it all for our honored guests. Of course there are always those we do not honor who have other choices. Coffee! Otto, see that Captain Schleiter has a cup of coffee!"

Soon a small tray bearing a coffee pot, identified by the rich aroma it emitted, and necessary accompaniments rested close to Carl's elbow. The high official began his inquiries.

"And just how have you been? Not well it seems. But as you know I am a quiet man and not like our friend Goering. Just give me a full report."

Because a "report" had been demanded, Carl decided to concentrate on official matters within his area. "All has been unusually quiet in our area. So much so some questions have arisen of which you probably are aware. We have had far fewer infiltrators than surrounding sectors; a fact for which I have no explanation. As was reported, one family was apprehended and executed when I first arrived in the Littach area before Ranck was killed."

"Enough of that! I do not want to be aware of those details!" Himmler insisted as he eyed the one Carl now knew was Schleiter's old acquaintance Major Otto Telge. "But do tell me why you entered the fiery building and how has your care been? The *Reich* needs all the good warriors it can find. You should not have done that!"

"I can not explain what came over me when I saw the children in danger. You know that I am a most cautious man when my own well being is concerned but there was something about the children—they looked so German, so much like me that something took over." Carl responded in truth although he would not use the word "Aryan' rather than "German" in his explanation.

Almost grudgingly the security chief of all of Hitler's *Reich* allowed, "I guess that speaks well of you. After all they were German children and you identified with them. I guess some will wear uniforms and some will be mothers of future warriors. You did save German blood!

"And your marriage? I understand that the organization was of some help in arranging that. It is reported that you have brought the damned aristocrat to heel! Maybe you should give lessons to all the German men who have trouble with their women. Are you aware that her father's good friend Bonhoeffer is working with the *Abwehr*? He has gone to Switzerland under their auspices ostensibly to make contact with intelligence agents but we are sure he is trying to arrange terms for a peace with England and America. Did he ever visit *Schloss Altburg* since you have been there?

"No," the *pseudo SS* captain responded, "He has not been anywhere in my district to the best of my knowledge. I also doubt that there are any true reports that he has been. Has he been conspiring?"

"We do not know definitely. If we did he might be singing another tune in another place. He talks far too much about Christian love and accepting the lesser races to suit any of us. You know, that Christian claptrap about loving your neighbors and enemies. That will be all, Telge, I would like to talk to Schleiter alone about some disturbing things I have heard."

"Yes, indeed, my *Reichsführer, Heil* Hitler!"

As the major departed Carl saw Himmler arise and put his ear to the door as though listening for retreating boot steps. He returned and beckoned Carl to come very close to him and turned a radio in the room to a higher volume. He then whispered literally into Carl's ear, "I have done much for you have I not? Yes, indeed I have. I sent the best doctor available to repair your face. You became a very young captain with my help. When Kaltenbrunner was after you by using that vermin Ranck, I interceded and blocked every effort to embarrass me through you. Since he became head of the R. S. H. A. Kaltenbrunner has tried to move up again and get my position. I do not know who his collaborators are and I am very careful. With you I know enough to have you hung on a meat hook at any time so you have to go along with me. This is what I want, if things get to going bad I want to be able to depend on you to control your sector in my behalf. I'm surrounded by a bunch of hyenas like Goering, Goebbels, Frank and Kaltenbrunner and at any time I may have to move against one of them so I want to be sure of those I can count on, do you understand?

Carl was able to get "Yes, my *Reichsführer*," out of his throat and then hear "That's all, Captain, get back to your work. Oh, by the way, your reputation must have penetrated even to England for prisoners have told us that they were warned to stay out of your area because you would shoot them after interrogating them. But do leave us some for interrogation purposes. We sorely lack intelligence from England." Then the head of the SS added, "I would not want to have your dossier if we do not win this war but I guess mine will be even worse if the Jews can manage it. Goodbye." At the wave of a hand Carl was dismissed from the bureaucratic presence.

On the drive back to Littach Pfefferkorn volunteered, "May I say something, Captain?"

"Of course."

"There was something about that building that made me nervous. It was…it was…kind of like there was a dark spirit there. I do not ever feel that spirit around you or the countess. Why that is I don't know. Can you explain it?" he finished rhetorically.

Early spring darkness had fallen by the time they approached Littach and Pfefferkorn drove straight to the *Schloss*. As they arrived Carl commanded, "I want you to come in, Pfefferkorn. You must have a warm meal and I know that Annaliese always had one prepared for me. The baroness always waits to share our meals together. There is always plenty for three or more. So you will come in. Possibly my wife can answer the questions about dark spirits that you have."

As he entered the residence his spouse directed, without hesitation, "Go wash your face, you look like death warmed over," as she reached up to plant a kiss on his lips. This spectacle of the feared SS captain being ordered about and simultaneously kissed by the smaller human brought a delighted smile to Pfefferkorn. The noblewoman then cautioned him, "You had better not laugh because you are going to get some of the same!" planting a kiss on his cheek. As Carl crutched his way to the wash room, she asked his driver, "Did all seem to go well at Kislingen? Did you see the *Reichsführer*? I am exceedingly glad to see you both back safely…you know, with the roads and aircraft and such."

"Yes, I did see *Reichsführer* Himmler in the office but did not speak to him and he did not speak to me. The captain spent some time with him. I must say that I had a depressed feeling all the time we were there. It was like there were dark spirits, even demons, present in the building. You know so much. Can you tell me why? It just makes me wonder about everything."

"All I can tell you, dear Ludwig, is that there is good and there is evil in this world. There is love and there is hate. It is better to speak of love like my Lord Jesus did than to speak of hate like His enemies did. The Bible speaks far more of love than hate. When guests are absent we have a time of devotion with the evening meal and tonight I will ask that we read the thirteenth chapter of the first letter to the Corinthian church from the New Testament. I trust that my husband will approve."

"You are a wonderful lady. I can see how any man in association with you could change. The captain is not at all like he is described by those who know him only by reputation. Those who know you both say that he has made you submit but I know that is not true. You are a wonderful couple and you together have encouraged me about the human race. Here's the captain."

Carl was correct in his prediction of the amount of food that Liese had prepared. After the meal Marli asked if they could read the chapter she had described to Pfefferkorn and all assented. So Carl read:

Though I speak with the tongues of men and of angels, and have not love,
I am as sounding brass, or a tinkling cymbal.
And though I have the gift of prophecy, and understand all mysteries, and all knowledge;
and though I have all faith, so that I could remove mountains, and have not love, I am nothing.
And though I bestow all my goods to the poor,
and though I give my body to be burned, and have not love, it profits me nothing.
Love suffers long, and is kind; love does not envy. Love does not vaunt itself,
Love is not puffed up, does not behave unseemly, does not seek her own,
Is not easily provoked, thinks no evil, does not rejoice in iniquity, but rejoices in the truth.
Love bears all things, believes all things, hopes all things, endures all things.
Love never fails but where there be prophecies, they shall fail;
Whether there be tongues, they shall cease; whether there be knowledge, it will vanish away.
For we know in part, and we prophesy in part.
But when that which is perfect is come, then that which is in part shall be done

away.

When I was a child, I spoke as a child, I understood as a child, I thought as a child:

But when I became a man, I put away childish things.

For now we see through a glass darkly; but then face to face:

now I know in part; but then I shall know even as I am known.

And now abides faith, hope, love, these three; but the greatest of these is love.

The *SS* corporal responded, "Those are wonderful sentiments but who has ever lived them out? It is a nice thought but no one ever achieved it. We all want to get even with our enemies."

Carl corrected gently, "You are wrong, Pfefferkorn. There was once a man on this earth that not only said to love your brothers, your neighbors, and your enemies but when He was falsely put to death, He begged, 'Father, forgive them.'"

"Aha, it was the Jews who murdered Jesus! You can not deny that!"

"Actually it was the Roman ancestors of the Italians, who are the former allies of the Fatherland, who did it when demanded by some, but not all Jews. In fact though His death was necessary because of me and my own sins, I, through my sins am as much to blame for His death as anyone. But Pfefferkorn, for reasons beyond our knowledge, He loves us and wants us to be His, to have fellowship with Him, to be his companion, to be His bride and reside in His arms of love. If you sense a difference between this house and the building in Kislingen it is because He and His love are here between the countess and Annaliese and Hans and, yes, me. This is what I have learned and this is what changed me. It has not been the love of a woman that made any change in me but His love. That I know I have for all eternity and that has made a difference with me."

At the end of Carl's sermonette, Pfefferkorn remained silent and his face still other than his eyes studying first Marli and then Carl and then back once more to Marli. "Have I gone too far? The message of Christ is certainly not the message of Hitler. Do I feel too secure with Pfefferkorn? I have violated our commitment to security but, somehow, I think He told me to do it. I do not believe that he is but he could be an agent of the *SD* luring us into complacency. Is he? I do not think so but all things are possible."

The next weeks passed quietly with the usually outgoing Pfefferkorn contributing to the quiet as he seemed to have periods of silent meditation in the office. There was much reason for Germans to be quiet for almost all sensed the fate of the Germany they knew hung in the balance. The eastern enemy's presence pressured through Poland. The radio, however, increasingly dared the western enemies to make their move along the coast of France.

The number of pilots seeking refuge and escape continued to dwindle. Those in the castle questioned if this was due to a more effective German effort or if fewer Allied planes were being hit. They could not know that the British and American air forces had increasingly gained control of the skies of Europe. Now fighter planes provided protection for the slower and more vulnerable bombers as they breeched the defenses into the deepest parts of the continent. Even in Littach, so far south and so close to neutral Switzerland, the vapor contrails of vast numbers of bombers could be seen as they circumnavigated the Alpine nation to strike in Austria and the southernmost regions of the *Reich* from Italian bases.

In late April the young Walther Weber surprised them all with his arrival at the Littach rail station. It seemed that this young man, called "Wali" by family and friends, had a delay of four days on his way to Vienna. There, he informed his family, "I will be instructed in a new type aircraft that will be faster by far than anything in the air at this time. It is expected that this new plane will really mess up the enemy air fleets. But, my God, we really have trouble against the Russians! We can only operate out of an airbase for short periods of time because our front can not hold them back. If something doesn't happen soon they will be on our soil and there will be hell to pay when they seek their revenge. They are barbarians and we all fear to fall into their hands. If we can only keep the Americans and British from creating a front in France then maybe we can concentrate on the Russians and make them want to end the trouble there. From what I hear we have a better than even chance to keep the Tommies and Yanks out of France."

Later Carl asked Marli, "Did Wali always drink so much? He didn't show much outward signs of being drunk except that he really wanted to talk and I never saw so much liquor being drunk by one man. He was able to manage his tongue in front of me and he wanted to hold little Eric, so I guess he can handle it."

"No! No! Wali was never drunk before the war! He has seen so many comrades die. There is so much tragedy in this war. I think he just wants to forget what has happened to his friends and what will likely happen to him. When he was younger he was very tender and sensitive, particularly to me."

"You have seen much war, Hans, when do you think the invasion will come?" queried Marli as they entered the room to be with Hans and Liese..

As a taciturn Teuton, the older man responded with few words, "I do not know." His thoughts, however, spoke through him, "This war is so different from the old war that I fought in. Then we struggled for the next hill. Now cities are taken in hours. Then we moved by rail and foot. Now they move by track and wheel. That is, if soldiers are not moved by airplanes like the *Wehrmacht* did in Crete. Then we needed phone lines or messengers to communicate. Now everyone has tiny radios that both send and receive messages. The whole world is different. I am past my prime so how should I know."

As the long winter began to show signs of passing with the clouds and snows of winter surrendering more and more to the invasion of the light of the sun. Once more it became routine for the German noble lady to walk the estate with her farm-boy husband to the serenade of the rills gushing down the hills to join the waters of the Rhine. The advance guard of birds arriving from their flight across the sea from Africa and the Italian peninsula added their songs to the accompanying rushing of the waters. On those days when the sun claimed victory over the clouds, Carl relished the play of sunlight and shadow on the countenance of his love. During these forays into the forest a well wrapped Eric let his mind absorb the lessons of sight as he peered over a parent's shoulder. These moments of being together bounded by the clear forest, seemingly in a world of their own, were precious memories carried into the perilous future.

Messages received in Carl's office as March became April clearly indicated the tautening tension within the highest command of German forces. All elements of *Nazi* forces, and especially those even tangentially connected with gathering information, were ordered to be alert for any indications from the enemy of the time and place of the channel crossing. The dispatches left no doubt of the imminent invasion of the continent.

April skies became ever clearer as the edge of the winter coat of ermine white snow of the Alpine peaks to the south began to creep up the slopes. Now the vapor trails of hundreds, even thousands, of high-flying warcraft lined the skies above *Schloss* Altburg. But the isolated corner of Germany remained placid under the clearing skies as April became May. Each passing day increased the tension contained in the communiqués arriving at the office in Littach. It was, or should have been, clear that the immediate impact of any invasion on this area of Germany would be minimal. The news of the war's progress from the east grew constantly more dire to the *Nazi* cause.

Conrad's rare letters told increasingly of attacks on the communications, airfields, and roads in France by both enemy warplanes and by French partisans. For months the wounded from Italy and even the eastern front flooded into the small hospital in Littach. Higher headquarters instructed Carl to inform the local authorities that the local hospital was to be totally available for the wounded returning from Italy and even the Russian front.

Burgermeister Otto Schlenkmann, when informed of this development, lamented, "I know! I know! I got the letter too! But what am I to do with the sick and injured of the town, eh, Party Man? My own mother has tuberculosis and should not be moved! You just tell me what I am to do with her? And *Frau* Parotto? The poor woman is dying with cancer and has no family. What is she to do? What are we to do?"

Carl quickly determined to put forth a bold solution, "I authorize you, by the power of the *Reich,* to requisition any house and any unused labor to care for the civilian sick and injured. Your mother will live with you and your wife will care for her. If you need additional assistance during the night you will direct the citizens to provide that aid. Find a nice large house for *Frau* Parotto and have the owners provide care for her with the assistance of others where needed. You might as well get used to this kind of thing with the raids on the larger cities and the impending invasion. We may have to requisition many more houses. Just do your job as mayor and take care of your comrade citizens."

Carl reported to Major Foltermann, "I have obeyed the general orders to prepare my sector by using all resources available. I have not received specific orders for what I have done, but my actions have been in the spirit of my instructions. I have made every house in Littach and the surrounding area available not only for the civilian sick and injured but also for the military in the event the capacity of the hospitals is exceeded." He then gave the detailed instructions he had given to Schlenkmann.

"My God! You did well. Very foresighted. It appears that we are going to go through a rough time so you had better have everyone prepared. But you need to see that the *Hitler Jugend* are given some basic training, particularly in the use of the *Panzerfaust.* Those are the instructions I haave received to pass on to the *kreis* authorities. I am sending Sergeant Horst Graukop down to give the boys some training. And, yes, just how many beds can you provide at *Schloss Altburg* for the sick and wounded?

"Caught in my own rashness," Carl thought, but answered boldly, "We could take quite a number although the distance from town and accessibility to doctors and nurses would have to be considered. But anything we can do to help."

"Sometimes you confuse me, Captain. You have such a vicious reputation that it has spread to England but when I talk to you all I see is the sweet light of love. Yes, indeed you seem like two different men in your reputation and in your person. Oh, well, all things in life are not explainable. I'll be down for a visit and a beer when I can, until I see you again."

Three Tuesdays after this conversation an agitated and excited Heinrich Hühn hurried into the combination police station and security headquarters exclaiming to all he met, "The invasion has begun! It is on the Berlin radio that a diversionary attack has begun on the coast of Normandy and that the main attack at Calais, or in that area, is expected momentarily. Our lines are holding and it is expected that the enemy on the coast will soon be thrown back into the channel like we did at Dieppe. Finally we can get our hands on them. Nobody, and especially the English and decadent Americans, can stand up to our soldiers. Yes, we will roll them up shortly and then maybe we can have peace in the west and kill the Bolsheviks in the east."

"Normandy?" Carl repeated. "Pfefferkorn, do we have a map that shows Normandy?" Carl's schoolboy geography lessons had failed to burn into his mind the location of this French duchy.

Pfefferkorn assured, "Yes, sir, my Captain." True to his word a map of France with the ages old duchies and counties boldly outlined was flattened on his captain's desk. Carl, leaning on his crutches and rubbing his chin contemplated the chart while his eyes searched desperately for the word *"Normandie"*. The index fingers of several hands indicating the old duchy of the Normans saved him from his ignorance of French, even European, geography. He knew of Calais and had joined many others in assuming the thrust would come once and for all straight across the English Channel in the shortest over water route. He did not know that the German High Command, even Hitler himself, saw this route provided the shortest distance over the water and also opened the heartland of Germany to the invaders. Therefore it was the only logical site for the overwater landings. The German leaders ignored the range of the Allied fighters, the enormous availability of ships, and much of American military doctrine.

Carl mused over the development to himself, "Interesting. Interesting, indeed! I wonder how the battle is going?"

The desk sergeant of the police station seemed to have the same thought as he said, "I have a radio at my desk. I think it would be right to keep abreast of the situation. You cannot tell what might develop. Here, let's turn it on to the

Schaffenhausen station." All in the room knew that listening to the Swiss station was forbidden.

Time passed before any reports came over the air and some began to question the authenticity of the communique. But eventually a voice reported that Field Marshal von Rundstedt had informed the *Führer* of the attempted landings and that the forces of the German nation were holding their ground and had every expectation of victory in the vicinity of Caen, Bayeaux, and the Cotentin Peninsula where Cherbourg was located. The forces of the *Reich* were on high alert all along the coast and especially in the area of Calais where the main enemy attack was expected.

All in the station waited, all but one hopefully, for the news that the landing had been smashed and driven back into the sea. One voice asked, causing an involuntary shudder in Carl,

"I wonder how many of the British and Americans were killed and how many were captured?"

Another voice proclaimed, "Well, one thing for sure. There will be no breach of *Festung Europa*! We Germans are the best engineers in the world and *Herr* Todt and his gang will have made the shore impregnable. By the time those poor Allied *schweinhund* get into the mines, the wire, and the bunkers they will wish that they were sipping tea somewhere in New York. I almost pity them."

No report of victory had come over the air as Carl and Pfefferkorn traveled to the castle residence.

Pfefferkorn was constrained to remain for the evening meal and to converse about the conflict in France. The legal long wave radio occasionally interrupted its music programming that ranged from Mozart to old German *lieder* with news from the fronts and Berlin. Hans provided a map and again the northwest coast of France was examined. By the time Pfefferkorn left for his quarters even the exaggerated claims of the German propaganda ministry did not conceal the fact that the landing site had not only been maintained but had grown during the day. It was only in the privacy of their room that Marli and Carl let their exuberant joy be vented. Their patriotic feelings for their land and people and the safety of their sons made the defeat of German forces bitter to the Webers. Their loathing of Hitler did not extend to their nation.

The sun was well up on the next day that was June 7 when Father Nimitz appeared. Entering in silence he quietly informed his parishioners and the young couple, "I have been warned that I should flee. Please do not ask why the authorities will seek me or how I was counseled. You know that I have reason to believe that you have a way to help people get out of the *Reich*. Will you help me? I have contacts in Switzerland and once there I will be safe in the arms of the Mother Church. I am not afraid to die but do not want to do so needlessly. Will you help me get to Schaffenhausen?"

CHAPTER 12

❁

June–August 1944
The Count

"Of course, of course we will do what we can to get you out of our country," assured Liese.

"Did you bring our marriage certificate from the church?" asked Carl.

"Oh, no! It escaped my mind in my start at the news that some churchmen had been taken. I will go back for it for you will probably need it. I know exactly where it is."

"Never!" Liese was adamant. "You will not go back. It is not safe for you there. I go to the church to confess and pray almost every day. If someone were there to arrest you, I would not know that you would not be there in the confessional. But where are the papers so I do not have to ransack the place to find them? There should be one about the birth of dear little Eric."

"They are hidden under the blessed Mother and Child to the east of the altar. You can pull the top layer of the pedestal, which is only a few millimeters thick, up with good fingernails. I hid the paper there. Please be careful and do no damage to the Lady and her Child!"

"Good! We will do that but now you must trust us and we must trust you. You will now see the whole of our little operation. First we must go to the old ruins." The priest Nimitz expressed astonishment as Hans revealed the trap door to him, revealing the chamber below. After doing all he could to make the priest comfortable with blankets, water and food for his overnight stay, Hans urged the priest, "When you are out please tell no one about this little escape hatch. There must be some reason that you must leave our land right now. I assume that you do not want to tell us, but if it does endanger us we would certainly want to know."

"I flee for I do not want to compromise the confessional. Some are planning the assassinations of the very highest officials of the government. I cannot say more other than that the Countess Marlene's father is a good friend of many of those involved in the plan. I do not know when or where the attempt will be made but I do know of the intent of many of those involved. Some of them are fervent observers of the requirements of the church and so confess in great depth. I fear that I will be arrested and tortured and tell what I know about quite a few things."

Nimitz's awe increased when the second secret opening out of the chamber revealed the shaft down to the tunnel. Before he went down the ladder, he turned, made the sign of the Cross and exclaimed, "So this is how you did it! I hope those who fled through this means know that He inspired your minds and souls. Go with God and I know that we will fellowhip again. Maybe the next time He will be with us and teach us those things we know not. Goodbye." The man of God then descended into the darkness below.

None of the residents of the castle ever again saw the good priest who had married Marli and Carl. Liese successfully rescued the written testimony testifying to the marriage and the birth of their son and Hans hid them again behind a purposely loosened stone in the old castle wall that had served as an *ersatz* wall safe for decades if not centuries. There they would stay dry and hopefully not be discovered by any other than themselves.

Forty-eight hours later Carl entered the *Silver Swan* as the uniformed men within greeted him with loud cheers. "What do you think, Captain? How long before we throw the English and Americans back into the sea? Rommel has them blocked at the edge of the water and it will not be long before our *panzers* counterattack and crush them. Rommel is a fox, indeed. He knows what he is doing and behind him is the genius of von Rundstedt! We have the greatest military scientists in weapons, strategy, and tactics that the world has ever seen. And Germans are the best soldiers."

"If Patton lands at Calais," chimed in another, "he will get a dose of the same medicine. I think we are just waiting for him there and," slapping his hands together to make a sound like a rifle shot, "our panzers will come like the tigers they are. London is getting a taste of bombing with our new weapons. I hear that more new weapons are on the way. We will make them pay for what they have done to our beautiful cities. Then they will come to their senses and know that the Jewish Bolsheviks are their greatest threats and not their fellow Aryans."

With caution heavy on his mind Carl reacted, "You are probably correct but I do remember that the English and the Americans fought well in North Africa even against the Fox. It is a mistake to underestimate your enemies. Not that Rommel does, for he has faced them before."

When the conversation turned to other subjects among customers in the German public house, Carl listened and nodded with judicial sagacity. Their glances often turned toward him as they seemed to seek his approval of their opinions. A small nod of approval from the known protégé of *Reichsführer* Himmler brought smiles of gratification from the declaimer. As he emerged from the muted light of the *gasthaus* into the brightness of the afternoon one of his crutches went flying away in a collision with another person. He avoided an embarrassing fall only by seizing the shoulders and clothing of *Frau* Erika Randorff.

"I did not see you," he stated the obvious. "My eyes had not adjusted to the light."

She made no effort to retrieve the fallen crutch or call to another for assistance but noted, "You are wrinkling and stretching my dress. I would thank you to release me."

At this point, a boy of about ten seized the chance to serve one who might be a hero of the *Reich* and picked up the fallen instrument, dusted it off, and handed it to the *SS* officer said by the adults to be a hero of the *Reich*.

"Good day," Carl greeted as though to make peace. "Please forgive my clumsiness if I have done you or your clothing harm. You are not injured are you?" Even as he asked he knew the only thing that may have been damaged was her ego.

"No, I am not injured at all," she retorted. She pulled out imaginary wrinkles as though the slight contact had sealed in permanent ripples in her woven woolen dress. "But I do wish that you would look where you are going. You should have taken time to let your eyes agree with the light," she instructed.

"I am glad that you can forgive me for my thoughtlessness. Do you have any news of the war? Being so far from Berlin it is hard to keep up with the latest word. I have heard that the *Wehrmacht* is extracting a great price from the Bolsheviks, Have you heard the same?"

"Yes, but many of the people are acting like traitors. I have heard some say that they wonder if the war can be won. The *Führer* carries such a heavy load for the people! He has led us to many economic and military victories. Nevertheless, when the going gets hard many begin to complain and change their minds. The *Führer* even had to sack Rundstedt for his pessimistic views. That is the aristocracy for you. They only seek their own well-being and care little for the ordinary German. Maybe I should not talk to you. You have certainly changed in so many ways. I still do not see how it is possible for a person to change so much in essential qualities. Your aristocrat seems to have won you over. You hardly seem like the same person who first came here with the 'no-o-oble' Marli after your marriage."

Carl noted how she sarcastically stretched out the word describing her "friend's" social status.

Erika continued, "Is she a witch that can change men to have her own character? No, witches are for fairy tales and our scientists have abolished belief in things like fairies, angels and demons. Now we know there are no fairies and they have never existed. There is some other reason for the change in you and I believe the authorities should keep their eyes on you for there is something out of place."

It seemed not to matter that on the surface Carl represented the highest authority in the Littach area so he surmised that she had access to other authorities.

"Oh," he countered, "the word from France seems good for Germany. The *Wehrmacht* seems to have stopped them near the beaches."

"Well, we will see who stands fast and who turns on the *Reich* and the *Führer*. There are people watching, you know. *Auf Wiedersehen.*" She turned abruptly and marched away.

Within days the glad tidings for the Germans began to fade. First, news filtered out that the allied aircraft had seriously injured the great leader Rommel as he drove to the front. This calamity to the *Nazi* cause impacted the nation psychologically. Then within two weeks further disconsolation followed as whispers began that the Americans and English had broken loose into the open country of France. The western foes of Hitler and his followers had established themselves solidly on the continent. Carl observed dour faces in the streets as well as at the city hall.

Liese increasingly expressed concern for Wali. "The Allies have so many airplanes. What can the German boys do? One must fight ten! Wali said that he has a good plane but he asks what can one plane do? Everyday I pray for his safety and for Conrad's too."

Immediately following the dark words from both west and east and during a sunny day in July, rumors raced through the Littach community that a member of his staff had assassinated Hitler at his battle headquarters. The Ministry of Information issued corrections saying that the *Führer's* injuries had been relatively minor. Within hours the German leader gave a radio address to the nation to demonstrate that he had the power and ability to remain in control. The voice on the radio assured Germans that the failure of the attempted assassination showed that destiny's hand directed him and willed him to exterminate those who opposed his leadership. Doubters and defeatists were to be identified and removed from the greater German society.

That evening in their room Marli expressed fears, "The *Nazis* hate my father and all he stands for. From the beginning, his opposition to *Nazi* doctrine meant to the Party that he was opposed to Hitler as a man. They would have loved to have brought him "into line" because of his reputation of integrity and intelligence. Long before the election of 1933 he often expressed his rejection of the programs of paranoid psychology of fear and hate the National Socialists advocated. For years many Germans seriously considered his views and some accepted them because of his uncompromising character. He would never take an expedient route when it came to the law. On the key issues he never believed that the ends justify the means.

"I have been told over and over again that my father applied the law under our old constitution as written, although he knew that a law higher than any nation's law exists. He told me several times that many Americans applied the higher law to Congress's law requiring that fugitive slaves be returned to their owners in the south. These people of faith explained that divine law trumped man's law.

"I expect father will be arrested if he has not already been. This I know. If they arrest him and put him in a camp, he will not survive. There are real and vicious criminals there who he sentenced. I believe that most of them respect him but there are those so full of hate they despise everyone, including themselves. He will not protect himself and so he will die."

As she finished stating her apprehensions Marli broke into wrenching sobs quaking her whole body. Carl moved more quickly than he thought he could to her side and took her in his arms as he consoled, "Darling, that is not necessarily the way it will be. You, we must have faith."

He resolved to do all he could to discover the situation of Erich *von* Krönitz.

Classified messages, sent in duplicate form to the local police, instructed, "*Frau* Field Marshal Ulla von Rudel is to be taken into custody and brought to Berlin under escort. Her husband conspired against the *Reich* and the *Führer* and has suffered the severest punishment." While Carl felt he had to accompany the local police to apprehend Ulla Rudel he would not actively participate in the arrest by the police. When the now widowed woman came to the door, she exclaimed, "My Paul is dead. I know from your faces. Did he die a hero's death in battle?" While her eyes glistened with slight tears, her countenance would have done credit to the wife of a fallen Prussian warrior.

A policeman, just up from the Hitler Youth, blurted, "He died a traitor's death for trying to kill our beloved *Führer*. You may soon join him in the Valhalla of traitors."

Carl interceded, "You must go to Berlin. Please take a few moments and gather the things that will be essential to you. We have no idea as to what you can expect in Berlin." Moving closer and out of the hearing of the others he whispered, "Marli and I will remember you daily. Thank you for your past kindnesses."

Then pointing to a policeman in his late forties, he told her, "*Herr* Lerner will accompany you to Berlin. He served under your husband in the first war." Carl appreciated that he could do this little thing in consideration of the noble lady.

"Oh! No! No!" Marli reacted when told of the execution of the field marshal and the detention of his widow. "What does this mean? Do you know how many have been executed?"

"So far I have heard of scores, mostly in and around Berlin. Hourly reports are coming in that the circle of arrests is expanding into the countryside. So far most of the arrests have been of officers of the *Wehrmacht*." He did not want to tell her that he feared for her father's safety as the net thrown all across Europe brought more and more victims to the surface.

"Oh, this terrible war. It causes humans to do things that they would have never thought of in time of peace such as murdering a national leader. That in turn has led to the death of many good men who love Germany. This is in addition to the suffering in the cities and the deaths of many young men who would rather have stayed at home and worked the farms and factories. How long will this butchery continue, Carl?"

Having no answer for her painful question he attempted none and could only hold her close to his body. Her soft sobs wrenched his heart.

The next morning the news became more ominous as a telegram listed thousands of those who were to be detained. Among the names he saw that of "Count Erich Albert von Krönitz." The message from Berlin, however. listed many others of a higher priority to be taken into custody. For moments Carl simply looked at the long list of names on the classified document. His eyes focused on the name "Count Erich Albert von Krönitz." He had come to know the love, the sacrificial love, that Marli had for her father. She had protected him by entering into an odious marriage. She had subjected herself to an alienation from him because of that marriage combined with an equal determination to keep him from sacrificing himself.

Carl knew that although he had never seen, heard, or touched the father of his beloved he loved the count because of the character, the inner goodness and honor, that all ascribed to him. One thing he did know. He would not allow events simply to take their course. He would act to save this man.

The count had not been a member of the conspiracy to kill Hitler and had few connections with those who were. He only led the intellectual opposition and as such posed little immediate danger. The security administrators in Berlin determined that they would deal with him a little later. Nevertheless, Carl, feeling a sense of increased urgency about the peril to Marli's father growing with each passing hour, began his preparations.

Carl instructed Pfefferkorn to prepare the automobile for a thousand kilometer journey because, as he told Pfefferkorn, Berlin had given him a mission to apprehend someone in the north of Germany, an individual highly admired by the general population and covered by an umbrella of protection by the *Abwehr* and its chief, Admiral Wilhelm Canaris. He further instructed the driver that the mission required absolute secrecy and that they would not be able to refuel on the way to their destination. Pfefferkorn therefore was to obtain as many cans of fuel as he could without compromising their task. When his mind completed his plans, he had Pfefferkorn deliver him to the castle before returning to prepare the car and fuel.

Carl, taking Hans aside, asked, "How much fuel have you been able to put aside?" Hans replied, "Something over one hundred fifty liters."

Carl continued, "Ludwig Pfefferkorn will come to the castle to get what we need to get to Wendenhof and back. You see, Hans, I am convinced that Marlene's father is in great danger. The *Nazis* can get away with almost anything after the assassination attempt. They are using it as a reason for getting rid of the remainder of political opposition. Pfefferkorn is going to drive me north to 'arrest' the good count."

Hans volunteered, "I will go too."

"No!" Carl reacted promptly, "You must stay here at the castle to protect the women. Besides, you will try to confuse any snooping around the grounds. This is an extra SS uniform that I have. See if you can get into it. If you can and Liese makes the pants leg so that you can bend back your calf into the leg, you can pretend to be me for an observer from a distance. Now here is what I want you to do. If you hear a vehicle coming up the road to the castle, give them a fleeting sight of your figure flitting into the residence. I believe we can entice a visit from the curious and suspicious *Frau* Randorff. I want her to catch a brief sight of you in the uniform of *SS* Captain Friedrich Schleiter as you scurry back into the residence.."

"Finally, you must not talk to the countess about the danger her father faces."

As his plans progressed, the time came to tell his wife that he was going to be away for a few days. As he did he instructed, "You must call in to the city hall and tell them, 'The captain has the flu but will return to duty in a few days.'" After telling his wife that he planned this trip to retrieve her father he found the letter that *Reichsführer* Himmler had written to him.

He then typed out orders on the paper filched from the desk that bore the letterhead of *Reichsführer* Heinrich Himmler. These orders stated that for confidential reasons Captain Friedrich Schleiter was to proceed by automobile to the north of Germany to take an open and avowed enemy of the Party into custody. Security reasons prevented the placement of the offender's name in print. Carefully studying the letter received from the *Reichsführer*, he forged the signature of the leader of the *SS* onto the document. He also prepared an additional and more personal forged letter beginning "My young friend Friedrich" that informed one Captain Friedrich Schleiter that he had been selected for this mission. The *Reichsführer* wrote, "I am convinced that, knowing your relationship with the subject of this apprehension, or rather his opinion of you, I believe it deliciously humorous for you to be involved in his final fate."

The simple, scrawled signature consisting of a line with a few squiggles Carl found rather easy to duplicate to a satisfactory degree.

Having compiled the paper work that he trusted and prayed would enable him to negotiate through any checkpoints he then approached his wife, "Marlene, your fears concerning the safety of your father are correct. I am going to go north to see if I can secretly bring him here. I have been thinking and as the war winds down, I am convinced that your father would be safer in Switzerland than in Germany. In that country he could blend in with the German speaking Swiss. While the Swiss have an understanding with the Germans that they will return any Jews fleeing the *Reich* they apprehend, I believe your father would be safe there. I will pretend to arrest him as though I am part of the regime. Pfefferkorn has totally committed himself to us and will accompany me although he does not know exactly what I plan.

"Why now?" she asked amid a score of other questions. "How will you go to Wendenhof? Will you go by train or automobile?"

"By automobile."

"What of fuel? Where will you get fuel for the car?

"Months ago Hans and I agreed that he would save and hide as many cans of fuel as he could. We now have enough, with what Pfefferkorn gets legally, to get us to and from Hundefurt and Wendenhof if all goes well."

He continued, "This is what you can do to help. Tomorrow I want you to call the police station and the city hall to tell them that I have a little touch of the flu, nothing serious, and will be away from the office for a few days. Tell them also that if there is any paper work that needs to be signed that you plan on coming to town for some medicine for me and will stop by to get it. It will not hurt if you can delicately hint that my 'flu' is really a cover for some very important mission for the *Reich*. You could say something like, 'Sometimes there are reasons to miss work and then at other times there are other reasons.' If someone comes who wants to see me say that I have taken a strong medicine and am sleeping. I would not be surprised to have Erika Randorff or someone else make a surprise visit to you after I have not been seen in town for a couple of days."

Facing their first overnight separation since their church consecrated marriage their bed was filled with kisses and tears as they held one another close throughout the night. She wept, "Carl, if you are not successful I will lose two of the most precious people in my life. I love you so much for what you plan to do. I know that you do it for me. Please, please be careful. You are my life and I want you above all to live. Please use the greatest caution."

That night the life of their daughter, Teresa Jacinta Solms, whom they named nine months and some days later, began.

Although the car was loaded with additional cans of fuel so that the trunks and the back seat were completely full, both Carl and Pfefferkorn made room for one change of clothing. It was noon before they headed down the slope from the castle and were on their way northward. Carl had abandoned his crutches and had pulled the wooden prosthetic onto his leg stump inside his laceless boot. As an afterthought, he had placed in the pocket of his jacket a pair of spectacles someone had abandoned and he had found.

A simply arranged but anonymous phone call to Erika Randorff aroused her suspicions and inspired her to visit the castle to check on the "sick man." There was no allegation in the call that the captain was missing from the castle but only that the illness might be more serious than the castle dwellers informed the townspeople. The plan, that she would get a flashing glance at Hans in the *SS* uniform, succeeded perfectly much to the delight of Marli and Liese. The women almost giggled when Hans, after hastening to remove the uniform, appeared, in the sight of the *SD* agent in his normal dress to ask for direction in his work.

When asked as to why Captain Schleiter was out of bed, Marli explained, "Oh, yes. So you saw Friedrich. He feels that fresh air would be wonderful for him. I try to tell him that rest would do more for him but you know men. They have to be so tough and overcome everything. Even when he lost his leg he would not obey the doctors and stay in bed like they ordered but he got out almost a week before they said he should."

Within a relatively few kilometers following Carl and Pfefferkorn's departure there appeared the first checkpoint they would encounter at a customs station in Germany on a road from Switzerland. The guards took a quick glance at the identification papers of an SS captain and waved the Mercedes past this first hurdle of their journey. Carl knew that not every obstruction to their expedition would be so simple. This became clear as they attempted to cross a bridge over the headwaters of the Danube River. Here the guards asked for justification for being so far from their duty station. The forged orders satisfied the young soldiers on the post although there were curious glances directed at the back seat of the car with its blanket-covered load of fuel.

Carl navigated as Pfefferkorn drove. He decided that boldness was the surest course so stayed on the main roads and acted as though he had not a care in the world. Even these main roads wound up the hills Carl would have called mountains in Texas. As the evening darkened, the road bent and curved between the subdued headlights softly illuminating the trees that stood only a foot or two from the pavement. On through the night they sped clearing checkpoint after checkpoint.

As the summer dawn began to show promise of light in the east Pfefferkorn reported, "Captain, I need to sleep or else we might go off the road. May I pull over in some safe place and just get a little sleep?"

Filled with the excitement of anxiety, Carl, feeling no need for sleep responded, "I will try to drive so that we may continue. I have driven quite a bit in the past but will have to learn again with this leg of mine—maybe I should say without this leg of mine," as he smiled at his own little joke.

Starting slowly and carefully on the empty roads, he at first negotiated carefully but increased the speed of the vehicle to correspond with his increased dexterity with the pedals as Pfefferkorn seemed to have no trouble sleeping.

After driving for more than three hours and thinking that they were approaching a larger town Carl pulled over in a secluded spot and asked, "Do you think you are rested enough to drive us through this town ahead. At present, I would rather not attempt to negotiate the streets with my leg. I can not move my boot fast enough from the gas pedal to the brake to be safe in town traffic."

"Yes, indeed, Captain. I can take over at the wheel. Thank you for letting me sleep. Do you think we could get a bite of breakfast in this town ahead? I am hungry."

As they exchanged places, Carl pulled his jacket down straight to eliminate as many wrinkles as possible and saw Pfefferkorn copying his pulling and tugging. Answering the question Carl said, "Certainly we can get something to eat. Please pick out a place that you think will have a good meal and I will buy and let Himmler pay," he dissimulated.

Carl could discern the trace of the old walls that once encompassed the community in centuries past. Pfefferkorn directed the car through the rather narrow streets to the center square of the centuries old town and found a spot to park in front of a small hotel. Anyone seeing what appeared to be two German fighting men entering the hotel would hardly have noticed that one walked with a slight limp as Carl strained to walk in as natural a manner as possible. Entering they were directed to a table by a buxom country girl who smiled invitingly at the aquiline features of Ludwig Pfefferkorn. After submitting their food ration cards, bread and cheese were set before them accompanied by beer for Pfefferkorn and what in wartime Germany passed as coffee for Carl.

"Don't you know beer is a sedative?" Carl asked. "Here you were sleepy and now you are drowning yourself in that stuff."

"Captain, it's only one beer and these steins are not big at all," he answered before he saw the expression on Carl's face that said, "I am teasing, good fellow."

Halfway through their meal the sound of voices and hob-nailed boots pounding the floor drew the attention of all in the half-filled dining room. Led by a boy who appeared to be about sixteen a group of five or six *Hitler Jugend* armed with machine pistols advanced arrogantly into the chamber as the leader proclaimed, "*Heil Hitler*! We have been detailed to make an identity check of all in this establishment. You must present your identity cards to me for inspection. Hurry up about it and have them ready when I come to you. Don't give me any back talk or delay me."

Suddenly Carl found the muzzle of one of the weapons, controlled by a boy appearing to be about fifteen, in his face. Calmly and slowly he raised his hand to the muzzle. Pushing the muzzle aside, he commanded, "*Heil Hitler!* Young man, do you recognize this uniform and this insignia of rank? You above all should be able to identify a captain of the *SS*! Get that young leader of yours over here! Go!"

Hearing Carl's command to his comrade, the young leader of the group presented himself to the man in the *SS* uniform, "*Heil Hitler!* You requested to talk to me, Captain?"

Remaining bold, Carl commanded, "No, I ordered you to talk to me! I would like to compliment you on your and your men's enthusiasm. Who is your group leader and is he available?"

"Sir, *Herr* Reineke is our adult leader and told us to rise early this morning to check all strangers in this area."

"And have you checked everyone in this room?"

"*Heil* Hitler! Yes, my Captain. All seems right at the hotel."

"How can that be when you have not checked my identity or papers? Are not the good corporal here and myself in the room? Do you have any idea who we are? As far as you know, we may be American airmen in *SS* uniforms. What authority do we have for travel? You must learn to be more thorough, and without proof, trust no one, my good young man. I will credit these lapses to your inexperience but if you join the *Waffen SS* you will soon learn to be more conscious of detail. Here is my identification card and the sergeant will show you his. And these are my orders signed by a rather significant person."

Seeing only the name at the bottom of the sheet, the young leader's eyes seemed to take on the appearance of half an eggshell. Feeling apprehensive and thrilled that he had personally encountered someone with such connections the youth profusely proclaimed, "My most sincere apologies, Captain, I am very sorry. I will be more careful in the future. Thank you for your instruction! *Heil* Hitler!"

With the rearward jerk of their leader's head toward the exit the group quickly abandoned the hotel's dining room amid the sound and clatter of nailed boots on the square tiled floor. At the same time Pfefferkorn eyed his leader so intently that Carl thought, "He must see the beating of my heart and the pulse of my throat."

Pfefferkorn stated, "You handled that very well. Almost as though you believed it yourself."

"What do you mean?" Carl demanded.

"It might be better if we talked in the car while we are on the road. There will not be so many sharp ears to hear."

Leisurely they finished their morning meal, satisfied the reckoning for the food, and made their way to the Mercedes.

Once clear of the town Carl pursued Pfefferkorn's observation, 'What did you mean back there? 'Almost as though you believed it yourself?' Just what are you inferring?"

"Captain, I know this is a made-up trip. I know that you are not what you purport to be. I do not know exactly why you are the person you are now but you are certainly different. You do not have the character that *Reichsführer* Himmler thinks you have. You have compassion. I really think we are on our way to rescue the Baron von Krönitz from retribution for the assassination attempt. I have told you that I love the countess dearly but as a sister.

"You need not worry about that! I do not think I am harming Germany by helping to save a good man's life and from all I have heard the baron is as good a man as his daughter is a woman. I will violate the law of the land by helping you. And you will need my understanding help, I believe."

Tears, although only moistening, seeped into Carl's eyes at the internal struggle that he knew this young patriot had experienced as he dealt with the conflict between personal loyalty and loyalty to his group, the nation. Instinctively, the Texan knew that Pfefferkorn had separated his loyalty to his nation from any supposed loyalty he should have to the regime ruling his people. He had recovered from the intoxication of deceit and misplaced hope to which he had earlier been victim. Carl reached over, and in confirmation of many feelings and much thought, simply placed his hand on the shoulder of his driver.

They had decided that they would drive in four-hour stints with Pfefferkorn taking the wheel if they became aware of a checkpoint before they arrived at the obstacle. Slowly they emptied the gas cans in the back seat and discarded the empties well off the road in any available forest. By mid-afternoon the second day, they neared their goal of *Wendenhof* near the small city of Hundefurt only to encounter a roadblock at the edge of the built up area. Adjacent to the road and well camouflaged in an apple orchard were more than ten anti-aircraft guns. As the vehicle drew to a halt, a grim faced Luftwaffe major approached.

"Just what do you think you are doing here? Some damn American Thunderbolts strafed us last night. The Amis killed one of my men and wounded four others, one seriously, and now you come meandering up. Show me who you are and what you are doing here! Right now! I do not care if you are an *SS* stool. Why are you here at this time?"

Both Carl and Pfefferkorn pulled out their identification cards and gave them to the major who reacted, "I said I don't care if you are an SS captain! I have never seen you before and I do not know what you are doing in this zone! Show me your travel orders!"

Carl reached into the slim letter carrier that contained the false orders and gave them to the irate and frustrated major who examined them minutely before he declared, somewhat more subdued, "I do not accept these! I think they are false and am going to call the local authorities to check you out more thoroughly."

"Good," countered Carl, "That will give me more time to check with the *Reichsführer* to tell him how thorough you are in checking on his orders. I am sure that he will be pleased with your questions. Would you please give me your name so I can credit you accurately? Besides who would not like to spend more time in their hometown and renew old acquaintances with the Party big-wigs here. I think that they will all remember my fervor and how the *Reichs-führer* took me under his wing because of my total commitment to the *Führer* and the Party. Again, sir, if you would kindly give me you name and unit I will insure that *Herr* Himmler expresses his appreciation for your doubts person-ally."

"That will not be necessary, Captain. Your papers are in order, although I would never have recognized you from the picture on your identification card. Where is the one you are to take into custody?"

Carl would rather not have revealed his goal but in the interest of diverting suspicion thought he must answer, "Our target is the Baron von Krönitz, who at our last report remained at *Schloss Wendenhof*. I will not need directions for my orders are complete."

"Nevertheless I want to be as cooperative as possible so have asked some of the local police to come and aid you in the detention. They will arrive shortly and accompany you to Wendenhof."

The Luftwaffe major then began to make what seemed idle conversation, "So you are from this area? Have you fished in the stream west of the city? I hear that they really rise to bite there."

Thankful for the time he had spent talking to his cousin Anna as well as Marli, he answered, "No, but that little stream to the east has great fishing I have heard, but I have never had the patience to throw a line into the water time after time."

Soon two local police arrived on bicycles with subdued remarks that indicated that they indeed knew "Friedrich Schleiter" even though one Pietr Hassberg exclaimed, "Man, you really did get torn up in that fire. I do not think I would have recognized you if I had not been told that you were here at the road block. Are you truly my old friend Friedrich? I really find it difficult to believe—your eyes are different. But these papers say you are so I guess you are Friedrich. I had heard that *Reichsführer* Himmler had taken you under his wing but I really thought that you would be in prison first when we were in school together. But why are you back in town?"

"To take custody of Count Erich Albert von Krönitz for disloyalty to the state. I have orders to take him south for questioning."

"I am sorry to hear that but I can not say that I am surprised. I am sorry because I think the count is a good, righteous and just man. Not surprised because his opposition to the Party, from which he has never wavered, goes back to the 1920's. If we are to assist you, we will have to ride with you to Wendenhof."

In short order the police had secured their bicycles at the flak command post and entered the back seat of Carl's car. The spokesman exclaimed, "Whew, this car stinks of fuel! What did you do, spill some on the seats? We had better keep the windows down."

Thankful that sufficient fuel had been used that there were no cans in the back seat, although the trunk remained full for the journey back to Littach and the *Schloss,* Carl sidestepped the question. "Yes. When we refueled last night from a can we spilled some in the car." Then, wanting to keep the idle chatter to a minimum for fear that some stray remark might expose them, he continued, "Let's go and get this done."

Within a half hour they had turned off the main road into a lane that led in a short time to a view of a large beautifully designed building composed in its center of three floors with wings of two floors each. Small and proportionate turrets topped by needlepointed spires adorned each of the corners of the multi-storied buildings. The total area covered by the chateau, which brought to Carl's mind some of the great country houses he had seen in England, exceeded by a considerable amount the area covered by the new wing of *Schloss Altburg.* "This semi-palace," Carl thought, "is the home of my wife's father and where she spent many months, even years, of her childhood. This is what Friedrich Schleiter coveted as much as he wanted to possess the Countess Marlene. It is magnificent but…" Something of the practicality he had soaked in during his early years caused him to ask himself, "What could a family do with so much room and what must it cost to run this place?"

Pfefferkorn guided the car to a halt on the gravel immediately in front of what seemed to be the main entrance. The four dismounted with Carl remembering to limit his limp as they approached the portal. Continuing to act his part, Carl peremptorily banged on the door, ignoring the bell string. As a servant woman opened the door, Carl led Pfefferkorn and the two police officers arrogantly beyond the foyer and into the drawing room, pushing rudely by the servant woman. Marli had lovingly described this room where she had shared so much joy with her father so much in detail that Carl recognized it. Even as they marched in, Carl demanded, "Where is the Count von Krönitz? Tell me where he is immediately, woman! I come in the name of the *Führer* and I will know where he is!"

A voice echoed from the drawing room even before Carl could see the speaker. "I am here, sir. What can I do for you?" By the end of these words a man nearing six feet in height, with a receding and graying hairline, physically trim but with a melancholy look about his eyes, appeared.

From Marli's treasured photographs of her father, Carl immediately recognized his father-in-law, the Count Erich Albert *von* Krönitz. Closely following the count another and much younger man entered. Disciplining himself to appear hard, Carl announced, "Erich *von* Krönitz, you are wanted for questioning." Then, hoping that the others would not think his words as too understanding, he growled, "You have half an hour to pack one suitcase for the trip and your stay. You will be ready to accompany us!"

Looking at Pfefferkorn, he ordered, "Go with him! We do not want to take any chances. *Reichsführer* Himmler is personally interested in this case." Carl hoped the last, although addressed to Pfefferkorn, entered the ears and mind of every other person in the room.

Then, turning to the younger man with the count, he demanded, "Give me your identification papers! Just who are you and what are you doing in this house? Did you know that this man might be an enemy of the *Reich*?"

When silence prevailed and no answer came from the man, a policeman who had taken the identification card exclaimed, "Aha, this fellow is Christian Niedertal. The authorities have been looking for him because he fled from some secret project with compromising knowledge in his head. There have been all sorts of police bulletins to be on the watch for him. You have made a good haul, Captain Schleiter. I am sure you will be recognized."

"Schleiter? So this is what you look like now? You are finally going to have your full measure of hatred, eh, Friedrich. I think you live only to cause me pain. My days may be over soon but I have few regrets." Color but not dignity left the distinguished jurist.

Carl, thinking wildly, knew that he could not leave the other man; obviously a friend of the count's and possibly even of Marli, to the mercy of the *Nazi* regime. Certainly she had friends of whom he had never heard. He again commanded, "You too have a half hour to gather your belongings. You too will come with me to face the authorities. Move!"

He then turned to the police, "You will remain here and search the house carefully for any evidence. When I command 'carefully', I do not mean for you to ransack it and break everything up. Just carefully look under everything. You will be held accountable for any damage. I will follow my orders and take the Count and this Niedertal fellow with me. You may call the city hall and tell them what has happened. There is a phone in the house is there not, woman?" He recognized the servant woman as one almost as dear to his wife as Liese Weber so felt burdened at the harshness of his tone as he addressed her. With trembling lips, the woman nodded and affirmed barely audibly as tears stained her face, "Yes, there is a telephone."

"Good." Carl confirmed. Then, turning to the two policemen he commanded, "Start your search of the house in the east wing and work to the west. This must be done right away so that servants will not conceal anything. Would you please get to it!"

Then, again addressing the woman, he ordered, "Go into the kitchen and make sufficient meals for a day and a half for the four of us. And put something to drink into the sack. Weak wine, a little beer, or even some water will do. Hurry, woman. We must be on our way." The woman might not have muttered as she did if she had known that the salvation of the count necessitated this man's urgency more than anything else.

Soon the two detainees arrived and then a large sack of bread, cheese and sausage and beverages were brought in by the woman. Carl ordered, "Corporal Pfefferkorn, search these two thoroughly and when I say 'thoroughly' I mean thoroughly." When satisfied that neither carried a weapon, Carl with a drawn weapon directed the two men into the back seat of the car where he further directed, "Put the shackles on them, Pfefferkorn. We don't want them to choke us in the front seat." Earlier Carl had explained to the driver that they had to do this to maintain appearances. He had also cautioned that there would be no explanation until they arrived at *Schloss* Altburg for fear that something might inadvertently be revealed. The count and the man Niedertal had to be convinced that they had been taken into custody and display anxiety at the check points to support their charade.

As soon as the men were secure, with some slight ability to move their hands sufficiently to reach their faces if they bent their heads down, they began their trip back to Littach and *Schloss* Altburg..

As they departed Hundefurt they were able to leave a message for the *Luftwaffe* major thanking him for his courtesy and assistance and that the two policemen were searching *Schloss* Wendenhof. Kilometer marker after kilometer marker stones passed by the car's windows. They passed one checkpoint successfully, then another, and another, and another. Eventually where their road crossed an autobahn near Arsberg they were stopped and questioned by a most suspicious sergeant who asserted, after the omnipresent "*Heil* Hitler," "I don't believe these papers. There is something fishy here. I have known *Reichsführer* Himmler from the early days of the party and it is not like him to give such a paper. I will hold you here until I can get this sorted out. Consider yourself in my custody until we check all this out with the *SS* in Berlin. My men will shoot if you attempt to continue your journey without my permission. I do not intend disrespect and you will be made comfortable in the *gasthaus* just over there," as he pointed to the inn in question.

"Don't you understand, good sergeant, time is of great consequence in delivering these men. They may have information on those involved in the assassination attempt on the *Führer*."

"I do not care! This old nose tells me something is not right. My orders say that if anything rouses my suspicions I will call to inform my superiors…"

Suddenly a Volkswagen staff car carrying a *Wehrmacht* colonel drove up followed by a large number of trucks apparently heading west. Carl guessed that the commander wanted the convoy to gain the *Autobahn*. Their vehicle, blocking the road during the discussion with the sergeant, prevented the convoy from continuing.

"*Was gibt,*" yelled a colonel, apparently in command of the convoy, "Get that vehicle out of the way! What are you doing? Having tea and pastries? If that car is not gone in one minute, I will have my trucks push it out of the way. Now move it!"

Consternation and frustration simultaneously moved across the face of the non-commissioned officer. His mouth opened as though to protest, then closed. First, he faced the colonel, and then he faced the SS captain, then the colonel once more before finally saying to Carl's small but obstructing group,

"*Raus!* Get out of here! On your way! I will forget I ever saw you and please forget that you ever saw me. *Heil* Hitler."

Carl responded with the *Nazi* hail to the *Führer* to both the colonel and the sergeant, saluted the colonel and ordered Pfefferkorn to get the Mercedes moving.

Both of the handcuffed men in the back of the car observed all that had occurred at the checkpoint. The count's face remained impassive as he continued to look straight ahead and did not dignify the ruckus with his attention while the younger man's face became puzzled. "What was that all about? Why did he suspect your papers?"

Carl retorted with a show of impatience, "Just an over-zealous soldier impressed with his own responsibilities." He did not choose to add his thoughts, "A very good and alert old soldier who was obviously a member of the Party in the twenties. I am thankful that all the road blocks are not manned by such as him."

The guards at the other checkpoints appeared content to the point of complacency as they displayed only personal curiosity about the "prisoners" in the vehicle. Carl sensed the laxity of the subsequent guards were a reward for his thankfulness. As they neared Littach the count, ever alert although feigning aloofness, began to turn his head and for the first time questioned, "What is your destination?" Carl noticed first perspiration and then nervous movements from the count as they drew ever nearer the old castle of Altburg. "Where are you taking us? Has my daughter been arrested too? For pity's sake, have some mercy, man."

Carl motioned Pfefferkorn to keep silent. Count von Krönitz became increasingly agitated with each minute that brought them closer to his daughter. After their passage through the town, Carl signaled the driver to pull off to the side of the road and whispered additional instructions. He then removed the restraints of the men and had the count move into the front seat with Pfefferkorn while he took a seat in the rear to the left of the younger "prisoner." When all were settled, they continued up the winding road to Altburg with the count showing ever increasing animation although he now maintained his silence.

As the car wheeled around in a turn that placed the right side of the vehicle toward the residence, the door of the house flew open and Marli dashed out. She jerked open the car door and almost pulled her father out of the car to embrace him and kiss his face repeatedly and then once more embrace him tightly as she rested her head on his shoulder.

The nobleman slowly emerged from the stunning revelation of his beloved daughter and grasped her to his breast so that breath was forced from her chest as he returned her greeting kiss for kiss. Then, drawing back, he looked around and asked, "Are there other *SS* here? Where are the other guards?"

She then turned to Carl, tears of joy cascading down her cheeks, drew him as close as one human can be to another and whispered, "Thank you! Carl, Thank you!"

Overhearing the whispered name, the count demanded, "Carl? Carl? Is not this the *Nazi* Friedrich Schleiter? Who is this man, daughter? I do not understand. Marlene, I want to know what is going on. Where are the guards?"

"No, Papa, there are no other guards here. I mean, there are no guards! There is so much to tell you! Come inside."

By this time Hans and Liese, faces beaming with the laughter of their hearts, approached to be greeted almost as warmly as the daughter. Hans grabbed the bags as he looked curiously at the younger of the two "prisoners." Count von Krönitz, observing the enquiring look, introduced the younger man as Christian Niedertal. He further explained that Niedertal had fled a German research installation and the *Gestapo* sought him. Marli, knowing that a search would be made for her father and his friend, told Hans to place the two men in a room on the second floor where a confidential passage way led to the basement where a semi-secure room had been established more than two centuries earlier. While Marli instructed, Liese headed for the kitchen.

When Pfefferkorn, eyes slightly moistened, made motions as though he would leave, Carl and Marli responded as with one voice, "No, you don't! Where do you think you are going? You will stay here and have breakfast with us. We are one now by the threat that we all face." Even as he said this, Carl realized that Pfefferkorn posed a dire threat to their lives. He could use to his benefit what he now knew for sure. Carl then caught himself thinking, "If I had the slightest doubt of his loyalty and ability to keep silent, I would have no qualms in killing him, no matter how kindly I feel toward him. I guess I would execute anyone who threatened my wife and children."

As they entered the house to find seats in the sitting room, Carl felt the eyes of the count intently examining him in every detail. He had been told and he had been certain, that this *SS* captain, whom his daughter called "Carl," with such a scarred face, was Friedrich Schleiter. Had his princess turned a toad into a prince through her love? He could not believe that fairy tale but if not that, what?

His daughter began to enlighten him. "Papa, we have a long story to tell. Please sit and listen before I bring someone to meet you." While Carl sat quietly and the man Niedertal often gasped as a fish caught on a line and pulled from the water, the father listened with intensity casting an occasional glance at Carl.

When his daughter had finished, the Baron Erich Albert von Krönitz spoke calmly, but with power, to Carl, "You are then the husband of Marlene? And you confess Christ? From what Marlene has told me you are a man whose character is, it seems, of the highest nobility. Your nobility might not be by birth, it is true, it may be better. I believe I am honored to have you as a son. You are and will be my only son, you know. I would know more of you, of your family, although Marlene has told me that your background is humble as far as birth is concerned. I would know what forces have created your character."

While Carl recounted his parents' humble goodness, the impact of the great teachers he had at home and in the New Sendlingen High school system, and his encounter with Christ in college, Marli disappeared upstairs to return with Eric Albert Solms. She said as she entered the room, "Papa, you do have another son. But this one is a grandson. Papa, I would like you to meet Eric Albert Solms, your grandson. He is honored to bear your name although we altered the "Erich" to conform to the American style. He will be a year old in October and quit nursing about two months ago."

The depth of emotion felt by the still-faced nobleman could only be measured by the use of a napkin from the breakfast set before them to dab his eyes as he repeated, "Marlene. Marlene. My precious Marlene." He then rose and went to his daughter whose name he seemingly never tired of uttering and embraced her as he looked at the face of his grandson. The baby, looking up into the new face above him, seemed to find the face of a German nobleman humorous and actually chortled as joyful laughter from the six adults filled the room. Any restraint the man felt in the presence of Carl and Pfefferkorn melted as exposed ice in a New Sendlingen August, as he asked, "May I hold him?"

The emotion that flooded through the young mother's body made her feel as though she might faint for joy and she had a brief concern that she would collapse before she could have her son secure in her father's arms. Safely seated with eyes filled with moisture, she watched as her father walked about the room saying little but insuring that all in the room looked upon the face of her son and his grandson. The man, who would have been baron in fact and not just in name a century earlier, acted as though Carl, Liese, Hans, and Pfefferkorn had never seen the child before. By motion and stance, he seemed to demand that they admire this son of his daughter. Only when he came to Christian Niedertal did he signal that oral approval might be accepted as he said, "*Doktor* Niedertal, I would like for you to make the acquaintance of my grandson, Erich Albert . . Solms." It is 'Solms,' is it not?"

Carl, who had survived thus far by alertness, quick-wittedness, and guileful planning interjected, "This is well but we must make plans. It is certain, Marlene," (He could not bring himself to use the familiar "Marli" when it was obvious that her father gloried in being able to call his daughter "Marlene.") "that searches will be made here with the disappearance of your father. Everyone here will be under suspicion at least. I hope that is all. If there is anything I know about the *Nazis*, it is that they hate being foiled and their search and their questioning will be intense. I think you, your father and Christian should go to Switzerland until the war is over."

"I agree," joined in the count, "I have many friends who offer us shelter there and you and little Eric will be out of danger unless the *Nazis* invade the Swiss and at this stage of the war I don't think that is a possibility. Yes, we should all go."

Marli asked, "Carl, will you go?"

He answered, "My reason for not going sooner was that I thought I could help Jews and able-bodied airmen escape to get back into the war effort. I could have gone earlier and been very safe although I am so glad that I did not because then I would not have had you or little Eric. It might be the wise thing to go but I really believe that my duty is here so I will stay and if I can help one airman get way before the *Nazis* catch on it will be more than an even trade: a healthy man for a cripple. No, I must stay to continue the work. Maybe I can last to the end of the *Nazis*."

"Then I stay, too," Marli pronounced. "We said for better, for worse, for richer, for poorer, that we would stay together. I meant my oath and I would add to that wedding oath, in danger and in safety. I will be by your side for I believe that you and I, Carl, are one and that oneness is confirmed in our son. I would that he could be safe but in the oneness we have he will have to share our peril. You, with God's grace and assistance, have protected us and you have saved my father. I have trusted our Lord and your wits and I will trust now."

Although all were exhausted, the emotion and excitement of the reunion of those who deeply loved one another eased the escape from the claims of sleep and rest. Finally, in the small hours of the morning as they bid each other *guten nacht* the count came to the little family group of Marli, Carl and Eric and then the stoic demeanor crumbled as open tears streamed down his face and deep sobs shook his frame. "My daughter, my son, my heir! From the depths to the heights. Oh, how good, how gracious is our Lord Jesus. She who was lost to me has now been found! Thank you and praise you!" Continuing he prayed, "My Lord, thank you for this miracle and for those that you will accomplish in the future. Jesus God, You have so long ago redeemed us for a great price and saved us by Your blood. And now, Lord, You have saved us thus far from the perils of this present world. For all these great salvations, we thank You and praise You. Please help us keep the remembrance of this moment in the forefront of our minds that we might be faithful to return to You that which You have purchased and preserved, our lives."

As he carried little Eric, they climbed the stairs together. When they bid a final "*Guten nacht*," the fingers of father and daughter seemed reluctant to part.

CHAPTER 13

❁

August 1944–May 1945
The French

"Carl, isn't there a way that we can keep Papa here at the castle?" asked Marlene of her husband as she reverted to the more familiar name for her father.

"I woke this morning thinking how great it is to be able to talk to him after such a long time. Little Eric loves him so and the feeling certainly seems returned. Cannot our son really get to know his grandfather? The way that the war is moving in France and on the east I do not see how it can be long before the killing ends." The deep petition of the wife came to her husband the morning after her reunion with her father.

"Marli, that would be most unwise. In a day or two, I expect that there will be swarms of people of all sorts in and around Altburg and Littach. They will certainly not just politely question you, Webers, even Pfefferkorn, and me. Our only hope, as we have discussed with all, is that we stick with our story that I had the flu and essentially had to be confined in bed in the castle. Pfefferkorn stayed here to take any message that I might have to the office for the three days I absented myself. I was not up to getting my mind fixed on work. While Pfefferkorn remained outside my door in the upper hallway except for meals and other short breaks he had nothing to take to town. Really our hope is that the regime will have too much to do to bring witnesses against us from Wendenhof. After all your father was not a prime target."

He continued, "I am glad that your father has good friends that he can visit in Switzerland. It would be well for him and Christian to stay out of sight even there for some time. The Swiss do have some sort of 'understanding' with the *Nazis* about returning refugees other than escaping flight crews. We will signal our "friends" over there that some are coming through and your father must tell them where he wants to go so that he will have the necessary means to get to his friends undetected. Now we need to get this started so that we will have time to rehearse our stories and see if we can punch holes in them in any way. I am sorry, darling, that you can not continue to be with your father for I know how you have missed his company and wisdom."

Carl shared what he had told Marli with her father and the latter responded, "Oh, how I would love to take her and the little one with me to safety. Her absence, though, would attract even more attention to this place and the *Gestapo* would even tear the whole castle down to find how she got away. Now they can only suspect to some degree but if she could not be found, they would know that there is an escape route from here. Unless you forget what you think is your duty and we all go out, then she must stay with her man. That is our way and the way it has been for generations. I can not stay and she can not go."

In mid-afternoon, the father and his friend traveled underground to the safety of the neutral land. Tears streamed down cheeks not only from the eyes of the daughter but also from the eyes of the couple who had given her care and love all her life. Their love for her enabled them to share in the pain of separation so soon after the reconciliation. Even the countenance of the father glistened with tracks of tears for they all knew that those remaining faced a future of great peril. Erich Albert von Krönitz, a Godly man, gave his benediction to those remaining, "God has promised 'the Beloved of the Lord shall dwell in safety by Him and the Lord shall cover him all the day long, and he shall dwell between His shoulders' and I call this to remembrance. We acknowledge how His miracles have protected each of us thus far and we call again upon His Name and His Power in every expectation of His final victory over evil. May each of us sense His presence every moment by moment. In His Name and for His glory, Amen."

While embracing his daughter between restrained sobs, he whispered in such a way that all heard, "Forgive me, beloved daughter, for doubting you when you seemed to have given yourself to that. . that…Schleiter to save me. Forgive me for doubting your motives. The last few hours my mind has been full of how you two have given of yourselves to save me. What a burden I carry for my life." Then Marli saw the little party enter the "barn" and the cavern beneath.

When things settled down once more Carl called the little conspiratorial group, now with the addition of Pfefferkorn, into the dining room and had each rehearse their story. He instructed, "In the office I have studied the manuals and the correspondence on interrogation techniques of the SS, the *Gestapo*, and the police and so have some knowledge of how they work. One thing I know is that they will torture if they feel relatively certain they are correct in their accusations. We will soon be questioned by the authorities, maybe local, maybe the *Gestapo*, and who else nobody here knows. Now I want to hear the story that each of you will tell. We will all have to tell some authority what we have been doing the last five days. So let us tell what we are going to say have been our activities those days as convincingly as we can. Give as few details as possible and some of those you give should not be known by anyone else. Now you start, Liese."

After each had told their embroidered tale of their activities and each tale modified slightly, Carl invited all to attempt to catch any impossible or contradictory statements. He then took each one aside separately and questioned them individually. He tried his best to trip them up and identify contradictions although he made sure that their statements were not too perfect. After he and all the others were satisfied that all holes had been plugged as much as they could, he charged them all to be careful that they did not mention what the others were telling about their activities.

"For example," he cautioned, "I would probably not know that Hans had spent half a day caring for the animals or that Liese had spent a day cleaning the kitchen. If our story were true there would be some difference on what each remembered so do not get rattled if they say they have caught you in a differing story from some one else. Just insist that that's the way you remember it. Perfect stories agreeing on every point are suspect. Convince yourself that you are telling the truth and let nothing, again, I say, nothing, shake you."

"The authorities also will probably lie and say such things as, 'The Count, or Christian, has been apprehended and told us everything that goes on in this place;' or they might tell you that Liese or Hans have said, 'The captain was absent for three or four days.' Don't believe them but believe in one another and that we will not betray one another. Even if they tell you that your or a loved one's life will be spared if you tell, do not believe them. I have seen the records and for what we have done no one will be spared, not even little Eric."

The precautions proved justified the day after the meeting as three cars and two trucks disgorged SS soldiers who immediately set about searching every inch of the castle and its grounds even while Carl and Pfefferkorn had returned to their "duties". One squad, with a mufti-clad civilian in charge, searched for evidence in the interior of the residence. Another squad, similarly led, searched the grounds and the shell of the old castle wing and seemed to pay particular attention to the pen where the dogs had once been lodged. Another squad probed the woods and grounds inside the outer wall as they drilled holes in the floor of any out building. Inside the residence, the searchers moved each picture and piece of furniture and even required Liese to douse the fire in the kitchen stove so the searchers could move it to check underneath. Every book was removed from its place on the shelves of the library. It appeared that the searchers suspected that a secret passage lay behind the books. After much pulling and pushing at the shelves and many holes drilled through them to the stone behind them the disappointed faces of the searchers indicated the total lack of success they had achieved.

"What did your father say to you when you saw him two days ago?" was the first thrust made at Marli after she had been taken into a separate room. "Please help us. We do not understand why he developed such a scheme to flee his house. The government has nothing against the old judge."

Although not trying to appear cool, Marli questioned, "You mean my father has fled. That news fills me with joy, even though, as you should know from your sources, that he quit speaking to me when I married Captain Schleiter. He totally shunned me but I must admit I am glad he is gone and I hope he is safe."

On and on the questioning went for hours, "What fever did your husband have? What were his other symptoms? How often has he been sick?" Agents in civilian clothes also grilled Carl and Pfefferkorn for hours with particular attention aimed at the driver, the most likely weak link in the chain. Each member of the little group kept to his story and vouched for one another's presence at Altburg. Carl knew that the interrogators as thorough Germans had or would know that his "figure" had been seen during his three days absence from the office.

When questioned as to why the rescuers used his identity in seizing the count, Carl could only surmise that the count's hostility to him made his identity a perfect foil for those who knew of the relationship. He found that he had to explain the count despised him although he was the count's son-in-law. Portraying an informality of shared National Socialist comradeship, he shared with them of the coercion that forced the marriage, something Schleiter would never have shared with his superiors in Berlin. The questioners' attitude seemed to develop respect when they learned of the way that he had brought the reluctant bride to submission.

The questioning continued for three days with only a few hours of sleep being granted to those being questioned. Carl carefully hinted at his supposed special relationship with the *Reichsführer* Himmler and kept stating how ridiculous any suspicions thrown in his direction were. After all did not the whole town from whence he came know of his scorn of the Count von Krönitz and his ilk. In spite of the extended intense questioning, each member of the group kept to his story. The dirt and straw beneath the wagon but over the metal door leading to the cavern and its tunnel were undisturbed. After six days Pfefferkorn reported, "The inquisitors packed up and left last night, Captain. Everyone says that they are not at all happy that they did not find the count or those who helped him."

Insuring against the possibility that they could be overheard either by electronic means or simple eavesdropping Carl cautioned, "Don't get too excited, Ludwig, they will still have their eyes watching us and mouths to report on us here in Littach. Keep alert and do not let your guard down. Forget that you and I ever made that journey together. Wash it from your mind and do not speak of it to the countess, to Annaliese, or to Hans—or even to me. It never happened!

"You know that I have trusted you with our very lives because I sensed a very deep change in you. You had every opportunity to betray us in the last three days. Why did you not? You do love the countess with a brotherly love I realize but you have changed in more ways than that, why?"

The young man of the *SS* explained that he had come to realize that the war was lost for Germany and there was no need for continuing deaths. He knew of the destruction of the German cities he loved and the hundreds of thousands who had died in the ruins of the ancient communities. He then added, "Finally the love of Christ your wife and you displayed to me convinced me that the hatred of other races and people who held other beliefs, simply because of their race or beliefs, was wrong. You both taught me that the love of Christ toward me and my love toward Him constrains me to love and not hate. I must not be allied with or serve those who teach and practice hate."

Carl was able to restrain the moisture in his eyes at this statement but when he shared the conversation with Marli there was no stopping the tears of joy that flooded her face.

By the time that the investigators departed, the *Nazi* regime had a worry beyond the attempt on the *Führer's* life. Mayor Otto Schlenkmann, toward the last of August, entered Carl's office and queried, "Is it true what people who listen to the Swiss radio are saying? It is being repeated, not by me of course, that the enemy's forces have broken out and away from the beach. I have heard that the Sicilian devil Patton is rolling freely across France. Oh, that we could have our good Rommel to deal with such trash. Why did God have to take him just when we needed him. Are these rumors true, Captain Schleiter?"

"Most of the dispatches I receive are confidential and for only a few eyes. One I did receive though that you could know about is that we have been ordered to watch out for rumormongers and defeatists. If anyone insists on spreading false information, we have been instructed to take them into custody and send them to higher headquarters. Now, *Herr* Mayor, just who is spreading these tales?"

"Oh, certainly not me! I just wanted to check the facts so I could make right any false reports that I might hear. Right now, I cannot remember just who told me these falsehoods. But believe me; if I catch him at it again I will silence him. The nerve of some people. Spreading false information all over the town. You must put a stop to this, Captain! We all know the fates always protect the *Führer*. Do you remember what he said after the traitors tried to kill him? Well, he said, 'Anyone can see that nothing is going to happen to me. There is no question but that I am to continue on my course and bring my battle to a successful conclusion.' Even that incompetent Mussolini thinks that the cause of the *Führer* cannot meet with failure.

"I heard that the bomb went off right at the *Führer's* feet and his injuries were minor while others, a long distance away, were killed. It seems an invisible shield protected the great man. A miracle sent by the gods, that is the only way to describe it. A miracle, a sign that things will turn no matter how dark they appear at present. That is what it was! Do you not think so, Captain?"

"Some think destiny has been written and what will be, will be. There is no doubt that the success of the *Führer* and Germany surprised the English, French, and Russians. Until he attacked the Bolsheviks, it was success after success and it might be that way again. The future is hard to know and I am no prophet. It is good, Mayor, to get those who were questioning us out of our hair so that we can get on with our work. But what are you going to do with this call for the mobilization of the *Volksturm* and the *Jugend* over fourteen. How many men are available in Littach who are not yet sixty and how many boys do you have?"

"The men of Littach will rise to the occasion and flock to the defense of the *Führer*. This I know. Only this morning I posted the notices that all that this call applies to should get their affairs in order and report in four days. I also gave notice for publication to Hühn for the *Zeitung*. So you can report that this mayor is on top of things."

Only a few days following this conversation Carl informed those at the castle, "The Allies have made another landing in the south of France near that resort area, the Riviera. Intelligence reports that have come in say that the invasion force consists of American divisions from Italy and some Free French soldiers. They have made good progress it seems and are pushing up the Rhone valley rapidly. Our reports say that Patton's forces have captured Verdun and the English have captured Brussels. It seems that there is an increased need for manpower to repair and increase the fortifications along the West Wall. Many of the *Jugend* are being used for that kind of labor."

In mid-September as they prepared for bed Marli revealed, "Carl, if God helps us survive you will again be a father. I am sure that I am carrying a child and by my thoughts it will come in the middle of April."

Speechless for a moment, Carl's first thought concerned the well being of his wife, "So soon after the arrival of Eric! Is it good for you? I mean, is not having a baby hard on your health? You worried so before Eric was born"

"My husband, you are sweet, but don't worry." exclaimed the expectant mother, "This child follows Eric by eighteen months and I think God made my body special to carry and bear children. I have always been in wonderful health and Liese told me that Eric came surprisingly easy for a first birth. I am far more worried about the war and the killing that is going on and will go on until it ends. I pray for its end everyday."

Her husband, moving to her to hold her in his arms, comforted her, "There is death, yes. But there is also the new life that demonstrates our confidence and faith. There are only two basic reasons healthy people can have for not desiring children. The first is a selfish desire that their life not be altered by the child's needs. The second is that they do not trust God to provide on earth or even eternally for them and their children. Neither of these, in my opinion, reflects well." Then smiling, he added, "Of course, more than twelve might be too many," as his wife turned to hit him on the head with a pillow.

The day after Carl received this report a somber Hans asked Carl if he could talk to him privately.

"Of course," Carl answered and went into the small office. There Hans informed him that, "I am going to join the *Volksturm*. I have told Annaliese. I must defend the Fatherland against the French. I fought them in the last war at Verdun and on the Somme. It is the Fatherland I want to defend and that is all. Besides all those pups in the *Jugend* are going to need an old dog to show them how to be a soldier and how to take care of themselves. They cannot imagine the shock of artillery or the horrible sight of bodies being mutilated by enemy fire. Poor children, their dreams will be destroyed by death or experience."

If the taciturn Hans had told his innermost thoughts he would have added, "It is my land that I want to defend. I despise the whole herd of the *Nazi* swine. I despise their policies and programs but I hate the thought of French feet treading on the hallowed soil of Germany too. I love our dark forests and hill-sides that look like green velvet. And the clean little villages that nestle in the valleys like bathed babes in their bed or sit like crowns atop the hill. The cry of the cuckoo in the forest of fir warms my soul. My grandfather taught me how the conqueror Napoleon occupied our land and humiliated our people. He instructed me on how we evened the score in 1871 against his nephew and I know they got their revenge in 1918. If the English were coming it would be different. And if Americans like you come, I could understand. But the French frogs? No! I must fight."

Carl sensed, but, at the moment, could not understand, the deep emotion that filled Hans.

There was no reasoning with the quiet man of the woods and soil. The American could only say, "We all love you, Hans, and will watch out for Liese during your absence. Just be careful and do not get yourself hurt. Remember you cannot stop an army all by yourself. You will be in our prayers, Hans."

True to his word, Hans went off the next morning to become a member of the group of old men who donned uniforms to fight. In the evening, Hans returned in an ill fitting uniform and carrying a rifle left over from the first war in order to gather the personal things that he would need. With these items in a small bag, he walked from the kitchen followed by Liese onto the gravel to say his farewells to Marli and Carl. When he extended his hand to the countess, she would have none of it. Throwing her arms about his neck she cried, "I love you, second father. But I do not understand why! Why? Why must you go? You are such a good man! I love you so much."

Carl noted not only this exchange but also the quiet tears streaming from downcast eyes down the face of Liese toward trembling lips. With an equally aching heart, he put his arm around her shoulders as he shook Hans' hand. That gesture seemed insufficient for the sentiment he felt and so he thrust both arms around the older man and hugged him. He bent his head to touch Hans' shoulder as he promised with muffled voice, "Do not worry about Liese. We will care for her as though she were our mother. She is family as you are too.

She can go where we go and be what we are. Go with God and with our prayers for your safety."

With a last kiss on the hairline of his woman, Hans left the castle grounds as Liese turned and sped through the kitchen and into the apartment she and Hans had shared.

Marli, understanding more of her sex than Carl, reassured, "I will go to her shortly. It is good for her to grieve and weep for a while. I think I need to as well. I do damn this war to hell because it is so hellish. All of Liese's men think they are fighting for Germany but it truly is for the ideas that they despise." So Carl and Marli had quiet minutes together as each dealt with their own thoughts about life's vital matters.

Carl came late into the office that morning, explaining to those who directed questioning looks at him, "I wanted to say goodbye to Hans Weber, the good man at the castle, who has joined the *Volksturm*." The news that this man, a hero of the First War, a master of the forest, and the steward of the castle had put on the uniform of the Fatherland sped quickly as it was told and retold through the town. All open utterances commended him, "What a great old man for his commitment to serve the *Führer*." But many breathed silently, not giving their thoughts voice, "What a stupid old man! What does he expect to get from this? The enemy is racing toward us and the *Führer's* goose is cooked. What a stupid thing to do!"

Entering the store of Ludwig Randorff to re-supply himself with handkerchiefs, which he seemed to have a great talent for losing, much to his wife's dismay, Carl encountered the storeowner's wife.

Guardedly he wished her a good day, *Frau* Randorff immediately responded, "So that man from the castle has gone to the aid of the *Reich*. It is time someone from there did something for the *Führer* and the Party. You people up there are peculiar. Just when we think we have you figured out, you do something going the other way. One thing I do know, you had better watch out for those French frogs you have working around the farm. I have heard that some French military are moving up the Rhone toward us."

Carl thought, "She must get the same intelligence information I do."

Erika Randorff continued, "You can not trust them. They may be spying on us. Have you inspected their quarters for a concealed radio? Some speak of 'perfidious Albion' but I would prefer 'false France.' Have you heard how the partisan terrorists are defying not only our men but also their own legitimate government of Petain and Laval? They are destroying railroads and shipments, murdering our men in ambushes and even assassinating their own people for helping in this war against the Jewish Bolsheviks. What a treacherous dirty tribe the French are."

"You are right, *Frau* Randorff, we must remember that the French started this war and are our enemies," Carl stated but added in his own thoughts, "You are one to talk about falseness or perfidy as you spy on your own people." He could not resist adding, "When does your husband expect to enter the *Volksturm*?

"Enter the army? Never! Unless conscripted. He will not volunteer because he knows that he is needed here to provide for the people of Littach. People have no idea how hard it is to find goods to sell. You know they have needs too."

Later Carl realized that he might have given greater heed to the woman.

Hans wrote in a letter shared by Liese, "My boys and I have been assigned to a division and have moved to engage the enemy. The kids are not trained and I fear for them. We have heard that the American artillery supporting the French is devastating. Remember these boys. Enemy airplanes are active everywhere. It is hard to move during the day. It is good to fight on the soil of the enemy and not in the Fatherland. My regards to the countess and the captain. Thank you, loved one, for being the woman you are and have always been."

As French forces drew nearer toward Colmar and Strasburg the attitude of the French prisoner-worker Chalvet became bolder. Even the three other prisoners complained, "Captain, what can we do about this fellow Chalvet? He is always whistling the *Internationale* in our ears and talking of the dictatorship of the proletariat. You should know that he has said that you are the first one he is going to have lined up and shot when the French come."

Carl had noted a malicious smile on the face of the Frenchman. He thought on these moments, "He grins at me like I imagine I look at the turkey a week before Thanksgiving. I wonder what he might be up to."

The flow of fliers downed by German guns and seeking refuge in Switzerland had stopped but not because the English-American air presence had slackened. The *Luftwaffe* of Air Marshal Hermann Göring could not cope in either planes or even anti-aircraft fire with the overwhelming flood of Allied planes

As the great supply lines of the allied forces in France grew longer, it became difficult to provide the materiel that the combat forces required, particularly fuel for the armored columns. Slowly the Allied columns stopped their forward movement to await the re-establishment of the lines of supply. With stable airfields, the supply problem applied far less to the Allied air forces. The air war continued as Allied aircraft increasingly suppressed the defenses of the *Luftwaffe*. New bases in France lessened the travel to the area of conflict.

The pause of the Allied ground advance gave the German forces an opportunity to reorganize and re-supply their units with men and materiel. As part of this effort, orders directed Pfefferkorn to report immediately to the *SS Panzer Lehr* Division with a promotion to sergeant. Former *Hitler Jugend* and now *Volksturmer* Klaus Beidermann, forced to lie about his age in order to be old enough to be a part of the *Volksturm*, became to Carl as his driver.

As Liese prepared to tend her family burial plot on the eve of All Saints' Day, Carl had to tell her, "Liese, word has come that "Wali" has died as he took to the air in his jet. An American fighter plane destroyed his plane as he was taking off. Observers had no hope for his survival when it happened. I am so sorry, Liese." While he was glad that he informed Marli before he told the mother, at the same time he mused to himself, "Why am I sorry that one of my country's enemies has died? I know that it is because I know him. I have heard his voice, shook hands with him, seen the joy of life in his eyes. He is not an abstract stick figure but a real man, a son to a loving mother, a potential husband to a German girl who will never have that good husband that I think he would have been. This war is both necessary and stupid. Because it is necessary it is good, but at the same time, it is evil. Just as mankind is depraved but often does good and necessary things. War exists because mankind exists. My heart aches because I knew and liked Wali but Liese's heart is being broken bit by bit. Her suffering dwarfs mine. First Rudi and now Wali. Whom will she mourn next? Hans? Conrad? Or will it be me, Marli, or even little Eric?"

As Marli touched and held her substitute mother, she heard no wailing, no loud cries but saw only tears streaming from tired and anguished eyes. She felt low sobs shake the frame surrounding the heart that seemed to crumble within the body held in her arms. Demonstrative emotion held no sway over a clan that had seen deaths by wars for millennia. Centuries of culture had raised the model of Spartan motherhood to the place of expectation. The killing raged on with not hundreds but thousands dying every day. The hope for an Allied victory and a German defeat by Christmas first faded and then, for a three-week period, events expelled from all thought for a quick end of the killing.

Herr Mayor Otto Schlenkmann seemingly recovered from his depression to chortle, "I said so! I told everyone that our *Führer* had some tricks up his sleeve! People of Littach, we live in the age of one of the greatest military geniuses of all time. He exceeds the great Frederick and Napoleon cannot compare! He is better than Caesar and only the great Aryan Alexander could be his rival! The Gods did not choose to spare Caesar from the knives of Brutus and Cassius but they did spare our beloved leader from the bombs of Stauffenberg and the other swine of the *Wehrmacht* and *Abwehr*.

"And now he is dividing the Americans and Tommies and driving them back into the sea! Soon they will surrender and we can finally deal with the Bolsheviks! Maybe the Americans and British will come to their senses and join us in a crusade to save Aryan civilization."

Carl could only nod and be silent. "What if the *Nazis* did turn the tide completely? Could he protect his family by continuing his deception?" He decided that he could only continue moment by moment, day by day. By Christmas he cheerfully informed Marli, "The counterattack ordered by Hitler seems stalled and the Allies are wreaking great destruction on the German forces in Belgium and northeastern France according to the word that I am getting from several sources. The French-American forces have reached the upper Rhine. It seems only a matter of time until they will be pouring across the river and into the cities and countryside of Germany."

Marli responded, "The only thing I will like about war is its conclusion. Look at Liese. Two of her sons dead and another together with her husband are in mortal danger. Now she gives love and attention to Eric. I worried that she would withdraw from emotional ties but quite the opposite has happened. She seems to want to, even compelled to, hold the baby to her breast every moment.

"You are really right about the war, darling, but without it I don't see how I could have met you. It would have taken a miracle for us to get together and if we had not, there would be no Eric and no child that is within you. The war is terrible generally but for you and our children I give thanks."

The thrust to split the Allied forces and rush to the Channel coast had failed. In the middle of January a long-faced Heinrich Hühn warned Carl, "The *Wehrmacht* has failed the *Führer* again. He has to fight the officers in addition to fighting the Allies. Only you in the *SS* are true and that is because you are not in the "old" families and have loyalty only to the Fatherland. The aristocratic swine are always thinking of their aristocratic cousins in Britain and looking out for their own interests. But all is not lost. We can still hold them and keep a strong watch on the Rhine while we reorganize and rebuild our strength. Hitler will outfox them yet."

When news came in February that Hans had been killed while earning another Iron Cross in fighting against the French in the Vosges sector it seemed the last sorrow Liese could bear. Never leaving the kitchen she only sat in a chair and rocked herself and, if possible, Eric. With moisture ever-present in her eyes, she incessantly hummed German lullabies and only spoke when forced except when she wanted to ask of a memory. "Do you remember how wonderful that man Hans Weber looked the first time we saw him at the *fest*?" "No, mutti, I was not born yet." Another time she volunteered, "Conrad is a good child; I don't care what the teacher said."

Marli shared from the depths of her heart, "My Liese seems so broken. She does not cry aloud but I can tell she is weeping so much inside that it hurts me. It is as though her mind is leaving her. Carl, is there anything we can do?" Two weeks passed before the spell of despondency left the woman. That occurred only when Eric developed a childhood disease and coughed the whole night through. Then she left her chair in the kitchen and went to his room where she remained through the night. When she came out of the room in the early morning, she asked what Marli wanted for breakfast and then prepared that meal.

On a day in the middle of March Major Foltermann, the security chief to whom Carl answered, entered Carl's office and asked, "Where will you go in the last days? You do know that all is lost. The enemy is across the Rhine at Remagen and I think that other crossings are imminent. The army still has a will to fight but has little equipment and ammunition. You know that we will be treated as criminals simply for enforcing the law of our leaders. I think I shall slip over to Switzerland soon with my new papers and passport that I had the foresight to obtain some time ago. Are you prepared for life in South America? You have kept things quiet here and I have not been bothered by higher ups. Do you need anything? I have some assets in a Zurich bank that no one can find out about."

"No," Carl answered, "I have obligations here to my wife and others whom I cannot abandon. Thanks very much for your offer of assistance and I wish the best things of life for you."

Even as Vienna and the Prussian city of Königsberg were falling to Soviet forces and British and American troops surrounded the Ruhr, the death of the American leader Franklin Roosevelt in April gave at least Adolf Hitler a surge of optimism. This surge was very brief as French forces flowed around the Black Forest to the north and along the Rhine to the south.

In the middle of April, all doubt that the enemy approached ended for the remaining inhabitants of Littach. Erika Randorff and her husband Ludwig came to the castle riding bicycles and asked, "Do you have room for us here? The French soldiers are only a short distance away and we understand that they are from Algeria and are uncontrolled by their officers when it comes to Germans. The Greiders have fled to Switzerland and the Hühns seek religious refuge at St. Blasien. This place is not as good as either of those but we will be able to move further in the forest tomorrow. We are only asking for help for one night. Please grant it to us for old time's sake, my friend Marlene."

"Oh, my poor store. If there is anything there for them, the Africans will make off with it. But I always said it is best to think ahead and so moved most of my inventory into Switzerland to a colleague's store. Oh, we Randorff foxes were not born today and we know how to take care of ourselves. We tried to get over there ourselves but the Swiss border guards turn back all refugees. We were wise in that we never joined the Party. But you, Schleiter, will have a lot to answer for. It does look like you are going to have one born any day now. That's too bad with your situation."

Only the discipline of her faith permitted Marli to open her home to this friend of her childhood but she provided them with shelter and as much food as could be spared.

The majority of the people of Littach remained in their shuttered homes. With the shortage of medical care, Marli had only her old nanny Liese to comfort and aid her when the pangs of childbirth began. Isolated in the castle they had no idea that the French had arrived on April 21, 1945. Carl and Marli only knew that their daughter Teresa Jacinta Solms came from the womb on that day. The joy of the birth gave a new spirit to Liese for now she had added responsibility and knew that she was needed. Although Carl yearned to make contact with American authorities so they would inform his parents that he lived, he nevertheless sat with his wife for two additional days until certain that she and the baby Teresa maintained their health.

After he had put on civilian clothing to seek Americans, he heard a vehicle come to a stop in the courtyard. As he exited the door he recognized an American made four passenger utility vehicle that he thought he remembered as a "jeep." The three soldiers in the vehicle, though, he thought must be French.

One had stripes on his uniform and said in German, "Captain Friedrich Schleiter, you are under arrest for crimes against humanity and for murder! You will come with us immediately. Do not turn around and do not make any move other than being seated right here. We will have weapons aimed at your back so be careful."

Only Liese saw these events and hesitated before telling her mistress.

The little vehicle sped down the hill and in minutes Carl found himself once more in Littach. There he explained first in English then in German, "I am not

Captain Friedrich Schleiter of the *SS* but I am Lieutenant Carl Solms of the American Air Corps. You are wrong about this and I can understand but I really am an American."

The American-made small vehicle delivered him to the school, which, with its high windows, had, it appeared, turned into a place of confinement. He had expected that they would take him to the city hall and his old office building. There a man who seemed to be an officer had the German-speaking sergeant order, "Take off all your clothes and throw them to the soldier there."

"But you are making a mistake! I am your ally, not an enemy. I am an American! My name is Carl Solms, First Lieutenant, United States Army Air Corps," he continued to give his serial number that he had forced himself to remember for three years. He nevertheless complied with the disrobing and threw his clothes to the designated *poilu*. He clenched his teeth as he saw the seams of the clothing being ripped in a vain search for documents, poisonous capsules, or who knew what. As he removed the boot and prosthetic that Hans had so skillfully designed and carved the one in charge said only "Aha!" and reached over and appropriated the item. With the search finished the officer commanded, "Get dressed!" as the soldier insolently threw the ripped and tattered clothing to Carl's feet.

Carl in his indignation tried to explain but at the same time tried desperately to cover his nudity, "You don't understand. I am an American officer who has been posing as an *SS* officer. I have aided many to escape from Germany. You can talk to my wife or to Annaliese Weber. They will tell you that what I am saying to you is true."

The ember of a cigarette in the mouth of the French officer bobbed up and down as he sneered at Carl sitting on the floor because of his missing foot, "Your wife! She will back up any story you two have concocted. The whole town has already told us of, how do you say, the great love she has for you. You have changed her whole personality in the last three years. And the woman at the castle is so devoted to your wife that she too will lie to protect a swine from the *Gestapo*."

Now Carl realized, "Only Marlene and Liese know my true identity and are available. As far as the Germans are concerned, I have sold myself as the pet of Heinrich Himmler and an *SS* officer, even a war criminal. Count von Krönitz could vouch for me but we don't know where he is in Switzerland, The American general we helped get out could identify me but he could be dead and even if he is alive I have no way of contacting him. Who knows where Pfefferkorn is? Maybe dead and maybe in a prisoner of war camp. What a pickle I'm in!"

When dressed, using that word loosely, Carl hopped down the school hall balancing himself with one hand against the wall, escorted by a French soldier carrying an American made submachine gun. Even Carl had to smile ruefully, "Here I am, an American who risked much to help others escape from the *Nazis* and now I am considered a *Nazi*. What is the word I want? Irony! That's what it is, irony."

The soldier directed Carl into a tiny room, hardly more than a closet. Carl surmised it had been some sort of storage space, possibly for cleaning materials. Once in the closet the door closed and a key turned the lock. Carl took pleasure that there was one single bulb fixed in the ceiling providing light. Carl had to slide down the wall in order to gain a sitting position.

After some time, hours he guessed, as the fine Swiss watch he had taken from the arm of Friedrich Schleiter had been "liberated," the door opened and a bowl of what appeared to be stew slid across the floor to him accompanied by the single word question, "toilette?" He nodded in assent because he needed to use the toilet and it would give him some time from his confinement. A shout brought another soldier and while one kept the weapon trained on him, the other helped him to his foot. Impatient with the time it took the prisoner to hop along holding the wall the soldier without a weapon let Carl put his arm over his shoulder and acted as a second leg. Even in the circumstances, Carl felt any act of kindness deserved some appreciation so he muttered one of the few words he knew in French, "Merci."

Carl endured the humiliating experience and found himself back in the closet, the door locked once more. Sliding down to the sitting position on the floor again, he discovered that the stew, never hot, had turned tepid. Finding no spoon, he drank from the lip of the bowl. Five hours later the French repeated this procedure but with a roll of hard bread accompanying the heavy soup. That night, uncertain as to when night fell and the sun rose, Carl lay on the floor to sleep as best he could.

On the fourth day following his arrest, the guards took Carl from his improvised cell and led him to a chair that had been placed immediately in front of the closet door and motioned for him to sit. His boots were then brought to him and he could see that they had been examined thoroughly. He had to manipulate and adjust the prosthetic in the right boot, as it appeared that the guards had dismantled it as they inspected it. Nevertheless being able to walk on his own, no matter the increased discomfort, raised his spirits, "Maybe they have discovered that I am an American."

Those hopes died quickly as he entered a converted schoolroom where several French officers sat in a row under a chalkboard with two single officers sitting on separated chairs behind small tables. Under the windows, Carl saw not only Marli but also Francois Chalvet, Erika Randorff and several other townspeople he recognized but did not know by name.

When Chalvet saw him escorted into the room he leapt to his feet and began screaming in German, and Carl assumed, in French, "Murderer! Murderer! Fascist swine! You killed my friend and fellow citizen of the republic! Murderer! Dog of a Fascist *Nazi!*"

A French soldier saw the motion of his officers and went over to still the outburst and to convince Marli that she was to remain seated and quiet. Both were quickly accomplished. The officer seated in the center of the three, apparently the senior officer, addressed Carl in passable German, "Captain Friedrich Schleiter, you are accused of murder by this man who served as a worker on the estate of your wife. He swears that you murdered one Rene Dresser, also a worker on the estate, and moved his body to Switzerland. His body was indeed found in that neutral country. Only you, as an agent of the *Nazi* government, could have transported the body over the border and had it appear as an accident. Secondly, you are charged with the death of thousands of Jews, gypsies, and other "undesirables" in Hitler's Germany by forcefully evacuating them from the city to the death camps in the east. How do you defend yourself?"

"First, sir, I apologize that I do not speak French, but, sir, if you speak English better than you speak German we can communicate in English for it is my native language. I have repeatedly said and I say again that I am an American officer shot down three years ago. I deny the murder of Rene Dresser and if his murderer is in the room I believe it is Francois Chalvet because that was inferred to me by the senior French prisoner, Alois Ducite, who indicated that the Communist Chalvet had done away with the pro-Vichy Dresser. If you would bring Mister Ducite into the room, He would settle this quickly.

"Aha! Are your saying that a poor prisoner of war, on his parole, could transport a body over the border to a neutral country and deposit it there? Come, sir, we of this panel are not imbeciles. Please explain to us how he could have done this."

"Sir, my wife and I, she was doing it when I came to the castle, operated a secret tunnel from the castle that led to Switzerland. After Chalvet killed Dresser on the estate because, I think, he was a Fascist and a mortal enemy of Marxist/Leninism and an informer for Ranck, the local Gestapo agent, his body was taken through the tunnel to Switzerland to protect our operation.

Mr. Ducite as much as told me that Chalvet, who is very strong, broke the neck of Dresser. Again I tell you that if you will just bring Mr. Ducite into this conference he will tell you that what I say is the truth."

"Sir, that is impossible. As soon as our soldiers occupied this area, the prisoner farm workers were free to return to their homes or wherever they wanted to go. Ducite has disappeared to who knows where. And now we have some documents to bring to your attention. Here is a letter commending you for your relocation of certain groups to the eastern territories. Now we all know that means that you sent people to the camps in the east where most died either in the gas chambers or from disease or starvation. And we have a personal letter from Heinrich Himmler in which he expresses deep affection for you and commends you for your good work. This letter is dated late in the war. We also have witnesses from the local population who say you supervised the murder of a Jewish family.

"Now, Mr. Investigator, would you bring your witnesses and documentation so that Captain Schleiter can see them and hear them himself? Call your first witness."

"I call Erika Randorff."

Marli looked in stunned disbelief as her childhood playmate entered the room. She thought to herself, "I knew that in general she supported the *Nazis* but why is she now going to be a witness against my husband?"

Carl at the same time thought, "What a turncoat! This woman can change colors faster than a chameleon. What is she going to say now? She is certainly no witness to any criminal acts under the law of God or international acceptance. She only saw me acting out a role of an *SS* officer. What can she say that can be used against me?"

He learned that there were no bounds to the duplicity of the woman who testified after being sworn in. "I have known the Countess Marlene von Ritterbach and Krönitz really almost all the days of my life, no? She looked up to me as her counselor and guide when we were young. You cannot imagine my shock and sorrow when she married such a scoundrel and liar as the man sitting there. I truly believe that he is a Svengali or Rasputin in whom the devil dwells. He can make one think whatever he wants them to think. He made me think that he really cared for me as a woman until I learned that he cared for his Hitler more than me. I tried and tried to get him to admit that there were errors in the *Nazi* way but, no, everything was perfect with the *Nazis* in control.

"I tried to warn Field Marshal von Rudel and his wife not to take him into their confidence but he persuaded them to pay no heed to my warnings. We know what happened to that sweet man and heaven knows where his woman is now. No, butter wouldn't melt in his mouth when it came to discussing the *Nazis* and the *Gestapo*. There are many people in Littach who can say what they know about the murder of that poor Jewish family."

Marli, with little Teresa on her chest, jumped to her feet. "Sirs, only one thing this woman says is the truth. We played together as children and that is all. Everything else is the devil's lies and quite the opposite of the truth. Many in the town knew her as a secret informer for the *SD*."

"Silence, woman, we know that this criminal shared your bed and sired your children but we will have order in this room and will not permit our witnesses to be attacked." The senior officer then turned to Carl, "Because we desire to keep this hearing civil you may question the witnesses only through your counsel who is sitting there by your side. You may proceed with your questioning." The latter instruction was given both in German and in French.

Carl turned to the young officer beside him and asked, "Do you speak English?"

The answer was quick and brief, "Non."

He then asked, "Well, then, do you speak German?"

The answer was the same, "Non."

"Mister Chief, or whatever I should call you, how can this man defend me when I cannot communicate with him? I insist again that I am an American and suggest that you take my fingerprints and send them to Washington to see if they belong to one Lieutenant Carl Solms. That will definitely show that I am not Friedrich Schleiter."

The president of the tribunal responded, "Insofar as your ability to communicate with your defender, from what we have heard from the honorable Mrs. Randorff it is probably good that you cannot lead the young and inexperienced lieutenant astray with your quick wits and artful tongue. As to your second suggestion, we will not permit you to delay these proceeding and the results of this trial that I foresee occurring shortly on these grounds. We have won the war. We will not permit the soft and wooly headed Yankees to interfere in our area. There will be no delay for weeks or months to send things to Washington. Our sense of justifiable outrage might slacken by then."

Up jumped Marli again, "My colonel, if you will not give my husband a counsel with whom he can communicate, may I sit by his side and act as an interpreter? After all it is a wife's duty to be at her husband's side at his times of trial as well as his to be at hers."

"Oh, very well. Soon you may be sitting as the accused yourself so it may be a good experience." Then to Carl, "You are a fiend who has bewitched this daughter of a man who is known throughout Europe for his sense of justice, wisdom, and courage. It is true what that English poet said about things being too wonderful for him and one was the way of a man with a maid."

Both Marli and Carl rose to that error with Marli dominating, "Colonel, may I point out that it was not just an 'English poet' but that saying comes from the God-inspired proverbs of the Bible. Sir, both my husband and I are serious students of the Bible. Do you really believe that *Nazis* study the scripture. If so they would discover that the things they read there are so. That includes the words that vengeance is the Lord's."

"So, you admit, lady, that we French and others in this room have just reason for seeking revenge against your husband not only in our own cause but also for all those innocents that he aided to be slaughtered. I think we have heard enough to call a court martial that will meet in five days and will be capable of imposing the most severe penalty."

Carl remembering the sound of the wailing whistle of German trains, almost imagined that he heard them once more, and asked, "Sir, my wife had a child less than a week ago, as you can see, and it would not be good to ask her to do what I will ask you to do. Please send to the nearest headquarters where there is an American officer present as liaison, or whatever, and ask him to come here before any trial is conducted. That would not necessitate an extensive delay but could be done in one day if you act quickly."

"I say again," rejoined the French colonel, "I object to letting the Americans get involved. They are too proud now and will probably continue to interfere in the affairs of France and other European countries because they think they saved us. But I like to consider myself a fair minded man so I will think on it."

Carl then left the room escorted by the same armed guards without being able to touch or speak to his wife. The guards moved him to another and larger room than he had been in but Carl noticed that bars had been welded or in some way fixed over the windows. His chamber now contained a cot and a table and chair. When he was in the room, the guards signaled for him to sit down and remove the boot with the prosthetic. "They are taking no chances that this one-legged "*Nazi*" is going to get away," he considered to himself.

The soldiers placed a chamber pot in the room and each morning they added a washbasin and hot water together with a towel, soap and a safety razor.

The guards watched his every move as he washed himself and shaved. They then removed the chamber pot for emptying and the razor, basin, and water and left him to his own thoughts. His mind darted and scurried to find a way to persuade those who did not relish being persuaded that they had not captured a vile *Nazi* criminal.

On the fifth day after the first hearing, they provided him with new and simple clothes as well as his boots. After getting dressed, the guards again escorted him to the classroom that had now been arranged as a judicial court. Quickly he perceived that he was on trial for his life. The same witnesses that he had heard from or about were presented again as well as numerous documents that clearly implicated Captain Friedrich Schleiter in the deaths of thousands of humans. This time Marli was permitted to take the stand in his defense. She swore, "I swear by everything that I hold precious that this man is not Friedrich Schleiter. He is not and never has been a member of the SS. Here, I submit to you his American military identification tags. My marriage to Friedrich Schleiter ended with his death in a British air raid in April, 1942. I then married this man. Do you think I, a member of the Confessing Church, would testify for this man if he were truly Friedrich Schleiter?

The three judges provided by the legal department of the French army nodded sagely and countered, "You say you married this purported American aviator? We have searched the marriage records and have not found any record of such a marriage. His possession of American identification and the English Bible proves only that he is vicious and probably killed this American officer, Carl Solms. We know that you want to protect the father of your children. We feel, however, that you might be benefited by being rid of such a monster and live a better life."

As Marli testified, Carl felt a slight pressure on his back, and turning around, he confronted the malicious smile of Francois Chalvet who whispered so only Carl could hear, "You are going to die, capitalist Fascist swine. It makes no difference to me whether you are American or German. You are the enemy of the proletariat. I have done you in but there are many more like you yet to deal with. Now you will know that the masses will rise and the capitalist oppressors will die. You have been spewed forth from the stomach of the beast of capitalistic individualism but you will be smothered out first. I laugh at your call for truth and righteousness. I long ago signaled that your throat was to be cut."

After the retinue of witnesses and documents had presented their testimony Carl felt that even he would have been inclined to find himself guilty if he had not known that he was not Friedrich Schleiter. In his own defense Carl could only maintain that he was not an *SS* captain and had done none of the acts of which they accused him. He explained again the death of the French prisoner Rene Dresser and the execution of the Jewish family by the *Gestapo*. His identity as Friedrich Schleiter had succeeded beyond all expectations.

He also knew that the finding was a foregone conclusion and was emotionally shocked but not mentally surprised to hear the sentence,

"You will be taken two days from now into this school's yard and executed by firing squad for murder of the French patriot and soldier Rene Dresser, the murder of an unknown Jewish family, and complicity in the deaths of thousands of innocent Jews, Gypsies, and retarded people."

Faced with the strong possibility that he would die within hours, Carl spent the night in prayer and in reading the Bible that had been provided to him at the indignant insistence of Marli. He examined his life for all the sins, and even errors of judgment that may have injured others, and confessed them with deep repentance. In his prayers, he asked that if it were possible that this fate would not be his.

Knowing that the time of death was set for shortly after dawn he was surprised by a commotion outside the door of the room of his confinement as darkness was falling outside. The door opened and into the room strode the figure of a stalwart man in the uniform of a lieutenant colonel in the American army. It had been almost five years since he had last seen Bruce Wishart of west Texas but he recognized the man and the voice that demanded as he entered, "Just what the hell is going on here? I understand that you are claiming to be an American officer. What a crock! You made me drive all the way from General Lattre's command post to learn that you are an impostor."

He seemed about to leave when Carl could only smile and say, "Et tu, Brucey?"

The American colonel turned and said in wonder, "Just who the hell do you say you are? Why did you say that?"

"Oh, you don't know me," teased Carl, as an incomprehensible relief flooded though his body, "Just because I had a little face work done and had a leg shortened a bit you don't remember your "old lady" from New Sendlingen! Are you and Lois married or did she find someone she really deserves? Seriously, though, Bruce, don't you know me."

Stunned for a moment Lieutenant Colonel Wishart, Artillery, Army of the United States, wheeled around and shouted with the greatest command voice that he could muster, "Guard! Goddammit! Guard! Get in here, pronto, before

I kick your behind. Go get that frog-eating colonel or whoever now and I mean NOW! GIT!"

He then turned to Carl and all the command presence melted into the deep affection he felt for one who was lost and now, miraculously was found. "Is it really you, Carl Solms? I heard that you were presumed dead years ago. What happened to your face? And your leg. And what's this I hear about a *Nazi* wife swearing that her husband is not who he is? Could she be that woman sitting in the hall at the entrance with two babies and an older woman?"

Carl hastened, "That is probably Marli with our babies. Bruce, could you get her here to me?"

Again the roar, "Guard! Guard! Somebody better get in here right now or that French general will know about it!" Although the guards understood little English they clearly understood a voice used to command with assurance, even in flawed French quickly learned in an Army school and as liaison to the First French Army Headquarters of General Jean de Lattre de Tassigny and immediately appeared. The orders continued, "The women and babies down in the hall yonder. Bring them here! Now!"

With a scurry and a bustle the guards were away and before he even expected it, Carl heard the voice he loved saying "Carl! Carl! What's going on?" He turned and saw his Marlene entering that which was once his cell but now took on a wonderful glow, with the tiny Teresa in her arms followed by Liese carrying Eric.

Haltingly, with tightness in his throat, he introduced in English, "Bruce, this is my wife Marli and these are our two children, Eric and Teresa. This is Annaliese Weber who has cared for my wife since childhood. Marli, this is my college roommate and best friend from years ago. You know, I told you about him. He is apparently a lieutenant colonel now but I never thought he would look so much like an angel to me. I know now that we are...I am safe."

Shortly after this the French soldier informed the French-speaking American colonel that the French colonel, the senior French officer of that area, had arrived. That officer demanded to know what was going on. Bruce presented letters from the French army commanding general, General Jean de Lattre, authorizing him to take any actions he found advisable. After a little sputtering about, "The trial ordered..." Lieutenant Colonel Wishart asked, "If you like, I will call and you can discuss this with General de Lattre himself?"

The reply was a quick, "Non! Non!" and he signaled the guards they were dismissed. Carl considered asking for the arrest of the man Chalvet but thought better of it for the murder that Chalvet had probably committed had the approval of Carl at the time and probably saved the life of the man with double identity. "Let the wheels of divine justice grind away," Carl thought.

The American colonel stated, "I and my driver had planned to stay the night in that little hotel we saw up the street. I will make sure that they have room for you and your lady as well as the babies and the, uh, the, uh, woman. Tomorrow I think we should talk to the French colonel and make sure everything is okay in the interest of allied cooperation and relations. Tonight I want to hear the whole story or as much as you can remember off the cuff."

So it was that the lights of the hotel stayed on well beyond curfew and even midnight as old and true friends and comrades shared their lives of the past five years. Bruce reported that because he had taken four years of high school French because, "Gosh, that French teacher is a pretty woman." Two years in college, where "the teacher, Mr. Lenay, was not at all pretty" followed. Bruce clarified, "I had to take some language." The army thought him a linguist and sent him to language school in California.

In the morning after the usual breakfast of cheese and rolls, Carl remembered that this was about the hour that his death had been appointed. Joy of the time cast that remembrance from his mind. After eating, he clambered, assisted by the driver, into the front seat of the jeep while the complete legged Bruce leaped into the back seat almost as though he flew with wings of joy.

Carl did reiterate his charges against the woman Erika Randorff and a search was begun for her as the conversation with French officers continued toward noon.

Just before midday a roar erupted in the outer office, "What the hell is going on? I come to this town to thank a man who saved my life. What do I find? I find all is confusion and no one knows a damned thing about anything. Get out of my way! I want to talk to whoever is in charge of this skunk works." As these words filled the air, Carl immediately recognized that wing commander, now Major General David McDowell, who had traveled through the tunnel to the safety of Switzerland. Even as the situation was being made clear to the general another voice, more austere and reserved but with no less authority, was heard outside the door. Count Erich Albert *von* Krönitz, returned from Switzerland that morning, was asking about the location of his daughter and her husband.

Overwhelmed by it all the French colonel asked, "Is there anything I can do? I deeply regret the decisions that were made and am so thankful that nothing horrible happened. Please what can I do to recompense our conduct?"

"Please provide transportation to *Schloss* Altburg for all those who need it and that includes my wife, children and *Frau* Weber. We will, with the help of *Frau* Weber, have an afternoon meal there."

Epilogue

Major General David McDowell's interest in Carl and Marlene helped greatly in Carl's return to the United States accompanied by his wife Marlene, their two children, and the ever-faithful Annaliese Weber. The general overcame all obstacles created by Marlene's and Liese's German citizenship as well as with the more mundane problems such as the "no fraternization" regulations instituted by the headquarters of General Dwight D. Eisenhower. In addition, he pushed for and gained recognition of the fortitude and diligence of Carl by the award of appropriate medals for both bravery and meritorious service.

Marlene's acceptance of his parents and their style of life did not concern Carl because of her genuine gentility and his preparation of her expectations. Those parents, who never pretended to be anything but what they were, received her with ease and dignity although they used the better of the two sets of china in the house. While they treated their son as Jacob treated Joseph when he seemingly returned from the dead, they did not give preference to Eric and Teresa over their fourteen other grandchildren but insisted that they too stay out of the flower beds and put things back where they found them. Peter and Minnie Solms gave the same preference when the little brother and sister of Eric and Terri, as Teresa came to be called, came into the world..

When Carl and Marli saw Carl's cousin Anna Tubinger, he made sure that Marli recognized her as the person who had made their whole experience and exploits possible. Marli in turn commented on the origin of her name as corresponding to the university town where her parents had met. Anna in turn gloried in the remembrance of her first loved land.

The town of New Sendlingen had a special Fourth of July in 1945 at the American Legion building as they celebrated not only one of the first Sendlingen boys to return from the war but one who had acquitted himself so well.

Although some seemed at first tongue-tied in the presence of a countess, Marli demonstrated her true nobility and soon had them laughing along with her. Carl made sure that she had the honor of meeting those humble country schoolteachers who had so shaped his life, the former Miss Marie Benton, who was now Mrs. John Schroeder, and Miss Helen Altman.

Contact with the rocket missile engineer Christian Niedertal, friend of Marli's father, led to Carl's employment first with the rocket program in Alabama and then closer to home in Houston. Bruce, the Brucey, Wishart, left the army to live with his wife and seven children in his home county in West Texas where he became a pillar of the community as the county judge. He and Carl had many reunions on the campus of their college over the decades remaining in their lives. Even before he left Germany, he was grieved by the news given by his old roommate that the ethereal Lydia Cameron had succumbed to leukemia in 1943.

Count Erich Albert von Krönitz, with his estate restored to him, returned to service of his people first as a magistrate and then as a judicial advisor to Konrad Adenauer, Chancellor of the restored government of West Germany in Bonn.

Ludwig Randorff and his wife Erika prospered in the German economic miracle that began in 1948 as they exported the products of the wood carvers of the Black Forest. *Frau* Randorff became a social leader, famous for her outgoing personality and sumptuous tables, for the German state of Wurttemberg-Baden.

Alois Pfefferkorn, after his release from prisoner of war camp, became the steward for the estates of Marlene's father while Conrad Weber took the place of his father as steward of the restored lands of Marlene's Altburg castle. His mother was part of the Carl Solms family until all the children were beyond the age of needing a "nanny." She then returned to *Schloss* Altburg to be with her surviving son and his family.

Francois Chalvet never surrendered in his struggle to create a soviet republic in France until he died sorely disappointed following the collapse of the Soviet Union and the hopes of Marxism throughout the world.

Carl and Marli traveled to Germany yearly to visit her father until his death and to the castle near Littach where people not only remembered Carl but also honored him as one who kept his trust.

978-0-595-36926-3
0-595-36926-X